PURGATORY

Also by Guido Eekhaut

Absinthe

PURGATORY

A THRILLER

GUIDO EEKHAUT

Skyhorse Publishing

First English-language Edition

Originally published in the Netherlands by De Boekerij under the title *Loutering*

This is a work of fiction. As such, you needn't worry: it isn't about you. Nor is it about real organizations, corporations, or situations. Any similarity to real events or imaginary ones is purely coincidental. Opinions spoken out loud by the characters are not those of the author. At least not always.

Skyhorse Publishing books may be purchased in bulk at special discounts for sales promotion, corporate gifts, fund-raising, or educational purposes. Special editions can also be created to specifications. For details, contact the Special Sales Department, Skyhorse Publishing, 307 West 36th Street, 11th Floor, New York, NY 10018 or info@skyhorsepublishing.com.

Skyhorse® and Skyhorse Publishing® are registered trademarks of Skyhorse Publishing, Inc.®, a Delaware corporation.

Visit our website at www.skyhorsepublishing.com.
Visit the author's website at guidoeekhaut.squarespace.com

10 9 8 7 6 5 4 3 2 1

Library of Congress Cataloging-in-Publication Data

Names: Eekhaut, Guido, 1954– author.
Title: Purgatory: a thriller / Guido Eekhaut.
Other titles: Loutering. English
Description: First English-language edition. | New York: Skyhorse Publishing,
   [2019] | "Originally published in the Netherlands under the title Loutering."
Identifiers: LCCN 2019004386 (print) | LCCN 2019009338 (ebook) | ISBN
   9781510730700 (ebook) | ISBN 9781510730687 | ISBN
   9781510730687(hardcover:alk. paper) | ISBN 9781510730700(ebook)
Subjects: LCSH: Mass murder—Fiction. | Cult members—Crimes
   Against—Fiction. | Criminal investigation—Fiction. | Ardenne—Fiction.
Classification: LCC PT6467.15.E55 (ebook) | LCC PT6467.15.E55 L6813 2019
   (print) | DDC 839.313/64—dc23
LC record available at https://lccn.loc.gov/2019004386

Cover design by Erin Seaward-Hiatt
Cover photograph: © Peeter Viisimaa/Getty Images

Printed in the United States of America

Prologue

BELGIUM, THE ARDENNES FOREST, early January

An almost translucent fog hung low over the landscape and would not disappear anytime soon. It would probably last until midday if the sun came through the clouds. This was January, after all, the middle of winter, and it was a colder winter than anyone could remember. It had been snowing for a couple of days. Not much, but just enough to cover trees, rocks, and bushes with an irregular layer of crusty white powder that only the most optimistic of skiers would regard as real snow. Not that skiers would venture out here, in this thick forest. No marks covered the ground, no animals could be seen. Even the birds stayed away. Nothing in the landscape moved. It resembled a huge, dreary, life-size painting by an artist who had only white and black on his palette, maybe a spittle of brown.

Alexandra Dewaal glanced over her shoulder at Walter Eekhaut, who was carefully following in her footsteps, head slightly down, his attention on the placement of his feet. Today they would certainly be the only larger living beings to leave their traces here.

Eekhaut would have preferred leaving no trace at all, letting this part of the forest remain virginal. He preferred spending January in a heated office or his warm bed instead of here—somewhere in the middle of the Belgian Ardennes, isolated from any touch of civilization. Strange it was, being so utterly alone in this otherwise densely populated country. At times, he imagined he was in the Canadian north or Alaska, neither of which he had ever set eyes on.

Dewaal stopped and consulted the digital compass she held in her left hand. Eekhaut waited patiently. It was a sophisticated military compass that indicated coordinates and other useful information, describing within a few yards where on the planet a person had decided to lose themselves.

"And?" he inquired, his voice loud against the trees and snow.

She shook her head. They had not yet arrived at their destination.

"Still far to go?" He knew he sounded like a ten-year-old, trapped in a car en route to Spain or wherever with ten hours or so still to go. He was feeling chilled, as if death itself were forcing its way through the soles of his boots.

Death.

The thought seemed apt in these surroundings.

She shrugged, as much as she could in that heavy, almost polar-weight parka and backpack large enough for an expedition of several days. He wondered what she had in that backpack. Not that he cared much. His own parka was warm enough, and he carried only his small shoulder bag. He had assumed they wouldn't stay overnight, camping in the wild. He wasn't prepared for that, anyway, hadn't even brought an extra pair of underwear. She hadn't mentioned camping when they left Amsterdam that morning. She'd told him hardly anything. Just that he needed sturdy shoes and warm clothes. And gloves. And he had to bring his weapon. Which he had done.

He assumed even she didn't know how far they still had to walk. The compass didn't compute distances, only indicated location. For distances and directions, they had to bring a map and figure it out for themselves. And in a landscape like this, distances had to be relative, since it was not possible to walk in a straight line. It would be easy to walk a quarter mile across the frozen soil if they kept clear of trees and bushes, but farther on they would have to climb and find their way through the forest, where it became denser.

She inspected the map she held. She had it folded up inside a plastic sleeve, as protection against the elements. It wasn't the kind of map tourists would use.

"Can't be too far now," she said, each word condensing in the air.

He nodded and pulled his cap down farther over his ears. She had drawn up her parka's hood. She wore a two-piece ski suit under her parka, the kind a member of a SWAT team would wear. The suit had pockets in unusual places, allowing fast access. He had to admit she looked positively adventure-ready. Like a polar explorer on steroids. Maybe a polar bear would make an appearance. Maybe this part of the country would break away from the continent and drift toward the North Pole. Everything seemed possible in this eerie landscape.

She gestured for him to follow. Along their left side, the landscape rose and gradually formed a steep wall with protruding lumps of rock sticking out from between the roots of plants and trees. To their right rose tight pines, like an army of pale green warriors, forbidding enough to prevent access to that part of the forest, where ancient forces might rule the deep, dark woods. Under their feet, the floor was rocky and uneven. Eekhaut slowed down to choose his footing. He couldn't afford an accident. It would be easy enough to break an ankle.

Dewaal paused and peeked over her shoulder. Her face remained in the hood's shadow, and he couldn't see her expression. She had been mostly silent all day, even during the drive from Amsterdam. Now, with only the pale tip of her nose sticking out from the shadow of her hood, she looked like a ghost.

The forest seemed to grow still more impenetrable. Even the light disappeared between the trees, as if a veil had been pulled over the landscape. The wall on their left leaned over their heads. There was nothing farther on but more forest.

And wolves, he thought. *Or maybe wild boar.* There would be wild boar in the Ardennes. He'd better keep out of their way. Weighing several hundred pounds each, they were said to be fierce and attack at the slightest provocation. He wouldn't want to cross their path or aggravate them. He wasn't concerned about wolves. There had been no wolves in these forests for a hundred years. Not indigenous, anyway. But some might have migrated from Germany.

"We will have to cross that part of the forest," Dewaal said, pointing toward the right. "Otherwise, we'd need to take a long detour."

He didn't doubt her skill with map and compass, but crossing through the forest didn't seem an attractive option. All he saw was a wall of dead branches and dead bushes between straight trunks.

"And then?"

She glanced at the map. "We're almost there." She looked up. "You still got some of that coffee?"

He opened his shoulder bag and pulled out a slim aluminum thermos, unscrewed the cap, and poured her a splash of steaming coffee. He had filled the thermos in the cafeteria that morning, fresh out of the machine. Not that he was a fan of cafeteria coffee, but it was hot, and he had added lots of sugar. It had been seven in the morning.

She drank the coffee in one go. She glanced at him thoughtfully, then at the map again. He put the thermos back in his bag and zipped it closed.

"Let's move," she said, as if this were merely a stroll on a summer beach. Summer beaches were more what he had in mind, but he'd chosen the wrong place and season. He followed her, not having much choice. Chief Commissioner Dewaal was his superior. He might have expected her to remain behind a desk, but she chose to be in the field as much as possible. Here, in the field, she hardly acted like his superior. That was something she did only from behind her desk. And whenever she was angry at him. Otherwise, she applied the rules of the AIVD rather carelessly. She knew he had a problem with rules, both those of the AIVD and hers. She tolerated that as much as she could. She knew he, as the only Belgian officer in her department of the Dutch intelligence community, had no trouble with her personally; only with the way the government and police were run.

She crossed the open space toward the trees and penetrated the forest. It swallowed her up. He went in after her, determined not to get lost.

"You want me to walk in front?" he suggested.

She hesitated. Between the trees, snow had hardly penetrated. The floor was littered with dried leaves and small branches, forming a soft, dry carpet.

"Why would you?"

"Because I'm bigger than you," he said.

She glanced at him. Of course, she knew he was bigger and should walk first, but she was used to leading, and lead she would. There would not be any immediate danger, he assumed, but still.

"Go ahead," she said and stepped aside.

He regretted his offer right away, forcing his way through the dense undergrowth. It was uphill all the way now, enough to make him realize he was in poor physical condition. Soon he was hot in his parka, but he couldn't take it off or he would freeze.

He heard a loud click to his left and knew it was her firearm being loaded. Dewaal held her gun in her hand and frowned at him. He reached for his own weapon under his parka, pulled it out, and tugged the slide back. The sound carried a long way, even between the trees. To anyone around, their arrival was now clearly announced. They moved on. Nothing else moved.

And then, suddenly, without any noticeable transition, they stood at the edge of a clearing. Dewaal squatted down and Eekhaut did the same. Keeping their guns at ready, they looked around the clearing that was bordered by a wall of gray, forbidding trees. It was several hundred meters across. Under other circumstances Eekhaut would have looked up at the heavens, but now his attention was fully on the spectacle in front of him.

A terrible spectacle of apocalyptic proportions.

Dewaal, next to him, remained silent. He expected nothing less of her. She was a very disciplined officer. During her career, she had seen horrible things, just as he had. As police officers, they had both learned to distance themselves from their feelings, to objectify horror and gore, as if they were mere props in a movie.

But now. He didn't know how to interpret what was in front of him. Even if the corpses chained to the stakes had long lost the essential characteristics of their humanity, they still had once been living, breathing people.

There were the eyes, to start with. Or what remained of eyes. Or the *lack* of them.

And then the rest of the faces. Faces in agony.

"Seven," Dewaal said, as if an independent part of her brain were registering objective details.

Eekhaut couldn't utter a word.

It wasn't that these had once been people. That wasn't what it was about. What this was about was what they had had to endure, how they had been put to death.

The whole clearing was deserted. Even hope had long ago deserted this place. If ever silence could be deafening, this was it. Even the ice-crusted snow beneath their feet seemed to make a terrible noise when they got up.

"You get the camera," Dewaal said, holstering her gun. She sounded businesslike, even though she spoke softly. She too seemed impressed by the silence. "Take as many pictures as you need. All the details. We'll need details. Lots of them."

Eekhaut thought, *Why don't you snap those pictures? Why don't you get yourself closer to the details of this . . . these things, these horrors that used to be humans, even if we prefer not to see them as such? Why don't you?*

But he didn't object. This was not the moment to question her authority. He noticed her body, even under the layers of fabric, was taut as a string, her face white. She had pushed back the hood of her parka.

In the middle of the clearing, seven high stakes stood more or less erect, firmly planted in the ground. To each of them had been chained a human being. People and chains and stakes now seemed as if they were made of the same material: hard and black and jagged, like charcoal for the barbecue. Snow covered the soil around the stakes and all over the clearing, and there was snow on parts of the seven figures. He knew there would be more blackness under that whiteness.

He deferred the most evident question. The question he didn't want answered.

Had they been dead already when the fire began to consume them? Probably not.

Dewaal stepped up to the nearest figure. It seemed impossibly tall, taller than the average human. But this was an illusion. Each stake rose out of a cone-shaped mound, about half a yard high. Each of the fig-ures—male, female—was a caricature of a human being. *Matchstick men*, Eekhaut thought. He knew how only high temperatures achieved that effect. He had seen other bodies like that. Victims of aircraft fires. People burned to death in cars. The pictures the public never got to see, not in newspapers and not on TV. Because the media still possessed just enough discretion to withhold such horrors from their audience.

Although this policy might, at some point, change. When horror sold more newspapers or more advertising time.

He inhaled deeply. The air was odorless because of the biting cold.

Dewaal turned toward him.

He holstered his gun and took the camera from his bag. A small digital camera, perfect for this work. He took pictures of the nearest figure. He hardly looked at the display. Each of the pictures would show an almost abstract object, a grotesque piece of artwork.

A piece of artwork.

Who was the artist? Eekhaut wondered about that. Who was responsible for these *figures*? And would he want to meet that person? He would not. But they had come here to find answers.

While Dewaal inspected the bodies more closely, he continued to take pictures. That took a while. He observed, although there was little to observe. The worst were the faces—or what remained of them. On two figures, the flesh was largely burned away and only the blackened and cracked skull remained. Of the others, something that could pass for a face, ears, nose, and even lips were rudimentarily present. All he could identify was the horrible pain and the last desperate cry escaping from steaming lungs and the bodies contorted as in a last effort to escape the flames.

The worst hadn't been the fire itself, causing so much despair, but the realization there was no escape.

He closed his eyes and stepped back.

His question had been answered. They had been alive.

When he looked again, he saw Dewaal standing in the middle of the clearing. She too held her eyes closed for a moment.

He turned his attention back to the victim in front of him. He needed to be professional. It wasn't clear if this had been a man or a woman or what age the victim had been. Or what color their skin had been. Having these questions answered would need more detailed medical investigation.

He noticed Dewaal writing in her black notebook. She caught him staring. "I'm just trying to . . ." she said, as if she needed to apologize.

And she made a gesture, encompassing the clearing, as if she wanted to say: I need to write a couple of things down to give meaning to our presence, as if this is a routine police investigation. He understood, and he took some more pictures.

After a while he switched off the camera and returned it to his bag. They stood side by side in the circle of death. "It's a ritual," she said. "It serves no other purpose."

"You realize no one was supposed to discover this."

"Maybe not," she admitted. "A ritual doesn't need the attention of the outside world. And I guess if you do something like this, you want to avoid other people knowing about it. Certainly, if you have very, very personal reasons to commit a crime like this, this far removed from the outside world. In the end, it's enough that it's done."

"And your informant sent us here because he felt we needed to see this?"

"He wanted *me* to see this. Because he trusts me."

"A ritual."

She looked up at him. "That's what it is, I guess."

"We need to identify them."

"The victims? Right away? I don't think we can . . ."

"I mean, let's get a forensic team over." He inspected her pale face. She looked ill. They both were going to be sorry they came here.

"Our Belgian colleagues? I guess we need to alert them as soon as we can. We don't have cell reception here, but when we get back to the car, I'll alert them right away. Problem will be to keep this out of the press." She looked past him. "Is that a cabin or something?"

At the edge of the clearing, slightly higher against the slope, stood a small rectangular building that looked as gray and lifeless as everything around it. Dewaal stepped away from Eekhaut and approached the building. He went after her, keeping the camera ready.

A ritual. Nothing good could come of this. Seven bodies. Why seven? He had a bad feeling about symbolic numbers like that.

The cabin turned out to be a run-down and roughly constructed building made of thin tree trunks. It had a door but no window. It didn't look as if it would serve as a permanent residence. The roof was of corrugated iron, rusty under a partial layer of snow.

Dewaal stopped and made no move to open the door. Eekhaut could easily guess what she was thinking. Inside, there would be more horrors. More bodies. More evidence of a perverse ritual.

She was also looking at something on the wall.

He approached and saw what it was.

His blood ran cold. He forgot to use the camera.

On the wall of the cabin, close to the door, was writing. It took him some effort to decipher the words. Someone had patiently, probably with their fingers, left behind these three lines:

This world seems to take forever,
But it is only
The dream of a sleeper.

Dewaal spoke up. "It's blood. It is written in blood."

Someone had taken the trouble to write these words in blood. That same person, or persons, had probably chained seven people on stakes and set them on fire. The words on the wall were almost black. None of this had happened recently, but neither had it happened long ago.

"Maybe," Eekhaut suggested, "it's a collective suicide. We cannot yet exclude anything, however horrible."

Dewaal looked at him in surprise. He understood. Why had he wanted to comfort himself with such an illusion? A collective suicide? It was something he wanted to cling to, while he wanted not to believe how much evil there was in the world.

"Nobody," she said, "commits suicide this way."

She probably knew more about this case. She had an informant.

"Want to go inside?" she said.

"The cabin?"

"We have to. And we have to search the whole clearing, for clues."

"Clues? Right now?"

"This is a murder investigation, Walter. You're experienced enough to know how things work."

Her face had gotten some of its color back, except for the tip of her nose. "When I was carted off from Brussels to your unit in Amsterdam,

I assumed I'd left my homicide days behind me. I still remember what the assignment read: to investigate subversive organizations and to—"

"I know exactly what the terms of your assignment stated and what I'm responsible for, Eekhaut," Dewaal said sharply. The hood of her parka was still flat against her pack, but she didn't seem cold anymore. There was a fire in her eyes, a kind of fever. Considering the circumstances, he didn't find that remarkable.

"You want me to walk in there, into that cabin."

"Well," she said peevishly, "or I'll do it myself. I just assumed, with you being the alpha male and all, it would be obvious which one of us would walk in there first. You don't want a female officer running risks, do you? Would be an insult to your manhood?"

He would normally not let himself be challenged by her. At least not this way. But now, with the cold and the gruesome scene behind them, he couldn't refuse. What could there be waiting for them inside the cabin that could be worse than the charred corpses?

A lot of things. A lot of things could be worse.

He flicked on his flashlight and pulled out his gun.

He kicked open the door of the hut. It went easily enough, frame and all. Rotten, completely.

From the cabin an old, musty smell emerged, and Eekhaut knew it would linger in his nostrils for the rest of the day. And it would be in his clothes. And everywhere. A basement stench, a cellar kept closed for much too long.

He did what he had done in the past, under similar circumstances. He thought of Fox Mulder in *The X-Files* and stepped over what remained of the threshold.

"What do you see?" Dewaal asked, standing behind him in the grim light and clean air. Eekhaut kept his gun ready and the flashlight in front of him. The cabin had no window, and he blocked the light from behind him. The beam of the flashlight moved like a lingering finger on what passed for walls and then over the floor.

"It's dead," he finally said, over his shoulder.

He enjoyed the short silence before Dewaal said, "What is?" The timbre of her voice told him she expected the worst. It being dead didn't seem to reassure her. "What is dead?"

He stepped back, then stepped outside, turned toward her. "It has tentacles and the body of a spider."

For a moment, he saw horror in her expression. Then she frowned. "Tentacles?"

"One of the Old Gods," he said. "Never read Lovecraft? The details have eluded me, but it was something with tentacles and . . ."

She might have slapped him, under other circumstances. Like when nobody was around. Which was the case here. But she didn't. Because she held her gun in her right hand.

"It's a fox," he said. "His head shot off or something. Probably used for the bloody message on the wall."

She abruptly turned and stepped away from the cabin. He had behaved badly, as usual, although he felt a bit sorry for her. Just a bit. It had been, after all, her idea to come wandering around in the Ardennes, far from her jurisdiction, based on nothing more than a message from an informant and a set of coordinates. An informant who assured her something big was going on. Well, that at least seemed correct. Seven corpses and a dead fox in a cabin. That would not sit well with animal rights organizations. Things would go downhill after that.

Cut it out, he thought. *You only make things worse with your stupid jokes. These people died horribly.*

Dewaal holstered her gun again and turned toward him. "What's the time?"

He glanced at his watch. "Bit after three."

"Mmm. There's not much daylight left. We're not going to spend the night here. How long will it take to get back to the car?"

"An hour."

"We have to get back right now."

"And all this?"

"Nothing here is going to abscond on its own account, is it, Chief Inspector? What does this whole setup tell us? Tourists not welcome. I don't think anyone will come and meddle with the evidence before we can bring in the circus. Once we're in the car, I'll make calls to everyone, including the local authorities and our own people, and with luck they'll all show up by tomorrow morning. Enough people, I assume, to explore every square inch of this place. Can you live with that, Chief Inspector? Otherwise, I invite you to remain here, but on your own."

He wouldn't do that. Not even Fox Mulder would do that. Not here, with the hideous shrieking of the victims still resounding among the trees.

They walked back together. He wasn't surprised she'd snapped at him, considering the circumstances. She seemed furious—furious for the seven lives destroyed in this terrible place.

MONDAY

Amsterdam. Three weeks later.

1

"Two?" CHIEF COMMISSIONER DEWAAL said with a frown that seemed to have taken permanent possession of her. "Are you serious? It took them *three weeks* to tell us they found usable DNA for only *two* of the victims?"

Eekhaut, neatly dressed in gray corduroy trousers, a dark blue shirt, and a wool sports jacket, sat across from her in her stern and austere office at the Kerkstraat, in the heart of Amsterdam between Keizersgracht and Herengracht, two of the main *grachten* or canals around the center of the city. He had been going through a leather folder that contained documents and photographs, all pertaining to the Ardennes incident.

Eekhaut knew in advance what these pictures would show him. Things he had seen all too often for the past three weeks, which were gradually losing their meaning. Two or three of the barely recognizable faces might provide clues for the investigation. Until then, they gave nothing away but proof of unbearable suffering.

Brief suffering, Eekhaut hoped. He would probably never know how long it had taken these people to die, unless some specialist told him. But he didn't want to know. A look at these remains showed him more than enough.

As Dewaal had predicted, the clearing in the forest wasn't an isolated patch of the Ardennes by the morning after they'd found it. At one point, Eekhaut counted thirty people, who had all had to walk for an hour through the forest, as it was impossible for vehicles to get any closer. Which by itself was remarkable, given the effort of the murderer, or murderers, to get their victims to that place.

Local police, Belgian federal police, two teams from the Victims Identification Unit, a federal prosecutor who would lead the Belgian side of the investigation, pathologists, some members of the local fire brigade, two foresters, and four men in suits and black overcoats who avoided talking to anyone but each other. Probably State Security, Eekhaut assumed. All the members of the extended family in one spot, as if this were a picnic. He knew none of those present and didn't feel the need to talk to anyone, which suited him fine. It suited everybody fine, since Dewaal, along with her superiors, had decided to keep this discovery from the newspapers, at least until any real progress was made on the identity of the victims.

Three weeks later, and surprisingly—seeing the number of people who had been involved from the beginning—the press still had not published or broadcast anything concerning the affair.

Everyone present wanted to know how Dewaal and Eekhaut had ended up at this precise spot and what they knew. Dewaal kept them at a distance, referring to an ongoing investigation by the Dutch State Security. The prosecutor, who spoke Dutch with a thick French accent, reminded her she was operating on Belgian soil, without an international mandate. She reminded him that she represented an international organization and was accompanied by a Belgian colleague, so *no*, she wasn't intruding on anyone's territory. The Belgian colleague said he had no intention of interfering, not in the presence of the prosecutor. He had never been friendly with prosecutors. This being a small world, the man might at some point recall Eekhaut's reputation from his time in Brussels.

The prosecutor also asked why such a high-ranking Dutch police officer would want to come all the way to the Ardennes and do the field-work herself, instead of sending a team. Dewaal shrugged him off. She would not explain—she didn't want to jeopardize the confidentiality of her information.

Seven black body bags had been laid out in a neat row, as if order needed to be preserved to compensate for the terrible fate of the victims. As if it would make their final moments bearable. The members of the forensics team, clad in white overalls like ghosts crafted out of snow, gathered the stakes and the chains, while others walked the perimeter of the crime scene, looking for traces. Ultimately there was nothing helpful to be found, not even in the cabin.

Nevertheless, samples of everything were taken, because with a site like this, no one could afford to be negligent. A helicopter was needed to take pictures of the site and the surroundings. Even the dead fox was bagged and carried off. By the end of the day, a Dutch team of forensic investigators arrived on the scene. It was assumed that at least some of the victims could be Dutch, given the background story Dewaal had shared with just three people at that time.

The days after had been particularly busy, especially for Dewaal and Eekhaut, who drew up a strategy for dealing with the details of the investigation, although they were hindered by the lack of information about the victims. Dewaal wanted a small team from the Bureau only, making sure no information went out to other departments and certainly not to the press. She drew up requests for additional expenses, overtime, and an extension of the Bureau's jurisdiction. All this resulted in almost endless counter-requests for revisions of budgets, estimates for the extra work hours, and warnings against meddling with foreign law enforcement agencies.

Inspector Van Gils, an old hand at avoiding both red tape and annoying chores, was initially added to the team as the part-time third member. He would snoop around in Amsterdam and have chats with people he knew from the old days. He was not directly going to mention the Ardennes or the burning of seven people, but he would carefully ask around for missing persons and strange tales of abduction. The contacts he had, however, were usually petty criminals, not the sort of people who would go all-out on apocalyptic rituals.

All this had started, three weeks earlier, with Dewaal showing Eekhaut, in confidence, a piece of paper with some numbers on it. He had just finished his third coffee of the morning, more than his usual ration. He needed the caffeine, having come to terms with Linda, his girlfriend, having left the night before for Africa. They would be separated for several months, a decision that had been hard on him, but one she had made after much soul-searching. The previous evening, as a sort of farewell, they had visited several pubs, and things had gotten a bit out of hand. He had said a proper goodbye in the early morning, after which she left with her luggage.

"Do you know what these are?" Dewaal had asked him. She shoved the piece of paper toward him. It was half a page from a yellow pad, with a series of numbers on it.

"Numbers," he said. Good thing he'd had his coffee, since she seemed to want to test him with some trick question.

She sighed. "I know they're numbers, obviously, but what do they mean?"

He cocked his head. "Coordinates?" They looked like coordinates. But they could be anything. Winning numbers of last week's lotto, for instance.

"You're awake after all. Good. I had a look at a map. If they're coordinates, they point to a spot in the Ardennes. Your Ardennes, in Belgium."

He grimaced. "What's so special about that place? The whole planet has coordinates. There are tons of coordinates around. And the Ardennes these days are full of Dutch tourists. Whenever Belgium is finally divided between Flanders and Wallonia, the Dutch ought to buy the Ardennes from our Walloon brothers, since hardly anybody lives there. And it's high enough above the current sea levels, which can't be said for much of Holland."

"I have this informant, and he gave me these numbers. He didn't say what we could find there. Figure it out, he told me. He's usually very reliable, or I wouldn't take this seriously."

"Reliable? But about what? What's he informing you about?"

"Ah," she said. "Among other things, about the Church of the Supreme Purification."

Eekhaut frowned.

"Never heard of it?" she inquired.

Eekhaut grimaced again, needing another coffee. This day wasn't going to get any better. "Have to hand it to you Dutchies. You have almost as many Christian denominations as the Americans. I find that odd for such a godless people, to have so many churches and sects. Are you sure you need that many? I've never met anyone here in Amsterdam who's religious. And then there's the name. Who would come up with a name like that for a religion?"

"Keep your arrogant Catholic humor to yourself, Eekhaut."

"I'm not Catholic. Not anymore, anyway. I'm a godforsaken atheist."

"The Church of the Supreme Purification isn't a bona fide church or religion. You should be aware of it, though, this being one of the subjects you're supposed to follow up on. How long have you been a member of this team now? Four months? Five? Your status as the token Belgian member of this section of the AIVD is becoming a very thin excuse . . ."

He ignored her. *They* had asked *him* to come work in the Netherlands, mainly because the Brussels crime squad he'd been part of had gotten fed up with his personal brand of insubordination and capricious behavior (their words). That had been in September of last year. So he'd been here for four months. "So what? There's about . . . how many? How many Dutch organizations have you got tucked away in your filing system whose behavior you consider suspect? Close to five hundred? From private militia to people engaged in the practice of voodoo. So I haven't read about all of them yet. Fine, I'll get to it in the end. Give me some space."

"Let's concentrate on the main things," Dewaal said, ignoring his rant. She was wearing a sharply tailored business suit that made her look powerful and sexy. She could be tough, and wore this civilian uniform only as a compromise. She seemed to feel more at ease in jeans and a sweater. Or combat gear. "The Church of the Supreme Purification is an underground religious organization. It's very close to a cult, even in the legal sense. You Belgians are really tough on cults. You even banned Scientology from operating in your territory. We prefer a little more caution. We're a bit more concerned about the lawyers on our doorstep. The Church of the Supreme Purification has existed in its current form for about seventy years, a bit longer perhaps. At least as far as we know."

"That's pretty young for a religion."

"It's not a damn *religion*, Eekhaut. It's a *cult*. A *cult*. Shut up and let me tell the story. Their premise is that the world will perish in somewhat more than two years, in late 2020—"

He again wanted to interject but realized he'd better just listen. "In 2020," she continued. "And don't ask me why. That year, the world will perish by fire. Bad enough as things go, but the members of the church also believe that only a handful of the human population will be spared. These few will experience the ultimate grace of God, and so on."

"Yes, of course," Eekhaut said, "the usual idiocies of your common homegrown apocalyptic religion. Uttered by idiots who, even after centuries of enlightenment, still assume their personal creator will save them from their own stupidity."

"Something like that, yes. I'm sure they prefer an altogether different definition. Their original thesis was that only their followers who wielded the purification of the fire would be among the elect."

"Wielded the—?"

"That's what it says in the occasional snippets of information they choose to make public."

"Oh, all right. Let me guess, they had to set themselves on fire, ritually if possible. And why not, I say. Members of a cult choosing to commit collective suicide is by definition the way to ensure your cult dies out by itself."

Dewaal remained patient. They had come to know each other well by now. He was annoying her on purpose. She would not be drawn into his game. "No, Walter, it's actually a lot worse than that. The ritual of purification meant—and probably still means—the elect were assumed to destroy other people, the large number of unbelievers, if you will, through fire. People who were, in the eyes of the church, unworthy."

"Unworthy?"

"That's right. It isn't complicated: anyone who's not a member of the church is unworthy. It's classic. There's still no definitive proof that the ritual was ever performed. At least no one has come up with definitive evidence, and the church never publicly claims anything. The true believers keep quiet about it for obvious reasons, given the seriousness of the alleged crimes, and given the level of secrecy surrounding the church. In the end, we know almost nothing about their activities. There is, however, quite a bit of speculation about certain well-documented disasters being the work of the church. Los Alfaques, the plane crash at Tenerife airport in the Canary Islands, the fire at the Innovation department store in Brussels—"

"That one dates back to 1967!"

"Exactly. And there's a long list of other incidents where many people died."

"The cause of the Innovation fire was never really explained."

"No. And more than three hundred people lost their lives. The crash at the Tenerife airport where two planes collided was probably due to a technical problem, but there are still doubts about the real cause."

"And you assume this church is responsible? But why kill so many people? What makes random victims belong to the . . . unworthy?"

"I leave that to your imagination, Walter. Los Alfaques: a tanker filled with a flammable gas drives off the road and explodes near a popular RV park and campsite, again randomly killing hundreds of people. With a cult believing that public semi-nakedness is an affront to your god and a mortal sin, you may well have a solid if delusional reason for mass murder."

"I see. And if your religion tells you eternity awaits you after you're done the vengeful god's work on Earth . . . What about your informant?"

She avoided his gaze. He noticed she looked tired. She wasn't her usual dynamic self. Since when had she been carrying this burden? "The story," she said, "is even more complex as far as we could find out. Some twenty years ago, new people began to lead the church. Apparently, they were tired of the killings, the sacrifices. They replaced these sacrifices with a purely symbolic ritual, no human victims involved. A ritual cleansing, no more. And much less dangerous to themselves as well, for they were no longer doing something illegal. They had no wish to face lifelong incarceration."

"But still they claimed the planet and humanity were approaching its expiration date."

"It still was, and it still is, I guess. Anyway, the Church of the Supreme Purification disappeared for a while. Disasters still happened, but there no longer was any reason to suspect them, or so the international intelligence community assumed. Not that we had much proof earlier. Unfortunately, many followers of the church didn't agree with the new moderate doctrine. They convened around a new movement that became known under an equally unsavory name: The Society of Fire. It didn't seem much creative thinking went into that."

Eekhaut frowned. "Really? The Society of Fire? Appropriate, I guess, but with a name like that, there's usually no way back for people joining you."

"Meaning what?"

"About talking people into some stupid superstition. You give them an apocalyptic agenda and a set of prejudices, all wrapped in a seemingly sound doctrine, and you find yourself in the presence of followers who are assured they're the human elite. What amazes me is that you have an informant—and I assume he's well informed—who's probably one of these people. What else did he tell you? Names, places?"

"There's not much more in my file than what I just told you. Most of what the AIVD and other agencies have is circumstantial, mere rumors. No member of the church was ever found guilty of any crime, nor did anyone spill the secrets to the outside world. We cannot condemn people for adhering to a religious doctrine if they don't commit crimes or actively incite others to commit hate crimes or murder. We can only hope the new guardians of the church are as much concerned about the radicals as we are and are willing to reveal the truth about them at some point."

"And it's this informant who provided the coordinates?" Eekhaut said.

After which they found themselves, on a cold January day, in a clearing in a forest, with only each other and death as companions.

Now, three weeks after their initial foray, they were still nowhere.

"He hinted that what we'd discover was only the proverbial tip of the iceberg," Dewaal said.

"A sort of preview? Of what exactly?"

"I don't know, Walter. I've never had any real conversation with my informant, who isn't keen on stepping into the daylight after all."

"No, I assume he wouldn't want to," Eekhaut said.

"Are they telling us," she said after a moment of awkward silence, "that there's no way we can identify the other five victims?"

"We can't identify any of them yet, Chief," Eekhaut said. "We've collected usable DNA on two of the bodies, but there's nothing to match them with since we can't find anything in our databases. One thing's for sure: while alive, these two didn't commit any crimes. Or were never registered as criminals. They're part of the millions of people not in our or any other database."

"We need a transnational DNA database of all citizens in the European Union," Dewaal said. She knew citizens, in the Netherlands as much as anywhere else, were very uncomfortable with being registered by the authorities. It was the type of thing only totalitarian states do. It would never pass legislation. The words "police state" would be heard whenever the subject came up. "Any other clues, like dental records? We could try dental records, assuming the victims are Dutch. Maybe none of them are Dutch."

"Our technical people tried to reconstruct jaws and dentures, but under intense heat, any part of the body becomes too brittle for them to use. Anyway, we would probably need to search records abroad, and we don't have the workforce to do that."

Dewaal leaned back in her chair. Eekhaut kept his gaze away from her suddenly tightening blouse. "So far nothing much, then. What was used to burn them?"

"Material that can be bought in any hardware store. Kerosene as an accelerant, mostly. Nothing complicated, nothing that leaves distinct clues. And the scene was about two weeks old, as far as the pathologist told us. The only thing he can say for certain is that they burned alive, but perhaps they were no longer conscious."

"That's horrible enough."

"Three of them were women. Ages probably between thirty and fifty. And probably Caucasian. That's about it as far as details are concerned."

"Must have been a lot of smoke. No reports about that? Anybody seeing the plume of smoke? Foresters, hikers?"

"Apparently no one was around at the time. The police inquired in the nearby villages, but there's no human habitation around for twenty kilometers. You remember how long it took us to get there on foot. And around the time of the murders, there had been several days of overcast weather and snow. It's unlikely anyone saw the smoke."

"These people prepared this execution carefully. Everything seems thought through, even the weather conditions."

"Isn't that what we could expect from a cult with such an impressive track record? That they prepared carefully and wouldn't want to get caught?"

She shook her head.

He wouldn't let it slide. "At least your informant should know better. Where did he get those coordinates? What role does he have in the organization? Is he actually reliable?"

"Are you questioning my informant, Walter?"

"I don't even know who he is, Chief."

"We did find the bodies, after all, didn't we? So, in my opinion, he is reliable. Shall we leave it at that?"

"Maybe these people *wanted* the bodies to be found. Maybe the informant has played the role he was *intended* to play. Is he a member of the conventional church? Or is he one of the radicals?"

"I know only that he walks with the radicals, the ones who want to continue the grand old tradition, and those bodies are proof of that intention. Try to keep things clearly separate, Walter."

"But we don't have any names? Nobody we know that's carrying a membership card? We could check their alibi and so on. Rattle their cage or whatever. Can't he give us some names?"

"As I understand it, he's deeply involved with the Society of Fire. That's not the problem. The problem, apparently, is that no one ever uses real names. And my informant is scared, really, that they'll find out he's talking to me. Can you imagine what they'll do to him? That's why our contacts so far have been brief. That is the problem with all cults: nobody talks to outsiders. And don't forget, the outside world is due to be destroyed. The apocalypse is nigh and all that. These people know only one thing. If they want to survive the coming onslaught, they need to pray to their creator and do what their leaders tell them to do."

"Well," Eekhaut said, "don't expect any prayers from me, even if the sky turns black right now and the Four Horsemen appear. If there were a god, he'd be less bloodthirsty and more compassionate than that. What about the message?"

"What message?"

"The one written on the cabin wall. Does it make any sense yet?"

She inhaled deeply. "Your guess is as good as mine, Walter. I asked Van Gils to google the text, but he came up with nothing. Maybe it doesn't mean anything at all."

"It's an explicit message. *This world seems to take forever / But it is only the dream of a sleeper.* That's clear enough, by way of warning. And it sounds vaguely familiar too. We must ask ourselves how many people are connected to this event. How extensive is this conspiracy?"

"There's no way of telling how many people were involved, since we found no trace of anyone. But that's not unusual, given that the ground was frozen in the whole area."

"I can't believe just one person was involved out there. He might have been able to drug the victims by himself, but he couldn't possibly have carried them all to the clearing without help. That or the material needed for the whole setup, the stakes and the chains and the kerosene. This was done by a group of people, with a clear goal in mind. Punishment, perhaps. But one of the reasons you punish people is as a caution to others. So why do it in a remote area? After this thing, I'm really concerned we'll be hearing from them again, and soon."

"You're probably right," she said. "Incidentally, I asked Veneman to consult the missing persons' database for the last couple of months. He told me a lot of people in the thirty- to fifty-year-old group are getting lost in Europe."

"Why don't we look at the Dutch only?"

"We could. But the Church of the Supreme Purification has an estimated hundred thousand members around the globe, and we may assume that's where the victims come from. That they'd be people killed by the radicals for belonging to the actual church."

"And how many of these radicals are there?"

"We don't know. Not even an estimate."

He rubbed his hands down his face and thought of Linda, who had been delighted with the news that she'd finally get to go to Africa on a humanitarian mission, although regretting that she'd be separated from him for six months—which was nearly as long as their time together until now. Linda, who had gone to Schiphol Airport on her own, didn't want him to come along and knew she'd be able to communicate with him only irregularly from somewhere in Somalia, technology permitting. He didn't want to think about the seven bodies on stakes, knowing that scenes like that weren't at all unknown to humanity. Burning people alive wasn't the sort of thing he came to expect here in peaceful and prosperous Holland, though. Or in Belgium, for that matter.

Dewaal interrupted his thoughts. "You and Prinsen will conduct a search for Dutch nationals, or Belgian ones, who've been reported missing during the month preceding the incident. We have to start somewhere. If we can't find anyone who might fit the little description we have of the victims, we'll expand our search. The boy can use the experience."

Prinsen, Eekhaut thought. "Yes, all right."

"And it's not a question of him being my nephew."

"He's better off with me than with any of the other members of the team, isn't he?"

She knew what he meant. To the other members of the team, young Prinsen was too close to Dewaal, family-wise. Eekhaut didn't care about her family relations, however. He was the odd man out in the group, the only Fleming. "God knows what they'd teach him, anyway."

"I leave things as usual in your most incapable hands, Walter. Although I should know better. Anyway, I hope your bad habits don't rub off on him. Got that?"

So, I'm not babysitting him, Eekhaut thought. Actually, he was. Eekhaut didn't know where to start anyway. Prinsen could do the heavy lifting, and Eekhaut could keep him knee-deep in research. Interrogating relatives of the hundreds of Dutchies who had recently vanished from the surface of the planet. *Sounds like fun*. This would keep them both busy for a long time.

"How many of them are there?" he inquired.

"How many what?"

"People. Dutch citizens gone missing."

"Oh! About a hundred and forty. Grown-ups anyway. Maybe fewer if you omit the ones who are either too young or too old." She stood up. "Start here in Amsterdam. Good luck with it. Maybe you'll be lucky right off."

2

NICK PRINSEN HADN'T RIDDEN his bike for several weeks now. Not because of the cold so much, which was bad enough this deep in winter, but because the snow in the streets and especially the patches of dirty, half-melted ice made riding through Amsterdam hazardous on two wheels. The winter so far had been severe, despite global warming. Storms and snow had come unpredictably, as if the weather wanted to challenge the doomsayers and weather forecasters alike. For more than a month now, Western Europe had been in the grip of winter. And it wouldn't be over soon. Still, the season had its occasional better moments. At night, temperatures would drop to the mid-teens, but during the day the sky would be clear and the sun would cause the mercury to rise to the mid-thirties. Soon enough, though, came clouds and high winds with more frozen rain and snow, forcing people back inside.

Riding his bike wasn't fun anymore, so Prinsen took the tram from his apartment to Prinsenkade, where he walked the short distance to Kerkstraat. Parkas had been in vogue for a while, along with laced-up boots and thick leather gloves. Amsterdam, usually the city of cyclists, had become a city of slow, hunched figures in heavy clothes waiting for trams or walking close to the storefronts. Restaurants were more popular than ever during daytime and on the weekend, but at night most people chose to stay home. More movies than ever were sold or downloaded, and more booze bought and consumed. And books read. Books, more than TV or games, were popular. This was the new literary winter.

That morning, however, Prinsen didn't have winter on his mind, or snow, the tram, or work. Last evening, he had had a call, a call he had been waiting for. Eileen Calster had called from Groningen, up in the north, and she announced she would soon be back in Amsterdam. She had already rented an apartment, found a part-time job, and was planning to take up studies again.

As far as Prinsen was concerned, all this was excellent news. Four months earlier, following a previous case, he had driven Eileen to Groningen to stay with her parents. Her life was no longer in danger, but she didn't want to remain in Amsterdam. She was still getting over the trauma of seeing her boyfriend shot, her brother murdered, and being chased by the same assassin.

During these last few months, she and Prinsen had often talked over the phone. She had finally made up her mind and told her parents she was not staying in Groningen any longer.

Now she would be back. She would be back in Amsterdam, and she would be back in his life, though she hadn't said it in so many words. During their conversations, she hadn't made any romantic overtures. They certainly had not talked of love. They were good friends, as things now stood. But this morning, in the tram, squeezed between the other passengers, it had felt like a bit of spring was returning to the city.

The tram clattered over Utrechtsestraat and stopped at the bridge over Prinsengracht, where the florist shop was closed for winter. Prinsen looked up. He'd been daydreaming, as he often did, and had almost missed his stop. He wriggled quickly from between the other passengers and stepped out from the musty, oppressive interior of the tram into the fresh air.

He pushed Eileen from his thoughts and made room for his job. The day before he had been going through files sent over from the local police in Alkmaar, concerning a criminal organization active in that town with contacts all the way to Norway and Sweden. The files included the usual suspects: right-wing activists, anti-immigration networks and bunches of shady but dangerous neo-Nazis. He couldn't understand why people were opposed to immigration. He lived in the most culturally diverse city on the continent. Most of these people's ancestors had immigrated to this country. If Amsterdam could exist with its scores of minorities, then the rest of Holland and Europe could too.

But a lot of people choose to think differently. Mostly those too young to remember the Occupation and the Holocaust.

More and more people advocated restricting immigration. Or even halting it completely. Some wanted to return non-native residents to where their ancestors had come from or some stupid idea like that. Third- and fourth-generation immigrants, citizens of the Netherlands and culturally part of the country, returning to . . . ? Or only those refusing to integrate? And then what about the large number of Dutch living and working abroad who didn't care to use the local language or adapt to the local customs? Would they have to return to Holland as well?

The idea was preposterous. He wasn't about to participate in any discussion of the issue. He found it to be a matter of prejudice and unfounded opinion, not based on anything sensible. The whole of Dutch society seemed bogged down in personal views and opinions, not bothering with real information and knowledge.

Opinions, not dialogue.

And with social media, things weren't getting any better.

He entered the building in Kerkstraat, the discrete location of the Office of International Crime and Extremist Organizations, or OICEO, which was part of the General Intelligence and Security Service, the AIVD. Nobody called it the OICEO. It was the Bureau for all concerned. And although it was part of the AIVD, it was physically separated from the central organization. And as such, in the minds of all concerned, a somewhat independent organization as well.

When he had started working there in late summer, the building had been almost cozy. But now, in the gray winter light, it had lost its charm. It had lost its charm as a place of employment as well. He felt like those anonymous worker bees that flocked from the railway station or tram stop toward offices in the morning and back again late afternoon. The building itself didn't give any inkling of what went on inside or what sort or organization it housed. No mention on the doors or facade of the AIVD. Discretion was the Bureau's hallmark. The Bureau chose to operate with utmost discretion and out of sight of the public.

The automated access system was as whimsical as it had been for the past few months. It flashed at him *Verification Failed* as he walked past the detectors. It added, not without malice: *Biometric Data Not Found.* For weeks now AIVD technicians tried to get the system back online and operational, but it remained buggy. How exactly it functioned was a deep organizational secret, and it seemed even the specialists couldn't find their way around it. The members of the Bureau had nicknamed it Basil because just like Basil Fawlty (of the famous British TV show), it possessed an erratic temperament. It constantly needed the intervention of a human guard. "Excuse me, sir," the one on duty today said, "but Basil is having one of his off days again."

Prinsen still had no private office, unlike Eekhaut who had been assigned one of the four enclosed spaces. Prinsen had his desk in the middle of the open space on the second floor, away from the window. Van Gils had taken the desk by the window, along with Veneman, another of the veteran officers. They had seniority, and one of the perks was a view over the small park outside, Amstelveld. Prinsen knew they had a problem with Eekhaut getting one of the offices. Dewaal explained that the Belgian possessed the status of the international contact.

International contact. It meant Eekhaut kept in touch with other European security agencies and wrote reports about the recent Bureau activities. And he had been involved, dramatically, in at least one major investigation.

Prinsen quite liked the Belgian. They had worked closely together these months since his arrival, and Prinsen knew him as straightforward and outspoken. The man was fluent in several languages and was quick-witted, even when confronted with complex issues. Dewaal— Aunt Alexandra to Prinsen—was convinced Eekhaut could be trusted slightly more than the older veterans of her team. Veneman and Van Gils were all right, but she knew she couldn't trust any of the other twenty officers and technicians in the building.

The feelings were entirely mutual.

"Eekhaut is here because he was getting on the nerves of his superiors in Belgium," she explained, a month after the Belgian had taken up residence. "I read his file, so I knew what to expect. His own methods, his own ideas, and he couldn't care less if they clashed with official policies." She wasn't saying she approved of what she'd heard about Eekhaut, but she didn't voice disapproval either.

Prinsen appreciated that she seemed to be confiding in him. She didn't have to, but she was. She wanted to make it clear he could trust Eekhaut as much as she did. But also that he needed to be careful in how he approached the other Dutch officers.

Upon entering, Prinsen looked over to the window of Dewaal's office. She was talking to Eekhaut. These last three weeks they had almost constantly been working on one case. He was almost relieved they hadn't included him. People burned alive at the stake as if this were the Middle Ages all over again. Ritual murders. He could do without them. It is the stuff nightmares are made of. He strongly preferred ordinary cases, like financial fraud or illegal arms trafficking.

Van Gils sat at his desk, looking out. He was eating a pastry out of a box from the Vlaamsch Broodhuys, a traditional Flemish bakery conveniently situated in the western end of Kerkstraat. On his desk sat the usual stack of folders. He hated paperwork nearly as much as Veneman did. Old-fashioned detectives, they preferred working with people, not with documents. That's where Prinsen came in. He enjoyed reading through thick stacks of reports, interviews, background information, even legal documents. As far as both the seasoned detectives were concerned, however, he still was the rookie who would have to work hard to deserve their respect.

And in this field, among people of this profession, respect was everything.

"Are they still in conference?" Prinsen inquired of Van Gils, while taking off his overcoat and hanging it on the coatrack. Van Gils and Veneman both preferred to ignore the investigation of the Ardennes incident as much as they could get away with it. They were concentrating on the financial affairs of a large import firm that employed a number of shady but well-known characters from certain parts of Amsterdam. Money had found its way into the deep pockets of police and customs officers, who consequently ignored the dealings of the firm.

There had been a couple of late-night confessions, but the directors of the AIVD had decided to keep the whole affair away from the public.

This didn't sit well with Van Gils and Veneman, who were frustrated with what they saw as a cover-up. Bringing the illegal dealings of powerful economic players to light. this was their primary mission in life.

"Are they still in isolation?" Prinsen inquired.

"There's a lot of things us common folk aren't supposed to know about," Van Gils said, eyeing the two officers in the closed office. "A lot to discuss, I guess. The results of the forensic team have been disappointing, to say the least. They haven't made much progress."

"There's the corpses," Prinsen said.

"The corpses. When you set something on fire and make it burn fast and hard, there's not going to be much left for forensics to work with. Cremating people is an art, actually. Most experienced criminals know that. So do we after finding a corpse in an oil barrel."

"So, whoever did it was experienced enough to—"

"I'd rather not think about it," Van Gils said, grimacing. After thirty years on the job, mostly in the streets of Amsterdam, he had seen arson with human victims aplenty, but not people tied to stakes.

3

HER HANDS PLANTED FIRMLY on her hips, unconsciously taking possession of the African landscape, Linda seemed surer of herself than she felt as she overlooked the scenery. After three weeks, this scenery should have been familiar, but it still was very different from what she imagined it would be.

Still, it wasn't an unfamiliar view. Documentaries and photographs had prepared her for this landscape. The desolate, nearly empty expanse of the African savanna was turning into a desert with frightening speed. This might have been the original landscape her very distant ancestors had experienced, looking up at the murderous sun, and at night at the staggering number of unexplainable stars.

But what photos and documentaries hadn't shown was the way she would be engulfed by the landscape, from which there was no escape, and how this experience obliterated inner dimensions. It felt like she was standing on the surface of an immense table, as if the earth was flat and the horizon would go on forever. This landscape took over all her imagination.

She also knew she would never be part of this continent. The shape of her face and the color of her skin told her that much.

At night, the landscape could not be more peaceful. There was never complete quiet, but only rarely did something move. Occasionally, a nocturnal animal cried out or chattered with sounds that were more amusing than threatening. The camp itself was asleep soon after dark because there was never enough energy to keep the lights on. In the evenings, there was little else to do but sleep. Whoever still roamed around ran the risk of being intercepted by patrolling soldiers. There were few of them around, but they were more than efficient.

It was a good thing these soldiers were present. She had counted about a hundred, led by a lieutenant and three sergeants. Kenyans, sporting the blue helmets of peacekeepers. A small part of the African peacekeeping force in Somalia, which was supposed to protect the camp where a few thousand refugees had found shelter against rebels, looters, murderers, rapists, and kidnappers. And, if needed, against nonhuman carnivores. Maybe a hundred weren't enough, but the Kenyans acted professionally and with respect toward the refugees, and they were all headquarters could spare.

Perhaps their zeal exceeded expectations, because two officials of the United Nations were left in the camp along with a dozen members of Doctors Without Borders, including Linda. She knew, at some point, the guards would need to guard the guards. But she was willing to give the Kenyans the benefit of the doubt. The lieutenant assured the doctors that he and his men were paid sufficiently for this dangerous mission and that criminals would not stand a chance.

She had been brewing tea and now drank a cup. It didn't amount to much, just reheated water with a slight mint flavor. There was no milk or lemon, and she drank it because little else was available. Supplies were difficult to come by, and the refugees constantly teetered on the brink of starvation. Some people were digging a fourth well because the other three were not sufficient to provide water for the camp. The stock had dwindled rapidly. The supply trucks had not come in over a week. Everything reminded her this was still a war zone.

The region was a war zone. Yesterday these people had been plagued by war, exactly like the days and months before, and there would be war tomorrow. They had been on the run for most of their lives. Or had stayed, however temporarily, in camps like this.

The camp began to wake up. Fires were started to make some sort of porridge in large iron kettles. Officials wanted to exchange the iron kettles for steel or aluminum ones, but the doctors had argued that even the small amounts of iron that would end up in the porridge would be a dietary advantage for these disadvantaged people.

"Mrs. Weisman," a civilized voice behind her said in a formal English Linda hadn't heard in a long time. She turned around. Lieutenant Odinga stood behind her in his dress uniform as if he would, at any moment, be inspecting his troops on the parade ground in Mombasa. He insisted the Kenyan flag be hoisted every morning and lowered again every evening, and no one objected. Except for the two members of the UN, nobody was going to disagree with him. The few village elders in the camp and some priests regarded the Kenyans as a necessary evil, since they had been cut off from their traditional social structure anyway. Lieutenant Odinga was the highest authority in the camp, by virtue of his troops, a position he didn't seem to appreciate. The UN officials merely advised him, and he was willing to listen to them, but at the end of the day, he made all the decisions. As long as no rebels overran the camp, nobody objected.

"Lieutenant," she said, also in English. "You know I'm *Miss* Weisman, don't you?"

He smiled, showing all too perfect teeth she was instantly jealous of. "It is better people understand you have a steady partner, even if that partner is not currently present. That is why I shall call you *ma'am*. Do not underestimate the prejudices of the local people. A woman on her own without a man in her life, that's not a good idea. They foster very traditional preconceptions about a woman's place under the sun. We are not going to talk them out of it. We are here to protect them. That's all we do. To us, however, they are barbarians that have not yet seen the light of true civilization."

She didn't know how to react. Surely, she couldn't rebuke the lieutenant. She was the one on unfamiliar ground, not he. Her characteristic Dutch levelheadedness would come in handy when dealing with him, but for a long while she would continue to be challenged by the inexplicable newness of this continent.

No, this was not about Africa. She could handle the alien landscape. It was fierce and wild, but after these first weeks, it no longer presented a challenge. The people, however, turned out to be the true unknown factor, especially those skeletal ones who shuffled day in and day out past the tents of the medical team. These people, who avoided her gaze when standing close and didn't speak to her for lack of a common language. These people had lived experiences she couldn't even imagine.

"From where do you originate, ma'am?" he asked, with an engaging smile. "I can't remember if anyone has already told me."

"The Netherlands," she said, hoping that would ring a bell.

"The Netherlands," he repeated, looking thoughtfully into the distance as if expecting to see a glimpse of that mythical country, maybe have an epiphany. It would be, he assumed, a place for rich, white people, with sufficient medical facilities, where an African would be an outcast but could perhaps become rich quickly.

"In Europe," she added. The six-foot-four lieutenant was an impressive sight, even standing beneath her on the incline. He had regular features, a fine nose, and high cheekbones. His hair, cropped short, was already graying at the temples. She estimated he was about forty but was probably wrong.

"Oh," he said, almost cheerfully as if amused by her needless explanation. "I know about your country, ma'am. I had my military training in the United Kingdom. You know what the United Kingdom is, do you? So, I am aware of the Netherlands and of Amsterdam. My friends and I managed to spend more than one weekend there. Terribly noisy city, drugs everywhere, the stench of addiction in the alleys, the women almost naked in the windows. We've seen it all. Yes, I know about the Netherlands and Amsterdam. Ma'am."

She kept quiet. She wouldn't start an argument with the only man who stood between her and Somali rebels, rapists, and killers.

"You're a long way from the Netherlands, ma'am," he continued. "I did not want to offend your country. We, here in Africa, are aware of the good things Europeans do for us. You sell weapons to our armies and you sell weapons to the rebels, and when a war breaks out, you provide doctors and relief supplies for the civilians. Your help, as such, is always appreciated."

"Don't misunderstand my intentions, Lieutenant," she said. She wanted to say more, argue with him about some of his points, but she couldn't. He was right, in that imperturbable way of his.

"Ma'am, I don't have the slightest intention to interpret your intentions the wrong way. You are here because you want to help people. You are most welcome. You have noticed this country is poor and in need of everything. That is why we all are here. But *our* intentions are misunderstood as well. Are we in Somalia because Kenya wants to be the local superpower? Are we here to annoy Ethiopia and Tanzania? No doubt all that is true. But I don't care. I'm not into politics. I follow orders. The general says, 'Lieutenant Odinga, you are going to keep the peace in that part of Somalia, you and hundreds of your men because the United Nations pays your wages, and they give you that nice blue helmet to wear, and because the Kenyan government gets a few million dollars for its involvement.' So, I come here and make sure there's peace and people don't kill each other."

"Because you see this as your duty?"

He glanced sideways at the landscape as if on the lookout for his duty. "I have nothing whatsoever to do with these Somalis. Our mutual ancestors waged war with each other. We still wage war, and again with Somalians. But not these people here. With Muslims, we hate Muslims."

"You protect these people, that should suffice," she said.

He nodded. "But, ma'am, what happens to these people here in this camp, when suddenly the UN sends no more money to my government? Me and my men, we would simply leave. That's what would happen."

"Just like that?"

"Of course. We are not responsible for the fate of these people. Forget what you see in the movies. When the American hero feels responsible for black refugees because they are black and because they have not yet seen the light of civilization, just so the American hero—and with him his Western audience—feels better. That's what movies are about."

She hadn't realized he would be a talkative man. For their previous encounters, they had never exchanged more than three sentences. Maybe something had happened that made him talkative.

"People feel better when they see such movies, Lieutenant," she said. "It reinforces their faith in humanity. Why look down at that?"

His eyes focused on her face. He looked into her eyes. "Faith in humanity?" he repeated.

"Yes. Despite wars and atrocities and the hunger and the poverty. Yes, despite all that, there's still reason to believe in humanity."

"Right," he said after a moment of silence. "I am willing to believe in the rest of humanity. The Russians and the Americans and the British. And even the Dutch. For your sake. But the Somalis . . ."

"We also have had our hereditary enemies, Lieutenant. The British and the Dutch were once—"

"I am aware of your historical differences," he said. "That was part of our military strategy lessons. How the Dutch almost took their fleet up the Thames to London. Hereditary, you say. How long do countries like the Netherlands and England exist, ma'am? I will answer the question myself: about a thousand years."

"Yes, that's about it."

"Allow me to use crude benchmarks for the sake of argument. Most European nations have existed for something like a thousand years in their present form. Sometimes much less, like Germany. A few hundred years of strife, that's what we remember. At the most. Here in Africa, nations and cultures and their memories go back five thousand years. Even longer. We don't know how long, actually. It often seems our tribes have been around forever, and since humans originated from Africa, they might have."

"No culture can really go back uninterrupted for five thousand years, Lieutenant. Collective memories don't go back that far. There is no historical evidence to support that, not in this part of Africa. In Egypt, yes, but . . ."

She ran out of steam.

He said nothing. She had the uneasy feeling she knew nothing at all about history. As if every book on the subject she had ever read had been full of fantasies.

"There's something I need to show you, ma'am," he said after a few moments of silence. "But I must ask you to come alone."

She hesitated. She didn't like the *alone* part.

"Oh, you can tell your colleagues you will accompany me. There's no need for secrecy. We can't have people gossiping, can we? I'll take a couple of my men along as well. There's already a few of them at the site, guarding it."

"The site?"

"Yes. The place I want to show you."

"What's the matter with that place?"

"I must ask you to be patient. There are no words to adequately describe it. You will have to see for yourself. It will tell you something about Africa. But I warn you that the sight of it will fill your heart with dread."

"You *are* making me curious, Lieutenant," she said. *Is this why he's so talkative?* she wondered. Because he had discovered something extraordinary in the desert? An archaeological site, proof of the existence of a vanished civilization, perhaps? Something that might shed a whole new light on the history of Africa?

"Curiosity is not a good trait," he said. "We, here in this small part of the continent, are not a curious people, Mrs. Weisman, because experience has taught us that a lion awaits us behind the next tree or a snake in the grass. That is why we stay on the paths our ancestors cut for us. Perhaps that's why African nations have never reached the level of civilization of your glorious Western ancestors. That's why we still live in the jungle or the desert."

"I didn't mean to—"

"I know you didn't," he said. "I know white people—forgive me the expression—want to know everything. That's why I will show you the site tomorrow. You can spare the time, I assume?"

She had plenty of time, even after a full day of work. She had months. That was how much she had allowed herself to be away from the Netherlands and from Walter. And from herself. Walter had been the most important factor in the equation, after all. She would return to him after her respite. She hadn't left because their relationship was going wrong, but to avoid precisely that.

4

EEKHAUT INTENDED FOR PRINSEN to do all the heavy lifting in connection with the new investigation, since the kid was going to be part of the small team. Going through newspaper archives, comparing medical data, whatever. The boring stuff. And no, it wasn't fair. Prinsen didn't deserve this treatment, although he was the youngest member of the team and still had to learn the tricks of the trade. He had to learn that all police officers, even those of the Bureau, were often asked to chase ghosts and illusions.

Eekhaut would teach Prinsen to conform, precisely the sort of thing he himself wasn't any good at. But after that, he was going to pull the rug from under his feet. He was going to show him how little a half-decent officer achieved by toeing the line. He'd make him into the perfect little rebel in his own image. In this jungle, you survived by not following order too much, by not playing nice. That's what Prinsen needed to understand, and the sooner the better.

Prinsen still had a lot to learn. Social awareness, critical thinking, historical perspective—the boy lacked all this, in Eekhaut's view. He wouldn't have learned it in school. Not here in Holland. That much Eekhaut knew about the Dutch. The most interesting things came to you by coincidence, when you tripped over them. He would force the boy to think for himself. He had learned these things the hard way himself, by forcing his way through the ranks of the Belgian police force, one painful step at a time.

Now he would be sending Prinsen on a treasure hunt, a different kind of treasure hunt.

Eekhaut didn't care much for fieldwork. He had been out on the streets for half his professional life, first in Leuven and afterward in Brussels, and look where he'd ended up. The odd man out in this Dutch bunch. But he had come to terms with the way his nonexistent career had worked out. He'd been sleeping better than ever before these past few months. He was no longer frustrated with the stupid injustices displayed by former superiors. At least Dewaal had been free of those sins.

But he would send Prinsen on a wild goose chase. Well, not really.

He wondered how to find out who the seven victims had been. There was no telling where they came from. Could be from all over the globe.

He got up. Through the glass partition between his office and the common area, he noticed Prinsen reading documents. He had no idea what the young man currently was investigating. He didn't need to know, since Prinsen was Dewaal's problem, being family and all. But it seemed Prinsen was distracted. Eekhaut knew why. He had heard Eileen Calster would be returning to Amsterdam. Prinsen had not concealed his excitement.

He opened the door. "Nick," he said, "you have a minute?"

Prinsen looked up. He closed the folder and walked into Eekhaut's office. Eekhaut closed the door behind them.

"You're in," he said. "Dewaal wants you to go looking for missing Dutch citizens that could answer to the very general description of those seven we found in the Ardennes."

"I guess you have an idea how many people disappear in the Netherlands every year?" Prinsen said.

"You can narrow that down to the last few months, until three weeks ago, apparently."

"The whole of the Netherlands?"

"Start locally. Amsterdam. You're good at collecting information and discovering links between things. You're the smart kid behind the game console, the kid in the movies that sees things grown-ups miss. That's you. There's enough data on missing persons of every age and social background. Crunch the numbers, kid."

"Why Holland? Is there a reason why these people had to be Dutch?"

"The informant who led us to the crime scene is Dutch. It may not mean anything, but we have to start somewhere."

"Is there anything else I should know before I set off?"

"Like backgrounds?"

"That would be helpful."

"The whole thing seems connected to a cult or a sect, whatever." Eekhaut gave Prinsen a short review of what he and Dewaal had collected by way of information and what the young detective hadn't already heard.

"The Society of Fire? Creepy," Prinsen said. "Burning people and stuff. Don't want to know, really. Reminds me of Roman emperors and Christians and witch burnings. You wonder what brings people to hurt others in such a terrible fashion. What's there to gain?"

"Any strong conviction, any absolute form of religion, blurs the boundaries of what is acceptable, even in a civilized society," Eekhaut said. "Happens often enough. Read more Stephen King, and you'll know what I mean. Or the Old Testament. But the Romans hardly persecuted the Christians, and all that nailing on crosses and having them eaten alive might be a myth or Christian propaganda."

Prinsen looked ill at ease. He would be ill at ease, Eekhaut thought. "A vengeful and cruel god," he continued, "who demands human sacrifice, who has no problem with his flock engaging in genocide. Sound familiar? But I digress, Nick. You understand what it is we want?"

"I'm on it," Prinsen said. "Any other characteristic I ought to look for?"

"Only some general things like race and age, height, but no more than that. There's a memo in your inbox right now detailing what we need."

"Maybe there's another thing we ought to consider."

"Like what?"

"If this was a ritual," Prinsen said, "it might be possible the victims were not chosen at random. Maybe they have things in common. Maybe they even knew each other. Members of the same church, perhaps."

"Yes, we thought about that. You expect a ritual to have an inherent logic. But maybe not."

"How much time do I have?" Prinsen said, getting up.

"The victims aren't in any hurry anymore, but Dewaal needs results now. You know the pressure she's under."

"I'll give it my immediate attention."

Eekhaut looked at his watch when Prinsen had left. Ten thirty. He had a couple things he needed to do. He got up, grabbed his jacket and coat, and exited the building through the garage. Buttoning his overcoat, he stepped through Kerkstraat and rounded the corner of Utrechtsestraat. He was close to his apartment but wasn't heading there.

He entered Café Bouwman on the corner with Prinsengracht, overlooking the canal. He took a table by the window, where there was plenty of light, and ordered a brown Leffe beer that came at once—cold and frothy. Exactly what he needed.

On arriving here last September, he had been pleased with the south-facing terrace—actually a double row of tables and chairs along the sidewalk, barely enough for a score of people. The tables and chairs would be back, he hoped, as soon as the weather got milder. On occasion, he would come here for breakfast or grilled cheese sandwiches for lunch.

These past months he took time away from the office almost every day, late morning, to drink a Leffe and clear his mind. Get the gray cells working. He probably was an alcoholic but he didn't much care. In Brussels, he had drunk Duvel, the local brew. Or red wine. Here he had switched to Leffe almost at once, in part as a reminder of Flanders and its tradition of beer-brewing monks.

Also to forget the things he wanted to forget. Plenty of those around. Things he no longer needed in his life. Children bought and sold to end up in Moscow flophouses. Drowned children on a beach somewhere in Italy. People on stakes. Esther's death, ten years ago—his wife of so many years. Or having to miss Linda for six months. Having to spend his evenings alone again. All that was bad, some worse than the rest. He was nearly over Esther's death. Had taken him long enough. Things that had happened and couldn't be undone were better left alone. The same went for the people who died in the Ardennes. He needed to concentrate on Linda. He had to work on his relationship with Linda. That was a thing he *could* do something about.

"I really have to do this, Walter," she had said. She had made up her mind. They had had the conversation over dinner at the Segugio Italian restaurant, in Utrechtsestraat, not far from his apartment. He was eating boar shank stewed in Barolo for *secondi*, and she was having pheasant breast with polenta in a sauce of olives and licorice. "I know Somalia's like the end of the world, and I'll be gone for half a year, but I need this."

He glanced at her hands, then outside at the little garden behind the building. The Segugio was a tiny restaurant but intimate. The elegant tables had white cotton cloths draped over them. The floor was unevenly tiled in rustic beige.

"I need to get some distance between myself and Holland and Amsterdam and the corruption and all that," she continued. "Away from everything—except you, of course. I would ask you to come with me, but I know you can't just walk away. And I really want some time alone."

He had understood. They had known each other for—how many months now? Four? He had never been to her flat, but she had come to his, and they had made love there.

Made love. How formal that sounded now. It had almost been raw passion. Sweaty bodies, chaos, body fluids, thirst and hunger, expressions of eternal trust, and promises.

Too many promises, probably.

"I won't try to keep you here," he said. "Not if you feel so strongly about this."

He thought, *Damn clichés. It is almost impossible to be original anymore.*

"But you'll be out there on your own," he continued, while the waiter, in severe black and white, removed their empty plates, returning to fill their glasses again.

But there was no way around her decision. She wanted him, and she wanted him to want her, but still she needed to go.

He realized he knew little about her, even after four months. There were a lot of unspoken things between them. He hadn't even told her anything about his life, about Esther, who had been his companion for so long, about . . .

The waiter brought desserts—lemon and Italian meringue crispy pie with mint sauce for her and a warm chocolate cake for him.

"What will happen after your time in Somalia?" he wanted to know.

"I'll come back here, and we'll have long conversations about poverty and the state the world is in," she said. And then she smiled. "I'm coming back to you," she added.

There had been coffee afterward.

And they made love in his flat.

She stayed until morning.

He glanced at his watch. He was expecting a call from Linda, but she had warned him communications with that part of the world would be difficult. There'd be no post office and no internet and no cell phone she could use. She would have to borrow a satellite phone if available.

His cell phone buzzed. He pulled it from his pocket and said his name.

"Walter?" It was Prinsen. "I think I've found something. It might be nothing, but it seems—"

"You found something already?" He imagined Prinsen working through the night, sleepless.

"That's right," the young man said cheerfully. "I went through the Amsterdam reports first. And there's something you might find interesting."

"I'll be with you in a moment," Eekhaut said. A moment. Time enough to finish his Leffe. He was not going to hurry. Certainly not for Prinsen.

Fifteen minutes later he stood next to the young detective. He had bought a cheese and ham sandwich from Bouwman, had it wrapped to go, and was eating it while listening. Prinsen, used to Eekhaut's erratic behavior, made no comment about the snack, although it was not noon yet. One of the other veteran officers of the Bureau, Siegel, sat at the table across from them, moving his fingers almost without sound over the keyboard of a laptop.

"If this works out well for you," Eekhaut said, "I might put you up for promotion, Nick."

Prinsen held up three documents. Eekhaut noticed pictures, names, and text. Profiles. "Three missing persons," Prinsen said, "that might fit the bill."

"No more than three people went missing in Amsterdam in the month or two previous to—?"

It was Siegel who replied, from behind the computer, not taking his gaze off the screen. "No, twelve, to be exact. But these have something in common."

"What's that?"

Prinsen said, "All three live in or close to the center of Amsterdam. Ages between thirty and fifty. Each works at a management level of some sort. Each disappeared without leaving a trace, destination unknown, between four and five weeks ago. It might be a coincidence, but then again not."

"Excellent," Eekhaut said. "Add their profiles to the dossier. Is there a way we could get their DNA? Have they given blood recently? Or donated an organ?"

"I'll try to find out who their doctors were or if they were blood donors."

Eekhaut went back to his office and sandwich. Prinsen would do all right, although he wouldn't get his promotion right away. He was hardworking and eager to help. Eekhaut would have to warn him about that. Maybe his colleagues would take advantage of him. No, he was sure they would. He knew the old guard all too well. People like Veneman and Siegler. And Van Gils too. He knew how they treated the new detectives. He'd seen that happen in Brussels, and cops would be the same the world over. Siegel was of a slightly younger generation, having worked at the AIVD for only ten years. Neither he nor the other veterans had been delighted when Dewaal climbed up the corporate ladder and became their chief. Prinsen, as Dewaal's nephew, would be particularly vulnerable.

He threw the paper napkin and sandwich wrapper in the trash and sat up. He grabbed his keyboard and started typing. He googled the text they'd found on the wall of the cabin in the Ardennes.

The search engine told him there were no matches to be found. Not unusual when your search item is three whole sentences. There were a couple of suggestions Google made concerning parts of the text, but these all seemed to refer to self-help groups, religious organizations, pastoral care, aftercare facilities, and things like that. Perhaps some of those would be useful, but he would have to scan hundreds of pages. The separate words would yield hundreds of thousands of results. That was equally useless.

Most likely it wouldn't be a biblical text, he assumed. It wouldn't have a literal meaning. This was something a lot of these serial and hate killers had in common—a penchant for mystery, for the spiritual, for . . .

He pushed the keyboard away. He thought of Linda. He thought of Linda a lot. More than was good for him.

5

JAN PIETER MAXWELL HAD positioned his hands on his closed black leather portfolio. That portfolio contained no more than ten documents. That was all Maxwell needed for this meeting. Just a page with highlights and some short reports. All the information about this company and the way it functioned was in his head, like everything else that mattered to him.

He was a man who took care of his appearance. His clothes were meticulously pressed, his jaw and cheeks neatly shaven. There was not a gray hair on his head and no sign of fatigue. He was, after all, not that old. His résumé would say he was in his late forties, and if you listened to his mother, she'd tell you he was a bit over fifty. But official documents would assure you sixty was closer to the truth.

With an outward semblance of sympathy, he scrutinized the various members of the board as they entered the room and took their seats around the table. Their places were fixed. They sat down quietly. Planning and order: Jan Pieter Maxwell loved it. A clearly defined hierarchy of people and things. Only then, if this condition was met, would improvisation be allowed. That's how he managed the company. He managed it with his mind and his heart, since this was his child, the company he had founded. One of the many he had founded. But this was the first, and as such the eldest in his family of companies. Which made TransCom stand apart. As it should. As the chairman, he would never miss a board meeting of TransCom.

He moved his left hand over the front of his jacket, enjoying the softness of the fabric. He always wore dark blue suits made by the best tailors in Amsterdam or London.

He enjoyed traditions.

He enjoyed order.

He also enjoyed leather portfolios, with their superfluous documents. He carried a portfolio to give the impression that even he didn't know *everything*, that he was human after all. He liked mechanical chronometers and expensive pens and discreet but luxurious cars. He wasted no words; he rarely wasted energy.

"Shall we commence?" he suggested.

No one around the table disagreed. The TransCom board knew about his penchant for formalities. They knew that no more than a mere nod from them sufficed to have the meeting start.

"The first item on the agenda . . ."

An hour later the meeting was over. Meetings should not last longer than strictly necessary, that was his credo. After a while, concentration began to drop, attention waned, fatigue set in, stupid decisions were made. An hour was long enough. Explaining and arguing for an hour usually got him what he wanted. He occasionally had to force decisions. This way he could squeeze several meetings with different companies into a day, without having to work for sixteen hours straight. Sixteen hours, that would be a waste of energy.

The board members left the room, convinced as always that they had matters in their hands, an illusion Maxwell was all too happy to bolster. He followed them outside and felt his smartphone vibrate. He glanced at the screen and recognized the number. He retreated to his office at the end of the short hallway. All rosewood and copper—bookcases with glass doors, two paintings with ornate frames, a thick carpet, a humidor on the desk, and a small, expensive laptop.

He dropped the useless portfolio and answered the smartphone. "Courier!" he said. He had several other meetings planned, but if Courier called, there would be more pressing concerns—concerns of a very different nature.

"They found the scene of the ritual," Courier said.

Maxwell didn't react. He took a pair of reading glasses from the breast pocket of his coat and put them on.

"Are you still there?" Courier inquired. "Baphomet? Are you there?"

"Who found it, Courier? Who?"

"The police. The cops found the spot. Three weeks ago."

Maxwell thought about that for a short moment. "Three weeks?"

"Yes. Apparently."

"And I get to hear about it only now?"

"It was only brought to my own attention an hour ago. None of us went back to verify the place was still untouched. Now I hear from one of my professional contacts that the police discovered the location. There must be a full investigation already, although very discreet, since it's been kept out of the press."

"Investigation," Maxwell said. He sat down on his straight chair, which felt uncomfortable right now. "And those contacts of yours, I hope they have no idea of your involvement with—"

"Of course not," Courier said indignantly.

"And of course there's an investigation, Courier. What did you expect? The cops find the scene and the bodies, things become interesting. Did you think they'd shrug it off and let the matter slide? Our problem, Courier, is will they find any answers to their obvious questions?"

"No, Baphomet, they won't find anything. We didn't leave anything out there that could give us away."

"You seem very sure of yourself."

"I am," Courier said. "We've been extremely careful and thorough. Anyway, the fire destroyed anything we might have overlooked."

"Don't underestimate the technology available to the police. Experience has taught us to always hide our tracks carefully. Never allow anything to escape our attention. That's what we did in the past and why we've always been successful in staying out of sight, under the radar. But technology evolves. Police work evolves. I shouldn't have to explain that to you, Courier. The slightest trace can draw the cops to us. So my question is: will we succeed in remaining invisible?"

"I hope so," Courier said.

"You *hope* so," Maxwell repeated. "Then let me say this, Courier: I don't have much faith—actually none at all—in what you choose to believe. For my peace of mind, I rely solely on absolute certainty. That's how I tick. I want you to contact your friends inside the force, the AIVD, and find out everything we need to know about the investigation, about the people working the case, about what they already have. I want to know for certain if any evidence can be traced back to us. Because if that were the case, I'd be greatly disappointed. Very. Even more if any evidence led back to me personally."

"I'll do what's necessary, Baphomet."

"Of course, you will, Courier. Oh, another thing. Don't call me again on this number. This is a business number. You ought to know that. You also know how to reach me discreetly, even in case of an emergency."

"I just figured—"

"Sometimes you think too much. Too much thinking, not enough action. You need to know what to do under circumstances like these. Can you deal with that?"

"I certainly will, Baphomet."

Maxwell ended the call. The smartphone was secure enough. It was secure against viruses and against government snoopers. No one would be able to listen in. But he couldn't allow Courier or any of the others to just call him unexpectedly like that. He couldn't allow that. Order and security were what he needed.

6

"Could you send me those results right away, doctor?" Prinsen inquired over the phone. "So our lab can compare them with the data we already have." He listened to the reply. "Thank you. We appreciate that."

He got up and walked into Eekhaut's office. "We'll get DNA data from two of the three missing persons I mentioned. I'll have it compared with the DNA we have from the victims."

"Good," Eekhaut said. "Let's hope we get lucky. Get the information to the lab at once. We can expect a special effort from them after they took so long finding DNA on the victims."

Prinsen returned to the common room where one of the younger female officers, Thea De Vries, new on the team, was handling incoming reports from foreign security services. This was the sort of routine stuff handled by junior officers. Which currently meant Thea and Prinsen.

Eekhaut picked up his phone—the desk phone, a suitably conventional one—and punched Dewaal's number. "We're making progress," he said.

"Are you?" she replied. "And why are you calling me? I'm in the pigeonhole next to yours. Walk over."

He felt ridiculous, hung up the phone, and stepped into her office. Her door was, as usual, open. "Your young nephew has managed to get DNA from a couple of missing people. He's going to have it checked against our DNA."

"And I assume that's all we have to work with? Did those two have something in common?"

"The most general social profile. Same broad background. I've requested their full dossiers from the local judiciary, then we'll know more."

Dewaal sat back in her comfortable leather chair. "We're counting too much on luck. I haven't heard anything else from my informant. He could tell us more, but he's not coming to the surface. The whole sacrifice might be an act of revenge. Members of the society getting rid of the competition. This doesn't look random. At least not randomly chosen victims."

"There're still five others we probably won't be able to identify."

"So be it. I'm more worried about what this all means. It can't be just some weird execution staged by a couple of insane religious zealots. There has to be a driving force behind a ritual murder like this, someone who inspires people enough to make them commit atrocious crimes."

"Oh, history tells us there're always plenty of people around when atrocities have to be committed."

She slowly shook her head. He had seen that before—her denying the pure evil in man.

"In times of war, yes." Dewaal said. "Civil war, that sort of thing. But this? This isn't just a matter of blind hatred toward enemies or adversaries. There's something deeper and more frightening beneath this sort of senseless violence."

He thought, *You're in unfamiliar territory, Alexandra. You've never been in a similar situation.* Neither had he, actually. Having to deal with international organized crime as he had done in Brussels, and she had done over here, meant they had all too often witnessed terrible things. Organized crime attracts a specific brand of psychopath, someone who has their dirty work done for them by other psychopaths. You ended up with body parts in oil drums, informers flayed alive, organs removed from living victims—that sort of thing. But religious motives never had been part of the deal. Mass burnings either. "Like you," he said, "I've had my share of psychopaths, Chief. This is something, well—"

"I am familiar with what psychopaths can do," she said, gazing outside. "And then of course there's the circumstances when their sort let loose and drag others with them in a frenzy of—" She turned her head. "By the way, aren't *you* supposed to be the cynic of the team?"

"Cynic? Me?"

"No? Then I seem to have misjudged your role so far. Weren't you the one with an attitude problem toward hierarchies and people in general?"

"You do me great injustice, Chief. And you're clearly confused about me. High time we adjourn to a pub and have a beer. I can recommend one in particular. A dark Belgian beer that has proven its positive influence on the working of the human brain. Even the famous Inspector Morse knew that, although he might have drunk another brand of beer."

He noticed a subtle change in her demeanor. "Intuition—you know, that specific female secret weapon—tells me you already had your Leffe earlier today. And probably while on duty. But your secret is safe with me. As long as it was only *one* Leffe." She got up and pushed her chair back. "But you're right. We need something to drink. However, I'm the responsible police chief, and as such I cannot drink spirits or beer during the day. Let's go somewhere nice where other sins are available."

"Other sins? You don't mean . . . ?"

They left her office, and she ignored his remark.

"What do you have in store for me next? Concerning the, eh, investigation?" he inquired.

"Why not visit a specific very nonofficial religion tomorrow?" she suggested. "It seems this is the right time to start looking more closely at a sect we've already had in our files for so long." She noticed he seemed lost. "I'm talking about the Church of the Supreme Purification, Walter, what else? We could ask them if some of their faithful went missing recently. After that, we check the places where those two absentees used to work. By then we might know if there's some kind of match."

They left the building, their coats protecting them from the cold. He followed her toward Utrechtsestraat, where she turned right toward downtown. She headed straight for Patisserie Kuyt. Not the sort of place he would usually go—a coffee and tea house, serving the most delicious pastries and other frivolous stuff for those with an intense sweet tooth. The interior was colorful and fresh, with a large glass counter, clear plexiglass chairs, indirect lighting, several complicated coffee machines, and an abundance of patisserie, donuts, pastries, and tarts.

"It's not a substitute for lunch," Dewaal said, "but I assume it will do on this occasion. I'll have a cappuccino, and I'm going to get me some of those éclairs and a little fruit tart as well."

He got them both a cappuccino, and for himself, he ordered a cheese *kroket* that came with slices of bread.

"Any news of Linda yet?" Dewaal asked after they'd been served. "Did you manage to get in touch with her?"

"There's a satellite phone in the camp for official use, but even then it's difficult to get in touch. I didn't really expect her to call me every day. She's not the kind of woman who likes idle chat anyway. If something serious happens, I'm sure she'll find a way to let me know."

Dewaal carefully tasted the éclair, making sure not to spill the vanilla custard. "Things will turn out all right for her," she said, around a mouthful. "How's the relationship anyway? Not that I want to pry . . . but I must pay attention to the mental health of my people, not only their physical well-being."

"I couldn't talk her out of it, Alexandra," Eekhaut said, assuming he could use her first name under these circumstances. She would have been *Chief* if someone else were around. "I couldn't keep her here in Amsterdam against her will. You know how she quit her job and what a difficult time she has had. She wanted to give meaning to her life again. Her professional life. She wasn't going to sit around in her apartment, waiting for the right job to come along."

"So, when the offer came, she just—"

"Someone she knew from her university days was familiar with people at relief organizations, and they are constantly on the lookout for suitable employees. Doctors and nurses mainly, but occasionally they need people with organizational skills. Who speak several languages, if possible. Who have no problem with camping out in some absurdly remote part of the planet, far away from civilization."

"Risking her relationship with you."

"If our relationship can't handle this," Eekhaut said, finishing off his *kroket*, "then it's in bad shape and shouldn't be allowed to go on."

"Was that your conclusion at the time? I mean, three weeks ago?"

"Yeah, pretty much so. And hers, of course. We didn't exactly use those phrases, but, yeah, that much was understood between us."

"And what are the risks? Over there?"

"In Somalia? It isn't like you can be repatriated when you're in trouble, so you're pretty much on your own. But there are people around, peacekeepers and all that. Soldiers from some other African country. Kenyans, I believe. A peacekeeping force. They're responsible for the safety of the camp and for the safety of the foreign aid workers."

"There's a risk, then," Dewaal concluded.

"Isn't there for all of us?"

"I know you're thinking about those people in the Ardennes," she said. "But they're atypical. They might have felt safe, in daily life, but at the same time they were members of a church with a very disturbing past. They made enemies."

That brought them back to the reality of the investigation. Which he preferred over fretting about Linda, whom he wouldn't be able to help if she were in trouble.

"If tomorrow things don't work out as we expect, then what?"

"I don't want to think too far ahead, certainly not when I'm at lunch, Walter. A thing I'm worried about, though, is we found one place where a complex ritual was performed that might have taken considerable time and resources to prepare. Will there be similar sites not yet discovered?"

"I prefer not, if you don't mind."

"Our wishes aren't always granted. We must face certain facts. The doctrine of the Society of Fire, such as it is, assumes its members are supposed to deal with all those millions of unworthy people. That includes most of the population of this planet. That's also you and me, Walter. As in the past, most future incidents involving people burned to death will have to be treated as suspicious. But why is it different than what happened in the past? Why did the society choose to set up the sort of execution that couldn't possibly be seen as an accident? What has changed?"

"We don't really know if we were supposed to find out. If your informant—"

"Still, it wouldn't go unnoticed forever." She glanced at the counter as if considering another éclair. "Not even in the Ardennes."

"Your informant had nothing further to share about the subject?"

"He was, as usual, very discreet. And concise. I never get more than a few sentences on paper, a vague picture that might mean something, that sort of thing. It's not like all of a sudden a detailed map concerning the society lands on my desk. And a compendium with names and biographical details. I don't even expect his information to lead to a breakthrough. Coordinates, that's all I got. And I'm still in the dark about his motives."

"Can't you contact him?"

"He made sure I couldn't. It's a one-way street. He is careful, obviously. He's aware, I guess, of the punishment for treason. Can't blame him for being careful."

7

LINDA WEISMAN TRAVELED IN the jeep with Lieutenant Odinga, who drove carefully for lack of road. The vehicle seemed as good as new and was painted a pale reddish-brown to make it disappear in the scenery. They drove south with old, jagged mountains looming in the distance. The other members of the medical team had warned her about those mountains. That's where the rebels came from. At least according to the refugees. Since the arrival of the team and the Kenyan contingent of Blue Helmets, no rebels had been seen. A couple of times there had been gunfire in the distance, but sound carried far across the open plain. Perhaps it had been hunters or poachers, who didn't seem bothered by the presence of the soldiers in the area.

She glanced over her shoulder, but the camp was no longer visible. The jeep threw a cloud of dust that was heavy and soon settled again. It had a sharp, metallic smell, like blood. She couldn't escape the dust. This world seemed uniquely made from sand and dust.

For a moment, she considered asking the lieutenant again what he wanted to show her. But the stern look on his face made her decide otherwise. He would probably not find the right words to explain what he and the soldiers had discovered *over there*. She still wondered why he had spoken to her about it. For the last three weeks, he had hardly been paying attention to her. He conversed with his sergeants, with the doctors, with the two officials from the United Nations, and he even talked to some of the older refugees. But he chose to ignore her.

Then, suddenly, there was this. This special treatment. Even more unusual because he had asked her to be discreet about their sortie.

No, she hadn't told her team leader where she was going. In her spare time, she did as she pleased. She wasn't accountable to anyone. She wouldn't be patronized. There had been plenty of that in her previous occupation. An occupation that left her with the certainty that she was not, and would never be, appreciated. Not by her boss and not by the other employees. A job she had quit after four years.

She had been honest with Walter: she needed time away from Amsterdam and from the Netherlands. Her feelings had nothing to do with him. He was probably the only reason ever to return to Amsterdam. He had understood. She hoped he had understood. She wanted to distance herself from her former life, find new horizons, although she was ashamed of the cliché. At the same time, she could help people who were in dire need, she could help alleviate the world of poverty, or whatever. Walter believed that the solution to third-world poverty was to provide interest-free loans to farmers in particular, provide knowledge on a large scale, and open fair international markets for these countries. But these were not the things she could help with. She wanted to go over there and get her hands dirty.

It's a war zone, she told him. There's no economic activity. What they need is urgent medical care and equipment for digging wells and for tents, water filters, those sorts of things. She recalled that as a kid, she sold paper flowers for poor countries and aid organizations. Walter recalled almost the same things. He collected bottle caps for the missionaries to sell and collect money for poor people in the former Belgian colony.

But her main reason remained the oppressive feeling she had in Holland. It had become too small, too restricted. No free spaces, no real landscapes—just houses and office buildings and football stadiums and factories and more office buildings. Then there was the way people shuffled through life, bound by that typically Dutch necessity to conform, to be exactly like everybody else. It had driven her almost insane. On the job, people always watching you. Making sure you didn't stick out. Being afraid to be different. It permeated their entire society.

She looked skyward. She would try again to call Walter tonight. It hadn't worked out earlier with the satellite phone. The UN people had a shortwave transmitter, but she could hardly use that to call Walter.

She needed a functional mobile phone. That was what she was thinking, deep in Africa, in a jeep.

"We're not going far, I hope?" she said.

Lieutenant Odinga turned his head slightly toward her without taking his eyes off the nonexistent road. "We don't measure distances here like you do in Europe," he said. "We might travel two hundred miles in four days to meet a neighbor. Just for a chat, to see someone who isn't even related. Two hundred, that's a trip, not a voyage, to us." There was suddenly amusement in his voice. "We're a bit like Americans in that respect."

They approached the foothills of the mountains. Red rocks, barely affected by erosion. Sand and wind had had hardly any impact on the hard material. Or it was a recently formed rock formation, geologically speaking. Sometimes she imagined buildings concealed under these rocks. A lost civilization no one had ever heard of, deep in the African heartland.

The jeep slowed. She wondered how the lieutenant knew where to go. Maybe he saw familiar details in the landscape that escaped her. He drove confidently enough, as if driving on a paved road. Then she noticed he was simply following a row of stones, marking a path, set a hundred meters apart from each other. Primitive but effective, although eventually the boulders would disappear under the sand.

"How long do you intend to stay?" Odinga inquired.

The question was obvious enough. It was the sort of small talk people used to avoid more difficult subjects. Except that this question seemed to have a very specific meaning, in a country without past or history and certainly without much of a future. He wanted to know to what extent she felt connected to the refugees, to the land itself. He wanted to find out the extent of her commitment.

"I'm staying for six months," she said. This wasn't entirely true but not really a lie either. She could leave whenever she wanted. A plane would be expected every week. She could be on it anytime she wanted. Nobody could keep her longer than she wanted, and nobody would blame her for leaving.

He nodded. Six months had been an eternity to her when she arrived. If she went back earlier, it would be because of Walter and for no other reason.

But after these past weeks, she had come to realize people here depended on her.

No, she wouldn't be drawn into that trap. *Don't let things get personal,* as she had been advised before coming here. *Don't get involved. Emotionally or otherwise. Because there is very little you can do for these people, except for temporarily tending to their most pressing needs. After that, you need to return to your own reality.*

These people cannot be saved just by sending medical teams or soldiers. Their problems, and those of this part of the continent, are much more fundamental. It all comes down to the basic problems of global capitalism. The widening gap between the very few rich and the very many poor. Soon, there will no longer be a middle ground, no middle class, no upward mobility for most of the human race.

That's what she had been told in Amsterdam by the people who had contacted her. *What we do in places like Somalia,* they warned her, *is tending to the superficial wounds of the body, while that same body is rotting away. So while you might feel a personal responsibility to these desperate people, you must keep in mind that you're not part of the solution. And never will be.*

But then, after arriving here and meeting the people, especially the children, she knew the real world, the world of hunger and sand, needed mending. And that politics, exactly like global capitalism, was a ghost, certainly to these people. They were hungry, needed clean water and basic medical help. She wasn't a doctor, nor a nurse. She managed supplies, work schedules, communication, the practical stuff the medical team needed regularly. Quartermaster and occasional cook, pencil pusher and gopher. That was who she was. She didn't need to encounter any of the refugees at all.

But the children soon found out what she was responsible for and what sort of stuff they could beg from her, like a bit more food and luxuries—sugar, chocolate, tea, coffee.

"What you are going to see," Odinga suddenly said, waking her from her reveries, "will shock you. I want you to be prepared."

"Then why show it to me? If it's shocking, isn't it your responsibility to keep me far away from it? Shouldn't you be involving the UN people instead?"

"Nothing is ever that simple, Miss Weisman. I assume I'll need to confer with an anthropologist, and maybe I should get one from Mombasa. Or perhaps a criminologist or a pathologist. You see, I'm familiar with all these terms. But who knows what sort of specialists we need?"

She silently wondered what he was talking about. A criminologist? Here, in this place where crimes silently disappeared under the sand?

What was he talking about?

And why did he need her?

"Do you keep an open mind about things that are difficult to comprehend, Miss Weisman? In the sense that you do not jump to conclusions about certain things you might see?"

"I don't know. I see myself as someone who wants to learn about what makes people tick, I guess. Maybe, yes, I keep an open mind."

"Well," he said, "I assumed you are that person. Not at all superstitious."

The jeep climbed between sharp rocks. The track now looked like a narrow river, running between banks of rocks. At least there was some sort of track the vehicle could follow. Otherwise, they would have been obliged to climb on foot.

Lieutenant Odinga steered the vehicle confidently through tight corners and on slopes. They reached a small plateau in front of a steep cliff that seemed to extend all the way to the top of the hill. She glanced upward. The reddish peaks and fractures of the cliff contrasted neatly with the clear blue sky. She would have taken a picture, but she had no camera.

The lieutenant turned the engine off. A disturbing silence descended over the desert. All she heard was a soft vibration, perhaps from the blood in her ears or the atmosphere heating up. There were no other sounds. It was never quiet in and around the camp with so many people. So many thousands of them. And then there was the almost constant wind over the plain, whistling through tent flaps and dry brushes. Now and then some animal could be heard, in the distance.

There was nothing of that here.

Only silence.

Interrupted by the ticking of the cooling jeep engine.

She glanced at Lieutenant Odinga. It was already hot between these rocks, even this early in the day. No breeze blew in from the plain. "Is this it?" she asked, imagining he had brought her to admire the beauty of the landscape.

She felt a bit uncomfortable. Assuming his plan was less courteous, how would she react? Nobody knew where they were. No one would come to her aid. Why had she been this naive?

Or did she almost unconsciously hope for a little spicy adventure out in the wilds, if necessary with Lieutenant Odinga?

Don't be silly, she thought. *That thought never crossed your damn mind. Not in the least. Did it? Unless you're developing a second personality*—a concept she knew was scientifically unfounded—*that cherishes such intentions in its perverse soul.*

He turned his attention to her. "We have to walk through the gap," he said.

Gap? She wondered what he meant.

He pointed it out to her. In the cliff she noticed an elongated shadow. A gap?

"Come," he said. "It will only get hotter the longer we wait. And I've brought almost no water. My men are waiting for us."

This sounded even more ominous, but she followed him as he approached the shadow that turned into a tall, narrow chasm that seemed to split the steep side of the hill in half. Inside the gap the air felt cool.

They didn't have far to go. This was not a large mountain. After no more than a score of meters, they stood at the edge of another open space, larger this time, like a bowl with an edge of irregular rocks.

A dozen soldiers rested against the rim of the open space, and each of them got up when they saw the lieutenant. Their weapons stood neatly against the rock, in the shadows.

Nothing of this caught her attention. The soldiers, the sandy bowl bordered by rocks, the blue sky overhead, the shadows—all that belonged to the ordinary, everyday world. This was the world she was familiar with, even this far from home.

What she saw in the middle of the bowl made her doubt her own sanity and that of the world.

Instinctively, she counted them. Eleven. Eleven human figures, standing straight up, black as the night, possibly even more black, as was the ground where they stood. Eleven figures, each of them formerly a human being, and now the only witness to an intense suffering.

Nothing could be further from the mundane world.

She stepped forward. She knew the soldiers and the lieutenant watched her, but that didn't matter. She didn't even wonder why Odinga had brought her here. She didn't think about his motives. Perhaps he wanted to frighten her. Perhaps he needed a neutral witness. There might be a sensible explanation, but given what she witnessed here, it would be meaningless.

She stopped. The rational part of her brain registered details. The arms of the figures had been tied behind their backs with what must have been belts or wires or ropes, she couldn't tell. The heat had fused the material of these bindings, along with what remained of the clothes, to the bodies. She noticed wide-open mouths, heads with all flesh burned off, blackened teeth. These figures, arranged in a circle, once had been human, some time ago, but the fire had reduced them to almost abstract objects. The whole setup appeared as an apocalyptic sculpture, here in this remote part of the desert.

She turned toward the lieutenant, who stood back from her, his gaze fixed on the sand in front of him as if the sight of these figures were blasphemy to him.

"When did this happen?" she asked.

But she knew right away it was a ridiculous question. How could the lieutenant know? There should be other questions. Questions within the range of the lieutenant's knowledge.

"A long time ago," he whispered, not wanting to disturb the dead.

She said nothing.

"This is an arid desert," he continued in a normal voice. "The lack of moisture has ensured that the bodies remain well preserved. This did not happen recently. We have spoken discreetly to local people, as far as there are any local people, concerning things that happened in the past. About the stories they preserve for posterity."

"And?"

"They have no stories for this," he said.

"Nobody recalls having seen this, or heard about it, in recent times?"

"It isn't the discovery we want to share with local people," Odinga said. "This may have been a public execution or a ritual. I'm no anthropologist, Miss Weisman. Perhaps once there was a people here who burned others alive like this, as a ritual. But that is highly unlikely since the locals have no such tradition."

"But this didn't happen recently?"

"Not *this*, no."

"How old then do you think—" She looked at him intently. "What do you mean, not *this*? Are there other . . .?"

He pointed. She turned around. Behind her, on the other side of the bowl, the rocks made a dip, and she now noticed another gap. He stepped past her and headed that way. She followed him. The soldiers remained.

"I warn you again," he said, "for what you are to see."

But she knew what to expect.

They entered another depression, another bowl-like natural edifice between rocks. They stood in front of a large open area with rugged plateaus and cliffs that exuded in all directions. Behind a ledge, the almost colorless savanna stretched toward the horizon, never meeting the sky.

Again, a circle of bodies. Seven this time. These were not yet petrified like the others. Some were only partially charred. A few heads were still intact. The heat had been less intense. The victims were all Africans, and at least one of them was a woman.

She turned her head away. "Dear God," she whispered.

"Oh," Odinga said succinctly, "God had very little to do with this. This is the work of men, Miss Weisman. This is the doings of people. Cruel, perverse people who are led to believe it is necessary to torture and maim other humans."

"Who are these victims? Do you have any idea?"

"I fear the question will find no answer. And as to your inevitable next question, this second location is no older than a few weeks. Again, because of the climate here, the flesh hasn't rotted yet. I had one of my men take pictures of the victims that might still be recognizable, and we will again talk to the locals, but we . . ." He made a gesture, indicating the futility of the effort.

"When did you find this?"

"Three days ago, only. We didn't discover it ourselves. A couple of refugees entered the gorge in search of water and perhaps small animals for food, and when they returned to the camp, they told us about this place. I dissuaded them from talking to others, but I cannot guarantee they will keep quiet. This discovery will not remain a secret for long. This is great sorcery, ma'am. In this country, this is powerful magic. Whoever did this had a special kind of power."

She turned around and noticed now four other soldiers sitting on rocks next to the gap. In between them sat a man in dirty rags. His hands were tied together with rope. He seemed strangely unaware of the bodies.

"Who is he?"

"We found him here," the lieutenant said. "He does not talk. But he was not here by accident, of that I'm sure."

"Has he got anything to do with this ritual?"

The lieutenant suddenly looked bored. "He does not speak a word, so we know nothing, as I said. Everything is possible. Every story, however unlikely, might be true. Maybe he is a rebel, though he carried no weapons. We suspect he has been here for at least a couple of days."

"What will happen to him?"

"We will take him to the camp. He will talk to us. Maybe he knows more about these victims. Their identities, perhaps."

She couldn't bear to look at the bodies any longer. She wanted out. And she still wondered why the lieutenant had brought her here.

8

Eileen calster left a concise message for Nick Prinsen. She had arrived in her Amsterdam apartment. Nick sat behind his desk, surrounded by the remnants of a previous investigation still scattered around him like body parts after an air crash. Van Gils was absent, but three other officers were noisily discussing current cases—illegal arms deals with some of the more unstable Caucasian republics and human trafficking from the Middle East to Europe.

They appeared to be ignoring him, and just as well, since he couldn't hide his joy at the message. In her most recent missive, she had confirmed she would leave Groningen and her parents, intent on never returning. She avoided talking about her parents. Only once she depicted them as taciturn, not in touch with their feelings, and indifferent to her fate.

If anything, she was running from all her parents stood for. She had tried to educate them—to make them understand the dark nineteenth century was long gone, but now she had finally, or so he hoped, broken with them.

Prinsen glanced at his watch. He would clock out earlier today. He shut his computer down, locked his desk, and got up. Veneman glanced up for a moment but then ignored him. Prinsen donned his heavy coat, gloves, and scarf and walked down the stairs. Outside, the air was crisp and clean, close to freezing. There would be snow soon, judging from the smell in the air. A sharp, ragged smell of intense, Nordic cold. He walked down Kerkstraat toward the city center. A walk would do him good, even in the cold.

Would he get a bite to eat first? Would he ask Eileen out for dinner instead? Yes, he would do that. To celebrate the fact that she had chosen her freedom. Her return to proud, complicated, and sinful Amsterdam. He pulled out his phone and chose her number. There she was, right away, slightly out of breath as if she had been running.

"Hello," she said when she saw the caller ID. "I'm in the apartment. It's still a bit cold up here but heating up already. Where are you?"

"Just left the office. It's still early, but let's meet for dinner. My treat. To celebrate your return."

She didn't have to think it over for too long. "Good idea. There's nothing here to eat anyway. And I'm starving. Probably the change of scenery makes me hungry. Where will we meet?"

He needed to think that over. He rarely went out, and even when he went someplace for dinner or lunch, he hardly ever noticed the name. He needed to come up with something in a hurry, otherwise he might lose his appeal as a man of the world. "Somewhere around the Dam?" he suggested. "It has mostly tourist places, I know, but there's an Argentine steak house where we can get proper food."

"And where it's almost dark inside," she said, knowing at once where he meant. A subtle touch of semi-darkness would add to the culinary delight. "Is that in Raadhuisstraat?"

"Yes. In twenty minutes?"

"Of course."

"I'm on my way," he said. It would take him ten, at the most fifteen, minutes to get there. He wondered if he needed to bring a small gift. Flowers? No, flowers would be awkward in a restaurant. A present. But what could he buy her? A book? Music? He didn't even know what sort of books or music she liked. He had been in touch with her for several months now but knew nothing about her taste in books or music. What had they talked about all that time?

They had talked about her and about her parents and about their mutual feelings.

Maybe he would buy her a diary. A journal. And a pen. Perhaps she needed to arrange her thoughts and write them down. She needed a place, some physical place, to arrange her thoughts about her brother and her former boyfriend, and about her parents. A physical place like the pages of a diary. Where these thoughts could be properly stored away, safely, unseen by others, still close by if needed, but slightly at a distance from her daily concerns. He would never read her diary, wouldn't want to. He knew the powerful impulse of putting your most intimate thoughts to paper. He had done it himself for a long time. His experiences with his family had not been all that different than hers.

He entered De Bijenkorf, the main department store in the center of Amsterdam. He took the escalator up, shedding his coat. He found her a black leather-bound journal with lined pages and a standard Waterman fountain pen with some refills and had it all wrapped up as a gift. That took some time, too much time, and when he approached the steak house, Eileen was already there, waiting for him in the street, cold but happy to see him. "Sorry," he said, "things took longer than I anticipated."

"You're here, that's what counts." She forgave him at once. She would forgive him anything, so long as he was with her. She rested her hand on his shoulders and kissed him on the cheek. That felt inappropriately intimate.

They entered the restaurant, chose a table by the window. It was still early. They were alone, except for four young men at a round table, probably Americans. The young men were already halfway through a substantial dinner of steak, baked potatoes, and a salad, each drinking from an oversized beer mug, bantering about something or other.

She took off her gloves and parka and straightened her hair. She fixed her gaze on him and smiled an engaging, totally innocent smile at him. "Do I look different than last time?"

"Yes," he admitted. "You look different. I don't know why, just different." But he *did* know why.

"I may have gained a few pounds," she said. "And did something to my hair too."

He was convinced there was more to it. The changes went deeper. She was no longer the skinny, frightened, but resolute girl she had been months earlier when the police had taken her into protective custody. Not the girl he had met then, the girl he had driven all the way to

Groningen, to relative safety. She had clearly distanced herself from the fears she had known then.

"Why didn't you come back earlier?" he wanted to know.

She laughed. "It's just that I—" The waiter approached them with the menu. Prinsen ordered Mexican chicken and a salad, and she surprised him by choosing a steak, medium done. And beer. He ordered a beer as well.

"The period of time is just arbitrary," she continued.

"Arbitrary?"

"If I had been gone for *six* months, you would have asked the same question."

"I mean, why stay any time in Groningen, with your folks?" After her boyfriend, Pieter Van Boer, and her brother Maarten had been killed by a Russian hitman, she hadn't wanted to stay in Amsterdam, although she was no longer in danger.

"I needed to go back home. Hoping that things would change. They didn't."

"Their son was killed. This would only confirm their prejudices about Amsterdam."

For a moment, she looked out the window. The waiter arrived with the beer. "They didn't want to talk about him at all. He no longer existed. Maybe he never existed to them. There were no pictures of him anywhere in the house."

"They continue to deny—?"

"No, that's not it."

"What then?"

He noticed tears in her eyes. Maybe he shouldn't press the matter. But then, if he didn't, if he didn't know what had occurred between her and her parents, she would remain a stranger. Part of her would remain a stranger to him. A part that mattered most to him, right now.

She said, "If you leave their community, you leave their life, Nick. That's how it goes, and that's how my family sees it. That's what happened to both me and Maarten. He no longer was their son. I am no longer their daughter. I am no longer part of their community. They'll greet me when I visit, politely as they would acknowledge the presence of any stranger, and they'll talk to me, but it will be no different than greeting strangers and talking to strangers. They won't ask about Amsterdam or about my life there. I only exist when I'm present in their home. I have no existence elsewhere. And don't assume the talking amounts to much, Nick. Even as a kid I noticed the lack of real words, real sentences. They communicate, that is all they do. Signs, but not deeper meaning. More often they say nothing. I used to be afraid of them, on account of their silences. Because many things were left unspoken. And then my brother left. And I left. We both fled."

Nick knew all too well what she was talking about. He was raised in a strict religious environment, although not as extreme as Eileen's. There was a bond, nevertheless, between them. A bond he regretted. They both had had troubled childhoods. A bond should be about something positive. But this wasn't.

The food appeared at the table. Her steak was larger than he expected.

"And what about you?" Nick inquired after the waiter had left.

"Me?"

"In what sense do you exist? Do you exist only under the shadow of your parents?"

"Of course not, Nick. That's the whole point. I have, for a long time now, taken myself from under their shadow, or I wouldn't be in Amsterdam in the first place." She sounded as if he had trampled her soul, and he probably had. "Do you for one moment think they would have voluntarily let me and my brother come to Amsterdam? Do you think I went back out of nostalgia? I'm not homesick. I want nothing to do with them, and that's final."

She cut the steak and shoved a rather large piece in her mouth. She chewed on it. They remained silent for a short while. In the street people hurried by, probably going home. A light snow fell.

"You'll be looking for a job?" he asked.

"Yes. I had an offer even before coming here. It isn't much, but it'll pay the rent, and I can eat. I'll go back to the university in September if I can get a scholarship."

"Public scholarship?"

"No, private. A company. My mentor at the university arranged it for me. I wasn't idle, these past few months. I prepared my escape thoroughly. He's a really nice man, my mentor. He said, forget the current academic year. Come back, and we'll sort things out. Without him, I'd be lost."

Nick was working on his chicken and considering the necessity of mentors. He assumed he would need one of his own. Would Eekhaut be playing that role?

She said, "And what about you?"

"As usual." Which, he suddenly realized, meant absolutely nothing.

"I don't know what usual means. Police work, I assume?"

"Yes. Research, files, problems, crime, conspiracies. The usual thing. I mean, there's these long and boring bits in between moments of tension and excitement—"

"Why are we here, together, Nick?" she suddenly asked as if remembering what she had wanted to talk about in the first place.

He stopped eating. "Why do you ask?"

"It's a meaningful and totally appropriate question. Why are we here, the both of us? Do we have something in common? Is there something between us? I'll have to know if you're expecting something from me, Nick. Would feel better that way, if I knew and didn't have to guess."

He was confused. Mainly because he hadn't figured out what sort of relationship they were supposed to be in. He wasn't even certain exactly what he felt for her. He had presupposed a bond between them, assumed she felt like he did. But that assumption was perhaps all wrong.

The little voice in his head told him an insurmountable truth. *Of course there's something between both of you. Why else did you ask her out? Why else have you longed to see her again and waited for her impatiently these last few days?*

"I, uh . . ."

"Is it on account of you driving me home, the last time we met?"

"Because," he carefully said, "you looked absolutely vulnerable, and I wanted so badly to help you."

But he knew this wasn't what she needed to hear from him. She hadn't come back to him. She had come back to a brand of freedom only Amsterdam could offer her. Freedom from her parents, mostly. And then there had been Nick, whose presence would probably reassure her.

Not only, and certainly not firstly, because he was a police officer.

She hadn't come back to him. His being here was a secondary advantage.

"You are empathetic, and you love to help vulnerable girls," she said. "But I'm not the fragile type, Nick. Not at all. At the time I was scared shitless, I'll admit that much. My boyfriend was killed before my eyes. I was almost kidnapped, I was shot at. An assassin killed my brother. That's a bit more than a girl is expected to endure."

"Yes, I understand."

"Yes, I guess you do. But I'm not the fragile type."

He thought, *No, you're not. I know you aren't. Because you've come back. Otherwise, you would still have been hiding in Groningen.*

"You don't want me vulnerable, do you, Nick? I hope not. I don't want you hovering protectively over me. I'll suffocate if you do."

"I don't want you to be vulnerable," he said.

"Because that's what my parents did. They suffocated me. With their good intentions, but I had enough of their stifling emotional poverty."

He wasn't going to mother her. He wasn't going to hover over her. But then, Nick, what *do* you want from her? Wouldn't he do better to keep some distance from her, for the time being? Until she managed to settle more comfortably in Amsterdam?

9

NOT FAR FROM THE Argentine steak house, Eekhaut was at the Red Lion eating grilled chicken with fries and peanut sauce. He had a large glass of Amstel beer on the side. It wasn't real beer, in his opinion, but nothing better was served. He'd never been a fan of Dutch beers, used as he was to the stronger, more complex Belgian brews.

As usual, the Red Lion was busy. Even in the middle of winter, a loyal clientele ate there. It was the sort of eatery tourists would only seldom visit; a somewhat old-fashioned place where waiters were almost as permanent a fixture as the never-changing menu. This was a place of decent Dutch food, only slightly influenced by the culinary import from the former Indonesian colony (hence the peanut sauce).

On his occasional visits to Amsterdam before he moved here, this area, around the Dam and the Kalverstraat, had been like a home away from home. Now, these last four months, it *was* home, although he would always be a foreigner. He already had adopted the lifestyle of the better class and occasionally shopped in the Bijenkorf, the grand department store on the other side of the Damrak.

This wide but never enticing avenue was lined with tacky bars and restaurants, all catering to foreign tourists. Just two buildings made the area interesting. The first was the Beurs van Berlage, an old stock exchange designed early in the twentieth century by a Dutch architect whose name the building bore. It was no longer a stock exchange but served as a venue for modern art and design exhibitions and a conference center.

The other building was the Bijenkorf. Much like Harrods, it catered to the well off, although its prices were somewhat more democratic than its London counterpart. In the stiff-lipped Dutch democratic tradition, it sold its own fashion brands, and there was an extensive tearoom restaurant on the top floor. Eekhaut had bought clothes there a couple of times. That's what he'd been doing just now. He had also gotten a Stephen King novel, *Duma Key*.

He slowly enjoyed the chicken and peanut sauce. It wasn't a sumptuous meal, but he wasn't hungry. Even after three weeks, he still had the stench of burned bodies in his nostrils, which was impossible since there had been no smell at all. He didn't sleep well either. Perhaps he dreamed of corpses, but he couldn't remember his dreams. He still imagined those caricatures of humans united in death. He remembered the absolute silence that prevailed in the clearing. The message in blood, but what was its significance? So far, no clues.

He had warned Dewaal that they were staring into the void of a meaningless message. Or one that meant something only to those who'd committed the crime. That was solely for the members of the conspiracy, inside of the Society of Fire. Maybe it was meant for a specific person, even. Someone who was supposed to find the victims. Why leave messages in a place like that? Who was expected to read them?

And who was the so-called informant manipulating?

In the meantime, they had made little progress. They had some DNA. They would find people to whom it had belonged, and then what? They'd find out in the next few days.

Meanwhile, he was thinking about Linda. Not long ago they'd been drinking on a terrace here in Amsterdam, enjoying the last of the good fall weather. Unfortunately, their favorite bar, the Absinthe, had closed some time ago. They'd been amazed one evening to find it boarded up, with only a brief notice posted, informing them it wouldn't reopen. Part of their life had gone. Three weeks later a Japanese restaurant opened in its place. They decided not to eat there for sentimental reasons. There were plenty of Japanese restaurants in Amsterdam.

From another table a woman sat watching him. He noticed her and nodded to her and then looked outside. He hadn't spotted her attention at first, but now he couldn't ignore her. He had been deep in thought. He glanced at her again. She looked about forty. She was dressed in jeans and a white blouse and had her jacket hanging over the other chair. An extravagantly tailored jacket. And over that jacket, an overcoat, equally expensive-looking. He had a policeman's eye for such details. It had come in handy in his previous jobs. It was always the details that gave away who people were and what they pretended to be. Their physiognomy, the way they ate, the way they talked, the way they looked at other people. And the clothes. At times, they tried to hide their true selves with gestures, loud talking, and clothing that cost a lot. But underneath, under the veneer of loud or civilized behavior, he knew he could and would find their true selves: scared, lonely, perverse, cruel—whatever.

Next to her, on the other chair, she had deposited a Bijenkorf shopping bag. Maybe her car was in the department store's garage, which meant she had money or was spending someone else's money. She preferred a coffee in the Red Lion instead of the store's tearoom. That also was significant. She was probably alone, not waiting for anyone. She wanted to smoke a cigarette but could no longer do that in bars and restaurants. She wanted company, but he knew she would return home alone.

Like he would. Go home alone. He would return to an empty apartment, thinking of Linda.

The look she had given him had been full of implied meaning.

He wiped his mouth with the napkin (cloth, not paper here) and drank his beer. Then he looked at her again. He would simply walk over and speak to her. See if she wanted to join him for an extra coffee. Something stronger perhaps. Leave the car in the parking garage. *You don't need it.* He was making assumptions. Everything was an assumption. He wouldn't need complicated strategies. Not under these circumstances.

He got up, approached her, and said, "I assume you won't refuse another coffee, will you?"

She looked at him, really *looked*, showing only mild amusement. "A coffee would be a great idea," she said. Her voice was unexpectedly low. A warm voice. He knew he had not been mistaken about her.

TUESDAY

10

It felt to linda as if she hadn't slept all night. It wasn't comfort that was lacking, at least not considering the circumstances. She had part of one of the larger tents at her disposal, her part separated from the rest by canvas flaps, allowing for a certain measure of privacy. The rest of the tent was taken up by two nurses and a doctor. But still, it was no more than a tent, as no permanent buildings would be built, not even for the operating quarters. The French army had provided the tents. They were solid enough, but they were hot during the day, and chilly at night. They didn't keep the sand out, which simply went everywhere. The only tent that could be sealed hermetically was the one used for surgery, but even that didn't really provide a sterile environment.

Twice during the night she'd heard shots in the distance. Probably automatic weapons. She had no idea from which direction the sound came or who was responsible. Had it been the men Lieutenant Odinga had left to guard the corpses? Had they shot at hyenas or other animals, or at ghosts?

She hadn't bothered to get up. Nocturnal walks through the camp had been discouraged by the lieutenant. There were always armed guards around, but it was inconceivable they would shoot at anything near so many people.

That morning she sat at the breakfast table with the other members of the medical team. Organizing breakfast (and lunch and dinner) was Linda's responsibility, in which she was assisted by two men she had recruited from among the refugees. Tea was strong and sweet, and breakfast invariably consisted of homemade (which meant made by the two helpers) chapattis, jam, and a serving of hot beans in tomato sauce. There were no eggs, no meat of any kind, no fresh vegetables, and hardly any fruit. She handed out vitamin supplements. The refugees had to make do with a sort of porridge of oatmeal provided by the Red Cross. Once a week they were given a ration of cake flour, milk powder, and strips of dried meat. It was a very dull diet, but not much worse than that of the soldiers and the medics. You could die of boredom here eating that food, or you died of starvation. So much for choice.

"Lord Jim would do well to keep his troops under control," one of the doctors said in French. Linda understood what he and his French and Belgian colleagues were saying, although she was far from fluent in the language. Fortunately, the Belgian members of the medical team also spoke Dutch.

"Lord Jim" was the nickname the team had bestowed on the lieutenant long before her arrival. She never asked why. She had few questions, realizing that nobody could spare much time for the newcomer. Doctors and nurses usually worked twelve hours straight. There were always more patients than they could handle. And more than enough dead. Medical supplies were insufficient. The trucks didn't arrive often enough and never on time. The Kenyan soldiers and the UN men had their own supplies, with strict orders not to share, not even with the workers from the international aid organizations. And certainly not with the natives. The medical team had the same orders.

Linda quickly realized the aid workers needed to eat well and hydrate sufficiently, or they would soon be unable to work anymore. The desert was unforgiving. They had to make choices, setting priorities as to who would be helped and who would not. But they needed their strength, because without them the whole camp became useless.

"I wonder what's going on in those hills over there," one of the nurses said. There had been questions asked about soldiers driving to and from the hills. Nobody, however, had noticed Linda being taken there by Odinga. Which suited her fine. How could she explain the trip if she wasn't able to divulge the hills' terrible secret? How would she be able to explain the human sacrifice?

Odinga had asked her for complete discretion, as long as he had no answers. He had wondered aloud if the victims had been refugees kidnapped and killed by rebels. That would not make much sense. But nothing about the findings seemed to make much sense. And what about the man they had found over there? He had been discreetly transferred to the camp and locked in a military tent, some distance from the camp itself.

She noticed the lieutenant standing next to one of the military vehicles, looking out over the savanna that seemed empty as far as she could see. She saw an empty savanna, but maybe he, through his long experience, saw something more. She saw emptiness; he saw a potential threat.

"Will there be a transport today?" one of the doctors inquired. When he noticed Linda wasn't paying attention, he said, "Linda? Will a transport come? Or a plane? Can we expect anything today?"

She looked at him, roused from her thoughts. "Yes . . . yes, we're expecting a truck. The plane is scheduled for the day after tomorrow, depending on the weather."

The doctor stretched and yawned. Sleep deprivation was a widespread problem among team members. "I think I'll start with my appointments," he said, not even bothering to sound sarcastic.

Linda got up and started clearing the table. The local helpers would do the washing up—with sand instead of water—and would clean up the kitchen. She paid them in water and food rations. There had been more than enough candidates for the jobs. Linda made sure to rotate the helpers so that more people in the camp got a chance to earn something, even if it was only a little food and water.

Moments later the tent was cleared of people. Linda walked out and approached Odinga. He glanced at her, his gaze still full of the desert. Or savanna. She wasn't entirely clear about the distinction. It probably was a desert. "Something the matter, Lieutenant?" she asked. "You look worried."

"We might expect a storm later," he said. "I have a feeling it will be a bad one."

She wasn't going to discuss his feelings. "Did your soldiers use their guns last night? Was there a problem over there in the hills?"

He frowned at her. "What do you want, ma'am? My soldiers are there, keeping guard over those bodies. It's dark, even with the stars. Maybe there was a wild animal around. Maybe it was just their imagination. They might have fired some shots, as soldiers occasionally do. Maybe they were shooting at shadows. What do I care? I am not going to reprimand them."

She left it at that. In the end, the waste of ammunition was not her problem. "What will happen with the bodies?"

"What do you want me to do with them, Miss Weisman? Am I responsible for them? I do not think so."

Yes, she thought, *we have a bad temper this morning.* "You can't just leave them there, I guess. They should be buried."

"Buried? The local population does not bury its dead. Underground, the spirits of the dead drift for eternity, without a way out into the eternal light. You want that to happen? For your spirit to stumble around in the dark, aimlessly, forever?"

She ignored that. "So, the bodies remain where they are, on those stakes."

"For now," he said.

"Will there be a proper investigation?"

He grimaced and looked surprised at her naiveté. "And who would investigate? The local police? There aren't any. The government of this wrecked country? Certainly not. I have no authority to conduct a criminal investigation. I can question the prisoner, but he does not want to talk to me. What shall I do with him? Torture him, so that he either dies or confesses anything, any possible nonsense, to make the pain stop? And why should there be a trial? People are killed here all the time. We are in a war zone."

"They aren't killed like that."

"No, I hope this does not happen much. But they die and in large numbers. Despite whatever help the West thinks it can spare." The lieutenant observed the horizon again, on the lookout for his hypothetical storm. "Whatever your efforts, ma'am, they are merely an illusion. It does not mean anything in the larger scheme of things. This country, this continent. There always will be hunger and diseases and killings.

The tribes that passed this way earlier did not stay, and for good reasons. People cannot live here, not in these parts. No food, no water. You dig wells, they provide water, for now. Soon they will be dry again. Then you must move. And without the water we must move those three or four thousand people over there."

"They can't be moved," Linda said. "They're too weak, most of them. Even you know that much. And wherever we go, there will already be more people, more soldiers, and too many mouths to feed."

"I see you understand the problem." He looked away for a moment, across the savanna again. "I am familiar with large parts of Africa, as I have traveled rather widely as a soldier. There are no alternatives for these people. There are still a few good places, civilized places, but they are far off, and anyway, they don't want these refugees. Not any more than you Europeans want them on your continent."

"We're here to help. And to prevent—"

"No," he said. "You are here because your government does not want these people to emigrate north, to Europe. You encourage them to stay here, where they will all die. So they will not come in droves to your green pastures and your old, comfortable cities."

"You're being cynical, Lieutenant. Things are not that simple."

He sighed, but patiently. "Things never are, except here in the desert. Look around you, ma'am. Do you see solutions or a savior? Is there a god, or perhaps a secular leader who will help these people and their children to survive? They want to live, like you and me. They don't need much to live, but even that they are deprived of. But they cannot go anywhere else. That would disrupt the prevailing economic order. So instead, we have a natural order, which says that these people should die."

"But *we* want to keep them alive. The doctors and the—"

"Yes, *you* do. And so do *I*. But we are not important players. We do not get to decide who lives and who dies."

"Well, if I have anything to say about it, and even if I don't, I'll try to keep them alive, if that's all the same to you. And maybe they can, one day, return home."

His face, dark and smooth, bore an expression she did not recognize.

Had he expected her to react differently? "Return?" he said. "What does that mean? You don't even know where they came from. From a hell-hole, most probably. They are going nowhere, Miss Weisman. If they had a place to go, they would have moved long ago. There's no future for them here, and they know that."

She said nothing.

"We've got something like three, maybe four thousand people in the camp. It's a large camp, but within the wider scale of things, here in Africa, it means nothing. History had fled from this place, never to return. This is a void. Those bodies in the hills? Even they are meaning-less. The fugitives, the bodies, they do not exist."

"I wonder exactly why you're here, Lieutenant."

Odinga sighed, and the expression on his face was neutral again. "It is my job to maintain the illusion of continuance, ma'am. It is my job to act as if this camp is a permanent refuge. Because otherwise, these people would be completely lost. Still, it is only an illusion I'm maintaining."

She turned away from him. "That's cruel, Lieutenant. To give them hope when there is none."

"You should do as these people have been doing for so long. You should accept that things happen, as they are unavoidable. This may be called fatalism, and it probably is the most widespread religion on this continent."

"I can't do that."

"It's a matter of accepting reality for what it is. Your civilization is an illusion as well. Your civilization insists that in the end, everybody will be saved. That everybody has the right to salvation. You encapsulate people so as to *prevent* people from running risks. But that's not what happens in the rest of the world. Elsewhere people live their short lives, and then they die. Why bother so much about the inevitable? The only real difference between you and these people is that you will live a bit longer than they, and under better conditions. But in the end, we're all dead."

She remained silent. There was nothing more to be said.

"What happens here is an attempt to maintain the privileges of rich, Western society. Doctors, nurses, food, clean water, a hospital. Protection and eternal life. But nothing structural is going on here. No roads are being built, no real hospitals, no universities, no ports, no factories."

Linda said, "I have a different view of things like culture and life than you, Lieutenant. It all boils down to simple decisions. These people need help now. They need a chance to survive the next weeks, months. We offer that help. It is short-term planning, and we are building no roads. But we get them the stuff to survive, if only barely, for a while. That is enough for me. That is all I can do. I have no ulterior motives. Why is that not enough for you?"

He held out his left hand and squeezed it with his right. "That's why, ma'am. Because of the color of my skin. Because I'm black, as they are. These are not my brothers. These are not my relatives. They belong to a distant tribe with whom I am not related. We do not have the same ancestor, not even the same gods. However, we share that same color. It is not much to share, but still it is something that unites us."

"Then I'd assume you would be even more motivated to help them."

"That's why I understand your motives for coming here, Miss Weisman. I'm here because once other people came to Africa and stole the many riches this continent had to offer: humans, gold, metal ores, diamonds, animals. Local people didn't see them as riches to be plundered because they were part of the land. So many people, however, wanted to steal these riches, and they did, and afterward, after the plunder, nobody was inclined to solve Africa's problems."

"That's postcolonial bullshit, Lieutenant. That kind of rhetoric no longer makes any sense."

"Then I will not talk about the colonial age, however bad that was. I will talk about today. About the riches being stolen from Africa today. Today it is the Chinese. They are building roads and ports and railroads to drag away the raw materials they say they so desperately need for their economy. Meanwhile, local people must deal with all those alien ideas: capitalism, Islam, economy, radicalism, socialism, fascism. People flock to the cities, to the new centers of economic power, where they are hurled into the twenty-first century after having stepped out of the eighteenth. The new local elite is getting rich quickly, embracing capitalism. But the gap between rich and poor is as evident here, in many parts of Africa, as it is elsewhere. Perhaps even more so."

"We don't have the power to stop the IMF and others or the nations that—"

"And that's why there's so much despair here, elsewhere, in war zones, places where people live almost in the stone age, or in slums or as slaves of other Africans. And so many things will have to change before they become better, ma'am."

Some time later, after performing her duties, Linda strolled along the edge of the camp. When she did that the first time, she took some food and water for the children, but when she noticed their empty, indifferent stares and how resigned they were to their fate, accepting the gifts without so much as a smile, she refrained from taking anything the next time. It was the soldiers' duty to dispense food and water to the refugees at fixed times and in an orderly way. Her extra effort, however well meant, would only disturb order. Hundreds of children would flock after her. She would never bring enough for all.

She approached the military camp. The few soldiers present glanced up at her. Some acknowledged her presence, others ignored her. This was what she deserved, being the stranger here. Passing one of the tents, she noticed a face looking at her through a lattice of sticks. An inquisitive Kenyan, she assumed, but then she recognized the prisoner. The man found by the soldiers at the site of the execution. The man who refused to talk. He had, she noticed, cuts and bruises all over his face. The interrogation hadn't been as civilized as Odinga had wanted her to believe.

She paused, although she wasn't supposed to linger around the military camp. Nothing that was going on in there was her business. Just primitive rituals to favor cruel gods. Members of a hostile tribe to be sacrificed, a fate to deter others. Death in retaliation for cruel acts. None of her business.

But she couldn't just walk away. The prisoner was held in a sort of cage, primitive but efficient. She could see only his head and shoulders.

He just watched her, without apparent emotion. Nevertheless, she felt threatened. She was convinced he was involved, one way or another, with the ritual in the hills. With the deaths of those people. He'd had them sacrificed to some god, and he'd had help.

Which frightened her most of all.

11

"WE'VE FOUND A POSITIVE match between DNA samples," Prinsen said, as triumphant as if he'd contributed to the landing on Mars or anything of equal historical significance. Or a cure for all sorts of cancer. Something in that order of magnitude.

Eekhaut took off his coat and hung it up to dry. It was snowing, and during the short walk from his apartment to the office, he had become quite wet. And cold. He would feel better after a decent cup of coffee. Not from the machine, god forbid. He had had his breakfast at Café Bouwman, toast and jam with one egg and a cup of real, freshly brewed coffee. For these past few months he had started to eat healthier and more regularly after discovering there were plenty of food shops around catering to the concerned eater. He kept his refrigerator full of good and fresh stuff and cooked regularly, preparing balanced meals for himself and occasionally for Linda. His apartment began to look comfortable and even cozy. He had been thinking about his apartment in Leuven, where he used to live before coming to Amsterdam, but had not yet decided what to do with it.

"The lab worked through the night," Prinsen continued.

Eekhaut, like all seasoned detectives, recognized the need for decent forensic research, without which little progress could be made in many cases.

"They'll bill us accordingly, which is going to displease Dewaal plenty," he said. "We'll have contributed to the emptying of her precious budget. Expect endless nagging."

Eekhaut wondered exactly how early Prinsen had arrived in the office. He often was there long before the others, not bothered by the weather. He lived in Amsterdam, cycling ten minutes or so to get to work, but even then it looked as though the young man lived in the office. Eekhaut appreciated his zeal but would, at some point, need to warn him about burnout and things like that. But at least Prinsen was totally involved in the case.

"Even better," Prinsen said, "we have one name that goes with the missing person in question."

"We have?"

"Basten. Adriaan Basten. That's his name. Or *was* his name."

"Well done," Eekhaut said. A name. They had a name. An ordinary and mundane-sounding Dutch name. Adriaan. A name one wouldn't at once associate with criminal activities.

A victim who had been linked with a name became a real person, with a personal history, desires, aspirations. It was no longer merely a body from a crime scene. Not merely one of the bodies tied to a stake and burned alive somewhere in the Ardennes forest. The victim became a *He*, a real person with a background and relatives and friends. Which made things worse. As far as a detective was concerned, an anonymous corpse was easier to deal with than a victim with a name.

"You pulled his profile?"

"He worked as an information specialist for InfoDuct, a company based here in Amsterdam. Thirty-two, not married."

"That saves us from having to inform a partner."

"From a first impression, a clever but ordinary fellow. Two years of military service, athletic type, vacations, hobbies. His bio fits nicely on one page."

All our bios fit nicely on one page, Eekhaut thought.

"Are we going to pay a visit to his office?" Prinsen asked.

Eekhaut frowned. "Eight in the morning, Nick. We'll find very few offices open this early. Secretaries still in bed. Desk jockeys too. And managers. Maybe on the way to work at best. The city isn't alive yet, except for people like us. You're one of the lucky ones, Nick. And me. We're early risers."

"Raised on a farm." Prinsen grinned.

"As if I would believe your stories," Eekhaut said. "By the way, how's Eileen doing?"

For a moment, it looked like Prinsen would blush, and Eekhaut wouldn't have been surprised at that. He liked people who could still blush, showing real emotions. "She arrived in Amsterdam yesterday," Prinsen said. "She has an apartment of her own now."

"I assume you arranged that for her?"

Prinsen shook his head. "I didn't. She did it all by herself. She tried to live with her parents again, but that didn't work out."

"Things will turn out well for her," Eekhaut said. He knew Prinsen had eagerly awaited her return. He had dropped her name a few times, less than casually. Eileen Calster, an innocent victim in a sordid case of political corruption and multiple murders. Eekhaut felt inclined in this case to revert to clichés. Certainly when love was involved. Without clichés, life would become too complicated. There would be less fun as well. Risk-free clichés kept society afloat.

Prinsen wouldn't tell him anything more about Eileen. So Eekhaut left it at that.

"Find as much background info about Basten's company as you can, will you? What's it called? InfoDuct? Sounds slightly ridiculous."

"It's a problem these days to still find original names. Same problem for car models."

"Or you could just use numbers like BMW does."

"Too complicated for customers," Prinsen said.

"Let's return to the subject at hand. InfoDuct."

"I'll get you all the info you need, Walter."

Eekhaut retreated to his office but left the door open. He turned on his laptop, hoping for a message from Linda, hoping she'd found a way to email him. He had plenty of emails but none from her.

He consulted newspaper sites. Africa was almost completely absent. No massacre in Somalia, no aid teams threatened. But perhaps such incidents wouldn't be important enough for the press agencies. Even with civil war and the occasional massacre, Africa only rarely got attention.

Dewaal passed by in the corridor. "Nick just told me you've identified one of the victims."

"I wouldn't be surprised if this Basten turns out to be a member of the Church of the Supreme Purification."

"We could try them and find out," she suggested.

"I assume the church won't be giving us a list of members."

"They're required to deposit a list with the Ministry of the Interior. Contact them and see what you can get."

"What about privacy laws, then?"

She frowned. "Maybe you're right. Not my territory, I'm afraid. But since they might be considered a cult or something, they might still be required to . . . I'll try to find out." She disappeared.

Eekhaut glanced at his watch. Eight twenty. He wanted to get things done. He wanted to kick in doors, put suspects under pressure. He wanted to confront government officials and require them to turn over confidential information. This had always been a problem in his career. Rules always held him back.

He got up and asked Prinsen, "When exactly can we go visit InfoDuct?"

The young man glanced at his computer screen. "Nine thirty, or so the website says. Opening hours for visitors."

"How far is it from here?"

"On foot? Ten minutes, at most."

"We'll leave on time," Eekhaut said, frustrated. He walked up to Dewaal's office. "What does the law tell us about privacy?"

"Just a minute, Eekhaut. God! You're a pain in the ass sometimes. All the time, actually. Can't remember why I keep you. Here it is. Religious, political, and cultural organizations do not have to divulge their membership list unless they're categorized as dangerous or are under surveillance."

"That means they have to show us their membership list when we tell them they're dangerous and under surveillance. A rather Orwellian arrangement."

"Whatever," Dewaal said. "The Church of the Supreme Purification isn't listed as dangerous, which is weird. Anyway, we have no list of their members. And we won't get one either."

"While that same church is being investigated by us? They're not considered dangerous?"

"Apparently not," Dewaal said.

"And your informant? Can't he just—?"

"No, he can't."

"And we still assume those seven victims are connected with a not really dangerous cult?"

"We do. Or maybe we don't. If you're a victim of a terrorist attack, it doesn't have to mean you're an accomplice to the terrorists." Dewaal noticed Eekhaut's reaction. "This was no terrorist attack, and your comparison doesn't hold water, Eekhaut. This was an execution. These weren't random victims. Since there must have been an explicit reason they were killed, we can assume they were the victims of the feud between the church and that Society of Fire. Sound logical, no? Now when we dig deep into the life of this Adriaan Basten, we might find some link to the church. Do you need more help with that, Eekhaut?"

"I could use Van Gils, to speed things up."

"Speed things up? I'd like you to solve this problem well before 2020, when we'll be wiped away by the apocalypse."

"Twenty twenty? That gives me plenty of time. So I get Van Gils?"

"Tell him it is my idea."

"And I'll have him doing what he prefers: contacting his local informants about Basten."

He knew she didn't much like Van Gils. She didn't even trust him. There was a certain level of antipathy between the older detectives, the veterans, and the new chief, Dewaal. She had been dropped into this outfit because of a political move. Van Gils and perhaps even Veneman had probably hoped to get promoted, but that wasn't going to happen, not with their background. It was an old grievance between former beat cops and the new intellectual elite.

And Dewaal had her own problems to deal with. Her mother, suffering from dementia, not even recognizing her own daughter and residing in an institution. Not much family left, either. No partner, no children.

He'd done better, socially. At least recently. There was Linda. But what else was there in his life? He'd be fifty-five soon. No children, hardly any relatives left. He'd sit in an old people's home in perhaps twenty years, with nobody to visit him if the relationship with Linda didn't work out.

In the end, he thought, *we all are left alone. We die alone. Or we die, surrounded by our loved ones.* He'd have to find a bunch of those.

12

WHEN THE PHONE RANG, Maxwell pressed a button but didn't speak right away. He just folded his hands and waited, a model of composure. He knew people like Courier would become nervous when they heard nothing on the other end of the line. Especially since Courier knew Maxwell had picked up the call and didn't want to respond. He and the others should have realized by now this was nothing but a power game. But as far as Maxwell was concerned, these people hadn't learned anything. Nothing. They couldn't grasp the concept of power games, certainly not when they were the victims. They couldn't understand that he was playing with them and their innate fears. They were afraid of him. But primarily, they were afraid of Baphomet.

Of course, they had good reason to be afraid. Maxwell made sure of that. He would constantly feed their fears, make them worry endlessly. He played with them and their anxieties, ensured his dominion over them. Courier had learned to fear Maxwell ever since he had been witness to several of his sudden bouts of rage.

And, of course, he knows what happens to those unfaithful to me.

"Maybe we should intervene," Courier said suddenly, having decided to speak first. But he didn't seem convinced of his own argument. He sounded as if he were slipping away over a steep riverbank with black, cold water awaiting him. "Baphomet? Maybe I could—"

"You will do exactly as I tell you, Courier," Maxwell said, using a rational but uncompromising tone. "I am, as you are aware, driven by the divine inspiration. Do you not feel divinely inspired in my presence?

Then you will do what I tell you and nothing else. We will have no misunderstandings concerning this point."

Courier had told him earlier the police were researching the identity of the seven victims. He had told Baphomet they knew about InfoDuct and had requested information about Adriaan Basten. Courier had excellent contacts, as far as Maxwell knew. That was not the problem with Courier.

"You promised me," Maxwell said, "no traces would be found at the site of the ritual." He spoke without emotion. He merely summed up the state of affairs. "You assured me not even the police would be able to find traces that would lead either to the victims or to us. That was what you told me. You would make sure. And yet, now, things seem to be different. This might put our sacred mission at peril."

"I'm sorry, Baphomet . . ."

"You tell me the police not only found traces but have also identified one of the victims. Is that what you're saying?"

"The detectives were lucky. That's all, Baphomet. They went looking for people who went missing recently, and—"

"*Pure luck*," Maxwell said.

"They searched their files for missing persons and at once found Basten. Metagogeus and I made sure there was nothing, nothing at all at the site, nothing that could identify the, um, *chosen*."

"Pure luck," Maxwell repeated. "Luck does not exist. Not in police work. There's professionalism and diligence and hard work. Faith and trust and maybe intuition. We must remind ourselves of those principles. More specifically, we need faith and trust in what we, this society of ours, will accomplish. All these things exist in the world. Luck does not. It is an illusion, created to suit the stupid masses who believe sweepstakes will let them win big. Luck is for women who are certain the handsome postman is interested in them. You have underestimated the police and their methods. Metagogeus should know better. So should you."

"I will try to find out—"

"*Courier*," Maxwell said. And then he fell silent again because he didn't want to know what the man was planning. He wasn't interested in what plans Courier had. Courier's effort would be without any merit since it would not remedy the situation. And in fact, Courier had to do nothing. In the end, there would be nothing that could associate him, Maxwell, with those bodies. In the worst-case scenario, the bodies would be tied to Courier and Metagogeus, and perhaps to others. But not to him. Maybe if the police dug really deep, they would find some connections, but nothing that could harm him. At least, he assumed.

The thing was, he hadn't thought Basten or any of the others would be identified. But it happened anyway, making things more complicated. Making him just a bit more vulnerable.

Finally, he said, "The only thing we must keep in mind, Courier, is that we are on the eve of the ultimate catharsis. We need to take radical measures, if necessary, to protect our cause. Our interests."

"Just the thing I had in mind," Courier said. Probably glad to be off the hook for now.

"I can do without the things in your mind," Maxwell said, suddenly feeling the need for a cruel remark. "I'll tell you what you should do. What you should do is inform me about the police officers involved in the case."

"They're members of the Office of International Crime and Extremist Organizations."

"Are they now? And what sort of thing is *that*?"

"Part of the AIVD, the Information and Security Service. Organized crime and such. War on terror. Homeland security sort of thing."

Maxwell fell silent again. The AIVD. It seemed logical they would be involved. Ordinary cops wouldn't cross borders and investigate ritual burnings. A potentially dangerous enemy, these people. Extreme measures would have to be taken to protect the cause.

"Do you have someone on the inside?" he inquired. "Someone who will keep us informed?"

"Not on the inside, no. But I know someone who is close to the AIVD. Close enough."

Yes, Maxwell thought. *I know who you are and what you do.* He kept himself informed about all members of the society. "So, this is what you will do, Courier. You will collect as much information on the officers as you can. We are looking for their weak spots. We all have weaknesses, for sure. Cops are no exception. Then we make our move. We make sure their investigation fails. It's as simple as that."

"I'll get to it right away, Baphomet."

"Next time you call me, you will have results for me. But remember, you're only to collect information. Nothing else, is that clear?"

"Certainly, Baphomet."

For a while, Maxwell stared out the window of his office. He had a nice view over Amsterdam, desolate though it looked in winter.

He would have to eliminate them all, he thought. All the enemies of the society. These seven would be just the beginning. Seven, that was nothing. He had deemed it senseless to sacrifice only seven people. But Metagogeus and Tertullian and especially Courier had insisted. He had granted them some measure of freedom. It had also helped to get rid of some people who could damage the society. But it had resulted in a disaster—the unexpected and unwelcome interest of the security service, no less.

The plans he had were so much grander, so much more encompassing than just this one sacrifice. Maybe not everything could be accomplished. The clock was ticking. In the end, he needed to be ready, ready for the final moments. Ready for the greatest sacrifice the society could organize.

He considered the Church of the Supreme Purification their enemy, though before it became weak and meaningless it had accomplished great things. The spectacular, highly visible sacrifices people still talked about. Purification through fire. The breathtaking disasters with hundreds of people sacrificed, and nobody suspecting foul play. The church had been powerful for a long time, but then its leaders had mellowed, had retreated into a watered-down ideology. No more sacrifices, no more victims.

He, Baphomet, had restored the old order and earned the respect of a number of veterans and new adepts. Restored the old power. And he enjoyed that power.

His thoughts were interrupted by a knock at the door. He was old-fashioned and traditional in that way, obliging his staff to knock.

"Come in," he said. Nor did he care for the sort of technology that would only widen the gap between himself and his people.

A young girl walked in with a couple of leather folders. She didn't carry them in front of her, like the other secretaries would, but had tucked them under her arm. But then, she was no mere secretary to him.

"Yes, Serena," he said.

"Excuse me, Mr. Maxwell," the girl said. "These are the financial reports from last week."

"Thank you," he said. She had joined his office two, no, three years ago. She had been working for his company for a year already in another capacity. Their first meeting had been remarkable because of what she said. She said she admired a man who could still talk about God and faith, even in front of his staff. That had caught her attention, she said. And she had blushed while admitting that. There is no shame in speaking about God, he told her.

A few weeks later, she was back. They discussed religion. Inspiration, faith, education. He had given her time. He had her background checked. Nice family, exemplary educational record. White as snow.

Gradually, slowly, he fed her information. Just innocent bits at first. About a certain religious organization. About the fate of humanity. About being inspired by an all-encompassing divine inspiration. He watched her reactions. He liked her reactions. He became convinced she would be an asset to the society. A true believer.

Only after half a year had he confided in Serena. Well, no, not exactly. He had trapped her in the web he had been spinning. He spoke of the community of people who possessed the only true faith, free from any conventional religion. He continued to feed her information, bit by bit, less innocent this time. He spoke of the dangers to the members of such a community, the dangers from a secular, vindictive world.

And then, one Friday, he suggested she'd spend a weekend with some like-minded souls.

She hesitated for a moment. Then she said yes.

And so it had begun.

Now she was a member of the society. She was one of his most loyal supporters. Now she was convinced, like they all were, that humanity needed a final and all-encompassing purification.

Courier, who in normal life went under a different name and who was not a courier at all, dropped his red cell phone on his desk. In a few moments, he would have a meeting with the first secretary of the minister and two senior officials. What was that meeting about? Funding the local police support services and their needs for rolling stock. A mundane but unavoidable subject. He was never excited about such issues. But the police had to have their new vehicles.

Afterward, he would casually inquire with the two officials about certain cases he had heard about. He was most interested in those that had yet not been mentioned in the newspapers. Wanted to stay informed. The first secretary would be knowledgeable, but he wouldn't communicate with Courier concerning these matters. Too much gossip going around already. Courier didn't mind. He always found someone who would be indiscreet.

He knew it to be a matter of vanity. The most beautiful of sins, along with greed. If people were not led by greed or vanity, how could he manipulate them? Life for him would be less attractive.

The AIVD would have no idea, he assumed, how often their affairs were commented upon by minor bureaucrats and overheard by people like himself. Sometimes people had to be encouraged to share certain information with him, but more often they were glad to show how involved they were in police matters. Which they weren't. But they loved their own vanity.

Except they would not talk to journalists. There was a subtle but clear distinction. Gossip, yes, but only with people they saw as their equals.

Courier worried about his relationship with Baphomet. The man appreciated his efforts, certainly, but just now he had sounded less than pleased. Entirely understandable. Relations between them had cooled somewhat after the Ardennes disaster.

But Courier was certain he would remain part of the inner circle. Those who would, in the end, be purified. And that was all that mattered.

13

THE DOCTOR AND TWO nurses were watching the northern horizon with interest. All around them, the savanna was slowly turning into a desert, a process that would likely take another few years. The last green patches struggling against the inevitable change would soon turn to brown or spidery gray. Another sight, however, held their attention. In the far distance the sky had turned a dirty purple with a deep, disturbingly dark front below it.

"Storm coming," the doctor said.

"Is it a strong one?" the youngest of the nurses wanted to know. She frowned back at where Linda stood, without actually addressing her. "Maybe we should secure the tents with more rope," she added.

"Storms are always bad in this part of the world," the doctor said. As if he had experienced many African tornadoes and barely escaped with his life.

"What did the lieutenant say?" the other nurse inquired, a distinct tremor in her voice. "Do we have to worry?"

She had addressed the doctor but then turned toward Linda. Linda was convinced that despite her discretion they all knew about her little trip with Odinga, and so she'd become an authority on what the man thought. In the few hours they had of free time, all the doctors and nurses could do by way of entertainment was read or gossip. Few were readers. They liked gossiping, particularly about Linda. She didn't care. There was much they didn't know about her.

The doctor, a Frenchman with a stylish tuft of graying hair under his lower lip, shook his head as if he had made an important decision. "It will be all right, that storm. The locals don't seem concerned. Why should we?"

To Linda, he was a fool and his remarks proved it. He never spoke to the people in the camp. He tended their wounds and gave them medicine and asked them simple questions through an interpreter, but he only asked about their medical problems. He knew nothing about them. He was an idealist, surely, but he kept a distinct distance between himself and the locals, as if their poverty and suffering might rub off on him. Perhaps he had a career in mind, after this, but not in medicine. He would be a politician, perhaps. Linda put more trust in the nurses' motives; they would still be nurses after this.

The nurses the doctor had been talking to walked toward the tent, heads down. They had been here for several months now and had seen death under all its guises. They were not afraid of a storm. But they would be, later, Linda suspected, when the front was overhead and a direct threat.

They would learn to fear nature.

Linda stowed her logbooks and her inventory sheets in a steel coffin and folded the metal table she used as a desk. She glanced at the neat white tent next door, home to the UN representatives. Their equally white Toyota Land Cruiser was parked in front of it. They had planned to take it for a trip a hundred miles northeast and bring back supplies, but they seemed to have delayed their departure. Neither had the supply truck shown up yet, probably due to the approaching storm. Current supplies would last for no longer than a week.

Holding onto the logbooks and the inventories might prove pointless if the whole operation were canceled due to the storm and its aftermath. But then, wasn't everything pointless, in the end? A human life was like a grain of sand in the desert. In the Netherlands, newspapers would chastise politicians if twenty children a year died in traffic. Here no statistics about life and death were kept at all.

Beyond the tent, she noticed six Kenyan soldiers, torsos bare and without their weapons, keeping an eye on the approaching storm. She recognized one of them, a young sergeant she had seen at the gorge. Over there, he had looked frightened, confronted with an event he could not comprehend. He would not share his fear with the lieutenant or with his men, but she had noticed it. He had shared it with her as if he expected from her some rational explanation for the horrid ritual.

She had no explanation to give. She knew nothing of Africa. She knew nothing of Somalia and the local people. She had arrived here, her head filled with carelessly collected ideas about what would await her—images mostly remembered from films and novels. What she didn't expect was the smell. Nothing in the movies and novels had prepared her for the odor of the savanna, the heated, salty soil, the grainy sand, the dry hot air, and the subtle but raw organic smells from distant cadavers. Old smells that remained in the atmosphere for a long time. It was the smell from ancient times, before the ascent of man. The only odors missing were industrial smells, exhaust fumes, machines, hot concrete, and bitumen.

The dry heat was another thing she had to adapt to. It sucked energy out of her. Energy she could hardly replenish with food and water. She had been confronted by the unwillingness of the locals, the refugees, to see themselves for what they really were, fugitives. They seemed unable to understand what exactly their current situation was, displaced as they were, cut off from their known universe. Her position? She was a stranger to them, hardly worth their attention. The concept of foreign aid was almost alien to them, although they accepted the medical assistance.

"They're much stronger than we are, in many respects," one of the doctors had said, a few days after her arrival. "They are reduced to the bare reality of survival. And for their fatalism they are mentally stronger than we. But make no mistake, the grief of an African mother losing her child is as real as when a European child dies. Life counts as much here as it does elsewhere. Even despite their fatalism."

She realized Lieutenant Odinga was standing next to her. She'd been lost in thought.

"Do these storms happen often?" she asked. Her voice trembled a bit, and not because of his presence. To hell with the nurses and their gossip.

For a moment, he didn't seem inclined to answer. He wasn't from around here. How could he know about local weather? Then he said, "This morning it was explained by the locals what these storms can do. How extensive their power can be. The sky will be dark as the entrance to hell, they said. And there will be wind and thunder to match that. Sound enticing? The savanna will undulate as if coming alive. Animals hide where they can, if they can, or risk getting caught by the wind. Imagine what will happen to humans. The thunder gods show their anger by throwing the clouds through the sky, by blowing the sand of the desert around in great heaps. What else do you need to know?"

"Should we leave?"

"Leave?"

"Break up the camp and leave?"

He laughed hoarsely. "And go where? A storm front like that spreads its infernal wings over maybe fifty miles. It moves fast. Faster, perhaps, than we can travel. If the gods are angry, they'll be angry for the right reasons. We will not escape their wrath. They will deal with us and with the camp however they please."

She had never wondered before if he believed in gods or the supernatural. Was he a Muslim? A Christian? It didn't really matter. When you saw the darkest of storms approaching, it didn't really matter what sort of religion you adhered to.

"My men will secure the tents with extra lines. Everything valuable will be stored in boxes and crates. We still have a couple hours. Use them wisely."

She noticed extra activity around the army tents, but nobody seemed in a hurry.

"I will send you some assistance," the lieutenant said, and left.

She had wanted to know what would happen to the bodies in the hills, but he was gone. She knew the answer: nothing would be done about them. They would be left hanging there and would remain there for hundreds of years. As was fitting for a ritual.

She continued packing. She had no idea what was valuable and what was not. It was just administration. Order forms, lists of equipment, a list of medicines used by the doctors. Maps of the area—none of them reliable—and flight schedules for the plane, although it never flew on time. None of this mattered. None of what they had done mattered. Doctors and nurses would pack their instruments and medical supplies, which were the only things they needed to rescue.

Except for the people, of course.

But they couldn't rescue the people.

She left the rest of her stuff as it was. The time remaining was too short anyway.

Let the wind blow it all away.

She went outside. A dozen soldiers occupied themselves with anchoring the tents. Half the sky had already turned gray, veined with dark green and purple. Even the colors were alien to her. The end of the world was nigh.

The end was nigh for the people in the camp as well. They ran about, without purpose but equally without panic. She noticed women chasing their children into the tents, but what good would the tents be with the impending storm? Old men lugged mattresses, equally useless. She saw young boys helping the grown-ups with bags and pans. Nobody was going anywhere.

The soldiers dragged large olive-colored boxes and trunks into the trucks. But none of the vehicles were leaving. Odinga was right, she assumed: there was no escaping the storm. There was no escaping the wrath of the gods.

The medical team gathered in the main tent. It was rare to see the whole team together. "It's like Sudan last year," one of the nurses commented. "But those were sand storms. Bad enough, but nothing like this."

"We went through an earthquake in Pakistan once," another said. "Three years ago." All relieved from their usual duties, they suddenly had time to chat. Under normal circumstances they hardly had time for personal histories, too tired as they were for conversation.

Linda suddenly wondered again why Odinga had taken her to the hills, the only nonmedical staff member. If he'd needed a medical opinion on what he'd found there, he would have taken a doctor.

Was it on account of what she said earlier, that she didn't believe in the supernatural? Or did he merely want to impress her? Well, she had been impressed. No, she'd been *horrified*.

She became aware of a sound in the air. There had been the distant rumbling of thunder and the wind, but this was another sound, coming closer, as if a large airborne creature was approaching.

And it got stronger.

Of course, it got stronger.

One of the nurses looked out of the tent, but not in the direction of the storm. "Good God," she said.

"Yes," a doctor said. "Heavy weather ahead."

"No," the nurse said, "It's a helicopter." She pointed east. Low over the horizon a large and powerful helicopter approached. Only now did Linda hear its engine over the noise of the storm. It turned out to be a military craft, Russian in origin like all helicopters in this part of the world. As the helicopter banked, she noticed rocket launchers and machine guns and the faces of the pilots behind the plexiglass. With some difficulty, it landed a few hundred yards from the tent.

"A helicopter in this weather?" the doctor said. "They're not going to evacuate us, I assume?"

A man in military fatigues jumped from the cabin of the helicopter. Lieutenant Odinga hurried toward him. He spoke to the man without shaking his hand. The man showed him a document. Three other men disembarked, soldiers armed with automatic rifles. They scanned the horizon.

Odinga gestured in the general direction of the camp and then toward the medical tents. Then he pointed at the hills. What was said Linda could only guess. Odinga gestured some more, but the visitor didn't seem impressed.

The two men approached the tent and entered. "Ms. Weisman?" the newcomer asked, in English. He looked like an Arab, maybe he was Indian or Pakistani. He surely wasn't Somali or Kenyan.

"That's me," she said.

"I'm Colonel Saeed Al-Rahman of the Saudi Intelligence Service, and I need to ask you some questions."

She looked at him in surprise. Then at Odinga. "What is this?" she asked. "The Saudi Intelligence Service?"

"He has properly identified himself," Odinga briefly said. "He is authorized by the Somali government to visit this site. And ask questions."

"I was informed," the newcomer said to Linda, "that you come from the Netherlands, and you have seen the sites of the sacrifices."

She noticed the other members of the team had all departed, probably finding shelter in the trucks and vehicles.

They both sat down on folding chairs.

"Why," Linda asked, "would Saudi Intelligence be interested in what happens in a secluded spot somewhere in Somalia, even if human sacrifices are involved?"

"Mutaween, ma'am," he said with a winning smile. "I am, more precisely, an officer of the Mutaween. Which is the Saudi religious police. But such a designation has an unfortunate negative connotation in the West." He spoke English with a pleasant British accent. "These people— their sacrifices have a clear religious orientation, if that's the correct word. We investigate such phenomena."

"I find it difficult to believe that, Colonel," Linda said. "You appear here out of the blue, in this godforsaken place, with a helicopter, while none of our own pilots would dare fly, and all that on account of a religious matter?"

He slowly nodded and pressed his lips together. "The conditions are extreme, I grant you that. But I must work according to a . . . how do you say, a very strict agenda." He smiled again. "To us, ma'am, religion is very important. But I'm sure you're aware of that. However, I cannot give you any more details on why I'm here. This is not just about religion. We are dealing here with people with very sinister political intentions. It seems we all have an agenda."

"Are you talking about terrorists?"

"You could call them that. Now, questions?"

"Lieutenant Odinga seems to know more than I do."

"Lieutenant Odinga," Al-Rahman said, indulging her, "is an intelligent man. His experience and knowledge are very important, concerning the local situation. But he also does not stray beyond his narrow personal concept of religious phenomena."

106

She wasn't sure what that meant. "Oh," she said.

"Exactly," said Al-Rahman. "And you're an outsider. You come from a largely secular society. Your perspective is different than that of, well, me and the lieutenant. What is it you have seen? Your interpretation?"

"A sacrifice. People who have been sacrificed. What else could it be? Unless they were criminals, and their execution is meant to deter others."

"No, we don't think they were criminals. But, a ritual?"

"Probably," she said. Wondering why he asked her, as he was supposed to be a specialist in religious matters. But of course, he hadn't seen the site and the victims. "You're asking the wrong person, Colonel. I'm not religious, as you pointed out."

"That does not matter. I appreciate your rational answers." He smiled again as if he wanted to reassure her. "Did those people want to die voluntarily?"

She shivered. The suggestion frightened her. Would anybody want to burn alive out of their free will? "I can't imagine they would. Will you visit the hills and see the place?"

"Too late for that, I'm afraid. Not enough time, with the storm coming. It took a lot of effort to persuade the pilot to come here, under these circumstances. He will not fly toward the hills, I'm sure. Maybe he already heard about the dead people. Even the military are very superstitious in these parts of the world. Any details that struck you?"

"What details? People, bound to stakes, burned. How many more details do you want me to remember?"

"Like signs left behind. I mean text, maybe written in blood, or markings on the rocks."

"No," Linda said. "Can't remember. Did I miss anything?"

"Not necessarily," the colonel said. "I would not expect such details. The remarkable thing is, in fact, the absence of any message to the world."

"Are there more known cases?"

"There was a man? He was arrested by the soldiers?"

"Yes," Linda said.

"What did he have to say?"

"He didn't talk."

The colonel sat back. His chair wobbled dangerously on the uneven ground. He didn't seem concerned by the approaching storm. "He did not talk."

"No, he didn't," Linda said, annoyed by his insistence. "Maybe he's afraid to talk. He fears for his life, or whatever."

"He's local?"

"There are no locals, not in the strict sense of the word, Colonel. This is the desert, formerly a savanna. Occasionally smugglers and traffickers pass by, but that's it."

"So, you don't know where he comes from."

"I'm the local administrator," Linda said. "Ask the lieutenant."

"Yes," he said, "I did." He got up. "Thank you for your time, ma'am. I will now look around a bit."

"Why are you really here, Colonel?" she asked.

He glanced at her, surprised. "You assume I do not tell the truth?" His smile had disappeared, and she noticed he was not pleased by her question. "I come here in spite of the storm and with a military helicopter, kindly loaned to me by the Kenyans. Do you not think I would share only the truth with you?" He stepped outside, frowning at the sky. She followed him. He did not look back. She had offended him, but she didn't care. The colonel joined the lieutenant and started a conversation. They walked away from her.

The doctor came up to Linda. "Who's that funny guy?"

He isn't funny. He's dangerous. "No idea," she said. "But this is one weird story." She noticed both officers hurrying toward where the prisoner was kept. Then they disappeared behind a cloud of sand. Linda entered the tent again. Not much later the helicopter departed.

14

EEKHAUT DROPPED YET ANOTHER cream-colored cardboard folder on the stack of similar folders by his left elbow. After four months at the Bureau, he hadn't been able to browse through a quarter of the information about criminal organizations active in Europe. He was astonished by the lack of quality information. The AIVD and other security services seemed to have gathered little or no real background stories and intel about these organizations. The files were pitiful and inadequate. He suspected the most dangerous enemies of democracy and order kept their secrets well hidden.

Nobody, however, asked for his opinion. And he wouldn't volunteer it either.

What had he read about so far? Extreme right-wing parties and their violent but fortunately small private militia. So-called religious splinter groups founded on arcane belief systems. Radical left-wing movements preaching the violent overthrow of capitalist society (capitalism would by itself succumb to its inner contradictions, Eekhaut knew from his lessons on Marxism). Criminal gangs catering to all the perverse wants of wealthy clients. Syndicates providing young women (or boys, if requested) for the dark side of the flesh trade in large Western and Central European cities. Trafficking in anything with a high financial margin—from Chinese automatic weapons and stolen art to a wide variety of drugs. And religious sects with extreme predilections.

Van Gils appeared in the doorway. "What do you need me to look for?" he inquired. He wore a heavy winter coat and looked bulkier than ever.

For a moment Eekhaut had no idea what the man was talking about. Was he supposed to be clairvoyant? Then he understood. "Oh, we need information on Adriaan Basten. Prinsen has his file. Ask him what is missing. What you can find out about the man that we don't know yet. All that's publicly known about Basten we already have on record. What we need to know is everything he wanted to keep hidden and secret. Since he lived here in Amsterdam, you'll probably know where to look."

"No problem," Van Gils said.

"That's what I thought. Is Prinsen around?"

"He might be. I saw him talking to De Vries."

"De Vries?" Eekhaut couldn't remember any officer by that name.

"Thea De Vries. That brown-haired young woman, fresh from the police academy. You've seen her around. Clever girl. Sort of girl men notice."

"I hadn't noticed her."

"I'm sure you did. You're not immune to feminine charm. Don't you look at girls in the street? Turn around to look at them?"

"Shamefully enough, I do," Eekhaut admitted. "And often enough, here in Amsterdam. A lot of gorgeous women around, in Amsterdam." He got up. "Whatever. I need Prinsen. Can't bear to look at another of these files."

He found Prinsen by the coffee machine. "Forget this crap, Nick. Let's go out and pick up some decent coffee along the way."

Prinsen looked relieved. He wasn't keen on spending too much time in the office.

Outside, the air had cleared, and it had stopped snowing. The temperature had gone up a bit, and the snow in the streets was already melting into a watery gunk that would soon be a nuisance to pedestrians and cyclists. Eekhaut mused, for a moment, about some warm place by the seaside, Tenerife or Crete or wherever. He could have been in Somalia with Linda if he had insisted. He would go anywhere with Linda.

"You're talking about Sergeant De Vries," Prinsen corrected him when he inquired. They had a quick espresso in a French snack bar across Reguliersgracht, east of Amstelveld. They were standing at the counter, among the early crowd and the sleepless. "She's no inspector yet. You only get promoted on the fast track when you're family of the chief." He grinned maliciously, having learned to counter the gossip about him and Dewaal. That was also Eekhaut's usual strategy: simply acknowledge the rumors, whatever they were. That usually made people doubt.

"People gossip about you and De Vries," he said.

Prinsen eyed the pictures of French seaside resorts on the walls of the snack bar. Lithe girls bathing, or not, in the tiniest of bikinis. "Of course, they do gossip. She's often around me. Why should I ignore her? She's a nice girl, and she's barely younger than I am. She's not into older men, Walter. But you know I'm not interested in her."

"I'm sure you're not. But what about her? Is she aware you've got that girlfriend of yours safely tucked away somewhere in the city?"

"Haven't told her," Prinsen said. "Let's skip this conversation, Walter. It's leading nowhere."

Fifteen minutes later they arrived at a brick building dating from the early twentieth century. It was well maintained and had been recently refurbished with a large glass entrance and an ugly logo over the door. INFODUCT, it said.

The receptionist wasn't surprised to see two police officers showing their credentials, as if the law often came knocking at their door. Would the gentlemen leave their coats at the cloakroom and wait in the lounge? She would call someone from Human Resources at once. She indicated a herd of straight-backed leather chairs that might have been used recently as accessories in a Batman movie. Whoever had designed the furniture seemed to expect only anorexic twentysomethings to use them. Prinsen sat down, fitting neatly, but Eekhaut preferred to stand.

Five minutes later a tall woman, maybe in her late thirties (or maybe not), stepped into the hall and walked over to them on dangerously high heels. Her attire spelled a distinct amount of power. "Chief Inspector Eekhaut?" she said, evidently choosing the elder of the two police officers. "Madeleine Bunting. Responsible for human resources."

"We'd like to have some information about one of your employees, Adriaan Basten," Eekhaut said, skipping introductions. And he thought, *You will be. Responsible, that is. I'll make sure of that.*

For a moment, she closed her eyes, as if trying to concentrate on the name, as if there were thousands of people working for her company and many shared that name. "Shall we go upstairs to my office?" she proposed. "We'll be more comfortable there."

And, indeed, more private, Eekhaut thought.

She led them across the hall toward the elevator. Her office was on the third floor and overlooked the canal in front of the building. This meant she was high up in the company's hierarchy. The view, however, wasn't great—gray streets and passing gray people. Eekhaut largely preferred Amsterdam in the spring and summer, awash with colors, its streets bustling with tourists, young people in exotic colors, florists—and the outrageously attired crowd of people who wanted to be seen.

He wondered what sort of company this was that could afford offices on one of the *grachten*, the canals that surrounded the center, in the most expensive part of town. He would have to find out what exactly InfoDuct did. It probably was part of that elusive digital economy he knew too little about. Where the real money was these days.

But not as much money as in crime.

He sat down on a chair that looked more comfortable than the ones in the lobby. Ms. Bunting's desk consisted of nothing more than a thick plate of glass on a brushed steel frame, with a small, elegant laptop, a smartphone, and a leather agenda the same size as the laptop. Next to it rested a massive Meisterstück pen. He liked the subtle mix of high-tech and tradition. We can afford both, this mix said. We can afford expensive but ultimately useless writing implements, and we can afford top-of-the-line electronics.

The office told him the same story. The furniture was of Italian design, large abstract paintings hung on two walls, and the windows were flanked by panels of exquisite Japanese rice paper. A small fortune had been spent on this interior. And she was just the HR manager.

Prinsen, next to him, didn't seem impressed at all. He might have been used to this sort of decor.

"I already spoke to your colleagues about Adriaan's disappearance," Bunting said. "There is probably nothing more I can tell you."

"That would be the local police, madam," Eekhaut said. "We are here concerning an ongoing investigation of our own." She had seen their badges, telling her they were not local police.

Before Bunting could react, the door opened and a girl walked in carrying a white metal tray with cups, coffee, milk, and sugar. "You will have a coffee, gentlemen, I assume?" Bunting proposed. She didn't seem in a hurry to get rid of the annoying police officers.

They couldn't refuse. The girl busied herself with cups and coffee with a smooth elegance that spoke of experience. Eekhaut wondered if this was the only thing she did around here: providing visitors and management with coffee.

"Thank you, Annick," Bunting finally said. Annick quickly glanced at Eekhaut and then disappeared silently.

The coffee was excellent. Black, strong, and syrupy.

"Adriaan Basten," Bunting said. "He disappeared, now let me see, a few weeks ago? Is that right?"

"Four and a half weeks ago, indeed," Eekhaut said. "The thing that surprises me, ma'am, is that you were the one informing the police of the fact. That's rather unusual. We'd expect members of the immediate family to come forward."

"Adriaan had no family, Chief Inspector. We felt it necessary to inform the police ourselves."

"No family? Really?" The information Prinsen had shown him had indeed made no mention of the man's family. Eekhaut had, however, assumed the information was missing. Now it turned out the family itself was missing.

"How did you find out he was gone?"

Bunting spread her hands as if the matter was apparent. "He no longer showed up. As simple as that."

It could not have been *as simple as that*, Eekhaut assumed. They would have tried to contact him—messaged, phoned, even visited his flat. People don't just not turn up for work one day without several people getting worried. Even if they're not family. "Maybe he found another professional opportunity or decided to go on prolonged vacation?"

She smiled, indulgently. "He would have told us. In this company, there are no secrets among employees. He would have told his supervisor, his friends. We would have known. We have responsible employees, Chief Inspector. That's what alarmed us at once. I had somebody go to his apartment. See if he was ill or whatever. Nobody answered the bell. A neighbor let us in. The apartment was empty. So we called the police."

"And the police found no trace of him."

"I don't know what the police found. They haven't kept us informed, probably because we're not family. Now you turn up. Do you have anything for us?"

"I really cannot comment on an ongoing investigation, ma'am."

She didn't like that at all. Suddenly, he noticed she wore the same sort of outfit Dewaal usually did. Business suit, white blouse. Might they shop in the same place?

"Still," he continued, "a young man falling off the face of the earth, that should surprise you, didn't it?"

"Well, aren't the police supposed to solve mysteries like that?"

"You didn't feel concerned about his fate."

"I am responsible," she said, "for the well-being of our employees, but I keep well away from their private lives. And I had to find a replacement at once, I'm afraid. A hard world we live in, Chief Inspector. People like Adriaan are tough to replace, but in the end, they *must* be replaced."

"What exactly was it Basten did here?"

"He specialized in services to foreign visitors. Expats. Foreigners who have to settle in Amsterdam for a short while, a few months or whatever, and require specific services."

"Such as?"

She seemed annoyed by his insistence, as if she feared giving away trade secrets. "Housing, of course. Residence permit, cable TV, an internet connection, a phone contract, and whatever else. Health insurance if not covered at home, a bank account for those staying longer. All the legal paperwork. Basten arranged it, so our customers wouldn't lose time with local administrations and such. He facilitated their life."

"For which your company got paid. Handsomely, I assume."

"Obviously," she said. "We're talking about people who either can afford such services or work for companies that can. He worked for diplomats and embassy staff."

"Intriguing."

She breathed deeply. "And, of course, very useful. He was an expert in dealing with bureaucrats," she said, not without malice. "He got things done when they needed to be done. Made life easier for whomever his clients were. Anyway, how is all this relevant to your investigation?"

Eekhaut sipped his coffee. He had other questions, but Prinsen beat him to it, "Had there, to your knowledge, been any contact between Mister Basten and religious organizations?"

For a moment, it seemed she would ignore him. Then she said, "We take no interest in the private lives of our employees. As such, I have no idea what religion Basten adhered to."

Eekhaut deposited his cup on the glass surface of her desk as if moon-landing a fragile object. "The matter isn't frivolous, Ms. Bunting. Basten might very well have been a member of some organization with strong feelings toward immigration, for example. He might very well have been a passionate follower of extreme ideologies. Do you get my drift?"

She shifted in her chair, clearly uncomfortable. "Even then," she said, "this might not be relevant—"

"Depending on the sort of clients he had, this would be relevant," Eekhaut continued. "If they were, let's say, non-Caucasian, he might have been, well, embarrassed by the tension between his private beliefs and his professional responsibilities. Do you see my point?"

Bunting leaned back, surveying both officers. "We have a very diverse customer base, Chief Inspector. And we offer a wide range of services while considering the needs of these people, including dietary and religious. We are part of a larger structure, as a subsidiary of TransCom. You know what TransCom is? No? Maybe you should check them out and their reputation. We cannot afford the private predilections of our employees to taint their professional behavior. And that includes, of course, Adriaan Basten."

"But, as you just mentioned, you know nothing of his personal life."

"We know what we need to know. We scan potential employees, or have them scanned by TransCom, and that includes religion and political affinities. However, the law forbids us to dig too deep there, as you certainly know."

"Since you obviously know very little about Basten," Eekhaut said, "we would like to talk to some of his colleagues."

He made sure it didn't sound like a request.

"Adriaan had few colleagues in the strict sense of the word. His was a sort of one-man operation. Which makes him all the harder to replace."

An immense loss for the company, Eekhaut mused. What a pain it must have been to her when Basten no longer showed up. It surprised him she didn't wear black.

"There's no one who can help us with more information?" He locked gazes with her. "Come now, Ms. Bunting," he said with a somewhat malicious grin, "people talk, they gossip. In the coffee corner, during lunch, in the pub. He must have had friends, he must have had a private life."

"I would assume that all of this belongs to the private sphere, Chief Inspector," she repeated. "And as such—"

"I don't plan to concern myself with Basten's private life," Eekhaut said, "and neither with that of any of your staff. However, I'm conducting a criminal inquiry. We assume he was murdered. We will find his murderer, Ms. Bunting. That is what we do. And as officers of the AIVD, we have a certain number of plenary powers that include questioning people."

"In that case—"

"Furthermore," he said, rising from his chair, being fed up with her, "we do not need your approval, ma'am. We will speak to any member of your staff, if necessary, and you will make sure they're available."

She rose as well, and with her high heels proved to be taller than he. Prinsen, hesitantly, rose too.

"There might be a few people who knew Basten," Bunting said. "I'll send for them, and there's an office next door where you might question them in private."

"Thank you," Eekhaut said.

It had been a small victory. At last, Prinsen and Eekhaut met with five young employees, all of them careful in expressing an opinion and surprised to be asked at all. Eekhaut was familiar with the aspirations and hopes of their generation, torn as they were between personal self-expression and the need for individuality on the one hand and adherence to a group, a social medium or a company, on the other. Most of them would at some point go freelance, since they'd read it was the way forward for digital nomads.

In the end, there was little they could tell the officers. Adriaan had been an excellent colleague but hardly a friend. He had been a member of the team, even though there was no team, only a collection of individuals gravitating around a common objective. No, they never met outside of work. Neither did they have any work-related fun, like drinks at the end of the week. No, they had no idea of his private life. Did they care? They did not.

An hour later Eekhaut stopped for the day. The whole effort had been useless. Basten remained a mystery. Before leaving he looked inside Bunting's office, but it was empty. He left his card on her desk, certain she would throw it in the trash.

Back in the street again, he felt cold and depressed. The sky was overcast. Amsterdam was less than cheerful, cyclists hurrying over the bridges and along the canals, avoiding careless pedestrians. Some of the local shops were closed, except for a bakery doing a brisk trade in pecan pies and vegetarian specialties.

When they entered Kerkstraat again, fifteen minutes later, Prinsen said, "That didn't go well, Chief." He seldom called Eekhaut *Chief.*

"A wonderful and inspiring example of indifference, Nick. Let that be a lesson to you. But you're right, we didn't get much out of them. I hope Van Gils was more successful."

"That whole religion thing doesn't sit well with me."

"You think we should approach the case differently?"

"That's not the point," Prinsen said. "I have a problem with the sort of people who rely on God for their salvation. People who consider themselves at the center of the world, the universe. And claim a direct line to God. The Chosen Ones."

"That's the point of the religious experience, Nick, being able to talk directly to your creator. And assuming this buys you a ticket on the front row of whatever *He* has in store."

"I hail from such a community," Prinsen said, gloomily. "And Dewaal as well. We both managed to escape."

"Oh! Your God-fearing parents. Grandparents, in your case."

"Like you wouldn't believe. Foreigners often, if not always, see the Netherlands as this superbly modern secular and tolerant state, but outside of the main urban areas we're as religious, superstitious, and reactionary as . . . Well, I would compare us to the American South, if I were familiar with the American South. And we have a Bible Belt too. There are communities out there who still live in the nineteenth century, if not earlier. At least as far as their religious experience is concerned. They're not Amish, nothing like that, since they embrace technology. At least when it doesn't connect them to the outside world. Tractors and trucks and cars and electricity are all right. Television and all the digital stuff is the work of the Devil."

"And your father was a pastor or something like that."

"No, he wasn't. Not that it made any difference. They didn't read books except the Bible, didn't know anything about the outside world and weren't interested. It's all cliché, and you've heard it before, but I lived it. I lived the reality of the one and overwhelming truth that canceled out everything else—the truth of God and his creation. We did have books in school, but only those approved on a religious basis. I fled. I ran away. I ran as far as I could when I was old enough."

"At least you realized you had to run."

"Oh, a lot of young people get out. The older generation is trapped in their dead-end life and probably know it, which reinforces their stubbornness. They will be saved, that's the thing they're sure of."

"You're familiar then with the ideas of the Church of the Supreme Purification. Nothing strange to you."

"No, actually, I'm very familiar with everything those idiots believed in. And what the Society of Fire still believes."

"What happened to Dewaal?"

"She got out as well. Actually, she was my example. She lived in Amsterdam, occasionally returned for a few days. Locals hated her, of course, but we, the younger generation within the family, knew we would eventually follow her lead, her example."

"Your hero."

"Mmm. More like an example. Wouldn't call her a hero."

"Your folks didn't like her."

"My mother hated, literally hated, everything my aunt stood for. Because she was free. She was free in the sense that nobody told her what to think, what to do. My mother was always pretty upset when her sister came to visit. Tried to keep us kids away from her and her godless ideas. Didn't work, of course. I suspect my aunt came back so often to make sure others would imitate her."

"And in the end, you escaped."

"It was like emigrating to another continent. I had to learn another language. Almost literally another language. It's language that enslaves or frees you. There's a language of suppression and another of freedom. In *the Book* you're taught the language of slavery. You're the subject of a malicious God, whose name I still write with a capital letter. He's malicious because He allows suffering. He allows, even obliges His powerless subjects to suffer. Most suffer in many different ways. What God, having the power to let all His people live in paradise, would submit them to lifelong suffering? Where's the sense in that? Only a vengeful God would do that. And I reject that sort of God."

They entered the offices of the Bureau. Van Gils, red-nosed because he had just come in from the cold, sat at his desk, perhaps considering a holiday far away. "This fellow Basten," he said when he noticed Eekhaut and Prinsen, "was born in Zeeland. That's about all the registry office has on him. He's like a ghost. No car. He rents a flat and pays cash. Wonder if he truly existed."

"All I need to know," Eekhaut said, "is how he fits into that circle of bodies. Why was he there? Why did he have to die?"

But neither Prinsen nor Van Gils could provide him with an answer.

15

A FEW MOMENTS LATER Eekhaut was summoned to Dewaal's office. She asked him to close the door, indicating important revelations. Or intimate confessions—although he realized this was less probable. "You know I'm a control freak," she announced. "And I need to know where things stand. And I'm also somewhat time-pressed."

"There's actually little progress," Eekhaut admitted. "We've been to the place Basten worked. Got confronted by an HR manager with her own ideas about communication. Basten turns out to be as insubstantial as . . . well, perhaps a sort of ghost, I don't know. Everyone liked him, but nobody knows anything about him. A specialist in one very narrow field. The perfect employee."

"The only thing about him we're certain of is that he was one of the victims."

"That's right."

"That leaves us with all the other questions unanswered, Walter. Why did he die? What was the thing in the Ardennes all about?"

Eekhaut had nothing to contribute.

"How did Prinsen do?"

"Nick? He's very effective. Why?"

"Don't treat him differently because he's family."

"I won't."

"You know what people in this office talk about? Him and me. That I protect him and he wouldn't have a job here without me. That sort of thing. I would have preferred that he wasn't related so I could treat him accordingly. But there we are. He'll make promotion on his own merits, is that clear, Walter?"

"Sure."

She was angry. And it had nothing to do with Prinsen. He had, since he came to work here, grown antennas for the things that were left unspoken.

"There's this crap I have to deal with from the veteran officers, Walter," she continued. "For more than a year now. From before you came here. I told you I trust you more than any of them because you're the odd man out."

"I know I'm the odd man out."

"Yesterday Veneman deemed it necessary to comment on . . . It doesn't matter on what. But Veneman! I need all of them in order to keep this outfit running, Walter. And you and Prinsen. I felt let down yesterday. And I have to be sure you don't let me down as well."

"Why should I? I don't have any history here."

She sat back. "I know. I'm taking this out on you. You're the only one I can complain to. Sorry about that. 'Dewaal and her favorite nephew.' That's what he said. Thought I wouldn't hear it, but I did. He's not even my favorite nephew. He escaped his family, like I did. They're a couple of troublemakers, basically, Veneman and Van Gils."

"You don't have to justify your decisions, Chief," he said carefully.

"Of course I do. And I need to be careful with people with hidden agendas. Or colleagues who aren't clean. Know what I mean? Yes, I have my suspicions, Walter. Some of them, here in the office, have their own agenda. Anyway, enough of that for now. This morning, I had a call from the prosecutor."

"Our new, *female* prosecutor?"

"Her gender is not at issue here, Walter, nor should it be mentioned. Yes, *her*. And you'll meet her soon enough. She calls me and wants to know about the Ardennes thing. She's not happy. It's taking too long. Good thing it's been kept out of the newspapers. But questions are being asked. About missing people and so on."

Eekhaut got up. "Not my problem, Chief, political stuff. I get paid to catch criminals, not to fill in forms to satisfy prosecutors. I'll keep Van Gils digging around for details about Basten."

"Good idea."

"Anything else bugging you, Alexandra?" He hardly ever addressed her by her first name. And then only when no one else was near. Those were the moments he knew she needed him, not as a colleague but as someone to share her problems with.

"I've been witness to a great number of crimes, Walter. I know what people are capable of. What they do to each other. The madmen and the psychopaths. But these are exceptions. Most murders are . . ." She was looking for the right term.

"Within the limits of reason," he said.

"Yes, something like that. Understandable. But what we witnessed here . . ."

"I see what you mean."

"We can't imagine doing these things ourselves, that's what I mean. I might kill someone when I'm driven by, I don't know, jealousy or anger, ultimately. Defending myself or others. But this? A ritual? Everything about it is *contrived*. Planned. *Systematically* planned."

"I know," he said. Further comfort he could not offer.

Thea De Vries carefully sat down on Prinsen's desk, folding one shapely leg over the other. He glanced up and noticed two things: De Vries's legs would effortlessly pass any beauty test, and he and she were utterly alone in the office space. Veneman and Van Gils and the two other detectives occupying desks at the other end of the office were out. This situation—the legs, the absence—could not be coincidental. At least, that's what Prinsen presumed.

"Nick," De Vries said, in a confidential tone that appeared totally comfortable with her position vis-à-vis her colleague, "can't you get me involved in this big operation as well? The thing none of you are talking about?"

"You aren't in on it yet?" he countered. Frowning, making sure she would understand he was preoccupied with a more urgent matter.

"Not really. I work with Siegel on Chinese importers of counterfeit luxury goods. Boring stuff. Neither of us knows any Chinese, and the translators make us wait for days. Nothing seems to happen. I don't understand why it takes two detectives to work this case."

Why the hell would she talk to me about her problems? he wondered. Did she want him to speak on her behalf with Dewaal? That wasn't going to happen. "The Chinese are an important trade partner to the Netherlands, and you have to learn the ropes . . ." he started.

"You know what I mean, Nick," she said, amused and annoyed. "I'm at the computer most of the day. And Siegel has no intention of teaching me anything. I don't want his job either. I want to work on the big projects." She leaned forward. "I've seen the pictures, Nick. The Ardennes."

"You'd be better out there in the streets with the local cops. Or move to Vice. That's the kind of work you might like. Pimps and street workers and the undeserving rich with their escorts that get paid more in a night than you'll see in a month."

She sighed dramatically. "I'd rather stay here, Nick. I don't want to do Vice. I want to work with you."

"Dewaal is not going to add another detective to the team. Not now. There's already Eekhaut and me and occasionally Van Gils. There's more cases, and you'll be needed elsewhere."

He was wary of her. She had been given high marks at the academy. An exceptional student. Almost. But she was too much in a hurry. She would have to learn the basics first, however slow this process was. He said, "We should discuss this with the Chief. I'll ask her if she—"

"I don't really need this to be official," she interrupted quickly. "This is something between the two of us, Nick. You and me." That gave her game away. This was not about her career. Not yet, anyway. This was about him. She wanted to impress him. She wanted to wrap her shapely legs around him, wanted to drag him into her personal life. Everything else was a diversion.

A small but venomous spider. "Ah," he said. "There's only the official way. You either get on the team or you don't. I can pass the word to Dewaal if you want. If you want to move up from what you're doing now."

"Really?" she said.

"I can try," he promised. But he wasn't going to.

16

JAN PIETER MAXWELL CLOSED the tan leather portfolio and observed the man on the other side of the oval table. "These results are not what we expected, Pieters," he said. He spoke in a fatherly way, a habit he had mastered only after years of practice. He had come to understand how he could use his voice to influence people. How to find the right timbre, the right mode of speech. He knew there was a right way to reprimand and another to merely sound concerned. Today he would be the family patriarch. He would be the great leader. His words indicated there was a problem—not a major problem, but at least something Pieters had to be concerned about.

Maxwell knew exactly how to deal with his employees and how to make them *want* to serve him better. He encouraged competition among his slaves, his minions. Competition was good. It weeded out the lesser elements, without any effort on his part. It didn't matter to him if they obtained better personal results or their department made a huge profit. This was important only to the company itself. What mattered most was their subservience. He wasn't merely their employer, he was everything else to them. An example, a mentor, a father figure. He was all that.

He, on the other hand, needed their admiration. He needed their regard. He knew a master was nothing without the approval of his slaves. He needed to influence them, everything they did and thought. There was no room for their individual needs or longings or aspirations. He wanted an almost demonic grip on people around him. *Demonic.* Yes, the word was well chosen.

Pieters, his current object of intellectual torture, knew all too well what had been expected of him and why he had failed. He would have failed anyway, whatever he had tried, because failure was what Maxwell had in mind. His appreciation of his employees was random. They never knew when he would be content with their results. When he would punish and when he would reward. Pieters knew he was merely middle management and would never, never be good enough to satisfy the expectations of Maxwell. But he kept trying. Because—in Maxwell's opinion—this was what slaves did. They kept trying to satisfy their master until there was nothing left for them to give.

"But what, Pieters, are we going to do about this mess?" Maxwell inquired, in his reasonable voice. Still sounding just slightly annoyed by the lack of effort from Pieters, but not really angry.

Pieters took a deep breath and glanced at the portfolio his boss was holding. He felt as if the whole of his future could be summed up on one side of a sheet of paper.

"We ought to pay more attention to the Middle East," he suggested, not really knowing what the problem was. "Despite current armed conflicts in the region, several of these economies are worth following. But the present instability—"

"*Ought?*" Maxwell said.

"Excuse me, Mr. Maxwell?"

"You said, *ought. Ought* to pay more attention."

"Well, of course, we *should*, Mr. Maxwell," Pieters hurried to explain. "We *will* certainly pay much more attention . . ."

"Think Tunisia, Pieters," Maxwell said. "Think Egypt. Think the whole of North Africa. All these countries are so desperate to belong to Europe. To become one with Europe. Sooner or later this will be a reality. One large, pan-European market, without internal borders, from Helsinki to Cairo. That's where this company is heading, Pieters. Toward our prominent role in a grander Europe."

"Of course, Mr. Maxwell. Of course we are."

"Nice to hear you're on track, Pieters," Maxwell said. "That you are with us on this." He handed the portfolio back. "Let's look at this again at a later time, shall we?"

After Pieters had left, Maxwell considered other problems. Things more important than the grand new pan-European market that was never going to happen. In 2020, nobody would be interested in the European market anymore. Such worldly matters would by then be superfluous. He knew there was little time left and still so much to do. Those wanting to be chosen still had to purify their dark, diseased souls. Sacrifices would have to be made, grand ones. A vengeful god looking down on you and measuring your effort, that wasn't something you could ignore.

And then there was the old enemy, the church, which had chosen to deviate from the true doctrine, thereby slowing all ongoing projects. Projects so many people had died for.

The members of the church would not be saved. They would not. He would make sure of that.

Maxwell turned around and watched Amsterdam. He was furious now. He had already taken revenge on some members of the church, but that would not be enough. It needed to be completely defeated. His hunger for revenge was not yet stilled. He needed to consider his soul. Would the planned sacrifices be enough? Probably not. Never enough. But he would try.

There was the one sacrifice they all had been working on for so long. The one that might appease the Lord. An offering of truly apocalyptic proportions.

He would continue preparations, despite the danger from the police. Of the AIVD and that ridiculous Bureau. They would, at some point, find out about his plans, but by then it would be too late. Their plans. The society's plans. There had been risks in involving so many members of the society, but he had no choice. So many things to do. He could not do it alone. He knew the risk. People might talk. He assumed they would all be loyal to him and to the society, but still, so many people were idiots and, in the end, could not be trusted.

Many were like Pieters. Slaves, and permanently afraid. The sort of combination he preferred.

There had been a few new people. People he knew would lead the cause forward. People like Serena. Her passion for the society was nearly unparalleled. He needed more like her. Difficult to find. Given what would happen in 2020, she was one of his best assets. But also afterward . . .

Because if 2020 didn't work out, there would have to be a plan B. Another apocalyptic scenario if the first failed. He'd need young people like Serena.

17

THE STORM HIT THEM with an intensity none of them expected. It was as if a giant truck slammed into the camp.

Then there was chaos.

The only thing Linda was aware of was the immense sound filling the universe and the wind grabbing her and trying to drag her away. She had known storms along the Dutch coast, severe winter gales with rushing waves of seawater. This was nothing like that. This was all dust and sand and almost no air to breathe and the force of an alien life-form pushing at her.

In the corner of one of the tents, the one with the steel structure that she hoped would withstand the storm, she crouched close to a couple large wooden crates, with the other members of the team beside her. She could hardly see anything but the canvas of the tent flapping wildly. The world was a swirling vortex of sand and dust. She wondered why they hadn't taken refuge in one of the trucks, as the soldiers had done.

Too late for that now.

Nothing would be left of the refugee camp. None of their improvised tents or huts could withstand such a storm. Many people would die today, and others would lose everything. All efforts to keep these people here, and in relative safety, would now be in vain.

Some time later, when the wind fell and the noise died down, she glanced at her watch and saw that only twenty minutes had passed. It had seemed like hours. Deafening hours. The dust and sand settled quickly, forming layers on top of everything, boxes and crates and tents and people. When she got up and looked outside, the landscape had returned to a more primitive state, fully a desert now, no longer any traces of shrubs or trees. Angular forms stuck out of the sand where the camp had been.

Some of the stronger tents had remained intact, more or less, mostly those of the military and of the medical team, although much of the canvas had been torn or ripped. The trucks were partially covered with sand. Boxes and equipment were evidence of an alien city half hidden in the desert.

In the camp proper, figures started to move in between the tattered remnants of structures as if new life-forms rose from the dry dust. The storm front moved away from them, indifferent to the suffering it had caused. Overhead, the sky had cleared.

"What an awful mess," one of the doctors behind her said.

She didn't respond. She would now have to make an inventory of the remaining material and supplies, but she knew the expedition was doomed. Too many things would be broken, the organization itself disrupted. And the refugees would probably not stay. When the trucks and aircraft came, the team would likely be moved, out to Mombasa or wherever.

She went looking for Lieutenant Odinga but couldn't find him.

Then she noticed a figure moving through the remains of the camp, one among many figures, but this one convulsively bent, as if in pain. She at once recognized the prisoner, the man the soldiers had found in the hills. In his right hand, he held a rectangular object, like a box with a handle. He was free but made no move to leave the camp. He passed broken tents and collapsed sheds, cautiously observing his surroundings. Suddenly, he stopped. He stood no more than two hundred yards from Linda. He began to fumble with the box—it looked more like a metal can—and then made a sweeping motion, holding the can in both hands. He sprayed a liquid over a group of people, mostly women and children, who squatted helplessly among the remains of their tent.

At once she understood what had been in the can.

She ran forward. She wanted to stop the man but knew she would not reach him in time.

The man then threw something at the refugees, who started to get up, panicking. A muffled explosion and reddish flames flared up among them.

Two, three soldiers ran past Linda and began to extinguish the flames with pieces of canvas and sand. Someone grabbed her hand and held her back. She had eyes only for the man, who just stood there, observing his victims, fascinated by the screams and the fear.

Again someone pulled at her arm, and she realized she was still trying to reach the victims, although the fire had died down.

Odinga stood next to her. He had drawn his pistol.

The prisoner turned toward them. He observed Linda and the lieutenant as if unsure about what to do next.

Odinga raised his gun and shot the prisoner in the head.

"I should have executed him right away after we found him in the hills," Odinga said. "I should have known he would be dangerous."

He sat on an empty crate, head down. Linda sat on a metal folding chair she had recovered from the rubbish. It was a strange artifact, one of the last vestiges of a long-lost Western civilization, one of the last links to the industrial world.

She wanted sensible answers from him but understood there were no longer any sensible questions.

"These cults are very old," Odinga said, looking at her now. "Coptic influences, probably. Or much older. Christians from the earliest ages, who took inspiration from older Egyptian cults. And Gnostics, on the other hand. Gnostic apocryphal writings, never fully understood. Few remember the traditions except for a scattered number of scholars who have studied the desert communities, here and farther north. People here have returned to their natural religions, but are still influenced by Christianity. Earlier Christianity, that is, not the missionaries' brand. There's this cleansing by fire thing, it goes all the way back to old religious practices. Fire is a powerful symbol."

"That's what he was trying to do? Purify these people? Or himself?"

Odinga merely continued gazing at his feet. She wondered how much of the truth he would be telling her and how much would be lies. "Who knows, Miss Weisman? An outsider, contemplating these Christian myths, might be struck by the unfortunate cruelty of its god. I am talking, of course, about the God of the Old Testament. Of the books of Judaism. Things get somewhat better with the arrival of Christ, but then there's the matter of consuming his flesh and blood during Mass. I'm not sure what other cultures make of that."

"It's merely symbolic."

"Everything is merely symbolic. The cleansing by fire is merely symbolic. Still, it's a reprehensible practice, wouldn't you say? Not something any civilized society would allow. But then, these people, they are highly fatalistic. And wouldn't they be? Their life is not their own. There is little hope for them for a fulfilling life, even under the best of circumstances. Maybe things might get better when a man tells them they must burn other people and redeem themselves in the eyes of some god."

"That's cruel. For them as well."

"These are not the times for these people, Miss Weisman. This is now the time of the West. Of Western society. Look at it. Western society has killed hundreds of millions of people during the last century, or caused people to be killed. By fire, often. Massive wars, the size of which this continent has never seen. Nuclear weapons, unimaginable for most people here, engulfing whole cities. There's your cleansing by fire."

"Still, you shot the man, Lieutenant. You rejected his point of view in doing so."

"Yes, I did. Of course I shot him. It's a clear thing. I protect the refugees from his madness. I do not question his beliefs, only his madness." He furtively glanced at the remains of the camp. "But it seems I have failed. I could not protect them, not against another madness."

"You couldn't have stopped the storm," she said.

He got to his feet. "I will have to inform my superiors, ma'am. A lot of people died today. I heard the two UN representatives died as well. Soon everybody will have left. I don't know where they will go. They will probably disappear in the desert. That's what deserts do. They dissolve people."

"You are not their god," she said.

She didn't know why she said it. It seemed . . . excessive.

"No," he said. "Apparently, I'm not."

18

VAN GILS HATED DOING this sort of fieldwork in the middle of winter, ringing bells and more or less randomly speaking to people—not certain what Eekhaut or Dewaal wanted. He wore his leather jacket against the cold and thought about his wife, probably warm and cozy at home, drinking tea with honey and watching TV. Or reading a book. He was looking forward to his retirement, going on extended vacations with her and not having to walk the streets anymore and visit pubs and talk to people he was not interested in.

He had many years on the beat behind him, more than enough, and he was almost too familiar with large parts of the city and the people who lived there. He had old cronies and drinking partners in many of the inner-city bars and pubs, even those that now were mostly frequented by young tourists looking for soft drugs—in the wrong place. As often as possible, he could be found in De Pijp, south of the city, mostly an area for students and artists and free spirits of any kind. For many, this was the last real vestige of Amsterdam from the fifties and sixties, before mass tourism—and fancy shopping—invaded the center.

It was late, nearly five, and already dark. He would be home in an hour. A hot bath, hot food, a glass of wine, nothing special but exactly what he needed at the end of work. But duty called. It called, sounding exactly like Chief Dewaal.

Now. *Adriaan Basten.* The document in his pocket told him the boy had no social life worth mentioning and would probably be forgotten by now, so soon after his death, by the few people who knew him. In this way, he was no different than most of the human population. And yet good old Van Gils had to roam the streets and sniff around. Fortunately, the man had lived in the center of Amsterdam, not in any of the dreary suburbs.

Van Gils knew that even an isolated figure like Basten would leave traces. There would be people who remembered him in the area where he lived. A nice young man like that never went unnoticed. Amsterdam was a city, but it was also a village. It wasn't like, say, London or Paris or any other large Western city, where people were mere ghosts. It was a city of neighborhoods where people interacted daily, night and day. More than in the suburbs where they went only to sleep. A particularly stubborn kind of people lived in the city center, despite the high prices of real estate. Even those living just outside the center, say in Oud Zuid* or toward Rembrandt Park (and even beyond that), could easily feel part of the real Amsterdam, not least due to fast and convenient public transport—trams and, of course, bikes.

Van Gils knew a lot of people in these neighborhoods.

Basten hadn't been picky about where to live, though he wasn't the only Amsterdammer who didn't have a problem with living in the red-light district of the city. This was one of the things that made Amsterdam exceptional: its easy mix of people of different ethnic backgrounds and social profiles. Even socially mobile young people lived in areas that at night were mostly frequented by street workers and their customers. Although over the last two decades these areas were becoming more genteel, forcing out the seedy bars, replacing them with more upscale premises, and driving up prices.

Still, most of the street workers were dark-skinned, exotic, belonging to a mixed ethnic background, and most spoke several languages. Some of them, Caucasian, came from former Eastern Bloc countries, probably misguidedly believing there was much money to be made here in this free and prosperous city. Van Gils knew you needed to avoid people whose gaze never really focused, who never really connected with you.

---

* Literally, Old South.

Local police would, of course, do nothing about those who were here illegally, being on the take themselves. They would do nothing about the hard drugs circulating in the bars, so long as no bodies piled up behind the dumpsters. They would do nothing about pimps mistreating their girls so long as the girls survived. Some of these cops had retired early, moving to some subtropical island, sometimes with their favorite prostitute in tow. Others hadn't made it. Their last permanent residence was a small patch of grass at the local cemetery.

This was the dark side of Amsterdam, much like the dark side of any large city.

But at least you could buy your stash of soft drugs freely and unhindered. And not too expensive, either.

Van Gils had kept his hands clean throughout his career. It was not a matter of principle with him, nor of self-esteem, but of caution. He knew that once you were drawn into the game, you never got out. In the end, there would be either an early grave or retirement abroad, beyond the grasp of local crime.

He walked along Oude Hoogstraat. It was probably the coldest winter in years, or so people said. Lately, they complained about everything—the world was warming up, Holland would again disappear under water, polar bears were starving, winters were too cold and wet. A new ice age would be coming, or perhaps not. People mostly were addicted to bad news. They liked to read books about the impending global disaster, either through overpopulation or rising waters. Or something else. Anything would do. Any sort of apocalypse.

Harry's pub was still open. Harry had no last name, never had one, but everybody knew who Harry was and what Harry had done. His pub was typical of the neighborhood: small and dark, a little bit squalid but not really dirty, furniture bought at knock-down prices. Harry had quite a few foreign beers on tap, mostly Belgian. If you were hungry, he'd serve you *bitterballen* or *vleeskroketten* or fries with peanut sauce.

Belgian fries, not *French*. There's no such thing as French fries, Harry would always tell his American visitors. Fries were invented in Belgium. Even he, a Dutchie, would admit that.

Harry had been a sailor when shipping companies still used Dutch sailors. When there had still been ships registered in the Netherlands. He'd been around. Had been in all the major ports. In all the bars. Knew all the girls.

What most people didn't know, but what Van Gils knew all too well, was that Harry made sure the boys at home never were short of stuff. What the *stuff* was depended on who needed what. Cocaine, amphetamines, heroin, hashish, uppers, painkillers. Whole pharmacies full of stuff. Whatever you needed, Harry could provide.

He had done two stretches of five years, but even then, Harry made sure the boys never lacked *stuff*. Harry was good at what he did. At some point, Harry was no longer a sailor, on account of Malaysians being cheaper. After that he had stopped providing *stuff* to his friends because the Russians told him his competition was no longer acceptable. They worked on a larger scale than he, anyway, and could easily undercut him. He listened carefully to their arguments and bought himself a pub. He no longer provided *stuff* but bought illegal vodka and cigarettes from the Russians. They were best pals. Everyone made a profit.

Harry knew everyone. Everyone that mattered in the area. He didn't know the mayor or the chief of police or the editors of the major newspapers, but he knew people with real information. No one farted anywhere in this part of Amsterdam that he didn't know about it. He could even tell what the man had eaten the night before.

"Van Basten?" he repeated, eyeing the picture Van Gils held in front of him, over the counter. Harry was seventy, he was eighty, nobody really knew. His face had stopped telling the story of his age.

"*Basten*," Van Gils said, again. "Not related to the soccer player. Thirty. Works for a company on the Westerkade. No family, as far as we know. Lives over the shop of Douwer. Had something to do with providing secretarial services to wealthy foreigners. Diplomats and business people and the like. Big money."

"Sort of thing I hear now and then," Harry said. Harry had no problem with foreigners, not after working at sea for so long and judging them for their qualities, not the color of their skin or the place they happened to be born. "Basten. Seem to remember him. Comes in here on occasion. Drinks the occasional pint with other customers. Called him Addy. Didn't really belong here, but fitted in anyway. Kind of kid that had gone to college. You could see that right away."

"Was he, like, slumming?"

"You and I would not call this a slum, Van Gils," Harry said, reproachful. Harry stroked his famous but unnatural black mustache, his only claim to vanity. "Didn't boast about anything, though. You could hear he came from Zeeland."

"And then he disappeared? Just like that?"

"People said, long time since we saw Addy. Didn't turn up anymore. But people do that, Van Gils. Disappear. Maybe he moved. I don't keep records on people."

"But people keep an eye on each other in the area, don't they? The pimps keep the pickpockets out, and the police keep the heroin dealers out, at least those not associated with the Russians. The shopkeepers keep an eye on whoever walks in. Older people . . . There's a lot of social control."

"I heard there had been a problem with his boss, or whatever."

"His boss?"

"He often complained 'bout his boss. Probably his own fault. Admitted he often mouthed off, you know how it is with the younger generation. Bosses don't like being contradicted. And things happened, with money, and he wanted to consult an accountant himself to sort things out. I don't know. Rumors."

"That's what Basten said to people here?"

"Not to me. Never spoke to me about these things. I heard it mentioned, is all. Maybe he was in trouble at his job. I mean, disappearing like that, after having been in trouble with his boss . . ."

"He discovered fraudulent behavior, maybe?"

"*Fraudulent behavior*? You've been away from here for too long, Van Gils. Watch your language."

"I mean . . ."

"I don't know," Harry said, impatient. "It was just a word here, a sentence there. Something fishy, but what corporate business is not crooked these days, one way or another? More crime in corporate boardrooms than in the streets these days."

"Won't disagree with that," Van Gils said.

"You should know, with the line of work you're in."

"Any people he saw regularly? People I should see?"

"Kept to himself, except for the chat over beer. Lately he looked more . . . how would you say . . . depressed?"

"And then he disappeared."

"Happens to people. That's what Amsterdam can do to you if you're not strong enough. Cruel city, it is, Van Gils. People think it's nice, come here to see the museums and the parks and the little shops and the canals. Nice city for visitors. We live here. You live here. You know what I mean."

"You mean he couldn't bear it, in the end?"

"I see hundreds of people here, day in day out. They either fit in or they don't. Sometimes they're losers, sometimes they're winners. You can't choose. It happens to you. Addy? I don't know. I wouldn't fit him in with the winners. And you know what?"

"What?"

"I think he meddled with things he couldn't understand. Things too big for him. And the wrong kind of people."

19

EEKHAUT'S PHONE BUZZED INSISTENTLY, as if it had a character of its own—a malign character at that. It told him he'd better react at once or be visited by digital furies. He dutifully answered the call.

"Chief Inspector Eekhaut?" The voice of an unknown young woman, quite pleasant in a husky kind of way. "Are you the police officer who was here earlier?"

"What's *here*?" he inquired.

"InfoDuct, with Ms. Bunting. My name is Annick. I brought you coffee, remember. When you were visiting Ms. Bunting?"

He remembered. "Yes. A nice cup of coffee, by the way." The nice girl with the slender hands. He remembered. He had noticed her hands. Hands usually had stories to tell. *Hold on, Eekhaut.* This was a young girl. He would be, what? Thirty years older than she? *Don't go running after young girls, Eekhaut*, he told himself.

"I'm not calling because of the coffee," she said, sounding a bit impatient. "I do more than serve coffee, in case you wondered. But that's what the old hag has me do when she has visitors. As if she has a personal assistant all to herself."

So she doesn't like her boss. But that isn't why she called. "So you're not only serving coffee. Good for you. And you're also not calling me because you dislike the old hag."

"No. I'm calling because of Adriaan."

"Adriaan Basten?"

"Yes. Who else? I assume she had nothing to tell about him?"

"It was a rather disappointing session," he said, carefully. He was not going to discuss the finer points of an ongoing criminal investigation with her. She was not involved. And why did she phone in the first place?

"She hasn't told you anything meaningful about Adriaan because she knows nothing about him."

She sounded frustrated and angry. And hurt. *All right*, he thought. *She's in the right mood to tell tales on her boss.* He was willing to lend a sympathetic ear. "And I guess you know a lot more about Adriaan," he said.

"I do. I knew him quite well. And I am sure something terrible has happened to him, or you wouldn't have dropped by. Am I right?"

"I want to hear what you have to say," he said, avoiding her question.

"Not over the phone," she said.

Another one that's seen too many spy movies.

"We can meet," he suggested.

"We can. Right now? I'll be finished at work in half an hour."

He glanced at his watch. It was four thirty. He needed a Leffe anyway. "Where do we meet?"

"There's a pub next door at the Design Center in Leidsestraat. It's easy to find. It's the pink modern building."

"I'll be there."

The place didn't resemble any of the usual pubs in Amsterdam, or at least not the traditional pubs, but that could be expected of a watering hole connected to a design center. It seemed fashioned with a younger clientele in mind, the urban digital nomads that needed latte, internet, and music in equal amounts for their daily professional routine. These nomads wouldn't think about investing in something as senseless as a proper office, although they needed large and cosmopolitan cities as a backdrop for their creative endeavors.

More of these Starbucks clones were emerging in cities all over the world. Eekhaut had read about them, seen the glossy pictures of a worldwide culture, with the same sort of hangouts in Ho Chi Min City, Paris, Vancouver, and Los Angeles. The lighting here was indirect, the walls bare brick, the floor concrete. The furniture looked like it had been salvaged from a dump, and minimally restored chairs and tables were intentionally mismatched.

He felt almost at home.

The girl sat in the back, glancing up when he entered. He sat down at her table and ordered two coffees. She looked vulnerable, her pale skin matching her natural blond hair.

He was probably, and with some margin, the oldest person in the place.

"Is this some sort of secret meeting?" he asked, more or less as a joke. It was meant to put her at ease. "Something just between the two of us? Not to be mentioned in any official report, certainly not one of mine?"

"Keep me out of everything," she warned him. "I don't want anyone to know we've been talking. I stole your card from Bunting's office. She wasn't going to use it anyway. You don't even exist, as far as she's concerned. Which tells you everything about the way things are run there. Oh, they're very *social* and *empathetic* and all, to the outside world. But they treat us like dirt."

"And she doesn't care about Adriaan."

She glanced outside for a second before answering. "Exactly. She's not interested in the people working there. But *I* care."

"He shared things with you? Basten?"

"He did. We were, well, friends. Just friends. But that meant a lot to him, I guess. He wasn't the sort of person to make friends easily. What happened to him? Is he—?"

"I'm afraid he's dead," he admitted, not wanting to keep her in the dark about Basten's fate. "But I can't tell you more. The investigation is ongoing." He wouldn't share with her the gruesome details of his death. Not with his parents or other family either. What would be the point? It wouldn't change anything if they knew how he died.

"I am sorry," he said.

She focused on her coffee.

"There's not much I can do anymore," he continued. "Not for Adriaan. But I can catch the people responsible for his death. Is there any reason to suspect anybody within the company?"

She looked puzzled. "Someone from the company? A murderer? I don't think so. Why would anybody want to kill Adriaan? Management exploited all of us equally. And he was in a dead-end career. Nobody would want his position. He knew his activities would be outsourced within the year."

"Were you close to him? I mean, in a relationship?"

She looked up, smiling bitterly. "We were *friends*, Inspector. To Adriaan this had a special meaning, I guess. No, I'm sure it did. Most people found him strange. I didn't. He was a *spiritual* sort of person. That may sound corny, these days, I know. He adhered to some church, some religion, I never found out what. He never talked about that, not even to me. There was a side to Adriaan that was always hidden to other people."

Things were becoming clearer to Eekhaut. A church. A spiritual side.

"You really don't know what church?"

"I'm not religious myself," Annick said.

"But not any official religion? Protestant, Catholic?"

"I think not. He didn't have much patience for that sort of organized religion. Once he told me something strange, though. About knowing what would be the fate of humanity. That sounded . . . ominous to me."

"Apocalyptic."

"Yes, that too," she quietly said, playing with her empty cup. "But he didn't use that term. He said I was pure at heart and would probably be saved. And that struck me as weird, Adriaan talking about redemption and so on. Him being spiritual, I could understand, but salvation and all that? Rather strange. I didn't insist. And I'm sure he wouldn't have told me more."

She glanced up at him, wiping a tear away.

"Not even to you," he said.

"No," she admitted. "It wasn't that sort of relationship."

"I assume he didn't have these discussions with any of his other colleagues either?"

"Oh, no. He knew they would have laughed at him."

Exactly so, Eekhaut thought. *These wonder kids of the digital age would have laughed at him and his strange musings.* Salvation. *Certainly not.*

"Did any of this help?" she asked.

"Yes, it has. I appreciate your help, Annick. I do. It gives me a clearer view of who Adriaan was. Get in touch again if you remember anything more."

"I hope you find . . ." she said but left the sentence unfinished. She got up. "You know, Adriaan was good at his job. He told me he regularly found loopholes to get things done, whatever that was. Financial things, I assume. I guess nothing important enough to get him . . ."

Killed.

"But you have no idea what he had found?"

"All companies are involved in some sort of fraud, Chief Inspector. Management hiding income and assets from shareholders and from the tax inspector. That's common enough. Surely you know."

"I'm sure they all do that."

"But they wouldn't murder a mere employee to cover that up, would they?"

"No, usually not."

"Anyway, I won't be working for them for long. I want to get out. Find something else."

"Good luck," he said.

After she had left, he ordered a Leffe beer. There was a lot to think about. Basten connected to an apocalyptic religion, perhaps discovering corporate fraud. The latter might have been enough to get him murdered in such an awful way.

It was time to talk to someone within the Church of the Supreme Purification.

20

EEKHAUT KNEW DINNER AT the Grand Café Krasnapolsky, next to the Bijenkorf department store, would cost him dearly, yet he ordered starters, a main course, and dessert accompanied by a superior white wine, the price of which would have made him question his sanity under other circumstances. This was his second visit to this eminent establishment since coming to Amsterdam. The first time had been when Dewaal wanted to meet with him on his arrival, and she had picked up the bill. He remembered how she had looked: official but extremely feminine. She had looked much younger than she was. They had had mandarin duck, as he recalled. They had even drunk a bottle of wine.

This time he chose the salmon ceviche with coriander, radish, sour cucumber, and dressing; the spaghetti vongole with chili peppers; and the chocolade fondant with *yuzu* gel and vanilla anglaise and caramel-sea salt ice as dessert. And a bottle of dry white wine. While he ate, he observed. He observed the people who came here to have dinner, to talk, to watch those who wanted to be seen. It was a perfect spot for people watching. Amsterdam's high society. This was the place he would take Linda when she came back.

He had another reason to indulge this sudden longing for luxury. He wanted to be assured of the normality of the world, even if this part of it was mostly exclusive and expensive. He needed the certainty that the world of criminal activities, of perverse torture and murder, was counterbalanced by the extravagant spending of the privileged. Here, in this expensive restaurant, the veneer of civilization was as thick as it could get. Here, he was as far removed as possible from abnormality. Even if this rich lifestyle was far beyond his means. He was spending a considerable amount of money, but it was worth it.

But at the same time, he realized he was wrong. The glossy veneer of civilization existed only for people who were careful enough to hide their inhuman side. He assumed most of them had made their fortune on the backs of people less lucky. The glitter here was nothing but a shiny armor, protecting these people from their own conscience.

He settled the bill and walked back to his flat, wrapped in his heavy coat and thick scarf. He mused about whether Dewaal would agree to pay for his dinner as a research expense. She probably wouldn't.

He walked past Muntplein and wondered if he still could find a pub open for business. The wine had made him thirsty, and he needed a pint of beer.

On Rembrandtplein, several local cafés were still open, but most of them had a deserted look. Finally, he decided to go home. His apartment was warm and cozy. He settled into his easy chair. The evening before he had started reading Stephen King's *Duma Key*, which he wanted to finish. He thought about checking his email first, but he felt lazy and stayed in the chair. A few moments later he was sound asleep.

WEDNESDAY

21

"How many people are employed by the Bureau?" Eekhaut asked. "Your outfit here, I mean. All together?"

"Twenty-four," Dewaal said. "Us included. But not the temps—those on loan from various other departments."

"And how many knew about the details of the case?"

"About half of them. No, less, actually. Some others might have heard the rumors, but even then . . ."

The newspaper lay between them on the desk. The headline read: Dutch Victim in Ritual Burning. The article covered seven columns. There was an aerial picture of the circle of victims they'd found in the Ardennes. No real details, but the title and picture were suggestive enough.

"Someone earned himself extra income," Eekhaut said. "By leaking this to the press."

"I will kill him," Dewaal firmly said. "Or her."

"Might not even be one of our people," Eekhaut suggested.

"No, maybe not. Someone from headquarters or from the Ministry of Justice—potential leaks everywhere. But very few people outside this office have knowledge of these details. Anyway, here we are, in deep shit. If we assumed nothing would get to the press, we assumed too much."

The morning had been cold but sunny, and according to the weather forecast, it would remain sunny throughout the day. Eekhaut had treated himself to a generous breakfast in one of the cafés at

Rembrandtplein with a hot chocolate, two croissants, yogurt, orange juice, and a Danish pecan nut pastry. He had received an email from Linda. She had returned to Mombasa and would be back in Europe as soon as possible. Her mission had ended catastrophically, she wrote. A sandstorm had destroyed the camp. The refugees had dispersed, and the team's efforts to help them had been fruitless. She would be back soon. She would be back in his life.

He felt excellent. Until he read the newspaper.

"The press will be knocking at our door very soon," Dewaal said. "Or at the prosecutor's door, which is worse. She won't like that at all. I expect her call any moment now. She has issues, that woman."

Eekhaut thought Dewaal should have called the prosecutor herself. He wasn't bothered by what the prosecutor might think or do. He had dealt with her ilk for too long and had other things on his mind. Linda's short message had an ominous tone to it, something he couldn't place. As if she were telling only part of the story. The storm. The mission's failure. Something else was bothering her.

"Walter? You still there? Can I at least have your full attention?"

He returned to present time. "Yes. I'm sorry."

"I need a press strategy, and I'm counting on you. We need to keep as many details to ourselves as we can, but at this point we don't know how much has been leaked. We might even have Interpol looking over our shoulders, and I really don't need that."

"Some of the victims might be foreigners. We could use Interpol's help."

"Pure speculation, Walter. Let's keep to what we know. The Dutch victim. The message I read in the papers this morning is clear: one identified victim, the others unknown. Let's keep it at that as far as the papers are concerned."

"Right," Eekhaut said.

"Found anything on Basten yet?"

"The poor lad had no family as far as we know and almost no friends. We have to dig deeper. From what I understand he might be associated with the Church of the Supreme Purification."

"Go to their headquarters and get some questions answered. Dig as deep as you can."

"You want me to find out who leaked?"

"Not enough staff, Walter. And too many people involved. And it's too late anyway. The press might not be our main concern now."

"I noticed you added De Vries and Siegel to the team."

"Yes. And take along Prinsen. He seems a bit absentminded lately."

"You know why, Chief?"

"I'm not his mother. Don't want to be his mother either. And what about you? I can count on you?"

"Linda is on her way back," he said.

"She is?"

He told her what he knew about her aborted mission.

"Too bad," she said. "But you'll have her back in no time."

22

THE HEADQUARTERS OF THE Church of the Supreme Purification wasn't a fortress or castle or some sort of underground lair or even a temple. It wasn't anything like that at all. It consisted of a narrow, neat, nondescript semi-Victorian house on the Nieuwezijds Voorburgwal, along one of the canals, with similar houses and a few restaurants in the neighborhood. The area had narrow sidewalks, twisted trees, badly parked bicycles typical of this part of the city, and basement lodgings. A staircase led to the front door. This wasn't a secret location by any means: the bronze plaque on the door announced the existence of the church quite clearly, if discreetly. The bronze hadn't been polished in a long time.

Prinsen took off his glove and pressed the call button.

The plaque stated simply: CHURCH OF THE SUPREME PURIFICATION. No mention of business hours or rites or consultations. Nothing to indicate this was anything different than any of the few score other religious organizations in the city. No reference to secret rituals, no inkling of potentially thousands of past victims, nothing to remind people of the impending apocalypse. However nefarious the plans made inside this building—still an assumption the police couldn't prove—the entryway looked quite respectable, even dull.

Never had any arrests been made over possible connections between the church and the disasters Eekhaut had heard of. At no point had the church been charged with conspiracy, arson, or murder, nor had any of its members. No news about satanic rituals or collective murder had ever made headlines. It was as if all the rumors about the church were nothing more than myths invented by the church's enemies.

The woman who came to the door didn't look like a serial killer or an arsonist either. She might have been sixty, was heavily built, and sounded severely asthmatic. Maybe she had climbed up from a deep, underground cavern where the church's secrets and skeletons were kept hidden. Which Eekhaut deemed unlikely, unless the church had direct access to hell.

"Yes, gentlemen," she said, brightly, despite her shortness of breath. "What can I do for you?"

Eekhaut showed her his warrant card. "Security services, ma'am," he announced. "Chief Inspector Eekhaut and Inspector Prinsen." He had a new Dutch police ID, giving him authority on Dutch soil. "We've been announced, haven't we?"

"Ah, of course you were. Come in, please. It's cold out there, isn't it? Too cold, even for this time of the year. And after such a miserable summer." She stepped back and let the two officers in, carefully closing the door behind them. "Please, gentlemen, to your left. There's a parlor. We rarely use it these days. Parlors are so out of fashion, aren't they? I'm making tea. Will you join me?"

Not waiting for a reply, she disappeared across the hallway. Prinsen stepped into the room and took off his coat, hanging it over a chair. The parlor was small, and its furniture belonged to another era when Victorians needed parlors to entertain guests. Cabinets and deep armchairs and cushions aplenty and severely threadbare oriental rugs, in deep blues and reds, on the parquet floor. Eekhaut noted the absence of religious symbols. No crosses, statues of the Buddha, no Stars of David, nothing. Not even a portrait of a great leader.

After a short while, the woman returned. She placed a large tray with elegant cups, saucers, a teapot, cookies, sugar, and milk on a table in the middle of the room.

"I am Johanna Simson," the old lady said, pleasantly, "currently leading the church in the Netherlands. Ah, the pope would be angry if he heard us talk about a *church*, but then we aren't competing with any other religion. We are not even an exclusive religion. Our belief fits in easily with existing doctrines, Christian as much as Islam. Sugar or milk?"

The tea procedure took a few moments. The brew itself was strong and exotic, nothing like Eekhaut had ever had before. *Was that cinnamon?*

"Ms. Simson," he said, "we need to ask you a few questions regarding someone we assume to be a member of your church. Adriaan Basten. And we have some questions concerning your organization in general."

"Ah," she said. "Adriaan. He is, indeed, a member. And of course proud of it, although discreet. Aren't we all? For obvious reasons, we keep our membership list secret from the outside world unless we're obliged to divulge it. By law, for instance. There is no reason our many current friends should be tainted with the dark past of our ancestors. Neither do we want people to focus too much on the revelations about the End."

"In 2020, I believe?" Eekhaut said.

"Or thereabouts. It probably is a more or less symbolic date. Anyway, you're familiar with our teachings and with some of the vicious attacks on our organization by people who believe we're capable of mass killings. We have always denied any involvement, and nothing was ever proven, but still we are burdened by these accusations. Given this, our members prefer privacy and silence."

"We currently have no opinion on any of that, ma'am," Eekhaut stated carefully. "We haven't come to talk about the prophecies or the past. The thing is, we have bad news for you. Adriaan Basten has been murdered."

She gave him a look, suddenly distant and cold, as if he had offended some private god of hers. "What does this mean, sir? Murdered? I knew he had disappeared."

"I'm afraid we can only confirm his demise," Eekhaut said. "He died under suspicious circumstances. That's why we're here." She hung her head, but he continued. "He was killed in a ritual. Along with six other people. We found them in the Belgian Ardennes. All in accordance with the tradition of your church. Former tradition, if you will."

"You mean—?"

"Yes. They were all burned alive."

Ms. Simson drank her tea, focusing on it rather than on the two police officers. Her hand was firm. Eekhaut understood she had to process the information about Basten. She showed no emotion. He wondered if this was a bad or good sign.

"Adriaan," she said.

"I'm sorry to be the bearer of such bad news."

She deposited her cup on the table carefully. "Mr. Eekhaut," she said. "Our church has had a violent past. I will not deny that, as long as I'm not making an official statement. Previous generations managed to cover up many heinous crimes, to which none of us will admit. Crimes against humanity, it would be called today. All this goes back, well, a century or more. These people, previous generations, assumed their eternal salvation depended on performing certain rituals. Rituals that also ensured the survival of our church."

"How," Prinsen rejoined, "can people ever assume killing other people would ensure their salvation, ma'am?"

Simson tilted her head toward him. "Because, young man, faith is a very powerful force. Today, this is less obvious than it used to be. We live in a secular age. God is dead, and if not, He is forgotten. People believe only in material salvation. Stuff. *Things.* There is no spiritual sphere for them to believe in. Even the ones that still flock to the churches of their choice don't believe everything that is preached there, a small minority notwithstanding. In earlier times people died for what they believed in."

"But the Inquisition is long past, ma'am," Prinsen said dryly. "So are the Crusades."

Ms. Simson smiled indulgently. "We don't have to go back that far, young man. The Nazis murdered millions because they believed in their own superiority."

"That was on social and racist grounds, not religious."

"That hardly makes any difference. Belief systems need not be religious to be dangerous. Fascism and communism were belief systems without a god but with a strict set of rules and a central doctrine. Even today, we're reminded daily of the violence originating from radical religious zeal. It has always been rather easy to convince less than bright people they should follow leaders and commit crimes in their name."

"That's what happened within your church?"

"It is the tradition of empires, including spiritual empires, Inspector. And yes, that's been our own tradition, but I cannot make any official statements concerning this facet of our organization. I'm sure you appreciate that."

"You promise eternal salvation, don't you?" Eekhaut said.

"We believe people can and will be saved whenever the End comes, yes."

"That's not exactly the same," Eekhaut said.

"No," Ms. Simson admitted, "that's correct."

"And you would have been persecuted for your beliefs."

"Let me again take you back in time. As far as the earlier Christian leaders were concerned, Gnosticism was a dangerous aberration of the real faith. All religions had their schisms, their cults and sects. Christianity never was united, and never will be. Are you familiar with the Gnosis, Chief Inspector?"

"I might have read a book or two on the subject once," Eekhaut admitted.

"For Christians, Gnosticism was an evil aberration. Its origins date from long before the birth of Christ. There's a long tradition that precedes Gnosticism. Zoroastrianism, Chaldean astrology, Hellenistic philosophy, mainly Egyptian mythology, but also the Jewish apocalyptic thought. That's what we inherited, Chief Inspector. We are basically Gnostics. For the Gnostics, and therefore for our church, God is a kind of spiritual father figure, but He exists outside the cosmos. That cosmos, the world in which we live, is intrinsically bad, but it's not His creation. On the contrary, the universe and all creatures were created by another hostile entity, which the Gnostics, and we, call the Demiurge. That Demiurge is assisted in his pernicious work by a whole hierarchy of dark creatures, the Archons. In this way, the Demiurge is an evil and dark supernatural entity, while the real God resides outside the universe, where He reigns over the kingdom of light.

"And as in Gnosticism, this explains the malice in the world and why God cannot or will not intervene.

"As it is, man is a fallen creature, condemned to the material world where the Demiurge reigns. This is the God of the Old Testament, a vengeful, cruel, suspicious, and distrustful God. Man cannot escape this universe, not even by believing in the true God or by doing good. He can only escape by the mastery of a transcendent wisdom, the Gnosis, through which he can discover the intentions of the real God."

"That's quite an undertaking for a simple man."

"It is. Many have tried to find redemption this way; many have failed."

"And for your church, redemption consisted of burning people."

"I will not admit to that, as I already told you. Anyway, we left that behind us. The tradition, however, dates from pre-Christian times."

"Which in recent times remained largely unnoticed."

"People usually see us as charlatans. Our obsession with the apocalypse is utterly alien to them. The true depth of our fate, such as it still is, eludes them. That makes us go unnoticed."

"No more killing," he said.

"Not anymore, not for a long while. It all radically changed two decades ago. We are preparing ourselves for the salvation of the soul, as a matter of inner conviction."

"But the tradition proved to be strong. It survived."

"Not with us."

"No," Eekhaut said. "Not with you. A radical sect claimed the tradition for itself."

"We have no control over the new radicals."

"I'm sure you don't," Eekhaut said. "And they insist on calling themselves the Society of Fire."

"They are deluded in following the old ways. They have only cruelty in their hearts. They're drunk on power. It will be their downfall."

"It seems your friend Adriaan Basten was a recent victim of theirs."

Ms. Simson said nothing.

"We need you to help us identify them," Eekhaut said.

"There's only one name I can give you: Baphomet."

"Baphomet? And who might he — or perhaps she—be?"

"Their leader. The inspiration of the Society of Fire. The Devil incarnate, even. A dangerous man. He was once one of us when we all were younger. Already a dangerous man in those days. Driven by very selfish motives."

"And what is his real name?" Prinsen interjected.

Ms. Simson glanced at him, as though remembering why he was here. "I have no idea. I'm sorry. We never identified ourselves by our real names. I use mine these days, because there's no longer any reason for anonymity. But Baphomet . . ."

"Why do you call him the Devil incarnate?" Eekhaut wanted to know.

"Because, Chief Inspector, he is willing to sacrifice all of us if it serves him and his cult. All of us. You know what that means, don't you? What he really wants is for the world to end. Nothing less. Oh, he will have to settle for less, but even then, his plans might cause many victims."

"Can't say that went well," Prinsen said to Eekhaut as they stood on the sidewalk again.

"Not really," Eekhaut said. "Let's get out of here. She might be watching us. Those people give me the creeps."

"Suppose it's all true? The Demiurge, the apocalypse. A creator who is probably Satan. An absent god."

"Don't let me catch you believing this sort of nonsense, Nick. I'll have you locked up."

"I'm not saying I believe any of that, but just like you, it creeps me out."

"I'm thirsty. Can't face another world's end without a Leffe beer first."

Prinsen said nothing. They walked down the street, passing a kosher charcuterie on one street corner and a Lebanese bakery on the other. They stepped into a nearby pub that looked narrower than Eekhaut's hallway but had a room in the back with framed pictures of how Amsterdam must have been when people first started making pictures. The place was almost empty, save for two elderly couples sitting at the bar. Eekhaut and Prinsen took a table and ordered. There was no Leffe, so Eekhaut got a local, dark beer that tasted somewhat sour. But at least it was beer.

"They've always been popular, these predictions of doom," he said, wiping some froth off his upper lip. "Nostradamus, Malthus. And modern equivalents. Club of Rome. It's a sort of porn, really. End-of-the-world porn. And there's a lot of people who would just welcome the end of it all, mostly because they cannot get whatever their little hearts want."

"Baphomet," Prinsen said, his thoughts elsewhere.

"Ah, Baphomet. Yes, that's something new. Gives our opponent a name. Quite a name at that."

"It will be a problem getting an arrest warrant for that name."

"Come on, Nick. Don't be negative. We learned a few things. He's a man. He's probably over fifty. He might be powerful, even in real life. We may be looking for hidden patterns here."

"Why do you assume he's over fifty?"

"Because he was one of the bunch that separated from the church two decades ago. You don't do that sort of potentially dangerous thing when you're only thirty. He has to be a figure of some importance, being so successful in his role as anti-messiah."

Prinsen gazed at the passing pedestrians in the street. "She told us nothing about Basten."

"Basten was probably a minor figure. One of theirs, yes, but not important. But then he got entangled in a web of intrigue, and it cost him his life. There's a war going on between these two cults, Nick. The society tore themselves away from the original group and wants to purify its members the old-fashioned way. They kill several adversaries, leave them behind in the Ardennes, unconcerned whether they'd be found. Ms. Simson might have lost more adherents than just Basten. But she will not admit that much."

"We can't blame her for being a true believer," Prinsen said. "And all that involves."

"She might regret it when she finds herself in Basten's place."

"Maybe we should keep an eye on her?" Prinsen suggested. "Offer her protection?"

"We don't have the staff, Nick. Anyway, how many people do we have on that list?"

"What list?"

"The one of people who recently went missing."

Prinsen found it in his inner pocket. "You're looking for what?"

"Things they have in common. Patterns again."

Prinsen glanced at the list. "Not much by way of a pattern, except two of them, beside Basten, working for the same company."

"InfoDuct?"

"No. An outfit called TransCom."

"Oh," Eekhaut said. "There's a pattern for you. That's InfoDuct's parent company."

"These two disappeared a week apart." Prinsen looked intensely at Eekhaut.

"Three people working for the same corporate group, and all of them gone missing within the same time frame. You're telling me that's a coincidence?"

"We need to talk to some people," Prinsen said.

"We sure do. One can't have enough interrogations. Stalin said so."

"He did?"

Eekhaut grinned and finished his beer. "At some point, yes. And you can never be too paranoid either."

23

JAN PIETER MAXWELL ALLOWED himself to be driven back to Amsterdam. He hated public transportation, even taxis. There was always a private car and driver waiting for him. The companies he managed could well afford such a luxury. It wasn't really a luxury. Fast transportation between meetings meant he saved time, and not having to drive himself allowed him to work in the car as well.

Another advantage was privacy. Nobody noticed him, nobody interfered with him. He could use his phone undisturbed. Not even the driver could hear him. He was talking to Courier right now, who had been doing research on the detectives investigating the Ardennes case.

"Do we have any leverage?" Maxwell asked. "Something to slow them down or incapacitate them?"

"One of them is a Belgian on loan to the AIVD. We know little about him. He lives in Utrechtsestraat, in an apartment rented for him by the AIVD. I can send someone along if you need him followed."

"That might not be productive. And the other one?"

"A young detective, Nick Prinsen. He's from the north. And he is Chief Dewaal's nephew, which might be interesting. He has a girlfriend, here in Amsterdam, a young girl he met during a previous investigation. I heard she's a bit . . . unstable. She witnessed a murder in her apartment."

"That sounds promising. Concentrate on the young detective then. He's probably most vulnerable. What else?"

"That's pretty much it. The other members of the team are only partially involved in this investigation, so I was focusing on these two."

"You have carte blanche, Courier," Maxwell said. "You know what to do. Disrupt the investigation. Our enemies might have unlimited resources at their disposal. They're dangerous. They can prevent us from attaining our goal. This can't be allowed."

"Of course not, Baphomet," Courier said.

"That's why your mission is extremely important. Prevent any further progress in this matter, Courier."

"Yes, Baphomet."

"You know you *will* not fail, don't you?"

"I won't fail," Courier said.

"Do not doubt for a moment I am the one who will lead all of you into salvation, Courier. If you have any doubts, however, I will replace you instantly."

"I have no doubts, Baphomet," Courier said. "I have none."

After disconnecting, Maxwell remained thoughtful for a long time. He stared in front of him. It continued to amaze him how easily he could get useful idiots like Courier to do exactly what he wanted. This was his gift. This was what he was good at—persuading people. The same way he had persuaded Serena to join the society. Serena, who seemed fascinated by the idea of people like himself sacrificing human beings for a higher cause. She was thrilled she would soon be part of his grand schemes.

People like Serena didn't belong in any category of ordinary citizens. He himself didn't belong in any ordinary category either. We are different, he told her, because we realize how far passion can lead us. Actually, passion can lead us anywhere we want. And we are different because of our bond with the ultimate Creator. We are different because we are true believers, in a world of heretics and of cold cynicism.

We are different.

And in this case, it simply meant they were *better*. Because they were prepared to sacrifice everything, even their own lives, for a glimpse of divine infinity.

That's what he told her.

These were also the exact words he used for other followers. With these words, he had broken from the regular church two decades ago. From that lukewarm pseudo-religion.

Serena had that same dedication. She truly was a celestial being, and she had rapidly become one of his most loyal supporters. Maybe she was some sort of *gift*. A divine gift to them all. A good omen that meant everything would work out well for them. She would be with them, and with him, in the final days of humanity. Yes, her arrival in their midst had been a good omen.

The Society of Fire was ready for the last days and would soon bring on its final, all-engulfing offering. He was ready. He had done everything humanly possible to prepare for the final days.

24

Johanna simson sat at the end of the rosewood table. All around her, in the old leather chairs, eight members of the church watched her. She had known these people for a long time. Some of them as kids. She had helped raise some of them, too. She had explained the Purification Doctrine to them but had prevented them from executing it. She had been a young woman then, unable to have children of her own. She had found relief in working with the children of other people. She knew the church would never disappear as long as there were children. Her own parents had raised her with that same doctrine but had avoided telling her about the actual sacrifices. She had, as a child, never heard about the death by fire ritual.

By the time she became an adult, she knew for certain this was the only true faith. There was no going back. Not even after the terrible truth of the church's inhuman activities had become clear to her. There was only one way forward. The end would arrive soon.

Johanna was one of those who, twenty years ago, took the initiative to break with the tradition. Her parents had strong objections to the rituals, although they couldn't stop them from happening. But killing tens if not hundreds of random people, including children, was no longer a viable option in the minds of the younger generation. When she was nearly forty, she led the church in the Netherlands and heavily influenced decisions abroad as well. No more burning. No more death by fire. She hadn't made the decision lightly and had reached this point only after years of contemplation and soul-searching. She could no longer raise children to become multiple murderers. She knew the doctrine necessitated it, but she didn't want these children to be accomplices to the worst of crimes.

She had discussed this with other members of the church. Many appreciated her point of view. Many shared it. The world had seen two devastating wars, a century of upheavals. They were faced with a world that wanted to move on, away from vulgar violence and avoidable suffering.

The older generation was pushed aside while the newcomers renounced all violence. Every chapter of the church abandoned the old doctrine. That had been twenty years ago. Years in which the new doctrine had become an intellectual challenge.

However, some small parts of the church opposed the change. Former members, unhappy with what they saw as the all too lax religious view, formed an underground movement: the Society of Fire. It went unnoticed at first, but then suddenly became violent and returned to the practice of the ritual. Small events at first, a few people dying here, a few people there. Things happened. Accidents, mostly. Or that was how the external world saw them.

But somehow, the members of the church began noticing a pattern. They *recognized* the pattern. Someone outside the church had been reviving the old ways. All this took several years. But in the end, it could no longer be ignored.

The people around the table were those most concerned. They knew they were being targeted by the society.

"They're hiding successfully," a blond woman in her forties said. "And once again they found some of our brothers and sisters and killed them. We should remember."

"We *do* remember them," a young man said.

"The situation," Johanna said, intervening, "is very serious. Even some of us who usually sit at this table are missing. Maybe they're simply in hiding. Maybe they're already the victims of this terrible sect."

"Seven bodies have been found by the police," the young man reminded her. His hair was thinning on top, and what was left was a pale ginger.

"We should inform the police. Work with them," another man said.

He was older than the others, about the same age as Johanna. "Why did you not inform them of our concerns, Johanna?"

"There's the issue of secrecy," she said.

"We will soon all be dead for your secrecy."

"Not if we take matters more firmly into our own hands."

"And how do we do that?"

"As we did long ago. We hunt our enemies down."

The young man laughed, without pleasure. "And what resources do we have? Look at us. We are a poor remainder of what we once were. There's less than a few thousand of us in this country, hardly ten times that much in Europe. We can run and hide, but not forever."

"We don't need to hide," Johanna repeated. "We need to hunt."

"And who will do the hunting?"

Johanna Simson smiled benevolently. "Help is on the way, my brothers and sisters."

25

"ISN'T THERE ANYBODY FROM public relations to deal with this?" Maxwell said. "Or human resources?"

"They're asking for you, sir," Serena insisted. It seemed to trouble her too, having to bother him with police matters, but she said these gentlemen insisted. They seemed to know Maxwell was in the building. "They're in the room next to reception. I could tell them you're in a meeting and have them wait. That would give you time to—"

"I'm not into procrastination, Serena," he said. "Bad habit. Let them in at once. And change my other appointments. I'll be late by, oh, twenty minutes at the most. This can't take any longer than twenty minutes. What is it about?"

"They didn't say, Mr. Maxwell. I inquired, but they refused to comment."

"Well, let them in."

Moments later, Serena opened the door to Maxwell's office and introduced the two detectives. Maxwell noticed the off-the-rack suits, the plain ties, the shirts too often washed and carelessly ironed. He recognized the lack of taste in clothing from a mile away, as much as a lack of imagination. These were plain cops, as ordinary as their clothes.

But another part of his brain warned him. An older and less forth-coming part of his brain. They were potentially dangerous. *Don't get fooled by the look.* They wouldn't be here merely on account of some minor criminal case. These were cops from AIVD, and they were after him.

"Thank you for seeing us and taking the time, Mr. Maxwell," the elder of the officers said, without really trying to seem accommodating. He identified himself as Chief Inspector Eekhaut, and he clearly was not Dutch. Flemish, Maxwell noticed. The odd man out. Courier's information had been correct. The other, Prinsen, said nothing.

Here they are, Maxwell mused.

"Gentlemen," he said cheerfully, as if he expected no real problems from these two cops. "What can I do for you? Let's hear your questions. Coffee, something stronger?"

"Thank you, we'll keep this as short as possible," Eekhaut said. Maxwell noticed impatience and displeasure in the man's attitude. Which was fine by him. *Let him be uncomfortable*, he thought. "We need some information about two of your staff." He glanced in a little black notebook. "Karl Desmedt and Daniel Brecht. They both work for you, don't they?"

"I should think so, gentlemen. They work for this company. Is this about their disappearance? Your colleagues have already been over. Local police, I assume. Did they find anything? We are very much concerned about both men."

"You are, in general, always concerned about the fate of your employees, are you?"

"Of course," Maxwell said. He didn't like the way this interview was going. This Eekhaut fellow was rather insolent.

"Concerned," Eekhaut repeated. "Like a father would be concerned about his children. When one—or in this case two—of his children go missing. Isn't that what you're supposed to do, Mr. Maxwell, look after the well-being of those who are in your employ?"

"They are staff," Maxwell said stiffly. "They work for a company I manage. I am not directly their employer, not in the strictest sense. I manage. As such, of course, I have responsibilities. Toward all who work here. And of course, I am responsible to the shareholders of this company."

"Shareholders," Eekhaut repeated. "You don't get involved with the private lives of those employed by . . . by this company, I assume."

"I manage several companies the size of this one, gentlemen,"

Maxwell said. "I have several offices and divide my time among them. Here today, in Rotterdam tomorrow. I have hundreds of employees. I do not, evidently, occupy myself with their private lives. I remember the names of these two men because we are all concerned about them. There is gossip, of course. I don't listen to gossip. And of course, I don't interfere with police work either."

That, Eekhaut thought, was a strange reply. "Have you seen their relatives? Wives, children, parents? Comforted them?"

"I . . . That is not part of my . . . obligations toward them, Chief Inspector. We have people in our HR department."

This time it was Prinsen who intervened. "And how did you feel about them, these men, I mean? Professionally. Since when did they work here?"

Maxwell glanced at the young man. "Both men have been with us many years, but I really can't remember the details, I'm afraid. As far as I know, they both were very satisfactory. Otherwise, they wouldn't have been with us for long. The HR department can provide you with details. Although that might be a matter of privacy. I should consult with them."

"We're a bit surprised by that," Eekhaut said. "Two of your employees disappear, and you seem rather unconcerned about their fate. Bright young men, both. Gone from the face of the earth. You inform the law, and that's it. I assume they've already been replaced?"

"This company needs . . ." Maxwell started, and then fell silent. He was not going to fall into *that* trap.

"No note, no message, nothing."

"We leave these things to the police. They seem even less concerned than we," Maxwell said poisonously, "judging from the lack of results. We have never been informed about any results of their inquiries."

"They simply walked away, and you don't want to know why?"

Maxwell avoided Eekhaut's stare by looking at his hands. *He is furious*, Eekhaut thought. *But he doesn't want us to know.*

"Where can I find your HR department?" Eekhaut asked.

"They have nothing to add to what I told you," Maxwell replied.

"We'll speak with them anyway." Eekhaut got up. "I ask politely but only once."

"My secretary will get you on your way, Chief Inspector," Maxwell said. "And she will inform them they must fully cooperate with you."

"I expect nothing less, Mr. Maxwell. Have a good day." Eekhaut left the office in a hurry.

Maxwell glanced at his watch. Damned cops. Twenty minutes? The conversation had taken less time, but it had been long enough. Desmedt and Brecht? Had they identified the other bodies as well? *Damn it to hell*, he thought. He would have to call Courier, who had assured him no traces had been left. And now, the cops had turned up. With two names.

It was time to make sure the whole affair didn't spiral out of control.

Prinsen shook his head. "Why did you get riled up in there?" They were waiting in the lobby, and he was whispering. He assumed the place was equipped with cameras and microphones.

"Riled up? I simply didn't like the man, Nick. Was that obvious?"

"You have a problem with authority," Prinsen said.

"With certain forms of authority. I dislike this kind of manager. Always have. The sort who see people as commodities. And something else bothered me. He lied. He lied through his teeth. Wanted us out of there from the outset."

"What do you intend to ask his HR department?"

"Nothing. I don't care what his HR department would want to tell us, which would be precisely nothing."

The secretary approached them. "Gentlemen? Is there anything I can do for you? Mr. Maxwell phoned to tell you—"

"We won't need anything further, on second thought, miss," Eekhaut said smoothly. "Thank you for your help."

She looked surprised. "As you wish," she said and walked back.

"You, my young friend," Eekhaut told Prinsen, "are coming with me. We're leaving this building. I'm going to find a pub and have a beer."

"And me?"

"You'll be returning here after a few minutes—without me. And you'll approach the nice young receptionist over there. The one that's been staring at you for a while. She clearly likes you."

"Very nice," Prinsen said, annoyed. "But I don't have time for her. Anyway—"

"You'll *make* time for her, Nick. You're going to ask her some innocent questions about the people who work here. Absolutely innocent questions. Maybe you mention the names of Desmedt and Brecht. Receptionists know a lot of things, all the more when they're young and pretty like her. Everybody talks to her. Everybody likes to impress a beautiful woman. Well, the men, anyway. And if necessary, you ask her out. Tonight. Drinks, something to eat, maybe a movie. I don't have to teach you the tricks."

"But I'll have to—"

"Oh, I'm sure Eileen will understand you have to do your job, Nick," Eekhaut said. "The sacrifices you have to make. You're a police officer, aren't you? And she's proud of you, of all you do. I'm sure she is."

"Go to hell, Walter," Prinsen said. But he would do as he was told.

Three beers later and Prinsen entered the pub again. Eekhaut enjoyed the way this job was turning out. No pressure, at least not at the moment. Time enough between whatever he had to do for Dewaal. Enough decent pubs in the central area of Amsterdam, with the right brands of beer.

That chat of Prinsen's had taken nearly an hour. "That was quite a chat," Eekhaut ventured.

"Nice colleague you are," Prinsen said and beckoned the server. "I'll have a pint too. She was all over me, that girl. Wanted a date. I had to promise I'd phone her soon."

"You've made a new friend, that's what counts in life. Friends are what make life interesting. What have you discovered while chatting with the poor thing, my faithful assistant?"

"She had a lot to tell. A lot of gossip. And time to spare. Anyway. There's this: both Desmedt and Brecht worked in the audit department of the company."

"That might be interesting."

"And in recent months, before their disappearance, there was a lot of tension between their department and Maxwell. Angry phone calls, angry people. Lots of late-evening meetings. Lots of aggravation."

"More detail?"

"Rumors of financial malpractice."

"*Malpractice*," Eekhaut said. "A word I treasure. Certainly, when it annoys the corporate suits. And it usually does."

"Is this in any way helpful?"

"Maybe. Two men who might have found discrepancies in the company's books. Let's assume something like that happened. Then they disappear. *Poof.* Gone. Their boss isn't concerned about their fate, their well-being. He doesn't give a shit, actually. Because he knows what happened to them, and good riddance. I'll talk to Dewaal about this, mentioning you procured this information while risking your life."

"Go to hell," Prinsen said again, still in a foul mood.

26

"I HAVE THE IMPRESSION, Chief," said Prosecutor Apostel, "that your investigation isn't going as well as we both might wish." She brushed her hair back as she spoke.

Apostel was fiftyish, ash-blond hair, slim, tanned as a former *Baywatch* model, and wore no makeup. She never raised her voice but spoke softly, with unmistakable authority. She was the new chief public prosecutor in Amsterdam, a position she had reached after a number of high-profile cases. Four months into her new job, she wasn't going to let anybody forget she had reached this lonely position all by herself, despite the old boys' network. She would never be one of the old boys.

Dewaal felt a certain kinship with Apostel. They both had climbed through the ranks, on their own, despite male prejudices. They both respected the other's professional qualities, without being friends. Or even allies.

But Prosecutor Apostel wasn't going to make Dewaal's life easy.

"And," Apostel continued, "any moment now the press will be crowding in front of my door, with cameras and microphones and all, and they'll be asking, among other things, why we kept this matter a secret for so long. I've never been comfortable with public attention. I don't like finding myself in the middle of a controversy either. Certainly not when the press, and hence the public, assumes we're covering things up."

"The Bureau doesn't function in public," Dewaal said dryly.

"No? Are you for real, Chief? Must I remind you your wages are being provided through the generosity of the taxpayer? It is public money; you are a servant of the state. And that state is the public. Of course, you work in public. Maybe not concerning the details of the inquiry, but when members of the public are murdered, well, there's a rather *public* side to that, isn't there? People might want to be reassured. They need to know you and the rest of the police force are making sure such terrible things cannot happen again. Burning people alive? That doesn't sit well with the man in the street."

"We're making sure those responsible will get caught, ma'am," Dewaal declared coldly.

Apostel said nothing for a moment. Maybe she was considering her options. Or what she was going to say to the press. Finally, she asked, "You've been working on a strategy?"

"No," Dewaal said. "Not as far as contact with the press is concerned. Not today, anyway."

"You haven't."

"I asked a member of my team to work on a press release, but something . . . got in the way."

"Something always gets in the way, Chief. That's a common excuse, but in this case it won't fly. Are you going to be talking to the press in a minute?"

"No, ma'am, I'm not."

"Then it will be *me* telling them the Bureau, as part of AIVD, is not currently planning to issue a statement about the inquiry."

"As you wish," Dewaal said.

"*No!*" Apostel exploded. "That's not what I *wish*! Drop the damn formalities, Alexandra! I never *wish* for anything. I *want*, and I *need*. That's the way this will play out between us, between the public prosecutor and the different police forces. Including, yes, the Bureau. The AIVD may consider you some sort of, I don't know, *elite* section, but you're no better than any other branch of the police once you cross the threshold of my office. Is that clear?" She took a deep breath and continued in a somewhat normal tone. "And now that I've spoken my mind, Chief, I will state my case more diplomatically."

Dewaal said nothing.

"The AIVD possesses a level of autonomy no other branch of the police enjoys."

"The nature of my investigation—"

"Yes, yes, forget about *that* for a moment. I'm familiar with the myth of the AIVD. However, its autonomy has its limits. And as far as I'm concerned, that limit has been reached in this case. I know what people say about me. I'm from the province, and I don't know how to deal with significant political issues in a city like Amsterdam. Let me tell you, politicians are the same all over. I know how to handle them, thank you. In that, I'm on your side, Chief Dewaal. At least until you either fuck up or leave me standing in the cold. Did either of those things happen?"

"No, neither did."

"Good. Then we're on the same page. But next time you come here, be prepared with a good story. A story I can use. One that sits well with public opinion. It's important, in our line of work, public opinion."

"I'll make sure I have something interesting to tell next time," Dewaal promised, choosing the easier path. Allies. On the same page. No need to make enemies here in this office. She was familiar with how political deals were made.

"What I want you to do, Chief Dewaal," Apostle insisted, "is to walk out of this building, go have a cup of strong coffee around the corner, take half an hour to write your statement, and then come back. I need to talk this over with you anyway, but I have another appointment just now."

Dewaal rose from her chair. "You want me to—?"

"Just stick around. I'll have you called. And write that statement."

27

EILEEN REACTED AT ONCE when two men attempted to grab her. She intended to turn around, collapse to her knees, and strike out with her right foot at one of the men's ankles. Previous experiences with violence had sharpened her reactions, and she'd had some training as well. Urban defense for women. She had had a hired assassin after her, which definitely changed her view of the world. A small but intense part of her mind was always focusing on potential danger.

But these men were no amateurs. Their victim didn't have a chance to react, or slip away. She had no time to scream. A strong hand in a leather glove was pushed over her mouth, and she was literally lifted off the ground. In one almost graceful collective movement, much like a dance, her abductors carried her off and into a large SUV.

An hour earlier she had phoned Nick to tell him she wanted to see some old friends. "Old friends" was a relative term, referring to the period of her life in Amsterdam before Pieter had been murdered and she had to disappear. It referred to an innocent time, although she had left most of her innocence at home, up north. Back then, she hadn't planned ever to return there.

Her childhood had been spent with her brother and sister in an old house and gardens near Groningen. She had known nothing about the rest of the world, living in the splendid isolation her family imposed on all its members. The outside world hardly existed, at least not during the first decade and a half of her life.

There had been Maarten, her brother, who was already showing the first signs of a slow-growing insanity, enveloping both of his sisters in a world of bizarre and sometimes downright sinister games and fantasies. Only later, almost as adults, did the girls understand the weak but stubborn and utterly alien intellect their brother had developed. He was weird in a world not prepared for weirdness.

Their parents were not at all equipped to deal with him and his resolute deviations from the rules they and their community imposed on all. He wasn't a rebel. He was merely *the Other*. God had shaped his mind differently, and they could do no more but accept that difference. At some point, the girls were confronted with a universe of things previously hidden from them: the universe of everything. They went to school, finding themselves the butt of jokes for their strangeness. Quickly, they adapted. School became an intellectual hiding place. Later, they left and moved to Amsterdam. It was a common enough story. It wasn't exceptional. Eileen and her sister became students, surviving on the little money their parents provided and semi-permanent jobs.

After Pieter's death, Eileen had returned home in one last attempt to understand her parents and make them understand her. It didn't work out. The only other place she knew was Amsterdam.

Where Nick greeted her with open arms. Although she intended to take it easy before committing to a relationship. A real relationship.

All this was far from her mind now, being abducted and all. This wasn't a joke. It was serious. Two men for one slightly built girl. Why would anybody abduct her? Had they made a mistake? Had they someone else in mind? Nobody would pay a ransom for her.

In the SUV, the hand was lifted from her mouth. "Who are you?" she asked. "What do you want?"

"Shut it," one of the men said, carelessly threatening. He had a scarf over the lower part of his face, but she noticed he wasn't young. Fifty maybe, judging by the lines around his eyes. The other seemed younger. Behind the wheel was the third man. The car sped through traffic, which wasn't easy in Amsterdam. She couldn't see anything because of the tinted windows.

The younger man pulled her arms behind her back and tied her wrists.

"Nobody's going to pay you money for me," she said.

"No ransom," the older man said.

The man behind the wheel said, "Blindfold her." A black cloth bag was pulled over her head. She thought she would get sick. But she didn't. She felt a sting in her thigh, and then there was nothing anymore.

The voice through the tiny speaker sounded civilized, despite the message. A refined voice making a business offer but leaving no room for negotiation. "Eileen Calster," the voice said. "She is currently our guest, Mister Prinsen. We know she's a good friend of yours. Currently, we're looking after her. There's nothing wrong with her—for now. Don't worry."

Prinsen couldn't think clearly. For a moment, he assumed this was a joke. Why would anyone want to abduct Eileen? Why did people get mixed up in sinister jokes like this? He had no friends who would play pranks on him.

"What do you want from me?" he inquired meekly. Because this was no joke. This was real. The man wasn't kidding. And this was about Eileen.

"You want her back?"

"Of course I want her back. Nothing must happen to her."

"Nothing will. As long as we agree on several premises."

Premises, Prinsen thought. *What is this? Who would speak like that?* "What premises?" he inquired.

The voice over the phone quietly explained what he wanted from Prinsen. Nothing that seemed complicated. Or maybe it was.

What he wanted from Prinsen *was* complicated because Prinsen would have to forfeit some of his principles. But he listened. He made no comment.

He listened to the voice until that voice was finished, and the conversation was over. Prinsen knew what was expected of him. The man hadn't made any threats. He hadn't spoken of what would happen to Eileen if Prinsen was less than forthcoming.

There was no need to make verbal threats.

28

DEWAAL FOUND HERSELF, FASTER than she had wished, back in Apostel's office. There had been just enough time for a coffee and a quick visit to the bathroom. Twenty minutes, her watch told her. Then her phone had chirped with a message from Apostel. She was expected back.

"Shall we move on, Chief Dewaal?" the prosecutor said, letting Dewaal in. A man got up from one of the chairs, a neatly dressed Arab gentleman with slick black hair and deep dark eyes. Or maybe Indian, Dewaal wasn't sure. For a short moment he observed her carefully, then extended his hand. "Colonel Saeed Al-Rahman of the Mutaween," he said pleasantly, in perfect Oxford English. "I am here, Chief Dewaal, by agreement with your own Ministry of the Interior."

"And we will extend all due courtesies toward Colonel Al-Rahman," Apostel added, also in English. As a warning to Dewaal.

"I am a member of the *religious police*, not just the secret service," Al-Rahman added, not without a certain irony. "In my country, this is an important distinction."

"I'm aware of that," Dewaal said. "Colonel."

The Mutaween. She knew what that meant. Or not. She had no idea why the colonel was here. Unless, of course, it was because of her investigation.

Mutaween, indeed.

"We will talk about the presence of the colonel in a moment, Chief," Apostel said, and continued in Dutch, "I told him we would have to discuss a few things between ourselves, but he didn't mind being present. So just ignore him."

"Of course, he doesn't understand Dutch."

"I assume not. There's a thing I need to warn you about: you have a mole in your organization. I mean, in the Bureau. How else can you explain how the news leaked to the papers?"

"From the beginning, dozens of people have been involved. I'm surprised things didn't leak earlier."

"Even so . . ."

"I know there must be a leak, ma'am," Dewaal said. "One of my people, or maybe not. Someone walks into a pub and shoots off his mouth, and there happens to be a journalist present, and when you mix alcohol with—"

"I don't want excuses. I want action," Apostel said.

"I can hardly dismiss the whole team," Dewaal said. "Maybe there used to be a problem with screening officers when siphoning them toward the AIVD and the Bureau. I don't know. The rot was always there in the force. We both know that. Too many corrupt officers, veterans usually. Give me a year to figure it all out."

"That's mighty long, a year," Apostel said.

"We might be talking about two or three people. I can trust only a few of the team. I have already taken certain measures. I've taken this up with the directors."

"I'll need to keep the minister informed. Anyway, now to the other issue. The colonel is here because a countryman of his has been killed here in Amsterdam." She looked at the colonel and continued in English. "We now come back to you, Colonel, with my apologies for this interruption."

"No need, ma'am," he said.

"I explained to the chief how a citizen of the Saudi state arrived in Amsterdam two days ago and met his unfortunate end," Apostel said.

"Is this something for us?" Dewaal inquired, also in English. "We don't get involved with murders, even when the victim is a foreign national."

"This is not just any citizen of our state, ma'am," said Al-Rahman.

"This is Prince Abdullah Ibn Faisal Ibn Saud. The name tells you why I'm here. He was killed in a villa just outside Amsterdam. It was rented for him by our government. He was here on official business, of course."

"This is highly unfortunate for the prince," Dewaal diplomatically said, wondering how the colonel felt about having to negotiate with two women. Or was *she* prejudiced? As if she cared about the sensitivities of the colonel. He looked sufficiently Westernized anyway. He might have left his sensitivities at home. "But I still fail to understand why we should be concerned."

"The colonel didn't just drop by to see us," Apostel said. "He arrived by military aircraft. His government is taking this very seriously."

The colonel kept his attention on Dewaal. "There are two major concerns in the affair," he said. "First, the Prince was killed in a most gruesome manner. He died in a fire, tied to a bed. Madam prosecutor seemed convinced that you would be interested in this modus operandi."

"I might," Dewaal said, not entirely ready to commit herself or her service. "And the second issue?"

"The other people present died an equally gruesome death, but in particular the fact that they were present disturbed my government highly. Disturbed the members of the royal household even more. And here we enter a delicate part of the story."

Dewaal said nothing.

"His Highness," the colonel proceeded, "was in the presence of three young Western women who had been paid to entertain His Highness, ma'am. This might not be something surprising to you, here, in this country. But in my country this significant detail will be extremely dis-graceful to the entire royal family. There will be dire consequences if this becomes public." '

"The prince was the second cousin of the . . . of the Saudi king," Apostel added.

"I understand," Dewaal said. "What you need most is discretion."

"Yes, ma'am," the colonel said. "The whole thing should not see the light of day, as the expression goes."

"And you are here as the representative of the royal family."

"I am not actually here, ma'am. Not officially. Officially, I am

179

merely an officer of the Mutaween, or the *Hayaa*, which is short for the Commission for the Promotion of Virtue and the Prevention of Adultery. It's sufficiently self-explanatory, I assume. We monitor the implementation of moral principles that are an intrinsic part of our society and our religion. All according to the wishes of Allah—the Almighty, the Merciful."

"You ensure people do not stray from the faith, I gather," Dewaal said, aware of Apostel keeping a keen eye on her. She would not be allowed to deviate from a cautious approach to this matter. Sensitive toes would not be stepped upon.

Colonel Al-Rahman smiled his most charming and endearing smile. He wanted to be liked. He clearly wanted to get things done his way. "Of course, I understand you have certain reservations about the way religion is so all-encompassing in my country. That much I understand. I've been in the West long enough to understand. But here we are. We each have our role to play. We are aware many in the West see the Sharia as incompatible with human rights. This is, however, not the case. The Sharia propounds a different approach to human rights. And the idea of human rights is not universal anyway, not in the Western enlightenment sense. Sharia has a great many benefits, even for women, and I advise you to study it, whenever you have the chance. But let us put this aside. I am a police officer, like yourself, and certainly not a religious zealot. We will not change my culture, and we will not change yours. I'm here because our two countries entertain excellent diplomatic relations. As things stand, I hope I can count on your professionalism to ensure that certain aspects of this unfortunate case will be kept between us. Officially, then, the prince was alone in the house, and his death was an accident."

"You don't want us to find his murderer?" Dewaal inquired.

"That aspect is solely your concern, ma'am. You now know where I stand."

"And," Apostel added, "seeing our diplomatic relations, we will operate according to Saudi wishes."

"Is the colonel aware we're working on another similar case?" Dewaal inquired.

"He is," Apostel said guardedly.

"Can we fit his case into our own, um, *framework*?"

"If you must."

The colonel rose. "I leave these details to you, ma'am," he said to Apostel. "I need to be present when the death of His Highness is investigated. I wish to be present during all phases of the investigation. Solely in the capacity of observer, of course."

"Of course," Apostel said, with a warning glance to Dewaal.

The colonel left.

"I have to babysit him?" Dewaal said. "Really?"

"Is there a problem with people looking over your shoulder, Alexandra? Because you better get used to it. *I* will be looking over your shoulder. And so will others."

"Oh," Dewaal said, "they've been doing that for ages. All right, I'll babysit him. By the way, he knows about the Ardennes."

"I told him," Apostel said.

Yes, Dewaal thought. *But he knew before you told him.*

"And do something about that mole," Apostel said.

"Twenty-four people," Dewaal said. "More or less. One bad apple."

"How many are absolutely trustworthy?"

"I've already assigned the one I really trust to the Ardennes team."

"Your nephew?"

"Yes, him too. And Eekhaút. Because he has no history here."

"No history?"

"No, at least not in Amsterdam."

29

EEKHAUT SAT DOWN ON the chair opposite Dewaal and crossed his legs. Some vague pain in his knee had been bothering him since that morning, but it wasn't bad enough to send him to the doctor. Remarkably enough, several folders and documents had been scattered chaotically over her desk, as if she no longer bothered to clean up. As if she had surrendered to the inevitability of chaos as an inherent characteristic of her line of work. This was so uncharacteristic of her. Her office had been, until recently, the cell of a post-industrial monk. All the technology had been there, but no paper. His office was the exact opposite.

She didn't look all that well, either. Her skin was gray, and she had dark shadows under her eyes. He wondered if this was the moment he'd have to take her to the pub. The cold air outside would do her good, as would a cold beer. She was working too hard. Spending too many hours in this office. She needed to relax, and he assumed she had little relaxation in her private life. Maybe she had no private life.

"An Arabian prince," he said. Arabian princes usually figured only in fairy tales and such. In the imagination of writers like Richard Burton. The Victorian traveler, not the British actor.

"Read the newspaper," she told him.

"You know I don't read the newspapers. *An Arabian prince.* You told me the story isn't in the news. Oh, only that the prince died by accident. Nothing about the—?"

"We're keeping it that way," Dewaal said.

"The call girls."

"They're all dead, Walter. As is the prince. And I have a prosecutor on my back. And a Saudi police officer. One dead prince is enough for me to worry about. Forget about the call girls."

"Too bad. I assume the Saudi isn't concerned about the girls either. Or he wants them to vanish from our reports. Is that what he wants?"

Dewaal threw him *that look.*

"And is there a link to the Ardennes file?"

"How would I know? This might be just a random murder. People who don't like Arab princes. A family affair. An act of revenge inspired by religion. But there are several details that remind me—"

"Burned alive. One nightmare after another, Chief."

"The preliminary report states all four suffocated before the flames reached them. Small mercy, actually. At least there's that. But that's as far as the pathologist was allowed to proceed. The prince's body remains in cold storage, pending further investigation. Chances are slim his body will be released to us. The Saudis cite religious reasons. They are already angry the pathologist touched it. Now, let's visit the crime scene."

No time for a beer, Eekhaut assumed. "I don't intend to take on every case the prosecutor throws at us, Chief," he said, feeling the need for some provocation. Tough luck—she was the only one around he could provoke. "Certainly not if it's political. What can we do at the crime scene? Get a whiff of barbecued human?"

"There's more to this than the death of a Saudi diplomat, Eekhaut," Dewaal said. "There's a full-fledged diplomatic incident in the making. A senior police officer flying in directly from . . . from wherever he came. A victim directly related to the Saudi royal family. I'm not going to wait till part of our government comes calling at my office."

"And why all this official zeal? Holland needs its crude oil to flow uninterrupted?"

Dewaal sighed wearily. "It hardly matters. We toe the line, like it or not. We keep a certain thing out of the newspapers. You're not getting enough action, Walter. It shows. You're getting cranky. Too much time behind your desk and not enough in the streets. I'm gonna change that. I'll kick you out. You'll come to love Amsterdam after you've walked all its streets for a couple of months. Actually, I liked you better when we were both in the field, getting shot at. You like getting shot at."

"I can arrange a shooting," Eekhaut said. "I can pay someone to shoot at me if you like."

She got up, all five foot four, adding an extra inch on account of her shoes. And dressed like she could handle any government representative or bureaucrat. What did she care about one dead Saudi? A lot, it seemed. She was under a lot of pressure. "It's not the bullets you need to watch out for," she told him. "People can harm you more than weapons. People, with their minds and mouths."

He wasn't going to argue with her. Not about this. He was experienced enough to recognize people for what they were. Untrustworthy, most of the time.

He accompanied her to the underground parking garage, where she clicked open the door of a small Volvo he'd never before seen. He hardly ever came to the parking garage. He almost never needed a car for work. The Volvo was new, and it was the right car for her. Not for him. He was taller than she, he needed a larger car. But when he stepped in, he was surprised the Volvo accommodated him adequately.

She drove carefully through the narrow streets. Even as a pedestrian in Amsterdam, he was always wary of the bikers. They'd come from all directions at once, swirling around obstacles and people and cars as if there were no tomorrow. For some of them there would be no tomorrow if they kept this up, this aggressive, chaotic behavior. Anyway, he didn't use a bike either.

In what seemed only moments but took fifteen minutes, they arrived at the ring road, driving south and getting off again after only a short while. The neighborhood they entered was starkly different from the center of Amsterdam. Large villas occupied parklike tracts of land, mostly surrounded by brick walls or fences. Plenty of camera surveillance as well, he noticed. Somewhere in the middle of all this, Dewaal slowed down and drove past a gate where two uniformed police officers kept watch. She stopped the car in front of a villa, which was large enough to entertain the guests of a major wedding, a royal wedding even. However impressive the house was, it had been severely damaged by the fire. On its whole left side, the wall and part of the roof were blackened, the grass and shrubs on that side largely gone.

"Seems these people invested a fortune in cameras," Eekhaut said. "What do we have on tape?"

"What do you want to see on tape?"

"Intruders perhaps? People sneaking around. Peasants carrying pitchforks and torches. Others carrying gas cans and flamethrowers."

"None of the cameras were functioning at the time."

He feigned surprise. "Oh, that's really bad luck, isn't it? The only time you need to have pictures of people setting your house on fire, and your cameras aren't working."

"Walter," she warned him. They were getting out of the car.

"Of course, if I were renting this place to Saudi Arabian royalty and I knew he would be frolicking about with three pale-skinned underage girls, I would make certain my cameras weren't operational. Wouldn't you? Perhaps there were dogs? Perhaps the premises were guarded by dogs? I'd have dogs. Dogs can stand guard and bite intruders, but they are not going to spill the beans about frolicking princes, are they?"

"He was a Muslim. No dogs."

"All right. He was a Muslim. No dogs. They can't have dogs around. Filthy animals. But girls? Girls no problem?"

He was wondering how long he could go on like this before she shot him.

On the other hand, she knew he was right. "I'm not Muslim," she said, patiently. "So I would not know. Now get off my back, Walter."

The front door of the villa opened, and another uniformed police officer let them in. "One floor up," was all he said.

Eekhaut noticed the man was carrying a submachine gun. *What the hell? Would anybody want to steal something from the premises? Wipe out traces?*

He followed Dewaal up the stairs. Stairs that begged to be called "monumental." The hall of the villa seemed larger than Eekhaut's entire apartment. The carpet on the stairs succeeded in muffling all sound. It showed a fleur-de-lis pattern. He sniffed. A pungent chemical smell hung in the air. And the stench of burned flesh.

Upstairs on the landing and in the corridor, a narrow pink carpet lay atop a deep red marble floor. The wall and ceiling had been painted gray but were now partially charred, as was half of the carpet. Dewaal and Eekhaut carefully stepped over the damage. Three doors emerged in the corridor, one blackened and hanging on only one hinge. Another police officer waited for them.

They stepped over the threshold and into the room.

None of its original colors had survived the fire. Most objects still retained something of their original form, like a bed and a commode and two chairs, but barely recognizable. Black, charred, melted.

"Imagine having to retrieve bodies from this mess," Dewaal said.

That, at least, they had been spared. The bodies, or what remained of them, had already been taken to the morgue. Even with the windows open and part of the outer wall gone, a cruel sour smell remained in the room. The house had suffered considerable damage. The fire had been hot, Eekhaut assumed, and accelerants would have been used. Remarkable enough that only this side of the building had suffered. The fire hadn't spread.

"Was there anybody else in the house at the time. Other than the—?"

"No," Dewaal said. "The servants who usually look after the place had been given time off. Privacy, what did you expect? The neighbors called the emergency services when they noticed the flames coming through the windows. Forensics identified the accelerant used: kerosene. Airplane fuel. Not obvious, and not impossible to come by, either."

She remained where she was, close to the door. She wasn't going to walk around too much in the black sludge, the mixture of soot and water.

"The fire seems to have been restricted to this part of the house. I assume its walls are more or less fireproof."

"Possible. I'll ask forensics."

"It must have been like an oven in here."

"Apparently."

"They didn't die because of the flames?"

"Not directly. The pathologist reported death by inhalation of toxic and hot fumes. Not a nice way to die, but probably somewhat less painful than burning up."

"That's going into his official report?"

"I assume so."

"And that's what the family is going to read?"

Dewaal eyed him suspiciously. "Again, I assume so. Why?"

"They'll also be informed of the fact that, if three extra bodies were mentioned, they would be employees of the embassy, helping His Highness with sensitive matters. If they're mentioned at all."

"If at all."

"I don't believe they died from asphyxiation," Eekhaut said. "They burned alive. The pathologist is embellishing the report, for the family."

"What makes you say that?"

"Because their death had to be horrible. Because it's another ritual. Like the one in the Ardennes."

"I don't see the connection," Dewaal said. "And, of course, you have no proof."

"It's the Society of Fire all over again, punishing those it deems unworthy. A Muslim, an Arab prince, fornicating with white whores. Let's punish him. Let's burn him. Asphyxiation is not enough as a punishment."

"What a fucking mess," Dewaal said. Although she still had reservations about Eekhaut's theory.

Behind them, someone was approaching. Colonel Al-Rahman entered the room. He quickly observed the damage and turned toward Dewaal. "Commissioner," he said, in English. "And Chief Inspector Eekhaut. How do you do?"

"Have we met?" Eekhaut inquired.

"Did they let you in, just like that?" Dewaal asked.

"No, and yes, in that order," Al-Rahman said. He smiled patiently, an advertisement for toothpaste. He wore a neat blue suit over a white shirt and a red tie. He looked like the manager of a respectable bank. "Do I need to explain? And why don't you introduce me to your colleague, Commissioner?"

"Incidentally," Eekhaut said, "it's pronounced 'ake-out.' Rhymes with *stakeout*. Easy to remember."

"Walter," Dewaal interjected, "this is Colonel Saeed Al-Rahman of the Mutaween, the Saudi religious police. He's here in connection with the death of the prince, of course. Colonel, my colleague, Chief Inspector Eekhaut, about whom you already have heard."

"Of course, Chief. I work for the Saudi intelligence services, as you know. We have access to the internet, and of course we trade information with police forces all over the world. At least those that are agreeable to us. Therefore, in a sense, I know Mr. Eekhaut, almost as a personal friend."

"Intelligence services?" Dewaal said.

"Certainly," said Al-Rahman. "What the Americans call Homeland Security: religious police, on our side of the fence. The violation of religious law is as much a crime as threatening the integrity of the state. Both acts are, in fact, one and the same in our book."

"Picking up heretics," Eekhaut said jovially. "We used to do that here as well, Colonel. In the good old days. That was before that thing we call the Enlightenment. We tortured them, occasionally burned them at the stake. You should try it too, enlightenment, I mean. Human rights and all that. A whole new universe opens up. Treating people decently and not on account of a belief in a god."

"Walter!" Dewaal warned him sternly.

"Oh, never mind, ma'am," Al-Rahman said almost cheerily. "I'm not hearing this for the first time. In every Western country I visit in my official capacity, I hear people telling me Islam and Sharia can't live under one roof with democracy and human rights. I will repeat what I always tell people. That Islam is the religion not of the sword but of the book, and a religion of peace and tolerance—the many radicals and reactionaries notwithstanding. I argue that women under the Sharia have significantly more rights than they have in many of your democracies and certainly more than under those primitive paternalistic and misguided cultures that still thrive in certain parts of Asia and Africa. I point out that, yes, we have severe forms of punishment, but they are rare and are applied only after long deliberation by judges and after due process. Not like in, for instance, the United States, where so many people are incarcerated, like animals, for the most common crimes. And in most if not all streets in Saudi Arabia and elsewhere in the Arab world, it is much safer, at night as well as day, than in many Western cities. That is what I tell people."

"Thank you, Colonel," Dewaal said. "We must keep all that in mind. I'm sure Chief Inspector Eekhaut will keep that in mind too." She glanced at Eekhaut, who was trying to keep these things in mind. He had now been warned not to mess with the colonel.

Al-Rahman glanced over the room. "A most terrible thing, is it not? Four people dying here, cruelly. This is an unbearable thought. Those responsible will be caught, I'm sure, and punished. I have read the preliminary report of the doctor in charge. And of the police. No cameras, and the alarm system was turned off."

"You have lived in the West, Colonel?" Dewaal inquired.

"A year in the United States and three years in London. Specializing in police matters. That is why I succeeded in resisting the American accent and cultivating the British. Many of my countrymen know it is an advantage to speak proper English. Especially in the Arab world, with its many variations of Arabic. Most of the Arab world is populated by backward peasants, who are mostly superstitious and do not understand the Sharia properly. Fortunately, the Saudi can show them the way to true civilization." He glanced at Eekhaut. "Or toward our specific brand of enlightenment, if you wish."

"What was the object of the prince's visit to Holland?" Eekhaut wanted to know. "Did he need to familiarize himself with Dutch customs?"

The colonel ignored the implication. He said, "He was preparing a diplomatic mission. The Dutch people are hungrier than ever for the oil of the Middle East. They have developed highly sophisticated technologies. They are masters at dredging, for instance. Architecture, port construction, you name it. All this knowledge we want to apply in Saudi Arabia. And for many political reasons, we want to avoid being too dependent on the Americans. Hence we seek European know-how."

"Might the murder have happened for political reasons, Colonel?" Dewaal asked, stepping out into the corridor.

The two men followed her. "I assumed," Al-Rahman said, "that you expected to be confronted with a clear-cut case. A case of religious fanaticism. Christian fanaticism, for once. People who want to assure themselves of a place in the mercy of their equivalent of Allah."

"We had been thinking along those lines," Dewaal said cautiously.

"If such is the case, we consider the investigation will be finished when you arrest the members of this group."

"Will that be sufficient for you? For your government?"

"That and the matter of confidentiality. We may offer to take some of the members of that group off your hands, to bring them to justice in my country, where they will probably get the death sentence. But your government will not stand for such a solution, so we will settle for a suitable conclusion."

"It is customary for the bodies of crime victims to be examined by a pathologist. Could you give permission, Colonel?"

"The prince's body?"

"Exactly."

"This is an extremely delicate matter, ma'am. The body of the prince will have to be brought before an imam and purified. I'm afraid no medical examination would be acceptable."

"As you wish," Dewaal said. "On the other hand, this property will be searched by our technical unit."

"Of course." The colonel lowered his gaze slightly. "We will soon meet again, Commissioner, I'm sure."

Eekhaut spoke up. "Colonel, I still have a question."

"Yes, Chief Inspector?"

"I understand there are many princes in your country."

"That is correct."

"About how many?"

"I beg your pardon?"

"I mean: how many princes are there in your country?"

"Oh," Al-Rahman said, "something like a thousand. I assume someone is familiar with the exact number, and I can request such information if you want. But something like that, about a thousand."

"Thank you, Colonel. That's very helpful."

After the colonel had left, Dewaal said, "You will attend the women's autopsy, Walter, for your sins. And what about those princes? What do you care?"

"Oh, I thought I'd ask. Just one of those things . . ."

"No, tell me, what prompted it?"

"*The Kingdom.* You should see the movie. It tells us a lot of things about the colonel's homeland. And the number of princes."

"Get on with that autopsy. Full report. On my desk. In a jiffy."

"Isn't in my job description."

"It is now."

30

A TAXI DROPPED EEKHAUT off at the morgue, an appropriate gloomy building, dating from the late nineteenth century. It was in a neighborhood he hadn't been to yet but that seemed affordable only to rich people. A cold north wind accompanied him inside, where decrepit 1960s decor welcomed him.

Behind a makeshift desk, an unshaven young man eyed him suspiciously. Pushing a cheap ballpoint pen into the breast pocket of his denim shirt, he raised an inquisitive eyebrow. Eekhaut asked where he might find the pathologist, who, two dimly lit corridors later, turned out to be a good-looking man in his early sixties whose name was De Vriend. "Guus," the man added at once, as if the use of family names were strictly discouraged in this institution. He gave Eekhaut a firm handshake. "Those three young women? Yes, or what is left of them. You people always seem most interested in the worst cases. Anyway, come with me."

From the cab Eekhaut had announced his visit by phone. He had spoken to a woman, who turned out to be the assistant pathologist, now waiting for them next to three steel tables in a cold examination and storage room. She looked pretty in a professional and distant way, but her legs under her lab coat offered Eekhaut a distraction from the inevitable horror he was going to see under the spotless white cloths that covered the tables.

"Are you aware, Chief Inspector, of what such an intense heat does to the human body?" De Vriend inquired. Eekhaut could not think of him as Guus, which sounded like the name of a favorite uncle. Perhaps this man was somebody's favorite uncle or grandfather. But here he was the man who had to witness the most horrific results of mayhem.

The assistant approached one of the tables and removed the sheet. The charred remains were those of a child, judging by its size. It had a roughly human form but could have been alien, as far as Eekhaut could tell. It lay in a fetal position.

"The human body," De Vriend explained, "consists largely of water. On combustion, most of this water tends to evaporate. Whatever remains of muscle tissue will contract, and the body shrivels." He looked at Eekhaut and held out a surgical mask. Eekhaut shook his head. He had seen bodies like this before. Recently. "Do you want to be present during the examination, Inspector? I thought I'd ask. Most detectives prefer to have a coffee in the waiting room while we proceed."

"I guess I can wait over there and hear what you have to tell me afterward."

"You needn't have come at all, Inspector," De Vriend said. "I would have mailed you my findings when I'm done. Won't take too long."

Eekhaut knew why Dewaal had sent him here.

"There's a sort of kitchen, back in the hallway, door to your right. Have a coffee. There are usually sandwiches as well and soft drinks. Help yourself. We are used to working long hours here, so it's a bit messy. I'll see you shortly."

Dewaal had wanted to teach him a lesson in humility.

That's what all this was about.

A lesson.

He found the kitchen, which looked like a set from a science fiction movie. White walls and kitchen cupboards, a high-tech coffee machine with a bewildering choice of beverages, a large fridge with sandwiches wrapped in clear plastic, and a plate of donuts and croissants. He didn't want to think about *Alien* and nonhuman life-forms. Not here, not after having seen one of the victims.

He waited about an hour, reading magazines and staring at the walls. He drank two cups of coffee, ate a donut, used the toilet (again, a high-tech affair), read more magazines. Nobody came in. He wondered who the food was for.

Finally, De Vriend walked in, peeling off his protective coat and gloves and dropping them in a wastebasket. He smelled strongly of disinfectants. "Clear-cut case," he said. He got a coffee from the machine.

"It is?"

"You'll get my full report later," De Vriend said. He added milk and sugar to his coffee. "We're both addicted to sugar, my assistant and I." He smiled. "That's the only thing we have in common. That, and the fact that we cut up dead people. It's almost like a bad joke." He chuckled and sipped his coffee. "Death by shock, cardiac arrest, and poisoning due to smoke inhalation. The shock and cardiac arrest came with pain, I'm sorry to tell you. Poisoning was only secondary, not the primary cause of death. But they died quickly, thank God. Or thanks to *whoever* had deserted them during those last moments. Attempted examination of blood and stomach contents, but you've seen the state they're in. From what my experience tells me, there's been alcohol and cocaine involved, but I can't be really sure."

"Anything else you noticed?"

"Are you kidding, Inspector? My conclusion is that the times of the Inquisition and burning at the stake have returned. That's my conclusion. That some really, *really* disturbed person did this to them, and that no sins these women may have committed can be bad enough to deserve such treatment."

"Nothing physical that struck you?"

"Not under these circumstances." De Vriend drank more coffee. "I see bodies all the time. It doesn't bother me. Neither does the way people die. To me, they're puzzles to be solved. In this case . . . well, I hope you find the animals who did this."

"Plural?"

"Oh yes. I'm guessing several people were involved. There needed to be several to overpower them and the man who was with them."

"How much alcohol and coke?"

"Like I said, I can't tell. It's just an assumption. But I hope they were stoned when they died—out of their minds."

"We should be grateful for the little things," Eekhaut said.

"Yeah. Usually, I'm the one to make that remark." De Vriend raised an eyebrow. "Don't want my job, do you?"

"I don't think so, no."

"I wouldn't want yours either, Inspector. Not really. I deal with the horrors after the facts. You, well, you have to deal with the real monsters."

31

IT HAD THE LOOK of a park but was the garden of a private estate. It was adjacent to a slowly ascending pasture. The house itself stood at the end of a long path, wide enough for a car. It was dark. The story went that an insane architect had constructed the house just after the First World War, to escape from the world. Which, to some, might have indicated there was some logic to his madness after all. Although he had no family and few friends, the house had exactly thirteen bedrooms and four living rooms.

A world war later, the building and surrounding gardens were purchased by a wealthy and much more down-to-earth industrialist who saw it as a sound investment. By then the architect had been dead for several years. The estate was in the hands of the industrialist's children now, who rented it out. They did so through an agency, so none of them knew who the tenants were or for what purpose the house was being used. For several months now, one of Maxwell's companies had rented it, supposedly as a venue for training top employees. In fact, it was the Society of Fire who used the house and the gardens as its headquarters and refuge.

It was cold in the garden. Most plants had shriveled, waiting for spring. Frozen drops hung from tree branches, even this late in the afternoon. One path meandered from the house through the garden, splitting several times. The paths would undoubtedly lead somewhere, but no current visitor wanted to find out where. All of them had already endured enough divergent paths in their personal lives.

Each of the visitors had a name, none of which had been given to them at birth. No natural parents had stood by the crib and whispered it with emotion. These names were given to them the moment they first joined the society, along with the message that they and only they were the chosen ones, who would live through the coming final ordeal.

Each knew the others only by the name given by the society. Previous, mundane names had been left behind, at least whenever the members of the society convened. There were just a few exceptions to that rule. The man called Baphomet knew the real names of all members, but none of them had any idea who he really was. Anonymity was a safeguard against enemies and intruders. Curiosity was a sin.

They all realized their way of life and the choices they had made would bring them into conflict with earthly powers. But these earthly powers would soon be of no consequence anymore. At the end of times, soon now, the Creator would make his final judgment, and few would be saved.

Baphomet came to meet them at the house. He wore a dark suit, a white shirt, no tie, and a gray wool overcoat. All of them were dressed for the cold in parkas or long wool overcoats, thick corduroy trousers, scarves, and gloves. They resembled not so much a religious cult as a collection of amateur explorers, bound for the North.

"My friends," Baphomet said, "may the greatness of our Creator envelop you all. His light will shine eternally on you."

All present repeated that last sentence. Baphomet waited for a moment. Silence reigned in the garden. Then he said, "Let us discuss our problems."

"You've chosen quite an interesting setting for this meeting, Baphomet," a heavyset man said. He had crossed his arms over his chest. His given name was Tertullian, and he was proud of it, as he considered it an honorary title. It was an old name as well, taken from an early Carthaginian Christian philosopher who lived during the first century. "Why not inside the house? Isn't it available? Or should we freeze out here before we're finally consumed by God's eternal flame?"

Baphomet pacified him with a simple gesture of his left hand. "We will enter the house in a moment, dear friends, and find there the food and drink the Creator has provided for us. However, this conversation we must hold in the garden. Remember the Garden of Eden? Look around you, my friends, and open your hearts. Do you not find the world beautiful, especially during this season? Is this material creation not a wonderful thing? Has not God inspired us to great deeds through his creation? All this, however, will soon end." He cast a quick glance at Serena, who was standing in the front row, not in the least ill at ease at her first meeting.

"Maybe we should attempt to save at least part of this wonderful creation," a small, blond woman suggested. "Why can't we?"

Baphomet ignored her. She was one of his critics he had to endure among the group. She had several supporters among the women of her own age. Most others, however, didn't think highly of her.

"Unfortunately," he continued, "dark forces are gathering on the horizon." He hated the cliché, but it seemed to work with this group. "We may have been overzealous, awakening certain members of the police force. We have always attempted invisibility, not appearing on their radar screens. Lately, however, we may have been somewhat careless. Some of us have, at least. I, however, bear full responsibility for this."

"We're all impatient," Serena said.

"We are proceeding as planned," Baphomet concluded. "The final and ultimate sacrifice that I promised you long ago is imminent. Meanwhile, we need to be discreet. We cannot afford the intrusion of the outside world."

"The great sacrifice must be made," a tall, gaunt man in his fifties said. "Otherwise, none of us will be saved."

"All will happen as we planned," Baphomet intoned. "I ask for patience."

"Everybody should have the opportunity to be saved," the blond woman insisted. "Everybody should have the same chances. That's what democracy is all about."

Why, Baphomet thought, *do I allow this stupid woman to make inconsistent and irrelevant comments? Democracy? This is not and will never be a democracy. And what is she gibbering about?* He knew that he could not silence her, though.

"The authorities are closing in on us," another of the believers said, a skinny man who seemed perpetually worried. His name was Horothetes, and he was the one who had joined Courier in the Ardennes, along with some of the younger men.

"Thanks to those who have been so careless in their duties," the blond woman chimed in.

Baphomet raised his hand. "The ritual we are all referring to was poorly executed. This could have been avoided. Again, I am taking responsibility."

"All because Baphomet wanted to take care of some of his personal enemies," Tertullian said. "He was the one who chose the sacrificed. He forgot a cardinal rule: not to let personal interests prevail."

"The doctrine," Baphomet replied sternly, "implies the unworthy should be punished. I made that choice, I did indeed. I found a number of unworthy in my proximity. Certainly, I did. Why would I look elsewhere, if these were available?" He looked around. "Is there anyone who doubts my choices? Let them speak now."

Nobody volunteered, though Tertullian glanced around defiantly when he didn't receive the support he was looking for.

"Good," Baphomet concluded. "Because there cannot be any doubt in our minds or hearts. Not with the finality so close. In a moment, we will eat together and cleanse our souls and pray we may remain pure."

"When will it be enough, Baphomet?" a frail older woman inquired. She seemed to suffer less from the cold than the others. "At what point may we consider ourselves ready for the purification?"

"Only when the last of days comes," Baphomet said. "Only then will we know we have succeeded. Until then we must be vigilant and act."

"Day by day the evil gains," Tertullian said. "Our enemies are closing in, as was said here a moment ago. The risks of defeat increase. In prison, we will be tainted by the presence of so much corruption and evil. We must at all costs avoid being found out."

"Last month's ritual was a dangerous gamble," the old woman insisted.

"There was a need to connect once again with the old traditions," Baphomet repeated. "Again and again, we must remind ourselves who we are. We must be aware of our tradition. We are nothing without that tradition. This implies the necessity of rituals. Otherwise, we risk deviating from the chosen path."

"Yes," Serena said, "let us concentrate on the final purification, Baphomet! To secure our salvation." This seemed to silence the critics for a moment.

He knew he had made the right choice in bringing her into the fold. "No other objections?" he inquired. "Let us go inside then. There will be food and drink."

While the others entered the house, a man in a long black coat approached Baphomet. He had been observing the procedures from a short distance, as if he weren't a member of the group. His given name was Metagogeus. Although only in the thirties, he clearly commanded respect, mostly due to his silence.

"What about the girl?" Baphomet addressed him.

"As promised, Baphomet, under our care. We've contacted her friend, and we made certain we have his cooperation in full. At least, we made clear what we expect from him."

"And he fully understood?"

"We have made our intentions quite clear, Baphomet. He knows what's at stake."

"Excellent. We should have done this earlier. It would have saved us a lot of headaches. Another thing, I heard about a foreign diplomat who was killed in a villa. A Saudi prince, no less. And with him a certain number of young women. This worries me, Metagogeus. I have the impression some of our members have been overzealous. I do not remember having given anyone permission for another sacrifice."

"Apparently, someone did indeed perform a ritual, and an improvised one at that."

"Any idea who?"

"I'm afraid not. It might be one who acted alone. Or with a small number of friends. I'm at a loss."

"This kind of creative destruction cannot be allowed. Discretion, Metagogeus, is what we need right now."

"The ritual in the Ardennes—"

"I knew very well what I was doing at the time," Baphomet snapped. "And I remember, quite distinctly, you and Courier promising all traces would be erased. I am disappointed, Metagogeus."

"I'm disappointed as well, Baphomet. We'll be more careful in the future, although we paid attention to every detail. I will of course make sure Courier takes this to heart as well. I sometimes have the impression he's sloppy."

"And now this new thing. The Saudi prince. The police, of course, are on it. Tell all members that initiatives of this kind will no longer be tolerated. We will focus on our final plan."

"I'll spread the word," Metagogeus promised.

Baphomet found Serena after Metagogeus had left. "You certainly have made an impression on the members," he said.

"This is important to me, more important than anything else in my life."

Good girl, he thought. She was possessed of the fire, within her. The all-consuming fire, as he had once been.

32

"AND WHAT'S THAT NEPHEW of yours been up to?" Van Gils inquired.

"Excessive speed on the ring road. Twice. Running a red light. Then talked back to the cop who pulled him over."

"Seems like he really did it this time," Van Gils said.

The man in front of him hung his head. Oleg had been living in the Netherlands for a full three decades but remained at heart a melancholic Slav. His melancholic character was probably the only quality he still had left over from the Ukraine of his youth. He had come to the Netherlands with a significant part of his family in tow and had settled on the south side of Amsterdam. There, after toiling for years, he now owned a chain of small laundries and grocery stores specializing in Eastern European items. He was doing well these days, judging by the expensive leather jacket over his shoulders and the golden Rolex on his wrist. That would be a real Rolex, Van Gils knew.

Oleg had the looks of a criminal, which he was. Over the past thirty years, he had been convicted seven times for smuggling cigarettes and alcohol, receiving contraband, and inciting prostitution. The latter bothered Van Gils the most, but Oleg had assured him he had left this particular activity behind. His wife had seen to that. "No woman will be your slave," she had told Oleg. Smuggling was all right with her, but a Christian should not force women to prostitute themselves. She had threatened to leave him. That and a year in prison had convinced him.

The nephew they were talking about was the youngest son of his sister. The problem child of the family. The kind of kid you found even in the best of families. Spoiled. Even Oleg knew the kid was spoiled. Too much pocket money from his dad. Fast cars and flashy sunglasses and girls and whatnot. Doing a hundred on the highway? Fast? Come on! Why that ridiculous speed limit? Why those stupid cops?

Oleg had tried to talk some sense into the kid. "But my sister is not very clever herself, Inspector, not the sharpest pencil in the box, and her husband doesn't care 'cause he's not the kid's real dad. You see? Things happen. Things go wrong. Kid lands in jail. Again. So, they come and see me. Want me to *arrange* things."

"There's just so much I can do, Oleg," Van Gils said. "Told you yesterday already. I know the police magistrate. I've taken care of business for him in the past. I'll have a word. The kid might end up with his license suspended for a year or so, but I'll try to keep him out of jail. You make sure he doesn't get behind the wheel anymore. At least not while he doesn't have his license. If he drives without his license, even I can't help him."

"You are a real friend of this family, Inspector," Oleg said. "You come with the wife, and we go somewhere nice to have dinner. I owe you that at least. I get tickets for the match between Ajax and Feyenoord this weekend in the ArenA."

"If you give me the info I asked for, I'd be more than happy."

"Oh, that." Oleg reached into his coat pocket. "Not difficult. We have contacts everywhere, don't we?" He glanced at the piece of paper he was holding. "Karl Desmedt and Daniel Brecht. Both worked at TransCom. The first one was an information officer, the other was chief accountant. Well-paid jobs, I guess. I heard there were problems."

"What kind?"

"These things happen. Look, Van Gils, there're many people working for me. In the shops I own. I tell them: do your job well. Or else you're out. Simple as that. They know me. They know I mean what I say. Almost never had to let anybody go."

"Good for you. Now, about these two? The rumors?"

"That's what they are. Rumors. Both had a fight with the boss. Threatened they would reveal *things*. What things, I don't know. There are always problems in big companies like that. Like my nephew, you know? People always want more, faster cars, nicer girls, more money. I tell him: you work, then you have money, not the other way around."

"So, if I have this right, both these men had confronted the management of TransCom. Does that information come from a reliable source?"

"Niece of my other sister, Inspector. Works there. You know, secretarial work. And making coffee, taking phone calls, that sort of thing. Someone has to do it. Big companies have money for that. I can't afford a secretary, so I do these things myself. But girls like her, they are everywhere, see everything. They're invisible like I am to the Dutch."

"No, Oleg, you're not invisible."

Oleg grinned, good-naturedly. "Perhaps I am not. Perhaps I should be more invisible. That is my problem. I am too obvious. But I love my work. Laundry business and small neighborhood shops. Earning good money. And I stay within the law too, Van Gils. You arrange this thing for my nephew? Then we have dinner together. Russian cuisine, here in Amsterdam. And what about that bottle of vodka?"

"I don't say no."

Oleg passed him a paper bag. "There's another thing, Inspector."

"Yes?"

"I know you're interested in trade in suspicious and hazardous materials."

"Yes. Like guns. And drugs. You got something for me, Oleg?"

"I don't know if this concerns you, but maybe, yes. You know I have much family. The thing I heard, this delivery of a truck of five thousand gallons of liquefied gas. That's what my uncle does, fuels and chemical stuff in bulk."

"And what's so special about a truckload of liquefied gas?"

"The thing is the client, not the product. Although this kind of gas, he doesn't often sell it. It's explosive stuff. Has to be kept refrigerated all the time."

"And who's the client?"

"A company called Real Estate Technologies."

Van Gils wrote that down. "And what does Real Estate Technologies do?"

"It manages large industrial premises. Like factories."

"Machines need fuel."

"No, not this kind of fuel. It's too explosive. It's used in certain processes in the chemical industry. Maybe it's for export, maybe to some country that wants to produce weapons with it. You know? They can use any kind of explosive to make bombs. In Syria or Afghanistan, wherever."

"I'll look into it, Oleg." Van Gils said, closing his notebook.

33

COLONEL SAEED AL-RAHMAN OPENED the bathroom door, stepped over the threshold, glanced at the mirror, and opened the tap. He fiddled with the water temperature until it was exactly right, pulled his hand back again, and then stood in front of the mirror. He inspected his face. Here in the Netherlands, he would not stand out too much with so many foreigners in the streets. He could easily blend in. But anyone looking carefully would notice he was not a Turk or Moroccan or Surinamese. Not that this mattered much. Nobody would bother him in the street. He would not be thrown out of a pub or a hotel if he dressed nicely.

But he was still an outsider.

He undressed and stepped into the shower. He closed his eyes and let the hot water run over his body. He wasn't used to the cold weather, the winter. He was unsure all the time as to what clothes to wear. He would not want to be underdressed and cold. But with too many layers of clothing, he would be hot in a building. At home, he wore cotton trousers and cotton shirts and at the most a light sweater.

The general had called him into his office and patiently explained to him what was expected on this mission, this very personal mission, and had issued a few well-chosen words of warning. There had been the unexpected and frightening discovery in Somalia, to begin with. That had been bad enough. But now there was the same uncomfortable situation in the Netherlands, first the discovery in the Ardennes and then the grisly murder of the prince.

These events were, of course, connected. And they could, as such, not be ignored.

Colonel Al-Rahman understood at once what was expected of him.

He was given both a public and a confidential agenda. The public agenda stipulated he would be an investigator, assisting the Dutch authorities with the ongoing investigation in Amsterdam. Finding the actual murderers and bringing them to justice, however, was not important. That would be a problem for the Dutch.

Keeping the body of His Highness out of the hands of the unfaithful would be part of his public agenda as well. No medical examination would be allowed.

The hidden agenda was more involved, as explained by the general. Colonel Al-Rahman was not happy with this part of his mission. But he was clearly aware of his obligations to his country, to the royal family, and, finally, to Allah. And he had seen pictures of the bodies in Somalia and in the Ardennes. So he had accepted the mission, hidden agenda and all. Because it was his duty to do so.

Duty was connected to honor. Doing his duty was serving the higher powers out of a profound and personal desire to preserve the sanctity of life as laid out by the words of Allah Himself—the Merciful, the Benign.

The hidden agenda, however, was not entirely honorable. The hidden agenda had nothing whatsoever to do with his obligations to his country or to the House of Saud. The general had made it clear that both of them—Al-Rahman and himself—had obligations beyond those of country and kingdom. Obligations of a very different nature.

In that sense, the hidden agenda was far more important than the public one.

He closed the tap and stepped from the shower. He draped a towel around his hips, dried his hair and then his body with another towel, and stepped into the bedroom. The TV was showing CNN. At home, he often watched CNN. It was American, it was biased, but you had to give it to them because they were well informed about what went on in the world. An Indian woman was discussing disturbances on the subcontinent. Al-Rahman knew three officers of his division were active there, and so he knew about the tensions in that region.

And the involvement of his government—unofficially, of course.

He sat down on the sofa, still damp from the shower. The curtains were partially open. He was on the fourth floor of the hotel, and he assumed no one could look in. An officer of the Mutaween standing half naked watching CNN was not a subject of interest to foreign security services, but of course he would still have to be careful. There might be microphones in his room, but he didn't care. He was not going to invite anyone in for a private chat. Officially, his job here was very low profile. Officially, he hardly existed.

The next day he had an unscheduled appointment, arranged by the general. The general had mentioned old friends and old friendships, and while Al-Rahman inwardly frowned upon such luxuries, he made no comment. The general had been concise about the arrangement, assuming the colonel knew how to handle such matters. He was familiar with the qualities of Colonel Al-Rahman. This was not his first foreign mission with a hidden agenda. The general knew certain matters would, in the end, have to be solved by the colonel, at his own discretion.

The only things that bothered Colonel Al-Rahman was how to stay involved with the criminal investigation and how to stay informed on the progress the security services made.

THURSDAY

34

EEKHAUT WAS STARTLED BY the shrill ringing of his phone. He didn't like the sound but hadn't yet figured out how to change it into something more agreeable. Like a Beethoven symphony. He quickly looked around, but nobody was paying attention. It was the tone associated with Linda.

"Walter," she said.

He knew this was one of those moments when no intelligent reaction would be expected of him. "Mmm?" he uttered, at once realizing he would never win awards for being eloquent.

It didn't even sound as if he was happy to hear from her.

Fortunately, she chose to ignore all that.

"I just arrived in Madrid, Walter. Direct flight from Mombasa. Can you hear me?"

"Yes, I can."

"Were you asleep just now? Did I wake you?"

"What's the time over there?"

"Nine," she said, sounding somewhat confused. "In the morning."

"That's what we have here too," he said.

"Oh, I didn't realize you're at work."

"Never mind," he said. "Never mind. You can call me anytime. Glad to hear from you. Forgive the grumpy old man I've become, but I've been worried. Was worried. But happy again when I heard you're safe and all."

"Safe since we left Somalia, actually," she said. "I'm waiting for a connection to Amsterdam. Next flight with a seat available is not until tomorrow morning. Can't be helped. Tourists fleeing winter, I guess. So I'll have to hang around here at the airport all day, which is . . . Anyway, I'll be at Schiphol Airport by half past seven tomorrow. Morning, that is."

"I'll pick you up. You'll be exhausted."

He almost heard her smile. Despite everything she'd gone through. "Don't bother, Walter. I'll take the train. It's no problem."

"You have a pile of luggage. I'll pick you up."

"I have almost no luggage left. It's all gone, and anything that was left that I didn't want to bring home again, I gave away. I have some hand luggage. I'll take the train. I'll call you from Amsterdam station when I get there. Can you pick me up there? In a police car? One with flashing lights and a siren? I'd like that."

"I'll see what I can do."

"I know you'll do your best, Walter. Like you always do. Look, I'll tell you the whole story later, but my phone battery is low now, and I have to go look for a place to . . . you know."

Then she was gone. The phone was silent. He leaned back in his chair. The morning was almost silent except for some sirens in the distance. He was glad the African adventure was over. He was glad she was coming home.

Prinsen walked past his office, lost in thoughts. The young man noticed Eekhaut and entered.

Something was wrong, Eekhaut could see. He saw the deep creases in Prinsen's forehead. Something was eating at him. Maybe he'd just slept badly. He was losing sleep because of Eileen, but it didn't seem he was spending his night at orgies.

"Anything new to report?" Prinsen asked.

"We went to the villa where the Saudi was killed, and I witnessed the autopsy of the three female victims. Or more precisely, I was around for the autopsies. I went for a coffee, and the pathologist did his job."

"I've never been present at one," Prinsen said thoughtfully. "I want to keep it that way."

"You know how focused pathologists can get concerning their subjects."

"I heard," Prinsen said, his thoughts drifting elsewhere.

"We're supposed to see Dewaal in a minute, to coordinate what everybody has found out. You all right?"

"Yes, just a little tired, that's all."

Van Gils walked in. "Morning, all," he cheerfully said. "Seems like the worst of winter is behind us. Spring soon again."

Prinsen walked out.

Something is really wrong with that boy, Eekhaut thought. *This isn't his usual behavior. We can't do with that now. We need everybody at their best.*

35

THE CROOKED OLD WOMAN carefully deposited the tray with a pot of tea, two cups, saucers, sugar, milk, and cookies on the table in the parlor. "Anything more, ma'am?" she inquired, her voice feeble.

Ms. Simson looked up. "Thank you, Dottie. I'll be fine." Dottie left the room again, carefully avoiding the furniture. She had served in this household for something like seven decades, since she was a young girl, in this same house where the masters of the church had come and gone. This house, where in her lifetime no less than three generations of masters had plotted and schemed. Dottie had always been there with tea and cookies and the occasional kind remark about small and insignificant things, never taking part but always observing. She also knew all there was to know about Amsterdam, having many contacts in the extended neighborhood. The masters would occasionally consult her about restaurants or people with specific skills who could be trusted. These days, and for some years now, she seldom went out because of her rheumatism and her failing eyesight. She was, however, still the living memory of the church.

Dottie had served the old masters in the days of the traditional rites and sacrifices, in the days of hope and fire. She would have seen the letters exchanged between groups, probably written in code, but she would have known what sort of instructions these letters contained. And she read newspapers, fully knowledgeable of these terrible, terrible disasters that befell humanity. She had never uttered so much as a word in defense of the victims, never gone against the will of the masters. She was a mere servant girl who knew little of doctrine and politics.

Although at night, alone in bed, she wept because of the children.

Dottie had also survived the schism in the church. The old guard had disappeared, most of them too old to act and some of them suddenly dead in bizarre accidents. The new masters had discontinued the old ideology. No longer would people have to die. The change had not affected her position in the house. She was as loyal to her new masters as she had been to the old. Maybe she was relieved no people would be killed anymore. Maybe she no longer cried in her bed. But she never shared her thoughts on the matter.

"Oh, Dottie," Ms. Simson said before Dottie could fully disappear into the corridor. "When the visitor calls, admit him to the salon at once. And, Dottie, he does not speak Dutch."

"That's not a problem, ma'am," Dottie said. She spoke several languages other than Dutch.

Simson hoped the visitor wouldn't notice Dottie's hands trembling. Ms. Simson thought, *We're all getting on in years. Our generation will soon be gone. With us, whatever is left of the old church will disappear. Hopefully. We once were introduced into the church as it was then, a vengeful and terrible cult. And then, too horrified to continue the ways of the elders, we revolted and we changed it. But our enemies prevail. Those who still believe in the purification by fire, those still in the service of that cruel God, have treated many of us cruelly. If things go their way, we will be exterminated.*

This was a war, and there would be only one winning side.

The visitor was of a much younger generation. His name was Saeed Al-Rahman, and he was an Arab. He was one of those who would continue the new tradition of the church, and at the same time he was a devout Muslim. There was no contradiction in this. He was one of those Ms. Simson hoped would be the new masters of the church. He would honor the rituals of the new church once the elderly members were no longer able to uphold them. He was sent here by an old friend of the church, a senior Arab officer who had introduced Al-Rahman to the ritual years earlier.

It might not matter much what Johanna Simson and the other members of the church planned. The end of times was near. These were the last years of humankind and the universe. Then everything would return to the Creator. All sins would be forgiven to those in His service.

But still, it would be a good idea to make sure the church would function beyond 2020, in case the prophecy failed. As it had failed before. The end of this world had been predicted many times, as often as not by the masters of the church. The world was still here.

Who would, in the end, be the chosen ones? Not the heretics who were still murdering innocent people. Not the billions outside the true faith. Not the masses who never spared a thought to their place in the universe.

Dottie closed the door behind her. She would go prepare fresh tea for the visitor. Mint tea with lots of sugar. Johanna Simson remained alone in the salon.

Simson tried to meditate and think of nothing. She had not read the Holy Book in a long time, knowing large parts by heart. Having its message in her head.

We are all the children of the book, she thought. That's what the Arab general had said over the phone. How long ago had that been? A couple of weeks? He had spoken slowly and had used simple English sentences because he knew she wasn't familiar with the language. They shared the same convictions. The same fire burned deep in them, across the gulf of cultures and languages. The same certainties enlightened their paths.

"I will send help," he promised. But not right away, he regretted. Sending someone at once would arouse suspicion. All had to be prepared carefully. But suddenly, a suitable if dramatic opportunity presented itself. He would send her a man who would help her. Who would help her deal with Baphomet. The general spoke comforting words to her. *We will survive*, he told her. *We will attain the eternity we are longing for. It will happen.*

The bell rang. Johanna heard Dottie shuffling toward the front door. She heard her voice but could not understand the reply. Then, after another moment, the front door closed again. Dottie walked into the salon, a man behind her. Simson got up. The man was younger than she had expected. Mid-thirties at the most. This was a good thing, but she wondered if he would be strong enough to see this through. On his face, however, she saw the determination he would need to confront their enemies successfully.

She addressed him in English, as best as she could. "Gratefully we welcome you into our house, brother," she said, somewhat stiffly. A sentence used many times before, like an incantation. The language lent itself perfectly to formalities. She loved it, remembering having read the classics in that language.

Saeed Al-Rahman lowered his head respectfully. "It is an honor to be welcomed by you," he said, his voice like wind through summer corn. "I heard you have problems."

"There are many things bothering us," she acknowledged.

Dottie arrived with the fresh tea. Simson and the colonel sat down while Dottie poured two new cups.

"I arrive here not by coincidence," he said, glancing at the old woman for a moment, then returning his attention to Simson. "My presence is the result of numerous events we do not fully control."

"We're aware of that. Our mutual friend, whose sensible judgment we appreciate, has done a good job. You know about our problem. We share the same enemies. I hope you can deal with them. The hour of the last day is approaching."

"Ah, it is," Al-Rahman smiled and drank his tea. "This is why I am here."

"We rely on the younger generation to . . . sustain us during these end times," she said. She wasn't familiar enough with the language to precisely express her feelings, but he understood.

"We both know," he admitted, "that the prophecy doesn't refer to an exact date, despite what many seem to think. It is a rough indication of the End of Times, which will come at some point, but perhaps not right now. There is still time, time for a new advent of the church."

She hadn't expected him to start a philosophical discussion about the basic concept. But then, she had probably misunderstood his intentions and those of the man who had sent him all along. Anyway, she felt there was no time for discussion about fundamental issues, with the society hot on their heels.

"But then, all this might not be a pressing issue," the colonel continued, unaware of her confusion. "We must convince all members of the church to follow the new line set out these recent decades. The Society of Fire is now our main enemy, not the rest of humanity. We must destroy the society or none of us will be saved."

This will happen, Ms. Simson thought. *This is what is going to happen.*

36

EILEEN WAS SURE SHE couldn't escape from the room. She had explored every corner of it by the dim electric light coming from the corridor through a small cobwebbed window in the wall above the door. She had cried and begged, but there had been no reaction from her captors. There was an equally cobwebbed narrow horizontal window high on one of the other walls, but she couldn't reach it, and it would be too small for her to crawl through. She assumed nobody would be around to hear and help her either.

Finally, bleak morning light crept through the window. The room was chilly and damp, and she assumed it was partially underground, the window just barely above street level. Street? There seemed to be no street around, no noise of any kind, no people who would hear her scream for help. She had wrapped the blanket around her for comfort and for warmth but had not slept much. In addition to the cot, there was a small wooden table and a chair, both under the window, both old relics of better times. She would not try to stand on the table; it would not hold her weight.

Why was she here?

It wasn't about money. Nobody was going to pay her abductors anything. Maybe they would sell her off as a sex slave or something. Russia? One of the Arab countries? She knew it was stereotypical, but even so, it might be true.

She had awakened earlier, feeling vaguely nauseated and light-headed after having been sedated. She had been lying on the bed, the blanket over her, noticing the world was cold and still. Since then nothing had happened. She still wore her clothes, including her jacket, but her kidnappers had taken her purse, phone, keys, and everything else. On the table had been a large bottle of water, from which she had already drunk half. Soon she would need to go to the toilet. Then what?

A sudden knock at the door startled her. Why would a kidnapper knock? Two men entered, dressed in black, each wearing a balaclava. That was a good sign. They were keeping their faces hidden from her. At some point, they expected to let her go.

The second man carried a steel tray with a china plate, a mug, a glass, a battered steel coffeepot, bread, cheese, salami, and a bottle of fruit juice. In her current situation, all of those were luxuries. She was hungry. She could refuse the food, but that would be foolish.

"Why am I here?" she asked. She managed to keep her voice down and nonaggressive. She preferred to be seen as a victim.

The second man deposited the tray on the table, the first remained by the door. Neither of them seemed inclined to reply.

"Eat," the first man said. "Then we will let you clean yourself up." He sounded like he came from South Holland. Both men were white, she noticed. They didn't bother wearing gloves. Their hands were large, but not calloused.

"What's going to happen to me?" she demanded. Not that she expected an answer.

"It won't be long," the first man said. The second retreated to the corridor. It seemed nearly as dark and humid as the room. "Don't worry. Nothing bad will happen to you." He sounded cultured, not the sort of man you'd expect to kidnap a young woman for sadistic purposes. But then, she had no experience with that kind of man.

But that, of course, was not entirely true.

The first man left too and locked the door. She sat down at the table and inspected her breakfast. They had even brought her hot coffee. Not what you'd expect from ordinary kidnappers. She knew she would need energy. Against the cold. And against boredom. She ate, and she drank the fruit juice and coffee.

What could she do? Should she try to escape? There seemed no immediate way out. Not through the window. And the door looked sturdy. The funny thing was, they'd given her potential weapons: the tray, even a knife, however dull.

But the men had looked strong and confident.

She would wait this out. For now.

37

Alexandra dewaal had asked several officers from the Bureau to gather in the small conference room next to her office. The room offered a view toward the back of the building, showing windowless brick walls of surrounding office blocks and, further on, a bleak landscape of chimneys, steel, concrete, and tiled roofs of some of the older early nineteenth-century houses. No one had ever been seduced by the view, and most of the people present in the room ignored it. The windows didn't open, not to prevent people from jumping out, but because it had been cheaper to build and easier to secure.

Prinsen and De Vries were seated in a corner with their laptops. On the table at the far end, white cardboard boxes from the Vlaamsch Broodhuys* offered croissants, éclairs, chocolate rolls, and small fruit tarts, all introduced by Eekhaut weeks earlier and since then appreciated by the on-duty officers. Everyone present looked serious, thoughtful, waiting for the chief to arrive. Some whispered together about family matters, sports, political events, the financial crisis. Some gossiped or complained about the weather. They looked like an informal gathering in any sort of business. The walls were bare, no AIVD posters. Nobody carried a weapon, none wore a badge. Not even their conversations identified these people as police officers.

Dewaal walked in and closed the door behind her. She glanced at the dozen people as she would have observed a soccer team of twelve-year-olds. *That's basically what they are*, she often thought.

---

* Literally, Old South.

"Good morning," she said and sat down in the one unoccupied chair. "This meeting is about the Church of the Supreme Purification and its breakaway sect, the Society of Fire, as it's aptly named. We don't yet have a code name for this operation because only the people present are working on it so far. That means all of you. And I have no inspiration for a suitable name either. I refer you to the briefings you received yesterday or this morning and which all of you read immediately. We have reason to believe the threat posed by the society is much more serious than the one or two collective murders we've seen so far. I'm referring, of course, to what occurred in the Ardennes a month ago and the recent death of a Saudi prince and three women here in Amsterdam. Because of the nature of these crimes and the assumptions we're making, we decided to expand from the original small team. And that's where all of you come in."

She ignored the growing murmur. "So far, we have very few leads, except for one particular and rather alarming item. What else we have is mostly based on assumption and a few witness statements or tips. One of the victims of the Ardennes is a young man named Adriaan Basten. He worked for InfoDuct, dealing with financial matters."

She glanced at Eekhaut, who ignored her. "Some people with a similar profile disappeared around the same time Basten did," she continued, "coinciding with the Ardennes event. They may have been among the victims. We're looking in particular at two men, Brecht and Desmedt, who both worked for another company, TransCom, a company related to InfoDuct. We spoke to their boss, Jan Pieter Maxwell, who did not seem too concerned about their fate."

"Because he's a capitalist swine," Eekhaut added morosely. "He's not interested in his employees, couldn't care less what people who work for him do."

Dewaal ignored him. "We can't identify either man as one of the victims. But it's clear now that both of them had discovered certain, let's say, *dealings* by Maxwell, unsavory financial dealings. That may be a motive for their killing. As for the other incident, the Saudi prince, we have good reason to assume there is a link to the Ardennes: motive and modus operandi, mostly. The primary motive for that event may be that the Society of Fire is eliminating members of the church because of profound religious differences. But this could be partly combined with Maxwell's personal motives, to want to eliminate people who know too much about him and his finances. All of this, however, is still speculation."

"And of course," Eekhaut added, "everyone is waiting for the apocalypse."

"Yes," Dewaal said carefully, "let's not forget the apocalypse. Chief Inspector Eekhaut won't let us forget that. For those new to the subject, there is complete background information on all elements of the investigation—including the, ah, apocalypse theory."

"And there's the tip Van Gils received," Eekhaut urged her on impatiently.

"Coming to that. It's the thing that has us worrying the most. Van Gils received a tip about a previously unknown company, Real Estate Technologies, which recently acquired a tanker filled with five thousand gallons of highly explosive liquefied gas. We have reason to doubt a legitimate reason for this transaction."

"The strange thing is," Van Gils explained, "the company bought both the transporter and the gas itself."

"What's more," Dewaal continued, it's especially alarming that Real Estate Technologies is in fact a full subsidiary of TransCom."

Veneman, from the other side of the table, said, "What about that gas, Chief? What can it be used for?"

"Whatever it's normally used for, it's not something we want to see in the hands of people who have a penchant for mass killings," Dewaal said.

"Shouldn't we bring in this Maxwell and have a long conversation with him?"

"We have nothing substantive on him," Dewaal said. "We can't link him directly to the tanker or the Ardennes." She looked around the table. "At this time, we're not arresting anyone. We observe, we delve deeper into their affairs, we try to find people who can provide us with more information. We stay aware of the ticking clock. The problem is, we don't know how urgent our problem is."

"And what does the prosecutor have to say concerning a feasible strategy?" Eekhaut inquired. "Because that's what seems to be lacking: a strategy."

"I conferred with her this morning, and she agrees with our strategy."

"And what about Baphomet?" he continued.

"Baphomet?"

Eekhaut turned around to where Prinsen sat. "Remember, Nick, Johanna Simson talking about Baphomet as the leader of the Society of Fire all the way back to its inception twenty years ago? The man has a problem, and an old one, with the church and its new doctrine."

"All the members of both the church and the society seem to go only by those sorts of names," Prinsen said. "We don't yet have real names to match them to."

"I assume Simson knows Baphomet's real name," Eekhaut said. "She knows who he is. She knows much more than she wants us to believe. She reads the papers, and she probably has informers both inside and outside the church. She knows who's behind these murders."

"But she won't tell you," Veneman said.

"We have enough to confront her again—"

The office phone on the table buzzed. Veneman took the call. He listened, then said, "The chief? Yes, she's here. We're in a meeting. Who did you say?" He glanced at Dewaal, held the phone away from his ear. "There's a Saudi gentleman at reception downstairs, Chief. A colonel something. Needs to see you."

"Damn," Dewaal said. She got up. "Another problem announcing itself. All right, let's take a break. Have some coffee and a snack. I'll be back after I've seen him."

She walked down the hall, determined to ask the colonel not to interfere with the ongoing investigation. But she already knew he would ignore that. He had political support, and he would push his way in.

Colonel Al-Rahman was waiting at the reception desk. He was inspecting some of the posters on the walls, holiday posters with tropical beaches and views of the French Provence. They were purely decorative and had nothing to do with the AIVD. Dewaal had kept them. Sometimes people needed the illusion they didn't work for a security service.

He wore a suit of dark wool and held a black overcoat over his arm, looking like a junior diplomat.

"Colonel," she addressed him in English. "You wanted to see me? I'm in the middle of a staff meeting, and I'm afraid I cannot help you right now. Could you make an appointment for later today?"

"This is not a personal visit, Chief Commissioner," he said confidently. "I have been instructed by my superiors, my very high-ranking superiors, to assist with and participate in your ongoing investigation concerning the Society of Fire and everything else connected with them." He conjured a document out of his jacket pocket. "Of course, I have here permission to act on behalf of my government on Dutch soil. I am certainly not going to disturb whatever activities you have planned, so please continue as you see fit. However, since I do not speak Dutch, I will need a member of your staff to translate things for me, or at least give me a concise summary of the proceedings."

She wasn't going to let him participate in her investigation if she could avoid it. "I'm afraid, Colonel, none of my staff will be available for translating purposes. We're short-staffed as it is, and we have more than just this investigation. This is the Netherlands, where public services are always understaffed."

He smiled at her patiently, ignoring her objections. "I am not merely expressing my wishes, Chief, but also those of the head of AIVD, whose signature is at the bottom of this document. And that of the minister in charge. So I'm afraid I must insist. I can easily adjust to your organizational structure, as it seems to be less complicated than the agency I work for in my own country. I am a nuisance, I'm sure, but I will try to keep a low profile. I'm sure you do not want me around, but we both must comply with orders given to us, mustn't we?"

She merely glanced at the paper. Whether she wanted it or not, the colonel was now a member of her team. Her extended team. What could she use him for? He would be nothing more than an observer. She couldn't ask him to interrogate people. She wouldn't even think of asking him for his opinion.

But she was stuck with him.

"Well, Colonel," she said, "it seems you're in, then. If you come along, you can meet the rest of the team."

They took the stairs. When they entered the meeting room, a silence descended over those present. The colonel merely smiled, aware of being the cause of the silence. "Your attention, everyone," Dewaal said, in Dutch. "This is Colonel Al-Rahman of the Saudi police." She wasn't going to complicate things by mentioning the Mutaween, religious police, secret service, or whatever department this colonel belonged to. Someone might take offense or something. "He's here because of the Saudi prince, and he will be part of the extended investigation team. Eekhaut, can you give him a concise translation of whatever is said in here, and also later on?"

"Me?" Eekhaut said, surprised. "You want me to act as interpreter?"

She shot him a look, warning him not to take his objections too far. "You are, after all, our international liaison officer, aren't you? Between the AIVD and foreign intelligence services. Isn't that your job description? And your English is excellent. It would be a waste not to use one of your many talents."

Eekhaut wanted to say something more, but she cut him off, still in Dutch. "And keep a lid on it now. Go and stand next to the colonel so he can hear you. Now, where were we?"

Eekhaut cast a glance at the colonel, who smiled at him. *All right, I'll play along, for now.*

"You're my interpreter, Chief Inspector?" the colonel asked.

"I am," Eekhaut said, staying firmly on neutral ground.

"Delighted," the colonel said, as if he meant it.

Not really sure about that, Eekhaut thought, but he kept that to himself.

"Sorry to embarrass you," the colonel added.

"No, it's not a problem. Just . . ."

"The prince had many interests and friends. Especially in Europe. I am here to make sure his murderer is caught. It is as simple as that."

"So, they are sending a police *colonel* . . ."

"Actually," Al-Rahman corrected, "I was an army colonel, and then I got a job at the police, retaining my rank."

"Army?"

"Special units, operations, infiltration, weapons training, explosives, and so on." He smiled. "The really interesting stuff. Counterterrorism and such."

"Shall we continue?" Dewaal inquired.

"Fine with me," Eekhaut said. "And with the colonel."

Half an hour later the briefing ended. Dewaal stepped back into her office, along with Al-Rahman. The detectives had received their instructions and gone on their separate ways. Eekhaut had been keeping an eye on Prinsen, who had seemed absent all the time, his mind and attention elsewhere. He had hardly spoken. Eekhaut knew something was wrong.

Could it have been Prinsen who had leaked information to the press?

Prinsen got up from his desk and donned his overcoat. He left the building. Eekhaut watched him crossing the Amstelplein. This didn't seem like a lunch break. It was too early for a lunch break. Something was going on.

He took his own coat off the rack and followed Prinsen.

38

"This is totally inadequate," the voice over the phone said. The man sounded annoyed, as if Prinsen had failed his expectations.

And he had.

"That's about all that was discussed," Prinsen said. He stood in a drafty phone booth where every surface sported scabrous messages or colorful stickers advertising dope or porn. "Really, it was. We have to be vigilant, we need to go through the files again, we must be ready for action. That's the drift of it. Then the colonel appeared." He hoped the man on the other end of the line would believe him. Was he good at lying? At pretending? Did he sound convincing enough?

"What colonel?" At once the voice sounded suspicious. The voice of the anonymous man who claimed he had Eileen. "What colonel are you talking about? Where does he fit into all this?"

"His name is Al-Rahman, and he works for the Saudi secret service or something. He's investigating the murder of the prince." He assumed his caller would know what prince.

"You're not all that well organized over there, are you?" the voice said, now with a trace of malign amusement. "But we need more coop-eration from you, buddy. Your girlfriend is cold and hungry. She'll stay that way, and maybe things'll get worse for her if you don't come up with better information. She's counting on you, Prinsen. And so are we. You got that?"

"If you hurt her—"

"Oh, cut the stupid clichés. Nothing will happen to her. We've all watched the same movies, and we know what our parts are, right? Mine is to threaten you. Yours is to comply with our demands. Her role is innocent victim. Got it?"

"I can only tell you what I know. They don't share everything with me."

"Really? They don't trust you? There's a certain irony in that, isn't there? Your chief doesn't like you? You get the chores nobody wants? Cheer up, Prinsen. You're young, and you'll get far. Show some ambition, dammit!"

"They know about the gas tanker," Prinsen said.

"The tanker," the voice repeated, neutral. Not giving anything away.

"They know about the link between Real Estate Technologies and TransCom."

"Do they now?"

"That's all they know. The rest is guesswork. They wonder why Real Estate Technologies needs highly flammable gas in such amounts. And the tanker to transport it."

"What else?"

"That's it."

There was a short silence. Then the man said, "You hear any names mentioned?"

"What names?"

"That's what I want to hear from you, dummy."

"No. No names."

"Don't fool with me, Prinsen. Think about the nice girl enjoying our hospitality."

"That's all I know."

Suddenly, the line went dead. Prinsen, taken aback, glanced around. He had been absorbed with the call and hadn't been paying attention to his surroundings. He now felt as if someone were watching him. Frederiksplein, where he stood, was almost deserted. Which was unusual, even in winter. Apart from a few elderly pensioners dressed in many layers of clothing and a bunch of young people who apparently didn't have to be in school.

Still, he knew someone was watching him.

He glanced around, but nobody seemed interested in him.

He hadn't spoken the truth just now. Well, only part of the whole truth. He had to assume they—whoever they were—wouldn't find out what he had kept from them. He was going to feed them bits and pieces, just enough to keep them occupied but nothing that would seriously jeopardize the investigation. He couldn't risk that. Couldn't risk them finding out, either. He was going to give them the impression that the criminal investigation wasn't advancing in any meaningful direction.

But he was balancing on a tightrope. Eileen was in danger. He wouldn't risk her life. He would sacrifice everything for her. Maybe he would even kill for her. He had no guarantee her captors would let her go, whatever information he fed them.

He left the phone booth.

They expected to hear from him again within a few hours. He had to sneak out of the office once more, which would at some point make him suspect. But they wanted him to use the booth, one of the last of its kind in Amsterdam, and phone a mobile number.

He turned around.

Eekhaut stood in front of him. Hands in the pockets of his coat and patiently waiting for a reaction from Prinsen. He knew. Eekhaut knew what Prinsen had been up to.

"Nick?" he said. "Is there something you need to share with me?"

They sat at a table in the back of Café Bouwman and drank coffee with a glass of brandy for medicinal reasons, at Eekhaut's insistence. "After all, police officers drink," he said. "It's a well-known fact they do. A law of nature. And laws of nature cannot be skirted. Personally, I'd choose a beer anytime, but in this case, I guess you need something stronger. The coffee, by the way, is just an excuse."

Prinsen stared at his now half-empty glass of brandy. "I'm sorry," he said. And then he realized what he had said. *Sorry?* What did that mean? Sorry he was caught? Sorry he was betraying his fellow officers?

"Your regret means next to nothing under the circumstances, Nick," Eekhaut said. "But please, do enlighten me. Who were you calling? And what exactly did you tell them? And why are you leaking information to the press? Don't tell me it's for money."

Prinsen looked up, surprised. Eekhaut, taking this to be proof of his guilt, went on: "Aunt Alexandra isn't going to forgive you, my friend. She hates it when the papers print stuff we want to shield from public view. What the hell were you thinking, Nick?"

"You've got it wrong, Walter."

"Do I? You sneak out and use public phone to—?"

"Not to the press."

Eekhaut sat back, sipped his brandy, and waited. "I'm waiting," he said.

"I can't tell you," Prinsen said. Although he knew he had few options. None actually. But, still, Eileen's safety was his primary if not his sole concern.

Eekhaut leaned toward Prinsen. "Nick, you have no choice. Well, you actually have two choices. Either you tell me what the hell is going on here, or I kick your ass all the way to Dewaal's office and you tell *her*. What's it going to be?"

"It's about Eileen."

"Eileen? What's Eileen got to do with this?"

"She has been kidnapped."

Eekhaut sat back again. He suddenly felt cold. This was any police officer's nightmare: your family being threatened by criminals. Or the family of one of your colleagues. There used to be some sort of honorary agreement between cops and criminals, not to touch the family. This worked so long as both parties occupied a common territory. A city, for instance. Once outsiders moved in, the whole idea about honor went out the window. Eekhaut had seen it happen in Brussels and Antwerp, and he knew it had happened elsewhere as well. The old consensus between the law and the criminal world evaporated when the Russians arrived, or the Bulgarians, or the Koreans. They had their own codes of conduct, but their codes didn't include the fair treatment of local cops and their families.

"Not the press then," Eekhaut said.

"No," Prinsen said. "She was kidnapped. By people who want to know everything, every detail of our case against the Society of Fire. They want me to keep them informed. On a daily basis if not more frequent." He peered over Eekhaut's shoulder, then fixed his gaze again on his fellow officer. His voice trembled. "A cult that burns people alive, Walter. What was I to do?"

Eekhaut was glad no one was around who could overhear them. Prinsen had tears in his eyes; he was desperate, which was wholly understandable. Eekhaut felt terribly sorry for the kid, but there was no time for sentiment. Some sort of action was needed.

"What have you told them just now?"

"As little as possible. That we found out about the firm buying the tanker and the gas. But I didn't mention suspects' names. They don't know we're trying to link Maxwell to the whole affair. I try to tell them as little as possible, but I can't risk telling outright lies."

"All right. So, they use you as a source of information."

"That tanker and the gas, that's probably some big thing for them. A main element in their plan. They have no reason to hurt her. She's not the enemy."

She's not, Eekhaut thought. But neither were all those thousands of people the church killed over the decades.

An awkward silence hung, almost physically, in Dewaal's office. Eekhaut told the story, while Prinsen remained silent throughout. Dewaal listened, not commenting at all. Not even a question. Not even a request for clarification.

Which, to Eekhaut, was not a good sign at all.

"There we are then," he finally said. "That's how it stands."

"I'm not really sure," Dewaal said, after a moment.

"You're not really sure about what exactly, Chief?" Eekhaut said. "There's no two ways about it. We cannot risk Eileen's life. The kidnappers should be left in the dark about . . . well, about Nick informing us. And we need to keep providing them with selected and edited information."

"There are numerous problems that might arise, Walter," Dewaal said. "For one thing, he might not be the only source they have inside our team. Have you thought of that?"

"No, I hadn't," Eekhaut admitted.

"So, we must be careful about what we feed them, while at the same time making sure Eileen isn't harmed. And believe me, both of you, I want Eileen safe and alive as much as you do. But we will have to take several precautions."

"They have all the cards," Eekhaut said. "The only things we have so far are hypotheses."

"Let's take the war to the enemy, then," Dewaal proposed. "Let's turn Maxwell inside out and see what he's made of. His personal life, the companies he works for, and those who work for him. Meanwhile, Nick will continue to provide his buddies on the other side with information, but only after the fact. He can concoct some story about being kept out of the loop, where certain things are concerned."

"We might find nothing on Maxwell."

"I don't know about the urgency of their apocalyptic agenda, but they haven't run the risk of buying a tank full of explosive stuff just to sit on it for months or even years. And when they're in a hurry, they will start making mistakes. Actually, kidnapping Eileen might have been a mistake." Dewaal glanced at Prinsen. "What's the number you're supposed to call?"

"It's a prepaid number," he said.

"Of course it is. And I would suspect these are pros employed by Maxwell and his ilk, not members of their own tribe. I'll instruct Van Gils to dive into his contacts all over Amsterdam and see if anyone knows about—don't shake your head, Nick. Van Gils might be a bit of a buffoon at times, but he's good at what he does. And he knows the local lowlifes like no one else."

"Chances are she was kidnapped by members of the society."

"Probably. But I want to look at this from all angles. All right with that, Nick?" Dewaal's desk phone buzzed. She picked it up and said her name. She listened intently. Then she said, "Just a second," and to Eekhaut and Prinsen, "I've got the minister on the line. Get lost, both of you. He'll tell me what kind of disgrace I am to the profession, and I don't want you near me when he does."

The two detectives left the office and closed the door behind them. "Put him through," Dewaal said.

"Chief Commissioner," the voice on the other end of the line said. "I'm calling you because of the Church of the Supreme Purification. As you may recall, this is not the first talk we've had on the subject."

"No, Your Excellency. That's correct. We also talked about the society—the infamous one we spoke about a few days ago."

"And today again I want you to tell me about your case. I keep getting anxious calls from my colleague in Foreign Affairs. He belongs to another political party than me, and, well, he is all too keen to express his discontent with the way things are run here. He's proposing, no, *threatening*, to express his opinions to the press. His impression is that we're not really doing what it takes to solve one particular crime."

Dewaal gazed up at the ceiling of her office. "We're currently investigating a number of very promising leads, sir. We're making progress, but the case is complex. It's linked to other cases I mentioned earlier. And we must proceed with a certain caution so as not to alarm the public. Or the adversary, for that matter."

"This is not what I need to hear from you, Chief. There are always leads, isn't that how it is supposed to work? It's a sort of Holy Grail with you people. When this goes public, I need something a lot better than leads. I want names, faces, and above all, arrests."

"Oh, names and faces we might have, Excellency. But we have no proof to link them to the crimes in question."

"In other words, you have nothing. You haven't been able to stop the killers from killing some more, including an important Saudi diplomat."

"And three Dutch girls," Dewaal added brusquely. No longer trying to sound amiable.

"Nobody, really nobody cares about three whores, Chief," the minister said, hoarsely. "They found themselves where they weren't supposed to be, doing things they weren't supposed to do either. Whatever. The Saudis, Chief. They're angry because we seem to be sitting on our hands. And for reasons you might better appreciate, I do care a lot about their feelings."

"With your permission, sir," Dewaal said dryly, "I personally don't care about the Saudi royal family or their diplomats. If their horny, adulterous nephew couldn't keep his dick in his pants—or whatever

234

he was wearing at the time—and needed three underage girls at the same time, then his worried relatives should have given him adequate protection. Maybe kept him at home. They have whores there, don't they? Probably not: they want to retain their sanctimonious . . . Well, whatever, *sir*. At this precise moment, my only real concern is the safety of the Dutch people. Because what we know right now sir, or what we don't know, is that the Society of Fire might be planning some big event, a major-scale barbecue perhaps, one that might eclipse all previous sacrifices they've organized."

"Commissioner!"

"It's *Chief* Commissioner, actually, sir, with all due respect. If Your Excellency is really concerned about his political career, you would do better to let us do our job. Otherwise, Your Excellency will soon need to explain to the rest of the Netherlands why the government failed to prevent a disaster of truly apocalyptic proportions."

She slammed the phone down. *Now there's my career going down the drain. Whatever.*

The minister didn't call back. He was a politician. He would hate her for this, but he would be too cautious to risk his own hide.

He would wait this out. If things went south, it would be the commissioner's fault. Chief commissioner. Former chief commissioner at that point.

But in the end, even if things were resolved without too much damage, she would come up for evaluation, and she would pay the price for her insubordination.

She opened the door. "Eekhaut, Prinsen, in my office."

They hurried inside.

"I need everybody and I mean everybody," she said, "in here early tomorrow morning. We're going to screen Maxwell and his companies to the bare bones. I'll ask Apostel for search warrants. And, if we need it, for an arrest warrant for Maxwell himself. But discreetly. No press. Clear? And as far as Eileen is concerned, Nick, we *will* find her."

39

"How many people will be available?" Maxwell spoke to himself in the full-length mirror, a precious heirloom that had belonged to his great-aunt, of whom he knew little other than that she had been vain. He repeated the question but with slightly different emphasis. "How many people do we have available?" He grinned broadly at his reflection. "How much people?"

He shrugged. It didn't come out well. It sounded like he was talking to the board of directors of one of his companies. He sounded like a manager asking for employment figures.

Which would be all right in front of board members, but not here. Not under the circumstances he had in mind. The Society of Fire was not a business. Its foundation was a spiritual one, based in faith and faith alone, not a desire to turn a profit.

He tried again. "About how many supporters do we have at our disposal, Courier?" He raised his head somewhat more, thrust his chin forward. That looked better, more commanding. "How many support-ers shall be willing to help us, Courier, in these dire times?"

No, that came out even worse. It sounded overacted. Not authen-tic enough. Why would these so-called supporters merely be willing to help? This was a serious matter, a matter of obligation. This was, after all, their guarantee of a catharsis that had not been made possible before. They should all come running, being given this ultimate chance for redemption. He, Baphomet, offered them an entry to eternity, and why would they not grasp that chance? They would, of course.

Perhaps the question would be unnecessary. He should simply assume all members of the Society of Fire would follow him, without reservation. When he explained the project to them—the project that had been set in motion some time ago and to which he was adding the final changes. They would follow him unconditionally, without asking questions. They would simply know it was to be grandiose and historical.

He grinned again at his reflection in the mirror. A world out there would be subordinated to the mercy of God, while he and his troops stormed the final hills on their way to eternal salvation. Stormed them without mercy.

Nothing would stand in their way.

No one would come between him and the certainty that he was one of the very few chosen ones. So much had already been achieved and in such a short time. He was not going to wait much longer to make sure he was attaining the most advanced degree of purification. In light of what the church in its former incarnation had achieved, he was still a minor figure, but that was soon going to change.

He stepped back from the mirror to better see himself. Then he walked to the door that opened into the hallway. He switched off the lights in the room behind him. Cold light fell on him from a few dimmed lamps in the hallway and from the garden. He walked down the hallway and opened another door to a larger room with sets of doors leading to other parts of the building.

He called out, "Metagogeus!"

The man appeared as if magically summoned from the shadows. "Baphomet," the man said.

"Is anyone there?"

"Yes, Baphomet, they all are."

"And where's Courier?"

"He's in the garden too. He seems to have a penchant for frozen plants."

"Oh, does he now? Well, I always expected something poetic from Courier. Can't blame him. We'll give him some leeway, and perhaps we should admit more poetry into our lives as well. Come on, let's join them all."

They walked into the garden, where torches and candles made a faint attempt at chasing the resident shadows. The smell of burning charcoal hung in the air, a special touch Baphomet had arranged. He needed the atmosphere to be right on this special occasion. These people needed to be impressed with the atmosphere, the light, the smell. That was why he used an almost archaic language when he addressed them. It was part of the tradition.

"Courier," he called out. All present looked up at him.

Courier stepped forward. He wore a simple wool suit and a sweater underneath. "Baphomet?"

"Will all true believers follow us?"

That, he was now sure, was the correct phrasing. Those who did not follow him would not in any sense be true believers. They would, as of today, be excluded from the future. They would spend eternity in the darkness of some personal hell, as would those who had doubted him openly in recent months. With some of those, he had dealt appropriately already.

A sacrifice was all the more sensible when you simultaneously deal with your opponents.

"All true believers will unconditionally follow you, Baphomet," Courier said stiffly. "Precede us, and all will follow. Enlighten our path, as you have done for so many years now."

That's exactly right, Baphomet mused. Enlighten their path. Courier knew exactly what that meant, and he knew the appropriate things to say under these circumstances.

"Friends, companions of the fire!" Baphomet called out. "All those present here will, as of the day after tomorrow, possess the certainty they will finally be cleansed. As such, they will be properly prepared for the final stage, without fear for the choices God will make at the end of times."

A few of the companions glanced at each other, but none commented.

"We have planned a great sacrifice for the day after tomorrow, companions," Baphomet continued. "It will be unprecedented. It will be the last and most definitive catharsis we have been waiting for. A sacrifice that will bewilder and horrify the world but that will take us up to the lowly place on the right side of God. And when the final hellfire descends on the whole of humanity, very soon, we will be the only ones saved from eternal damnation."

"But how does Baphomet know," the blond woman inquired, "that this one sacrifice will be enough? Does Baphomet have a direct link to God? Enlighten us further, Baphomet."

He had known dissidence would be unavoidable. He had expected it from her. She looked tense, afraid, but determined to question his authority. Determined, out of fear, or perhaps out of stupidity.

"No one dares to speak the words of God or claim to be a speaker in his name, sister," Baphomet said loudly. "But I reflect solely on the tradition of the former church, a tradition we are continuing. We all know and recognize the importance of the ritual in that tradition. All the past sacrifices have been, in many a sense, limited in scope. Often, if not always, the outside world was unaware of our involvement, and our predecessors kept it that way to avoid detection. The situation has changed. We step into the open, and our message will be heard by all. We can only attain the highest goal by exploring our possibilities to the fullest. This is what is happening now. Within this context, I urge those of faith to follow me."

Several of the companions cast angry glances at the woman. But, stubbornly, she would not back down. "I think," she said, "we should all have a say in this."

"*A say*," Baphomet repeated. "It sounds like you want to *interpret* the message I am conveying to you all. We do not *interpret* messages of a divine nature. We *act* upon them. We implore the mercy of God, and as such, we are merely his children, begging for His forgiveness. For acting as such, we will be redeemed."

Several of the companions spoke up and silenced the woman's reaction.

Baphomet stretched out his arms. "But if these companions deem, we should postpone the sacrifice . . ."

Several of the companions now cried out: *No! No!*

Baphomet addressed the woman again. "Sister, do you lack faith and courage to participate? We will then release you from your obligations."

The woman looked stunned. "No, Baphomet, that is not what I had in mind. I merely wanted to have a discussion about certain fundamental principles."

She was again drowned out by angry reactions.

Baphomet raised his arms to quiet them down. "Brothers and sisters, Companions of the Fire. In two days, all your doubts will vanish. Will we take that final step in unity?"

All cried out in agreement.

After the faithful had gone inside where sandwiches and wine were served, Baphomet had taken Courier aside. "I am tired of ignorant dissidence," he said. "This woman is not an asset to our cause. Keep an eye on her, and make sure she doesn't cause us trouble. Both inside and outside the society."

"I might suggest a more definitive solution," Courier said.

Baphomet shook his head. "I am fully in favor of such solutions, but time is short and we have other and more pressing concerns. Planning has reached its final phase."

"Metagogeus has acquired the passes needed," Courier said. "We have some faithful working security on the premises, which made things easy. Tomorrow we'll arrange the technical details, after which all is ready for the sacrifice."

"Nothing must go wrong," Baphomet insisted. "There's only this one opportunity."

"Nothing will go wrong, Baphomet. I will make sure of that."

40

SOME NINE HUNDRED MILES south of there, Linda sat on an uncomfortable chair in her hotel room. The room was dark. She had opened the curtains and looked down on the moving lights of Madrid, thirteen floors below her. The improbable, intangible glow of the metropolis seemed to her like the virtual projection of a world that had no right to exist. It was a strange, almost alien vertical world, estranged from nature. She had been living in its opposite—a wild, dry, horizontal planet.

She brought her right hand to her forehead, where too many thoughts fought for her attention. This had to stop, but it wouldn't. Although she would have to arrive at the airport early tomorrow morning, she didn't want to lie down and sleep. Not yet at least. There was too much to think about, and these thoughts wouldn't go away.

There was the African project. The whole team had been evacuated by the Kenyan soldiers. In a hurry, as if they feared all would be swallowed by the sands and the desert. Lieutenant Odinga had refused to give any explanation. Orders, he said. Orders to evacuate everyone.

And what about the Saudi gentleman? Who was he? Odinga didn't know or didn't want to say.

No real explanation had been given as to the reasons the whole project had been abandoned. But she had seen what remained of the camp after the storm, with a few hundred people, too old or too sick to move, left behind after the exodus of the able-bodied and young. These people still needed help, but most of the equipment had been lost. One of the doctors observed, "We're no longer useful here," and he left it at that.

The troops were no longer staying either, since there was no use for them. Perhaps they would be moved to other camps.

A single storm had erased so many hopes.

She was stunned by the efforts undertaken to get the whole team out of the desert and out of Somalia. They had been picked up by an aircraft on what remained of the airstrip close to the former camp and were flown directly to Mombasa. At that airport, on their arrival, air-conditioned habitations—refitted shipping containers—had been placed at their disposal, with real showers, real toilets, a café, and a pizzeria.

She tried to remember how long ago she had left behind such luxuries.

Little time was allowed for her to acclimate. A short while later she was on a flight to Madrid in clothes provided by the military. She had almost no luggage left, just an extra set of clothes and underwear. Nothing material seemed to matter anymore. She could have bought things in Madrid but didn't. She wanted to get back home, to Amsterdam, as soon as possible. Everything was confusing to her right now. A hotel room high over the city. A shower with hot water. Room service. A room in which thousands of people had lived previously and many more would live afterward. A city that didn't need sleep. A world connected by airplanes and internet. It had only been a few months since she had left all that behind, and already she felt estranged.

She hadn't turned on the television, knowing she wasn't ready for this world.

She was thinking about Walter. She was thinking about her impulse to create some space between them. Space and time. She had needed both to appraise their relationship. She wanted to find both space and time in Somalia, but things turned out differently. She could ask for another assignment but realized she no longer wanted to postpone a decision about Walter. About her and Walter.

What sort of relationship did they have? It had been based not on passion but rather on curiosity. It had been based on respect. He was old enough to want to take any relationship slowly. She was curious about him but still knew so little. They had never really spoken about what this relationship meant. Was he in love with her? Perhaps he was, in that strange and almost boyish way of his. Was she in love? Not really. Although she wasn't sure what exactly her feelings for him were.

Walter hadn't asked for anything other than her presence. They had frequented the Absinthe bar, had been to movies, took walks in the center of Amsterdam with autumn turning into winter. They had talked about books but hardly about family and even less about his career or hers. They had talked about a lot of things but seldom private stuff. It was a sort of relationship, and yet it was not.

Then she told him about her opportunity. Doctors Without Borders. Somalia. Leaving her job.

It had seemed like the most natural thing to do—put their relationship, such as it was, on hold and move out for a while.

He didn't try to talk her out of it. She wondered about that.

Now, she was on her way back. Sooner than expected. Sooner than *she* had expected. She had no idea what *his* expectations were.

And Madrid was surely not going to provide any answers.

41

Van gils had gotten it. Unobtrusive, the chief had said. Walking the streets and into bars, but discreetly. She confided in him. None of the other detectives knew about Eileen's abduction except for Prinsen and the Belgian. And it was supposed to stay that way.

Prinsen's girl kidnapped! He remembered her as he had met her briefly in connection with a previous case. The girl had endured quite a lot, the things she had gone through. And now, kidnapped. He could blame Prinsen for getting her into trouble, but it probably—as far as he knew—wasn't his fault.

But this idea, him going around to bars and cafés, trying to find out who knew anything about her kidnappers, that was a laugh. He hadn't said that much to Dewaal; she wouldn't have listened anyway. Ten years ago, he would have had his finger firmly on the pulse of this city. He would know what was going on in the streets and in the minds of the local crowd. Today, he no longer had his fingers anywhere near that pulse. He still had friends and occasionally foes he could talk to, but this was no longer the same as it had been.

The ones that would still talk to him were of an older generation.

He slowly walked through De Jordaan, the formerly proletarian neighborhood, now the new place for the new kids, a quickly gentrifying area with small houses and apartments and corner stores and old pubs. Small fashion boutiques had taken over grocers and mom-and-pop stores, selling outrageous clothes and accessories, secondhand design items, and old toys as well as homemade pies and health food.

After ten in the evening, it was still a nice place to have a drink and expect a good conversation.

Like in Rick's Bar.

"Bloody hell," Rikkert admitted, not even suppressing a yawn while simultaneously stroking his beard. He was an old hand at neighborhood gossip, an old mainstay of De Jordaan. Although somewhat younger than Van Gils, he had known this part of Amsterdam before the gentrification. And he still had his own bar. "You're still at it, Van Gils? Trying to amend or whatever? There's always going to be injustice in this world. And crime. We try to avoid crime now, these days. But it's going to be around forever."

"I'm a cop," Van Gils explained simply.

"You're asking 'bout men who might have kidnapped a girl? What sort of question is that? This isn't Colombia or Mexico or wherever they kidnap people for money."

"She wasn't kidnapped for money," Van Gils said. "And I didn't ask around, either."

"Yeah, and I'm the most discreet of bartenders, that's my reputation."

Rikkert was certainly discreet, or Van Gils wouldn't have been so direct.

"Nobody kidnaps anymore, Van Gils. Too much risk, not enough gain. There are the perverts, the pedophiles, and the gangs that pick up girls from the street, the girls that are lost and scruffy and have no place to go, but that's not what you have in mind, I guess."

"No. These guys would kidnap on order."

"Like, 'I need a girl this size and color, get me one'?"

"Something like that. In this case, a specific girl. And she's twenty, not underage."

Rikkert thought this over. "Some Russians might do that."

"Had enough of them Russians," Van Gils said. They all had. Even in De Jordaan. With the upwardly mobile young people moving in, things had changed rapidly, the dealers moving out, working people moving out. Although the new crowd wouldn't shy away from hard drugs for recreational use.

"How much time you got?"

"Not much. I need info tonight."

"Tonight? Like there's no tomorrow, eh? Well, things are not moving that fast anymore, Van Gils. The Chechens are in on the game as well. Moved out of Antwerp, coming in here. Not in De Jordaan, though."

"Chechens."

"They're worse than the Russians. Have known nothing but war all their lives. Why don't you drop by the Dead Sailor? You don't have old friends there anymore? It's a more likely place for this sort of information. But be careful. Your police ID isn't going to protect you against the Chechens."

The Dead Sailor wasn't a tavern for sailors but for people working in municipal services, mostly. Bus drivers, sanitation workers, maintenance, and so on.

"I'll give it a try," Van Gils said. The Dead Sailor was two streets down. He finished his beer and stepped out in the cold. The Dead Sailor was a busy place. He hesitated before entering. This was his seventh pub. He wasn't concerned about the expenses—the boss would take care of those. However, his wife would object to him being out this late. And returning with alcohol on his breath. He had promised her, a while ago, he was done with pubs. And alcohol.

He walked into the Dead Sailor and quickly got rid of his overcoat, as the place was hot and crowded. He would have a final beer, ask around a bit, carefully, and only if he met someone from the old crowd. He glanced at his watch. Quarter past ten. He ordered a beer, got it, paid for it, and walked away from the bar.

A powerful hand gripped his upper arm. "Van Gils," a deep voice said, sounding neither surprised nor happy, just registering his presence. A man much taller than himself. Van Gils looked up. This was not merely a man but a mountain of meat and bones and muscles who could have crushed him and probably had crushed quite a few people in bars, here in Amsterdam and all over the world.

"Sjaakie," Van Gils said. Not exactly the man he had hoped to bump into. Sjaakie had been big and imposing since childhood, or at least those were the rumors. He had worked in a great variety of places and jobs, mostly because of his size and nastiness. Occasionally he had worked for local mobsters, being the sort of bodyguard nobody was going to ignore. Van Gils had booked him twice for assault, and both times Sjaakie (whose name was a diminutive of Jacques, which happened to be his real first name, to everyone's surprise) had come without any fuss, as if the police simply had the right to arrest him.

Sjaakie had one redeeming quality: he was not vindictive. Van Gils had merely done his job by arresting him, as Sjaakie had merely done his by beating people up. This was the foundation for the respect both parties had for each other, on the one side the unarmed detective and on the other the imposing mountain of a man.

The man emitted a deep gurgling sound, which Van Gils knew was his way of laughing. "You still remember me, Van Gils? It has been a while."

"You're not the sort of person one is likely to forget, Sjaakie. How much time did you spend inside?"

"A year and a half in all. No problem, Van Gils. Nobody bothered with me. You still a cop?"

"Yes."

"No pension yet? You still on the street?"

"No pension yet," Van Gils said. "You want a beer?"

"Sure, why not. You're here officially?"

"I am."

"Ah." A big fist clutched the new beer. "I heard you moved up to . . . whatever it is you moved to. Great to hear. Now you still come to these bars? Missing us?"

"Sometimes I need to talk to the old crowd. Hear about what happens in the city. And you're probably the man I should listen to."

"Sjaakie knows everything," the mountain admitted.

"Can we sit somewhere where we can have a chat discreetly?" Although Sjaakie would never really be unobtrusive.

"Well now, mister detective. Would I want to be seen talking to you? I have to consider my reputation. Well, if you insist. There's a table free in the corner. Keep those beers coming, and I'll keep the news coming."

There would not be much privacy, even in the corner, but with all the noise, they wouldn't be overheard. "Young woman, twenty, kidnapped and held somewhere, to exert pressure on a colleague of mine," Van Gils said. "But keep this under your hat."

"What sort of thing is he working on, your colleague?"

"You read about these people in the Ardennes, burned?"

To the amusement of many, Sjaakie's face could manage a wide variety of facial emotions, but this time if showed only revulsion. "Read about it," he said. "Pretty fucked-up shit. And now they pick a girl off the street?"

"Professional guys, I guess."

"There aren't many who would do this," Sjaakie said. "I heard about three men interested in a building with a basement they could use for a while. Isolated, too. Would that be something?"

"Could be. Did they find the building?"

"Friend of mine rents these things out, even if they don't really belong to him, you know what I mean?"

"Where?" Van Gils said, although he suspected it was a long shot. Still, it was the most promising thing he'd heard all evening.

"You know where Bickersgracht is? At the Westerdok?"

Some place around the harbor. "I do. One of those places we'd be keen to visit on an evening like this. Us and Customs."

"You won't find much. Been unused for ages. But that's where they got a place all to themselves. I don't have names or nothing."

"We're talking three men?"

"Maybe. I could ask around."

"No, don't, Sjaakie."

"Was that helpful?"

"It might be. Much appreciated. Another beer?"

FRIDAY

42

JUST BEFORE LINDA'S PLANE took off from Madrid, she called Eekhaut, waking him at three thirty in the morning. She would arrive at Schiphol Airport around six. She only had hand luggage, and she would be in Amsterdam Central Station no later than seven thirty.

"Good thing you still have your passport," he said, trying to get fully awake. "But I can pick you up at the airport."

"I don't want you to drive all the way to Schiphol."

"Early like that? There'll be almost no traffic." Although he knew that would probably not be the case for the return trip.

"I hardly have any luggage. Pick me up in Amsterdam."

By seven fifteen he had parked the unregistered police vehicle in front of the Amsterdam Central station. He had picked up the car earlier from the underground parking garage below the office. It had a discrete AIVD logo on the windscreen, so a parking guard would leave it alone.

He entered the busy station. He was still fifteen minutes early, so he got himself a coffee, which turned out to be worse than the ones at the office. Nevertheless, it was hot and caffeinated, so he drank it. He used to be a morning person, but lately he needed caffeine to start the day. And a decent breakfast as well. This morning he had neither. He hadn't slept after her call.

Finally, the train from Schiphol was announced, and he hurried to the platform. Passengers got off, most of them with suitcases. He spotted Linda at once. She waved. She looked different, he noticed, but exactly as he would have expected. A long trip, a stay in a totally different environment. Where things were done differently than in the Netherlands. Somalia. Africa. She wore casual clothes that didn't suit or fit her. That didn't suit the Linda he had known.

They embraced and kissed and embraced again.

He looked her over. Carefully. She smiled. "Is that grime or do you have a tan?"

She laughed. "It might be grime. I can't remember sunbathing. The hotel in Madrid had a functioning shower, but I guess I couldn't rinse off weeks of dirt." She held up her bag. "This is all I have left. I need some new clothes, Walter, but not right away."

"You have to tell me everything. Every detail."

"I will. But not here. I want to go to my apartment. I want to sit on my own couch. I want a decent Dutch breakfast, if such a thing exists, and I want to talk to you. How much time do you have?"

"For you? All the time we need. But Dewaal urgently needs us in the office by ten. Crisis meeting. Really bad shit going on."

"Aren't there crises all the time? I didn't get the chance to follow the local news."

"I'll tell you later. It's confidential anyway. Most important is that you're back. I'll take you home so you can have a decent shower, and I'll make you some breakfast. We can catch up later today."

"I'm still in shock, Walter. From all that happened over there and from the sudden adjustment to civilization."

"I imagine things are very different over there."

"You have no idea." He really had no idea, and she couldn't blame him. She had gone there with misconceptions about how life would be.

She tossed her travel bag into the back of the car, and they drove off.

"What went wrong?" he wanted to know.

"There was a huge storm," she said. "Something not even the locals seemed familiar with. The end of the world, almost. Afterward, the camp was gone, and so was most of our equipment. The soldiers got us out, in the end. There was no sense in remaining since the refugees had left the area."

"Soldiers?"

"Part of an African peacekeeping force, Kenyans. United Nations mandate. I don't know if the dead were buried. We were ordered out at once."

"And no one stopped the refugees when they fled?"

"It was chaos, Walter. We couldn't. And the soldiers weren't going to keep them there either. Everything was simply gone. Everything we had set up." She was, she realized, close to tears now. She hadn't shed a tear before this.

"I'll get us something to eat. Your apartment?"

"I don't know if there's electricity. Probably still cut off."

"We'll use mine then. You can take a shower there. You got an extra set of clothes?"

She nodded.

"Good."

He parked the car around the corner on Utrechtsestraat. Then he went to the nearest shop and bought bread, eggs, ham, cheese, instant coffee, milk, sugar, tomatoes, onions, and a can of baked beans. And two bottles of wine for later.

"All that?" she said, surprised.

"Full breakfast. I don't know what I have in the fridge, so I just bought what I think we need."

He left the car on Utrechtsestraat, close to the tram stop but in a spot that wasn't exactly a parking space. They carried her bag and the groceries to his apartment, where she went right into the shower. She came out twenty minutes later dressed in her other set of clothes. He had turned the heat on, and the apartment was quickly getting warm. He was now occupied with eggs, bacon, and beans in tomato sauce. "You can stay if you want. I have a spare room with a bed I don't use."

"I'll have to think about that." She watched him preparing breakfast. "This shit . . . I mean, I'm not used to such abundance anymore. Hot shower and personal breakfast service and all."

"Guess you aren't," he said. "Sit down."

She sat at the kitchen table next to the window. He brought coffee, toasted bread, and an almost complete English breakfast. "You'll feel better with a full stomach," he said. "Trust me on this."

She ate with an appetite that surprised him. Or not, actually. After the second cup of coffee she said, "I think this is what I needed. Breakfast and you." And suddenly tears ran down her cheeks. She hid her face.

He held her by the shoulder. "That's all right," he said. "It's a delayed reaction and shock. After all you went through, and you didn't have the time to let it really sink in."

"There's so much . . ." she started but couldn't finish her sentence.

"You can't help them all, Linda," he said softly. "There're too many."

"There were literally thousands of refugees there, Walter. Men, women, old people, and children. And we let them all down. When they needed us most, we let them down."

She pushed away her empty plate.

"All that time they were just sitting there. Before the storm, all those weeks. Those who were ill came to us, the others just sat there. They had nothing to live for. They'd reached the end of the road. And there was us. A handful of medical staff. We meant nothing. We didn't make any difference."

"That's not true. You helped those who were sick."

"We might have made a difference for some of them, for a little while. And then, after the storm, nothing remained of our efforts."

He poured her more coffee and kept an eye on the clock. He couldn't afford to miss this meeting with Dewaal.

"Tell me about you," she said. "We need to talk about you too. I want some normality in my life."

"Compared to what you've been through," he said, "things have been rather routine here." Which was a lie, but he wasn't going to burden her with tales of immolation and murder.

"Be more precise, Walter. You're being evasive. You haven't been doing nothing."

"I guess you'll read about it in the newspapers anyway. We're looking into the criminal activities of a cult."

"A cult?"

"Not just any cult. This one sacrifices people. We've found examples of their work."

"Sacrifice?"

"We came across the remains of a ritual murder somewhere in the Belgian Ardennes. Seven victims. All tied to stakes and burned alive. That's the sort of thing this cult does."

She stared at him. He realized he shouldn't have brought this subject up. Too many horrible things in her life, and now this.

"I think," she said, "I've seen something similar in Somalia."

He frowned. "What are you talking about?"

She described what she had seen in the hills. Both circles of bodies, old and new. She described what Lieutenant Odinga had told her about these sorts of sacrifices having been performed for centuries in the most remote places. How the old bodies had looked petrified. Literally. "It's as if that sect you're talking about had been active outside Europe and for some time already."

He wasn't surprised. He told her about how many disasters were supposed to be the work of the church, and how a new group, the Society of Fire, had continued the tradition.

"That's . . . I don't know what to say. How can people do that? Are we going back to, I don't know, the Middle Ages?"

"We're after these people, and we'll get them, but there are probably many of them, and not just here. It's evil, Linda. We're fighting extreme evil."

43

SAEED AL-RAHMAN DIDN'T WANT to imagine how life would be if he had to stay in hotels all the time, as some of his colleagues in the diplomatic service did. He didn't care to envisage such a life. It was bad enough he was obliged to stay in hotels from time to time. Getting dressed alone and then having breakfast with strangers wasn't the sort of habit he enjoyed. Waking up in the morning without the familiar smell of his wife, without another human being next to him, was unbearable.

He had sacrificed enough for his country, more than enough. He shouldn't be obliged to endure this life anymore. He wasn't planning to share this reflection with his superior, though. Colonel Saeed Al-Rahman was first and foremost a high-ranking officer in the police force of the House of Saud and only secondly a citizen with a personal life.

But he had always known what was expected of him. At seventeen he left his home, not to study medicine like his parents wanted, but to join the military. The military needed bright young men, especially when they had a talent for foreign languages. And if they proved to be God-fearing and hardworking and attended Koranic school regularly, their career would be guaranteed. Saeed walked from cadet school right into active service and became a lieutenant in five years, graduating in the top ten of his class.

This is not Iran was his observation when the professor of international history confronted his students with world affairs. If this had been Iran and not Saudi Arabia, the young lieutenant might have been killed on the battlefield during that long and cruel war against the Sunnis of the tyrant Saddam, who was supported by the Americans for the wrong reasons. This was Saudi Arabia, the cradle of Islamic civilization, where eventually every Muslim would return.

His family had found him a suitable wife, and they were married three weeks after his graduation from the academy. His first assignment took him to Jordan, where he advised the local security forces. He was a young lieutenant without any experience, but he soldiered on, stubbornly, quickly acquiring a reputation as a passionate and headstrong officer. He learned how to work with weapons and explosives and how to make people talk about things they wanted to keep hidden. He learned how to use pain—of others—as a weapon. People always, in the end, talked when they expected more pain.

For four months, he had lived apart from his young wife. They communicated through letters. They weren't allowed to make phone calls because he wasn't officially in Jordan. He admired her love and affection for him, a man she barely knew and hadn't seen before her marriage.

He would no longer be separated from her, not for long anyway. After the job in Jordan, he got another assignment in Rihad. They lived there together and had three children. Terrorism, wars, espionage, and civil unrest occasionally drove them apart, but not for long periods.

All this happened before he had the conversation with the general who was an old friend of his family. This current assignment was simple, without personal risk. But he'd needed to go abroad again, first to Somalia, then to the Netherlands. Al-Rahman at once saw the necessity for this operation when it was explained to him.

Both he and the general adhered to the same faith, which was not Islam. Although both were strict followers of Islam.

He was standing in the bathroom, shaving. The general had discussed the future with Colonel Al-Rahman. The veteran officer could, within two years, likely join the palace guard. That would be a special honor, and it meant more money and a larger house for the colonel. The colonel had been flattered, although he preferred real work. And what about his eldest son, Ahmed, who wanted to study in America?

This seemed more important than a larger house. Al-Rahman knew the government annually allowed a limited number of students to study in the United States, and most of them would be children of the House of Saud. Exceptions would be, well, exceptional.

"I have no authority there," the general had said. "I will file a request for your son, but of course, one way or another, this will have no impact on your zeal."

"Of course not, sir," Al-Rahman had said.

44

VAN GILS PHONED DEWAAL early in the morning with the information he had gotten from Sjaakie. "Westerdok?" she said. "Is that where they're keeping Eileen, you think? Are you sure your source is reliable?"

"No reason I should doubt him, Chief. He's been very reliable in the past. We need to get out—"

"I can't spare the manpower, Van Gils. Not this morning. I know this is important to Prinsen. It's important to me too, but we'll have to deal with this later, after . . ." She hesitated. "I'll see you at the Bureau, Van Gils. I need you to be discreet for a little while, until we've arrested Maxwell. After that, I promise, we'll see about Eileen."

Most of the team was already present when Van Gils arrived on the second floor. He poured himself a coffee. "Are you coming with us to the ArenA or what?" he pressed Veneman, whose expression almost formed a question mark. "Just asking," Van Gils went on, "because last week you said you wanted to see the match. It's tomorrow, remember? if you don't go, I'll sell the ticket to someone else."

"Told you I'd come," Veneman said. "I already said it twice."

"What about you, Eekhaut? You can come if you want. We'll find extra tickets. The opportunity of a lifetime to see decent soccer. *Dutch* soccer—best in the world. You know about Ajax, I guess? A completely different class than those Belgians whose names I can't even remember."

Eekhaut, who was staring outside, wondering if the thaw had already set in, looked surprised. "Soccer?" His thoughts had been elsewhere.

"An internationally admired sport played on a large field by twenty-two participants from two opposing teams and a leather ball as a prop."

"I have absolutely no interest in sports," Eekhaut said.

"No sports?" Veneman responded, horrified.

Siegel, closing his laptop, chuckled. "A Flemish police officer who doesn't like sports? Not even cycling?"

"What? Spending hours watching a bunch of grown-up men running behind a ball, or other men biking around the same circuit time after time? And then wasting more time discussing strategies, like we're experts on something? I've got better things to do than waste my life that way."

"All right!" Van Gils said defiantly. "Didn't expect you to feel that way."

"While those same people, having wasted their energy watching and commenting on sports, let themselves be exploited by their bosses, by politicians, by the rich! You'd think they'd be more, I don't know, more critical about their working conditions?"

"People like to relax now and then," Veneman said mildly. Although he cared little for Eekhaut's opinion of sports.

"Relax?" Eekhaut said with a grimace. "Yeah, that's what they do, all right. Using the time they could spend educating themselves so they'd no longer be vulnerable to lying populists with agendas. But the same critical thinking they apply to sports, they abandon once their real life is at stake and they have to think about society and their future. They let themselves be lied to, exploited, misguided."

He knew better than to go on like this. They didn't want to hear what he had to say.

"What do you want, Eekhaut?" Van Gils replied. "That's how people are. Most are too stupid to think for themselves. Can't even differentiate between opinions and facts. Yes, we know, politicians, or at least certain kinds of politicians, are deceitful, narcissistic psychopaths at worst, or interested only in their personal priorities at best. You gonna change that by denying people their sports events?"

"Maybe you should go into politics yourself. Back in Belgium," Veneman chimed in.

"It's nothing personal, Van Gils," Eekhaut said.

"Wasn't going to assume it was. *I* like soccer. So, tomorrow, I'll be joining thousands of like-minded idiots in the ArenA, unless Dewaal really is going to make us work seven days a week."

"Saturday is a sacred day, Van Gils," Veneman said. "Ajax is playing Feyenoord: the game of the year. There're going to be a lot of people to see that."

Dewaal marched into the common area while the others were chattering. She wore black pants with lots of pockets and a sort of combat jacket over a black T-shirt. She held a gray parka over her arm. Eekhaut was becoming somewhat paranoid about the varying manifestations he had witnessed of Dewaal so far. When she dressed differently, she acted differently. Today he wouldn't risk having an important discussion with her. Not the way she was dressed.

"Good morning," she said firmly. "Are we all here?"

The detectives gathered around her. Most brought their cups of coffee.

Several photographs decorated the whiteboard. Dewaal had written names under each: Maxwell, Basten, Desmedt, Brecht, Simson. All players in this infernal game. Some of them victims.

"These are the people that matter to us," Dewaal said. "The main players, although some are dead. We're convinced everything revolves around this man." She indicated Maxwell. He looked rather harmless in the somewhat out-of-focus picture. "Jan Pieter Maxwell, scion of an almost extinct family, whose grandfather made them all rich. He was—the grandfather—a classic patriarch like the ones who only live in novels. Children in and out of wedlock. He lived in Dutch India for years and made his fortune there, went into politics afterward. Not much of the family is left. Not much of the family spirit either, it seems. Jan Pieter is the exception: manager of several businesses, some partly owned by him, others by his less intellectually inclined relatives.

"What we suspect about Maxwell is that he's the leader, or at least one of the leading figures, of the Society of Fire, though we can't prove it. We don't have enough for an arrest, but we can get a search warrant, which might, just *might*, provide some evidence of his association with the society. I'll question the man myself, knowing that without decent proof we're obliged to release him within six hours after his arrest."

"Let's get him then," Van Gils said. "Let's get him off the streets."

"Which will happen very soon now," Dewaal said. "Apostel isn't happy with the way things are going, but at least she got us the warrants. Including for his offices. We'll raid them all, along with local officers from Amsterdam-Amstelland CID. Six of his offices in all."

Eekhaut's attention was drawn to a movement to his left. Colonel Al-Rahman had appeared at his side. The man seemed to possess magical powers, in his country's tradition. The Saudi police officer leaned toward him. "Could you inform me what is happening here, Chief Inspector?"

Eekhaut tried to keep his attention on Dewaal and gestured to the colonel to be patient.

"I want everybody to carry their weapon," Dewaal continued. "Local police will be in uniform, but this is not a raid. We will not force doors. We ask nicely to be let in, show the documents, and that's it. And we have a warrant for Maxwell only, remember. Everybody clear?" She opened a folder and passed some documents to the officer standing closest to her. "Pass these out. Partners and cars and destinations. Radio contact at all times. And an emergency frequency. Remember Maxwell belongs to a group that has killed in the past and will do so again. We're leaving in fifteen. And remember, follow the plan. This is a coordinated action."

The detectives started to leave the room.

"Are things progressing now?" Al-Rahman asked Eekhaut, who was studying the document.

"That's correct, Colonel. And it seems we're still joined at the hip."

"Beg your pardon?"

"We're assigned to the same vehicle and destination. You come with me. To Maxwell's house. And along with Dewaal herself. Seems we're in the main group."

"Is there cause for amusement?" Al-Rahman inquired, puzzled. "Being in the presence of one's chief is a matter of trust, but one has to be extra careful not to make mistakes."

"We try to avoid mistakes at all times, Colonel," Eekhaut said. He wondered if the colonel was being ironic, but clearly not. "We'll pick up a prime suspect, even without decent evidence, and bring him in for questioning."

"Ah," the colonel said. As if his deeper suspicions had been confirmed about the methods of the Western police.

"Exactly. I don't know how this works in your country, Colonel, but here it means we can grill him for six hours without a lawyer present. At the end, we have enough to indict him, or not, in which case he walks."

"That seems rather undemocratic, Chief Inspector," Al-Rahman said. "Without a lawyer being present? Under Sharia law having a third party present is a solid human right."

Eekhaut wasn't sure how to comment. He knew almost nothing about the way police worked in places like Saudi Arabia. "Well," he said, "such is the law in this country."

"And of course, the law is always right," affirmed Al-Rahman.

Eekhaut was sure the colonel's royal family would work around any law if the potential murderer of one of theirs was picked up and made to confess. What would they do if it turned out Maxwell was responsible for the death of the prince? What would the Dutch government do? Extradite? To a country with a death sentence? A Dutch citizen? That wouldn't happen.

And the colonel probably knew it.

"Sharia is not a cruel law," he said, following Eekhaut downstairs, toward the underground parking garage. "It is a law concerned with what is right under all circumstances. It evolved in times of hardship, times much different than now. People were vulnerable, as was society itself, with greater personal risks. Psychology and so on have evolved, of course, giving us a better insight into what drives criminals or the insane, but these laws were written long before that."

"Hands no longer chopped off?" Eekhaut inquired. But at once he regretted that remark. It was a stereotype, although it still happened in countries where Sharia was applied. As did stoning and hanging. "Incidentally, Colonel, I assume you have your weapon with you?"

The colonel opened his coat and showed Eekhaut a black nylon holster and a semiautomatic pistol.

The detectives gathered around the vehicles. It was cold in the parking garage.

"Everybody ready?" said Dewaal. "Now, one last thing: Van Gils has a lead on the whereabouts of Eileen Calster. We'll see what we can do with that information after the raid."

The detectives took their places in the cars. The vehicles left the parking garage and drove in different directions. Eekhaut was in the front seat of a BMW 7 next to Siegel, who was driving, with Dewaal and Al-Rahman in the back. Siegel drove with lights flashing and siren at full blast. Even then, in the narrow streets of the city, they didn't move fast.

"We are going to arrest the main suspect?" Al-Rahman inquired.

"That's the idea," Dewaal said. "According to our most recent info, he's still at home. That's where we are going now."

"On suspicion of murder?"

"On suspicion of a lot of things, including multiple murders and incitement to commit murder."

"Ah," the colonel said as if this explained everything.

The BMW sped up once it had left the center. *Why hurry?* Eekhaut *wondered. Either we find Maxwell at home or we don't, and then he'll surface somewhere else.* But Siegel seemed to enjoy the speed. Eekhaut would never have driven a car that fast in an urban area, not even in Brussels.

"Kill the siren," Dewaal said, with the car now traversing a long, straight street in one of the more expensive suburbs of Amsterdam. Siegel turned right and then left, led by the GPS, and finally parked the vehicle in front of a house that was perhaps a bit larger than the surrounding properties. Eekhaut assumed the better part of middle-class Dutch society lived in houses like these, in a country where extravagance of any kind was frowned upon, at least by the older population. Most of the houses were early postwar, all surrounded by extensive gardens, which even now, in winter, looked green.

The street itself was empty. No strollers, no kids, no cyclists. Maybe even pedestrians were frowned upon.

"Number thirty-three," Dewaal said, checking her phone. "This is the one." They all got out. Dewaal spoke a few words into her phone. At the same moment, the other teams all around and in Amsterdam would take action.

Dewaal walked toward the small gate that separated the sidewalk from the garden. It wasn't closed. Siegel followed. Eekhaut had Al-Rahman in tow somewhat behind them. He expected a sudden volley of shots coming from the house, eliminating at least two of them. But nothing happened. Dewaal rang the doorbell.

The house seemed deserted. Nobody was going to answer the bell.

"Let's not waste time, gentlemen," Dewaal said. "Siegel?"

Eekhaut expected the man to use a crowbar or another heavy object and apply it to the door, like in American movies. But Siegel turned out to be a specialist in picking locks using only a small tool. The lock yielded at once.

Dewaal noticed Eekhaut's surprise. "Why destroy a door when almost any lock can be picked?"

The house seemed deserted. No alarm, no one coming downstairs. "Police!" Siegel shouted, loud enough for anyone to hear him. "We are entering the house."

"Eekhaut, Colonel," Dewaal said, "search the ground floor. Siegel and I will take the upstairs."

They spread out. Eekhaut noticed the colonel had drawn his gun. That seemed unnecessary. Eekhaut kept his weapon in his holster. Maybe the colonel had had nasty experiences with searches like this. Eekhaut assumed he might have had to confront terrorists.

The house was empty.

"He probably left early this morning."

Eekhaut wondered about that. Why had Dewaal, experienced as she was, assumed Maxwell would still be at home? A busy businessman like him, at home after ten in the morning? That made no sense at all.

Why were they here?

"He seems to live alone: bed made up, no breakfast on the table." Dewaal spoke on her phone. She got replies. When she talked again, she seemed angry. "He's nowhere to be found. Even his secretaries—plural—don't know where he is."

"Do a thorough search of the house?" Siegel suggested.

"We'll turn it upside down. We have a warrant; it would be a shame not to use it. Take everything that can be useful."

It took them a couple of hours before all the material they could find had been stowed in boxes and taken to the Kerkstraat offices. Eekhaut reminded Dewaal that they needed to look into the info from Van Gils concerning Eileen's kidnappers.

"I know. I haven't forgotten. We assumed we'd catch Maxwell. That didn't happen. All we have is his stuff. And it will take weeks, maybe months, to sift through it."

"Eileen might be in direct danger."

"They won't kill her, Eekhaut. That would make no sense. Try to calm Prinsen. And let's concentrate for a moment on Maxwell. When we find him, the problem with Eileen might be solved."

One of the detectives shouted out for her. "Chief, you have an urgent personal call in your office."

Dewaal hurried away.

"Her mother isn't well," Van Gils said. He surveyed the documents, the boxes, the computers. All of it stacked in the main room on the second floor. "How much time do we have?" he inquired. Thea De Vries, in the same kind of combat vest as Dewaal, said, "The computers are mine. I'm the resident geek."

Dewaal appeared again. "Your attention, everyone," she said. "You know I have an informant within the society. Yes, Veneman, I really do. Now, this informant tells me the society is planning an attack tomorrow, somewhere in Amsterdam, with the goal to kill a great many people. That's all my informant knows at this time."

She lifted both her hands to silence the sudden murmur in the room. "Quiet, please. This is all we have to go on. Any ideas?"

"At least we know how they'll use the gas tanker," Van Gils said.

"You just can't explode a gas tanker," Eekhaut said. "You need an explosive device first."

"As if there aren't experts in explosives in Amsterdam," Veneman said.

"Who would they be targeting?" De Vries said. "The people they consider unworthy?"

"To them everybody might be unworthy," said Dewaal. "Some place where there are a lot of people. Places that draw large crowds."

"Central Station. Always packed."

"The Dam, during the afternoon rush and the shoppers. Tomorrow is Saturday."

"Red-light district? A lot of unworthy people there?"

"The Kalverstraat. To get back at consumerism?"

Dewaal again raised her hands. "A lot of interesting ideas, folks, but we can't have all those places evacuated simultaneously. Where would they park a gas tanker anyway? They would want to hide it, keep it out of sight. They can't even drive it around. It would be too conspicuous."

Nobody had any useful suggestions.

"Major problem," Dewaal said. "I'll call the minister of the interior and the chiefs of police and the highest level of the AIVD. You all look for something that will lead us to the tanker."

Colonel Al-Rahman was leaning against a filing cabinet. He already felt at home in the office, despite the fact that so far only a few members of the team had acknowledged him. Apart from Eekhaut and Dewaal, most had ignored him.

"Can't we get rid of him?" Veneman whispered to Eekhaut.

Eekhaut shrugged. "The chief wants me to babysit him. What can I do? I follow orders like everybody else. That's what I'm good at."

"Yeah, sure," Veneman said. "You should offer him a place to sleep."

"In my apartment? No way. He's staying in a hotel, and I'm fine with that."

"Yep, I heard he's staying at the Hotel de l'Europe, of all places. Most fancy place in the whole city. And commutes in a taxi."

"Again, not my problem," Eekhaut said.

"Aren't you supposed to be keeping an eye on him night and day?"

"You pulling my leg or what? I keep an eye on him when he's here, and I translate for him, and that's as far as my involvement goes."

"You know what I'm thinking, Eekhaut?"

"I have no idea, and I don't care, but you're going to tell me anyway."

"I wonder," Veneman said, "what the colonel's real mission is.

Investigating the murder of the prince? There's gotta be more than that. He didn't come here because someone in royalty was concerned about a murdered nephew. They've got plenty of princes over there."

Exactly what Eekhaut had been thinking.

Eekhaut kept an eye on Prinsen, whose thoughts would be with Eileen and not so much on the case at hand. He would be especially stressed out now that Dewaal had moved against the society and against Maxwell. In Prinsen's opinion, she was risking Eileen's life, even if she saw it differently.

Prinsen got up and left the room, while the others were going through the material from Maxwell's house and offices and Dewaal was in her office, on the phone. Eekhaut followed the young man. Prinsen stood in a hallway, leaning against the wall and making a phone call. He noticed Eekhaut approaching. "That's not my fault," he was saying into the phone. "I wasn't even informed in advance. The chief told us to get to the cars, without so much as a suggestion about what would happen. I would have phoned you, but there was no time."

He listened and looked at Eekhaut. He nodded. "Now wait a second!" He hung his head. Defeated, he said, "If you hurt her I'll—" But it was clear the other side had hung up. He dropped the phone in his pocket and looked at Eekhaut. "They're angry because I didn't warn them."

"You explained you couldn't," Eekhaut said. "Nothing you could do."

"Still!" Prinsen glanced over Eekhaut's shoulder. Dewaal had appeared, as if out of nowhere.

"What's up?" she inquired.

Prinsen told her.

"I promised you we would look for Eileen as soon as we got Maxwell."

"We can't wait," Prinsen said.

"All right then. Eekhaut, take two men out to Bickersgracht. Do it right now. If Eileen isn't there, we have to think up a new strategy. And someone ought to speak with Ms. Simson. See what else she knows about Maxwell that she forgot to tell us earlier. I suspect her of having her own agenda."

45

"Not so brave, that lover of yours, after we had a talk about his obligations and responsibilities," the man with the balaclava said. He sounded as if he had a cold, or smoked too much.

That the man continued to wear his disguise gave Eileen hope. *They won't kill me. They won't. Things will turn out all right. I'm just merchandise in an exchange. Nick will make sure nothing happens to me.*

They hadn't touched her, so she assumed the men were professionals, not amateurs. Working for a fee or something. She knew that much from watching movies. They hadn't tied her up either. She was free to move about in the room but hadn't been let out. They seemed convinced she couldn't escape.

The other man, behind her, said, "But he didn't respect our agreement, and that'll be held against him."

"He's a cop," the other said. "He should know how this works. But he isn't the tough guy we expected. More like a wimp, isn't he? Are you sure you want him as your boyfriend? A spunky girl like you?"

"That's not what's on her mind right now," the first man said. "She doesn't even want to *think* too much, anyway. Thinking hurts under these circumstances. Because she knows horrible things might happen to her if her lover doesn't cooperate."

Eileen knew it was better not to react. Not to give them the satisfaction of her doubts. She let them talk. They might let slip clues about what would happen. Or who they were. There were only two of them, but she assumed there must be a third man somewhere, keeping a look-out and contacting Nick.

"She's not really a talker, is she?" the first man said. "That's what I like about women, personally, knowing when to shut it. That cop's a lucky one, isn't he?"

"Well, what would you do?" the other one said. "Alone, in a room, with the two of us. You wouldn't have much to say either, would you?"

"How long will I have to stay here?" Eileen asked.

"Now let's not get too intimate," the first man said. He opened the door and walked out into the corridor. She noticed a wall of aged, dirty bricks, with gray light coming from an invisible source. Daylight. Whatever this was, it hadn't been used in a long time. Maybe a former factory or warehouse.

The first man looked over his shoulder at his partner. "You coming? Or do I lock you in there with the girl?"

The second man left the room. The door closed with the unpleasant echo of old steel against brick. A large, empty, hollow building. If she could make contact with the outside world, this description might be useful.

She was alone again. No more human sounds. She sat on the chair. She had already examined the room for a means of escape but found nothing. She didn't even know where she was. Maybe still in Amsterdam, maybe abroad. She'd been unconscious when she arrived here, for how long she didn't know. And she wasn't going anywhere.

46

"ARE YOU SURE?" EEKHAUT asked. He was worried because the situation wasn't entirely under control, which he hated. From experience, he knew accidents happened when the situation wasn't under control.

"Absolutely," Van Gils said. Eekhaut had sent him to reconnoiter the scene. This area with the hulk of a closed-down factory and empty quays seemed deserted. *Decaying* would be the better word. From his vantage, it appeared as if no living soul had been here for some time. But Van Gils had found evidence of occupation—and occupants.

"You can't see them from where we're standing," Van Gils continued. "A black Land Rover and two men smoking, as if on a break. There's a third man somewhere inside. I saw him through the windows. None of them seemed to bother about observing the surroundings. As if they're sure it's the perfect hideout."

"She's here," Prinsen said.

"We don't yet know that, Nick," Eekhaut warned him. "Let's be careful about this. There's three of them, there's three of us. Whoever these men are, they must be armed. We need assistance if we want to proceed."

"There might be more of them inside," Van Gils said. "Although, if it's only the girl involved, they wouldn't need more than three men."

"Calling in assistance takes too long," Prinsen said.

Eekhaut looked at Van Gils for his opinion. "Armed officers?" Van Gils said. "An hour, at the very least."

"Can't we ask Dewaal for help?" Prinsen wanted to know. "It's her problem we're solving."

Not really, Eekhaut thought. *It's mainly* your *problem, Nick.*

"Not with that many people occupied with Maxwell," Van Gils said. He studied Prinsen carefully.

"What's in our car?" Eekhaut asked. He knew, from previous experience, that the Bureau's cars usually held a small arsenal in a hidden compartment in the back.

Van Gils frowned and glanced at the Mazda sedan they'd come in. "This isn't one of the better-equipped Bureau vehicles. No, there's no weaponry in there."

"That means it's just the three of us, each carrying a pistol."

"We have the advantage of surprise," Prinsen insisted. "We don't need backup."

"There's risk involved," Van Gils said. "We're not supposed to use force if a hostage is present."

"What's the usual operational procedure the Bureau has for such cases?" Eekhaut asked Van Gils.

"We rarely have to deal with a situation like this. There's no procedure other than whatever's improvised."

"Let's just sneak in," Prinsen suggested. "How hard can it be? This building's full of holes."

"It's probably full of dangerous situations as well," Van Gils said.

"Hold it," Eekhaut said. "I still outrank both of you. So it'll be my responsibility. We go in. Get Eileen out, shoot the bastards if we need to. Prinsen, you see that wall over there?"

"Yes."

"There's a large hole to the left. Go in and proceed toward the men, and make sure you can see all three of them. Then I need a signal from you."

"What signal?"

"Message on my phone."

"Right."

"Van Gils goes to the right and enters the building. I'll walk up to the men and keep them occupied."

It wasn't anything like a decent plan and Eekhaut knew it, but this was the best he could come up with on short notice.

Both detectives disappeared. A few moments later the message from Prinsen pinged on Eekhaut's phone. It said: *I see 2. Not 3.*

Can't be helped, Eekhaut thought. He walked toward the back of the building, turned a corner, and saw two men standing next to the Land Rover. They seemed relaxed, up until they noticed him watching. He had drawn his gun but kept it out of sight. The man who saw him first threw his cigarette away and nudged the other. Both were young, maybe in their thirties, and athletic. Both would be armed.

"This is private property!" one of them said, loud enough to cover the distance.

The other, apparently less confident about the sudden intruder, stepped from behind the car and felt under his coat, presumably for a gun.

Eekhaut raised his weapon. He was familiar with the kind of men who were hired for these purposes. They were a special kind of mercenary who weren't likely to risk their lives.

"Police officer," Eekhaut said. "Keep your hands where I can see them. The building is surrounded." Which sounded hopelessly melodramatic.

The first man's hand appeared from under his coat holding a gun. It moved upward and would end up pointing toward Eekhaut's head.

He reacted almost on instinct. He had neglected to hold onto his gun with both hands, and it jerked violently; the bullet seemed to end up nowhere. But this was his lucky day: the man with the weapon didn't finish his movement but stepped back, two, three steps, then collapsed.

His partner cursed and reached for his own gun. Too late. Eekhaut now grabbed on with both hands and fired his gun a second time. But the man was moving, and he missed.

The man ducked behind the Land Rover, aimed at Eekhaut, and opened fire.

Then two shots came from Eekhaut's right flank. The man behind the Land Rover fell sideways and didn't move anymore. Van Gils stood at the other end of the building, gun still raised.

"Did I get him?" he asked.

"Two down," Eekhaut said.

He saw Prinsen inside the building through a gap. He was moving fast.

Eekhaut went after him, while Van Gils quickly frisked the two men for more weapons.

Inside, the air was cold and stale. Eekhaut heard sounds. Hurried footsteps over concrete and broken glass. He found his way into an enclosed area under a large jagged opening in one wall. Prinsen stood in a corner, pointing his gun at a man who looked eerily similar to the two men outside. "Where is she?" he asked, his voice hard as the glass under his feet. "She'd better be OK."

Eekhaut stepped closer. "We got the other two, Nick. And Eileen will be around somewhere. Don't shoot him."

"She's over there, behind that door," the man said.

"Keep an eye on him," Prinsen told Eekhaut. And hurried toward the door.

Prinsen wanted to ride with Eileen in the ambulance, but Eekhaut told him he was needed elsewhere, and that he needed to face Dewaal now more than ever.

"There's going to be a lot of explaining on your part, Nick," he said.

"She's in on it," Prinsen said. "It's not like we did this without her knowledge."

But he knew what Eekhaut was referring to.

"Eileen will be all right," Eekhaut replied. "Van Gils will keep her company. After this, we have to go see Ms. Simson. And after that, your aunt will certainly want to have a word with you."

Prinsen hung his head.

"It'll be all right," Eekhaut said. Although he was sure it would not.

47

THE UNDERGROUND AREA HAD walls and a ceiling of grainy reinforced concrete and steel that appeared able to withstand a nuclear war, but Courier told Baphomet much of this strength was an illusion. "What you see is the support structure, and there's not much weight on top of it. The weight of the aboveground part and of the whole complex is carried by the external framework, the walls and the arches around the outer walls. All this steel and concrete? Because it's the cheapest way to build. And it requires no maintenance."

Baphomet turned toward the gas tanker. He wore black jeans and a sweater of the same color under a dark blue parka, hanging open now. "And why is this underground space so large? Is it used as a parking garage, or what? I don't see the need for it."

"It's used when there are concerts going on aboveground. The stage builders park their trucks here, and the stuff goes into the large freight elevators. Sometimes this is where buses park for visiting groups. I've chosen this place because much of the time hardly anyone comes down here. We won't be disturbed."

They stood at a distance of no more than fifty feet from the parked tanker, in the middle of the large space. The looming vehicle consisted of a tractor and a semitrailer with a matted steel cylindrical tank sporting the gold-on-red name of a transport company. Metagogeus climbed out of the cab of the tractor and carefully shut the door.

"Any doors or gates we need to lock?" Baphomet asked.

"Four," Courier said. "They're already locked. A single entrance will remain open for our use. This facility can be hermetically sealed, Baphomet. Don't worry. And it will be fully closed once we have set the timer."

"Nobody gets in once the timer is started?"

"Nobody. I made sure of that."

Baphomet glanced toward Serena, who stood a couple of yards from them, admiring the tanker. She didn't seem interested in anything else.

"What do you think, Serena?" Baphomet asked her.

She was lost in dreams. Or deep in thought. "I don't know," she said. "I can't imagine . . ." And she made a wide gesture that encompassed the entire underground complex and probably all the future victims. Clearly, the whole concept was too big for her.

"I'm sure you can't," Baphomet said. "And you're not supposed to. Let us deal with this. In the end, you'll see why this is happening. For now, you must trust us. And I'm sure you do."

She smiled. "Of course, I trust you," she said.

Metagogeus joined them. "All is ready, Baphomet. Do you want to check the installation one last time?"

"Courier will do that. Won't you, Courier?"

"At once," Courier said. He walked over to the tractor and opened the cabin door. His upper body disappeared from sight.

"Everything to my specifications?" Baphomet asked.

"Exactly like you wanted," Metagogeus said. "Things are ready to go."

"I still wonder . . ." Serena said. "I still wonder if this much is necessary to . . . achieve purification?"

"These people," Baphomet said, "are the unclean, and as such they hardly qualify as people. As humans. It is unfortunate we will end their lives, but they will serve a much greater cause than they would have served otherwise. In fact, these people are already dead."

"Will we ever be sure we've done the right thing?" she insisted.

"Don't you feel the grace of the Creator within you, Serena? Is there a sudden doubt in your mind now? Could it be you suddenly are less confident than before?"

"I apologize, Baphomet," she said. "I'm acting like a spoiled child.

I'm humbled by the presence of my Creator. As I'm humbled by the presence of people so much more worthy than I could ever be."

"Now, child, do not despair. The Creator sees all intentions and will judge you with mercy and compassion." Baphomet added, "Can you wait for us at the exit?"

She knew she was being dismissed and walked away.

"Courier," Baphomet said when she was out of earshot, "keep an eye on her and make sure she talks to no one."

"Leave that to me," Courier said.

"Is there a problem with the girl?" Metagogeus asked. "Something we should be aware of? I seem to remember she's one of our more recent converts. Do you have any reason to doubt your judgment about her?"

Baphomet had always admired the younger companion, who now seemed rather nervous. That was not surprising, however, with all that was happening. *But,* he thought, *we can't afford to be nervous. Nervous people make mistakes. Too much at stake. No time for doubts either. The machine is set in motion and past the point of no return.*

"I see no problem with the girl," he said. "I have taken her in on account of her passion. She is, of course, young and inexperienced. And Courier will keep an eye on her."

"Yes, about Courier . . ."

"What about him?"

"Can *he* be trusted sufficiently? He's the one who saw to all the details. We're putting all our trust in him."

"He is worthy of our trust. Is there anything in particular you are worried about?"

"I've lost contact with the men in charge of Eileen Calster."

"And she is?"

"The young girl linked to that police officer who's providing us with information."

"Ah, him," Baphomet said. "And what seems to be the problem?"

"These men are supposed to report back to me after they've consulted with the officer. He's supposed to keep them informed about the plans of the Bureau. I haven't heard from them for quite a while."

"That is most worrisome, but in the end it will not stop us.

Everything we need is here. The setting is secure. Soon all of us will be purified, and then we will prepare for eternity."

"I don't have to worry about Serena, then?"

"Sometimes it feels like you lack faith, brother. I'm sure that's not true. Forget Serena. Forget that girl and her police officer. We will prevail. And we will make sure Serena will follow us into the moment of our own sacrifice. Until proven otherwise, she is to be trusted."

48

IT WAS LESS COLD than the previous day, and Eekhaut was hoping for an early spring. But it wouldn't arrive for another month or two, so he'd have to struggle through more cold days ahead. He pushed aside all concerns about the seasons and the cold and concentrated on Johanna Simson, at whose house he arrived with Prinsen. The house on the Nieuwezijds Voorburgwal seemed darker and more silent than before and more possessed by ghosts from the past—ghosts appointed to guard the church's secrets.

Before ringing the bell, he turned to Prinsen. "We're only discussing her involvement with the church," he said.

"Sure. What else?"

"Later, after this thing is over, I'd like to discuss with her some of the finer points of their tradition. About why so many people had to die, why so many sacrifices were made in the past."

Prinsen knew Eekhaut had certain hang-ups, and one was religion. More precisely, the madness of religious feelings and traditions—all superstition as far as he was concerned. Prinsen wasn't planning to be present for the talk the Belgian would have with Ms. Simson.

"Sacrifices and the like are also part of Christian history and tradition. Does it matter in whose name people are murdered?"

"I don't know, Nick. This is, or was, recent history. We're talking about things that happened—what?—forty years ago? That isn't ancient history, that isn't the Middle Ages."

"What do you expect? A confession of guilt from her? That would be nice, but I don't expect it. And neither should you. Let's get on with it. I want to get back to Eileen."

Eekhaut rang the bell. An elderly woman opened the door, hardly surprised to see the two men. Eekhaut and Prinsen showed her their IDs. "Security services," Eekhaut identified himself. "We would like to have another word with Ms. Simson."

"Ms. Simson is ill," the woman told him. "Better come back on Monday."

"This cannot wait, ma'am. Ms. Simson knows who we are and what this is about. We need to see her immediately."

The old woman hesitated, frowning deeply. "Well," she finally said, "I guess I'll let her decide. Come in, gentlemen. What are your names again?"

"Eekhaut and Prinsen."

"Please proceed to the drawing room. I will speak with Ms. Simson."

"Will she realize how important this is?" Prinsen said after the elderly lady had gone.

"I don't want to drag her all the way to Kerkstraat, Nick. She'll have to talk to us. What's the time?"

Prinsen glanced at his watch. "Quarter to four."

"And another day lost."

"We've just begun, actually."

"No, we haven't. This thing has kept us occupied far too long already. What's going to happen tomorrow? We're looking at a potential disaster, and we have no idea where it's going to happen."

He was interrupted by Johanna Simson entering the room. The elderly woman assisted her. "Gentlemen," Simson said, "I hope this is important. You'll have to excuse me, I seem to have the flu."

"This will only take a short while, ma'am," Eekhaut said. "All we need to know is the whereabouts of Jan Pieter Maxwell. He's not at home, and we couldn't find him in any of his offices. Do you know if there are other places where he can hide?"

"You are asking me about Maxwell, Inspector? Really?" Simson grimaced. "That I, of all people, should know where he is?"

"You understand a lot of things about him, ma'am," Eekhaut

insisted. "You know he goes by the name of Baphomet. That's his moniker in the Society of Fire, isn't it? And you have knowledge of many things, none of which you've shared with us."

She sat down carefully. "And what are you going to do with all that information you assume I possess? If I tell you where he hides? What will happen? You send in armed police, and there's a shootout with him and those faithful to him, and many people die. Because you will not catch him alive. He wants to die a martyr. That's what they all want. All the people who ever believed they were the chosen. You should know that, if you've been following the news these last decades."

"We want to catch him alive. The lives of many innocent people are at stake."

"The number of hiding places the church once used is not infinite. But this is Amsterdam, Inspector. Ask your older colleagues familiar with the city. There is no city with more hiding places invisible to the outside world than Amsterdam."

"We'll never catch him, is that what you mean?"

"He will prove to be the most elusive man in police history, gentlemen," said Simson. "I wish you good luck. On that, the whole church is with you. They are our enemies as well. They are much more our enemies than yours. What do you think will happen to all those remaining members of the church once a man like Baphomet has completed his purification?"

"I have no idea," Eekhaut said.

"He is the serpent, deceiving mankind. You remember your Old Testament, I assume. He is the serpent. He will be a leader, and people will follow. He will tell lies, and people will follow. He will turn people away from the truth, from science, from common sense. And people will follow him. That's who he is. And as such, this serpent must die before it can cause harm."

"There's no longer a death penalty in the Netherlands, ma'am. But he will go to jail for a very long time."

Johanna Simson shook her head. "It doesn't matter to him. His lies penetrate walls. There exists no prison that can hold him. You must kill the monster. A wise man knows what to do. Separate the head from the body. That's the only way to be certain."

"Today, we're concerned about one event, a terrorist attack we fear is in the making. He has the means, he has the people to do this. It will happen if we don't intervene. We have no idea where."

"A sacrifice?"

"Yes."

"He will need a whole lot of victims for this sacrifice, Inspector. If this is the ultimate event he is planning."

"That's what we fear."

"His supporters are blinded by his apocalyptic reasoning, Inspector. He is a strong leader."

Eekhaut was becoming impatient. He'd had enough of this prophesying. Ms. Simson either knew nothing or wouldn't tell.

He had one last card. From his jacket pocket he produced a document. "There's something I want you to read, Ms. Simson," he said. "We found it earlier at a crime scene. It's the text of something written on a wall." It was the text he and Dewaal had found in the Ardennes.

"Hand me my glasses, Dottie," Ms. Simson said. She read aloud: "This world seems to take forever, but it is only the dream of a sleeper." She looked up. "You want to know where this comes from?"

"Borges?" Eekhaut said.

"*La vida es un sueño*, you mean? Indeed, you know your classics. But Borges got the idea from another poetic master, the Persian Sufi poet Rumi, who lived in the thirteenth century. He preached tolerance and founded the whirling dervishes. Those are his lines."

"And what exactly does it refer to?"

"I told you before of the Gnostics, Inspector. Where the tradition of our church originated."

"This Sufi tradition doesn't teach you to burn people," Prinsen said.

"Which we realized much too late, indeed. We have tried to hide our past sins, adding sin upon sin. We have recanted. However, that will never bring these people back."

"*As in a dream*," Eekhaut said. "Like in the text."

"It is, indeed, all a dream. Our traditions were perhaps not meant to survive the twentieth century."

"That's not what a dogmatist like Maxwell believes."

"He can act as he wants because, in reality, he believes in nothing but himself," Simson said bitterly. "He uses other people to better himself. Even in the spiritual sense."

"And yet you won't help us catch this man. Even if he's your worst enemy."

"I thought I already explained, Inspector," she said. "There's no way I can help you. This house is empty except for my old friend and myself. Everything we know belongs to the past. I'm tired, and the world will soon end. It will end when I die, becoming that dreamer. I have nothing to offer you."

She rose, with difficulty. Her petite elderly companion helped her out of the room.

49

CHIEF ALEXANDRA DEWAAL WASN'T easily disturbed. Not even now, sitting across from Van Gerbranden, the silver-haired interior minister. His office was as impressive as government offices came, including an original Rothko on one wall. Next to her sat the uniformed chief constable of the Amsterdam-Amstelland police region, Edward Mastenbroek, who kept at a strategic distance from Dewaal. On the other side of her, at an equally measured distance, was her own director-general, Stuger, in a conventional dark blue suit. This was the exclusive male company she preferred not to meet with too often.

At the very worst, she thought, they would simply fire her. They would not, however, make her change her opinion or talk her into changing her strategy. Not these men. She had lost any trust in paternalistic father figures a long while ago, when she understood their position was maintained by a system of mistrust and repression. Men like these were often without any redeeming human qualities, narrow-minded and full of themselves as the great saviors of society. If she showed any weaknesses, they would hurt her. They would certainly humiliate her, and even cast her out, just because she was a woman. And a woman who wanted to be their equal. To her, however, they were as pathetic as they were vulnerable.

"You ordered searches at different locations simultaneously," Director Stuger said cautiously, as if he were still unsure whether he liked the idea or not. "Then you dispatched three detectives to another location. Shots were fired and members of the public were hurt."

"They weren't members of the public, sir," Dewaal said "They were criminals. They had abducted a young woman."

"So it appears. However, the three criminals apprehended at the scene have little or no connection to the rest of the operation. Which, by the way, resulted in exactly what? Nothing. None of the searches brought anything to light in this case."

"We're still examining the material we confiscated," Dewaal said, maintaining her calm.

"The main suspect in your case, Chief, is still missing. You assume a terrorist attack is imminent, but you cannot tell us where this will happen, or even *what* will happen. All you have is an informant, who remains anonymous, and a vague plan by some even more vague religious sect."

At the very worst, she thought again, they would kick her out. She suspected they were already preparing their case against her. Destroying her investigation. *If there's no terrorist attack, then I'm screwed. And if there is one, they'll blame me for not having prevented it. And I'm screwed anyway. So, they fire me. But first they'll parade me in front of the press as a scapegoat. In either case. And when that happens, I'll start my own independent security firm. Maybe I'll employ people like Van Gils and Veneman, possibly Prinsen too, and Eekhaut, why not, because they'll get booted as well.*

"There's a real threat out there, Director," she said. Warning him. Making sure all present had heard what she said.

"We do not underestimate this threat, Chief," Minister Van Gerbranden said. He had that look he always had, even in official pictures: a tight-lipped and characterless bureaucrat. He wouldn't defend her. He would be the first to shove the blame in her direction. "And," he continued, "if there is an attack of the size you, uh—"

"Suggest," Stuger suggested quietly.

"Suggest," Van Gerbranden continued, "then we should alert all our security services. Nevertheless, it is impossible and unjustifiable—as you know best—to completely evacuate the whole of Amsterdam tomorrow, when we don't even know anything will happen. What we could do is close the center to all traffic, increase the mobile patrols on the streets, and helicopters in the air, maybe alert the army . . . And we need a list of all large gatherings or events, so we can alert the organizers."

"Isn't there any other evidence? Any other information that tells us more precisely what will happen?" Chief of Police Mastenbroek asked. "What sort of target these people have in mind? Because we're in the dark here."

"All we know is there's this truck involved, gentlemen," Dewaal said. "Five thousand gallons of liquefied gas. If that goes off, there'll be a big bang, a lot of casualties, and a lot of damage."

"What kind of impact would such a blast have if, for instance, it were to occur in the city center?" the minister asked. "Or anywhere else, for that matter?"

"We haven't yet had the opportunity to consult specialists, Excellence," Dewaal said. "My estimate, and I'm just an amateur in this matter, is that most if not all buildings will be leveled within a radius of, say, a half mile. What this means in terms of human loss, we can only guess. It will depend on the area where the blast is located. If it explodes somewhere around Kalverstraat on a Saturday afternoon with all the shoppers, there would be thousands of casualties."

The three men sat in silence for a moment.

Then Van Gerbranden asked, "Are there any other proposals, gentlemen?"

"Could you contact your informant again, Chief?" Mastenbroek suggested.

Dewaal shook her head. "I'm afraid that will not be possible. My contacts with the informant are one way only. He's in a difficult spot. He only talks to me when it's safe for him to do so."

"Too bad," the police chief said. He knew about informants and how that worked. And he knew AIVD politics concerning them. Informants were an important aspect of police work. You didn't trust them, yet you had to, to a certain extent at least. The point was that, in the end, no police officer was comfortable having to rely on informants alone.

Minister Van Gerbranden eyed the police chief suspiciously and then concentrated on Dewaal again. "I won't deny there is reason for concern, but maybe the whole thing is merely a matter of . . . bluffing."

"Bluffing?" Dewaal was astonished. Had the man not been listening?

Van Gerbranden didn't seem to notice her reaction. "Maybe this, uh, cult . . ."

"The Society of Fire," Stuger said.

"Yes, this cult or sect or whatever, maybe they want to pressure the government into . . . whatever."

He's an idiot, Dewaal thought. Nothing said here today would change her ideas about politicians and police chiefs.

"They haven't yet, nor have they ever, contacted the government or the press with any demands, sir," she said. "On the contrary. In the past, all of their sacrifices remained unclaimed."

"So-called sacrifices," Van Gerbranden said. "I've read the files. There was never any proof this society, or church or whatever, was ever implicated."

"We have information to the contrary, sir," Dewaal said.

"From an anonymous informant! And from people who were members of this church long ago and thus were themselves implicated in those assumed crimes."

"And what about the men you arrested in connection with that . . . the girl that was abducted?" Stuger asked.

"They were contracted through criminal channels, sir," Dewaal explained. "We can eventually figure out who's behind the contract, but that will take us . . . much too long, anyway."

"We need to get this thing cleared up, gentlemen," Mastenbroek intervened. "Even if we're not convinced there will be an attack of any kind, we still have to take measures. I suggest all security forces be put on alert, also the fire brigade and civil defense and the hospitals in the larger Amsterdam area."

"I'm on the same page as the chief here," Stuger said. "Not doing anything is going to put us in a very difficult position if something happens."

"Let's do this, then," Van Gerbranden said. "We'll be on full alert without having to paralyze the city. Are we all agreed?"

Dewaal didn't feel the need to comment.

Van Gils was drinking a large mug of coffee—spiced with some other liquid from the small canteen in his office. He raised the mug in a mock toast when Eekhaut walked in. "Did you lose Nick on the way?"

"I drove him to the hospital," Eekhaut said. "That's the very least I could do for him, wasn't it? How's the girl?"

"You know, she'll be all right. Feisty little thing, she is. Would be nice to have her as a daughter." Van Gils kept his attention on his mug. "You know, she didn't for one moment doubt he would come and save her. Isn't that a nice story? She knew Nick would save her. If anything good comes out of this whole fucking operation, then at least there's that."

Eekhaut had nothing to add. "Where's the chief now?"

"Defending her case—and ours—with the bigwigs at the ministry."

Van Gils drank his coffee and got up from the stool, with some difficulty. "Let's call it a day, Walter. There's nothing more we can do, not till tomorrow. Actually, there won't be a thing we can do tomorrow either. Except when there's the emergency we hope won't happen. Anyway, I was thinking about going to see the soccer match with Veneman. If we're needed, we'll hear about it."

"Have fun. Hope you don't get called in."

"Probably nothing will happen. These people, they're warned off, is my guess. They store the tanker and the gas and wait for better times."

"What will you do after the game?" Eekhaut asked. "You won't come in?"

"On a Saturday? I don't know. Maybe. I have a wife who wants to know why I need to work on a Saturday."

Van Gils left Eekhaut alone in the cafeteria. Eekhaut considered having another coffee but finally decided against it. The rest of the team wanted to go out for a bite, but he wasn't in the mood. The whole operation seemed so useless now. He would see Linda and take her out.

Thea De Vries came strolling in, by appearance already in weekend mode, followed by Siegel.

"Oh, hello," she said. "I thought we'd be the only ones here by now."

"The colonel is still around somewhere," Siegel said. "And the surveillance people, but otherwise the place is deserted."

"How's Nick doing?"

"Well, under these circumstances. Got his girl back, so . . ."

"And what about tomorrow?"

"There will probably be a general alert, I guess," Eekhaut said. "Which will keep a lot of people on their toes for the weekend. If nothing happens, we'll all be back here Monday and start over. Hunting for Maxwell and so on."

De Vries looked around the empty floor.

Siegel said, "Well, I guess we're off then."

Eekhaut was left alone. He returned to his office for a moment, scanned a few news sites, then closed the laptop.

50

TOON, THE RETIRED POLICE officer who lived one floor down from Eekhaut, greeted him as warmly as ever. "I haven't seen you in a few days, Walter. Pressure, as always? No time for a drink?"

"I'm always in between things and obligations, Toon. My girlfriend returned from Africa earlier than expected. I'm going to see her now."

"Ah, always difficult to catch up on things in life, I know," Toon said. His old face full of wrinkles spoke of the many years of experience in personal relationships. "Talking to each other, nothing as important as that. Africa, is it now? No place I would go to. Where exactly?"

"Somalia."

"Oh, Somalia. I read about that unfortunate country. Worst place to be in. Cursed continent, too. Worst country in a cursed continent."

"It's not all that bad, Toon. There're many places in Africa where democracy and peace have been around for quite a while."

"Yes, you're probably right. I might be behind on my reading. But still . . . No drink, then?"

"No, Toon, not this evening. Like you say: gotta keep her company."

Wrapped up against the cold, Eekhaut made it to Café De Engelbewaarder on Kloveniersburgwal, with its barred windows on the basement floor and the main floor, where the actual café was situated. Inside he quickly shed his winter coat. Linda was waiting for him at a table with what appeared to be a glass of water. "I'm sorry about this morning and having to leave," he said.

She smiled at him as if she would forgive him anything. He ordered one of the Belgian unfiltered beers for both of them and calamari, spring rolls, and sausages.

"I often catch myself looking over my shoulder," she admitted.

"People are following you?"

"Not really. It's just a feeling I have."

"Afraid African spirits will come after you? Did you get in trouble with a local shaman or whatever?" But he noticed she was serious.

"I saw a sort of . . . magic. Or perhaps something akin to that. A cult that made a habit of burning people alive. And then I discover the same thing happened here."

"It's complicated," he said, not willing to go into the details of the case. "It used to be a worldwide cult, and now they are performing the old rituals. It's ignorance coupled with irrational fear. I'm glad you're back."

"I don't want to be treated as a victim," she said. "Don't treat me as one of those people you need to protect. I can't bear to belong to the ones in that corner."

He took her hands in his, but perhaps that wasn't the most appropriate gesture. This wasn't just about something she had experienced in Somalia. "I rarely, if ever, have had to deal with the victims, Linda. They're all dead."

"Things have . . ." She lowered her head. "I don't know, Walter. Coming back here . . . Things are so much *different*."

"They don't have to be. Not between us."

He felt as if he were losing her.

There was no reason he should feel that. And still, there it was: a growing distance had already manifested between them.

"Did you feel threatened at any point? By the—"

"I know now I should never have gone there. That by doing so, I created a gap between us. And all because I needed time to contemplate our relationship. While doing so, I was explicitly distancing myself from you."

"And then you came back."

"I was *forced* back. Nothing happened because I *wanted* it. Or maybe that's exactly the problem, I *wanted* that distance. I *needed* it. And now, well, I feel as if there's nothing but distance."

Her glass was empty. "I'm an alcoholic," she said, as if suddenly realizing a terrible truth.

He had never seen her drink too much. She wasn't an alcoholic.

"You needed some time alone," he said. "I mean, time without me. I understand. You left because of that. I don't mind. I don't mind being by myself a bit longer. I had taken that into account, you being away for, what, three months? Why don't you take a vacation? France, perhaps. Or Belgium. I can arrange something for you in Belgium, where you'll be on your own. And you can call me anytime. I'll be over there in no time. But only when you want."

"We haven't talked about you yet," Linda said. "I've been talking only about myself, my feelings."

"My feelings are simple. I love you. I want to live with you. I'm not a complicated person in that regard. But I understand."

"I'll think about a vacation," she said.

Eileen had said, "Neutral ground." Which meant not in her apartment and not in Prinsen's either. Neutral ground. He donned his sweater and his parka, walked to the pub she had mentioned, and found her at a table in a quiet corner where they wouldn't be overheard. There weren't many people around anyway. A quiet evening in the center of Amsterdam. In the middle of winter.

"They'll probably close early," she warned him.

"Mmm?"

"I don't know . . ." she started. And then fell silent again, lacking the right words. She had been discharged from the hospital less than an hour after being admitted, as the doctors could find nothing wrong with her. There was the announcement of a general alert, and the medical staff needed as many free beds as possible.

"I'm sorry you got involved in this, Eileen," Prinsen said. "It should not have happened." This was the only thing he could do: apologize. Although nothing was his fault, he blamed himself.

"It had nothing to do with you," she said. But she realized what she was going to say next would sound harsh. "But I know, Nick, I know having a relationship with you will always involve some risk. I will be in bed, every night, and if you're not there, if you're out doing this work you do, I'll be worried. I'll be terrified by the idea that one day you won't return to me, and two of your colleagues will come knocking at our door."

"These things happen only rarely, Eileen."

"How often do girlfriends of police officers get abducted, Nick?"

She had a point. She had a damn good point. It had happened once. It could happen again. Or something much worse.

"I can't make any demands on you, Nick."

"Yes, you can."

"No, I really can't. I know where you came from and what price you paid to get here. About your parents and your home and everything. I know what you left behind. So you're not going to sacrifice all that for me. I can't expect you to do that, and I won't ask. And I know all that because I've been there, Nick, where you have been. So, there we stand."

"You're wrong, Eileen. It's not a matter of choice. I've chosen in life what I want to do, and whom I want to be with. I'll be with you, and I'll be a police officer, and things will turn out fine for the both of us. We both have left one life behind us. We will live the new one together."

"And what if—"

"If what? What if you, Eileen, cross the street, here in the middle of Amsterdam, and some idiot in a car, driving too fast or not paying attention, kills you. Kills you there, on the street. Should we make decisions about what we want, based on that assumption? On the assumption that, yes, some idiot will kill you in some stupid accident that could as well happen in that village of yours or mine?"

"This is different. Don't do this. Don't reduce the problem to simple assumptions, mere speculations."

"You'll be dead just the same. And I will tell myself: if I had let her go back to her folks, she'd still be alive. But you know what's the difference?"

"What?"

"That we'll have shared part of our lives. If only for weeks, months, years, maybe even decades. If the accident doesn't happen, if I don't get shot by a criminal, then we'll have all that time together. And nobody is going to take that from us."

"Nick . . ."

"That, Eileen, is why I want to stay with you, and I want you to stay with me."

Meanwhile, nobody had taken notice of Colonel Al-Rahman. Surely, the colonel himself would not complain about this lack of interest. It allowed him to remain unobtrusive while around him the drama evolved. He had assessed the strengths and weaknesses of each of the members of the Bureau, had evaluated their capabilities, understood their mutual relations. He knew which of the detectives were most passionate about their job. He tried to understand what they talked about among themselves, even when he couldn't understand what they said. He relied on his extensive and specialized training.

He was back in his hotel room now and had just taken another shower. He turned toward the mirror in the bathroom. What he saw taught him nothing new about himself, except that he was getting older. As in a fantasy, he felt a cool evening breeze, smelled the sharp, bitter smoke of wood fires the street vendors used to grill beef on iron skewers, as they had been doing for centuries. The intoxicating aroma of freshly brewed coffee lingered in his mind, and his wife's hand touching, barely, his arm. They would sit on the couch and eat delicious sweet cakes, which he had bought for her.

None of this was real, not here in Amsterdam. In this large and overly decorated hotel where he slept with British executives, German technical engineers, French wine merchants, and Italian shoe designers in the adjoining rooms.

Today he had learned a few things, the least of which was how the Dutch police were organized. About human nature he had, however, learned nothing new. Like everywhere, men protected the women they loved but were less concerned about the well-being of people they did not know. People worked hard to better themselves, but this betterment was almost exclusively seen in terms of material gain and influence and only seldom as a way of attaining spiritual wisdom. Chief Dewaal was one of those who concentrated mainly on extending her circle of influence.

Colonel Al-Rahman dressed in the bathrobe provided by the hotel. Underneath, he was naked. The heating in the room was on high, but he would soon turn it off, allowing him to sleep in a cooling room. He didn't favor artificial heat, but as this was a cold country, he had no choice. From his time in the United Kingdom, he recalled the drafty rooms, the insufficient heating system, and the watery beer. All prejudices, of course. The Dutch beer wasn't any better.

Of course, as a Muslim, he wasn't supposed to drink beer.

He sat down at the table and opened the leather portfolio his wife had bought him for his birthday three years ago. "Every time you open this portfolio," she told him, "you will be reminded of me." And now he thought of her, picking up his pen and writing her a letter. He often wrote her letters, preferring the old artisanal communication over email, even if it meant the letters had to go through official channels.

The mission was almost at an end, he wrote her. Tomorrow he would mail her the letter. It would arrive in a few days. He was going home soon. It was still a matter of finding the serpent, and he could leave that to the Dutch.

But finding the serpent was only part of the mission. The serpent also must die. There was no doubt in the mind of Colonel Al-Rahman. His mission would only be completed when the serpent could no longer do harm.

He hesitated for a moment, glancing at what he had already written. He was sure the letter would be read by other people as well. Nothing in his life was private. Or at least very little. Still, he continued writing.

SATURDAY

51

DEWAAL HAD GATHERED THE entire team into the large open office space on the second floor where, under normal circumstances, only Veneman, Van Gils, Prinsen, and three other officers worked. A persistent fog covered most of Amsterdam. During the morning, the team had gone through Maxwell's computers and phones with no significant result. They'd found quite a bit of intel on the workings of the society, but that would hardly land anyone in jail. However, they found nothing on the final sacrifice, whether on the event or its imminence.

All in all, Eekhaut counted eighteen people present, including the unavoidable Colonel Al-Rahman. Even the technical staff was busy. Everybody's input was appreciated. But both Van Gils and Veneman were absent, a fact that had enraged Dewaal. "Fucking unbelievable," she had said on arriving and finding the two men missing. "They can't be bothered to turn up while we're living under the threat of a terrorist attack?" Eekhaut would have liked to make an excuse for them, but he knew better than to pipe up.

"There will be consequences," Dewaal said. "I'm not kidding. There's no excuse for their absence. You wanted to add something, Walter?"

Eekhaut might also have warned her about too much excitement, rising blood pressure and so on, but he kept his head down for this one. He declined to respond.

"Chief," one of the other officers said, "as long as we don't have any certainty about whether or not there's a real plan and *where* something might happen, there's no sense in being here. It's not like we'll find anything in this heap of shit."

Silence fell over them all. They had all been thinking the same, but even Eekhaut wouldn't have said it aloud. Not again, at least.

He knew Dewaal needed the support of the veteran detectives, whether she liked them or not. Whether she trusted them or not. She didn't, actually, and that was now the main problem. It would have to be solved, but only after the current crisis.

He noticed Al-Rahman turning to Prinsen, probably because he needed translation.

"The tanker truck still hasn't been found," De Vries pointed out. "Although there's a nationwide alert out for it."

"Hidden somewhere," Eekhaut suggested. "They didn't have to drive it out into the country after they bought it—another indication that whatever happens will happen here in Amsterdam. No more news from your informant, Chief?"

"I told you already, Walter, if he doesn't talk to me, he doesn't talk to me. Maybe he's dead, as far as I know."

"That right there's a problem with his reliability, Chief," De Vries said.

"He was reliable when he told us where to find those bodies."

"We need him now more than ever," Eekhaut said. "But nobody seems to be talking. Not your informant. Not even Johanna Simson."

Colonel Al-Rahman listened to the brief explanation Prinsen was giving him, but he'd only get the general drift of the conversation from Prinsen. Eekhaut wondered why he stuck around.

"If we brainstorm long enough," one detective said, "the whole day will have gone by, and Van Gils and Veneman will be the only ones to have done something worthwhile."

Eekhaut let his gaze wander out the window. The fog was lifting just a little, and the skeletal trees in the square were becoming visible again. He could even see the houses to the left of the square.

While gazing, he realized there was an idea in the back of his mind. *Why haven't I thought of that before?* The thought had been skulking and prowling among a collection of cast-off scenarios, presumptions, premonitions, and theories. Occasionally, it would raise its head and wink at him, but all this time he hadn't really taken notice of it.

A terrorist attack. A tanker filled with highly explosive gas. A mass sacrifice. This ghost of an idea—of a solution—trying to catch his wandering attention.

And now it stood there in full light, and he knew how the details connected.

He lowered his head and groaned involuntarily.

"What's wrong, Walter," said Prinsen. "You all right?"

That got everyone's attention.

"Is he ill?" the colonel inquired.

Eekhaut lifted his head again. "The ritual," he said. "Think about their tradition. The tradition of the church. Los Alfaques. The Innovation department store in Brussels, the Tenerife plane crash. All those accidents we assume the church was responsible for. Killing hundreds of the unworthy. Unworthy: which means anyone not belonging to their cult."

"That's such a broad definition, it can apply to—" Prinsen said.

"As many victims as possible. The maximum. Here, in Amsterdam."

"Oh God," De Vries said. Frightened.

"The Amsterdam ArenA," said Prinsen.

"The most important soccer match of the year . . ."

Everyone started talking at the same time.

"What's the expected attendance?"

"When does the match start?"

"We have to contact Van Gils and—"

"Maybe the underground train station—"

Dewaal raised both arms for silence. "All right, everybody!" she shouted. Order returned almost at once. "Is this really the site we've been looking for?"

"If the gas tanker is somewhere on the premises," Eekhaut said, "and its contents are ignited, there'll be thousands of casualties. No one has ever carried out a more extensive sacrifice in the church's history. Anything before this was like a dress rehearsal."

"Are we sure this is it?"

"If it isn't," Eekhaut said, "then what else could it be?"

"Someone tell me when the match starts," Dewaal said. "Come on, all you soccer freaks! And text both Van Gils and Veneman!"

"Three o'clock," Binnendam said.

"Less than an hour from now. I'll call the police chiefs and the ministry. Eekhaut! I want the whole team outside of the building, in the vehicles, with weapons and vests and ready to leave!"

"You heard the boss," Eekhaut said.

52

THE SIX UNMARKED POLICE vehicles drove to the Amsterdam ArenA, the flying saucer–like soccer stadium south of the city that had been, since its opening in 1996, the largest of its kind in the Netherlands. Large enough for a crowd of some 52,000 people, it had been home to international soccer matches and pop concerts by the likes of U2 and the Rolling Stones. Now the two main Dutch soccer teams were playing an eagerly anticipated match, attended by the combined armies of their respective fans.

Stadium security staff and stewards had been alerted that the officers were coming. About three-quarters of the spectators were inside the stadium. Many others were waiting in line outside, but were kept from entering by stewards and members of the riot police. Supporters of both Ajax and Feyenoord booed the arriving officers. Because of the rivalry between the clubs, the atmosphere was heated and would quickly turn openly hostile.

The black BMW with Dewaal, Eekhaut, Prinsen, Siegel, and the colonel stopped in front of a small building outside the perimeter that had been set up by the police. The other Bureau vehicles parked alongside. Eekhaut surveyed the area where more police vehicles were arriving—official ones with more officers in riot gear. Off to one side, two large Mercedes Saloons, each with a uniformed chauffeur and tinted rear windows, stood waiting. He also noticed a trio of equally black SUVs driving by, parking further on. It seemed a lot of important people intended to get involved, although Eekhaut would have preferred that they create distance between themselves and the ArenA.

A gaunt, gray-haired man stepped out of one of the Mercedes and approached Dewaal. "Mastenbroek," Prinsen whispered to Eekhaut. "He's the chief commissioner." Dewaal stepped forward, meeting the commissioner. They talked while surveying the area. More men in uniform and in suits gathered around, some of them talking on phones, others on police radios.

Mastenbroek nodded to Dewaal and talked into his phone. Further on, a riot police officer with a megaphone shouted directions at the waiting fans. They shouted back at him, and Eekhaut could tell they weren't pleased, even without understanding what they said.

Dewaal beckoned Eekhaut. "There's thirty thousand people inside," she told him. "We can't evacuate them all at once, and we can't tell them how serious the threat is. It's going to be difficult. And we must get them away from the ArenA. Much farther away."

"And we don't know whether the truck is actually inside or when it might explode."

"If at all," Dewaal said. "But let's assume the truck is there, and if there's a timer, then it will go off anytime during the match."

"Less than forty minutes. Where would the truck be?"

"There's a large underground garage. Stadium security just told Mastenbroek there are no CCTV cameras in the area. They wanted to have a look themselves, but he told them that's our job. Actually, there's the possibility some members of the society were left behind to make sure nobody could intervene. And they could be armed."

"We have to get in and find out," Eekhaut agreed.

"The bomb squad hasn't arrived yet," Dewaal said. "I'd want them with us, even if we aren't sure about the truck yet. We don't have much time."

"We have our own explosives expert," said Eekhaut.

"Do we?"

"The colonel. He told me he worked with explosives when he was in the army."

"You sure?"

"Best we can do for the moment, Chief."

"Go get him."

Al-Rahman was standing with Prinsen. "We need you, Colonel," Eekhaut said.

"I can help?"

Eekhaut took the colonel to Dewaal. "Do you know anything about explosives, Colonel? Bombs, IEDs, that sort of thing?"

The colonel glanced quickly at Eekhaut, then said, "I was at one time quite familiar with them, Chief, yes."

"We need you in there."

Al-Rahman eyed the ArenA. "I suppose," he said, "as Prinsen told me, you cannot evacuate within a reasonable time frame. So you need to disarm the bomb, whatever it is."

"We don't know what we'll find there, Colonel. We're still guessing."

"I'm with you, Chief," the colonel said.

"Right," Dewaal said. "Eekhaut, Colonel, Prinsen, Siegel, Binnendam, and myself."

"What about Van Gils and Veneman?" Prinsen asked.

"We haven't located them yet, and they're not answering their phones or their messages. Let's move, people. And I need to see the supervisor for this building's maintenance, whoever's in charge of it." She made a gesture toward the ArenA.

Several officers around them all at once drew their phones and started typing or talking.

Moments later an older man in dark blue overalls was brought forward. He seemed confused, uncertain about what all these people wanted from him. Yes, he had worked in the ArenA since it had first opened, did general maintenance of technical installations, and of course knew his way around.

"Underground area? Yep. Large enough for several trucks. The pop groups that come to play drive under the field and unload. How else could they set up their equipment? But it isn't being used now, not when there's soccer."

"We need access to it at once," Dewaal told him.

"I've got the keys," the man said. The six members of the team followed him, with Dewaal ignoring Mastenbroek's advice to take a larger and more heavily armed contingent of police personnel with them. Meanwhile the evacuation was proceeding, but only small groups of fans were being escorted through the exits. This would take hours, Dewaal assumed.

The technician opened a double door and led them into a musty-smelling concrete-walled hall, switching on lights as they went.

"Careful," she said. "They might be waiting for us."

They walked hurriedly behind the technician, guns drawn.

"And remember, no shooting near or at the tanker," she added.

The technician frowned and eyed her suspiciously. They all went down a winding corridor, down a ramp, and then down steel stairs. Dozens of pipes and cables, coded in striking colors, ran along the ceilings. Everything else was painted a dull gray. The area smelled of oil and disinfectants.

"Still far?" Dewaal asked.

"It's a big building, ma'am," the technician said.

He stopped at a door, no different than the ones they had passed. This one sported a number: XT554, white on gray.

"This is it?"

"Behind it there's an access to the large parking area beneath the field, ma'am."

"Open the door, but slowly."

The technician pressed a lever, but nothing happened. The door didn't open.

"What's the matter?" Dewaal asked.

"It won't open."

"God, man, don't you have the key?"

"There's no key, ma'am," the technician said. "Someone on the other side blocked the door."

"Come on, guys," Dewaal told the officers. "Give it a push."

They tried, but the door didn't budge.

"Seems like they locked themselves in," Prinsen said.

"Is there another entrance?" Dewaal asked the technician.

"There's another door, down the corridor, and there's the main gate itself opening into the garage, for the trucks."

"Let's move on then."

The next door didn't move either. Then the technician led them to a twenty-foot high gate, which also remained shut when he engaged the mechanism to open it.

"What options do we have left?" Dewaal asked the technician. "Come on, we don't have much time."

"There's a technical passage, where the cables run into the parking area," the man said. "It's a tight fit, but you could use it."

"Show us."

The technician led them to a row of steel plates on the wall. He turned a lever, and one of the panels moved sideways. Behind it was a passageway from which hundreds of cables of all sizes and colors disappeared into the dark behind them.

"What are they for?" Eekhaut asked.

"Everything," the technician said. "High-tension energy supply, data transmissions, alarm systems. Everything runs through here."

Dewaal pressed forward. "We'll skip the guided tour. It's just straight in or what?"

"Into the dark," the technician said.

She drew her gun and climbed into the passageway. There were only a few feet between the wall of the passageway on one side and the cables on the other. Eekhaut went in second; the others brought up the rear. The narrow space was cramped for Eekhaut. He felt uneasy, and it seemed difficult to breathe. But what he felt most was fear—of the immediate danger from the bomb and of a potential welcoming committee.

Dewaal had turned on her flashlight and was guiding them. In front of her was the corridor. She stopped.

"What you waiting for, Chief?" Eekhaut asked.

"We have to assume they're familiar with the layout of this building," she said.

"Perhaps not in detail."

"This Maxwell is crazy."

"Undoubtedly. In many senses of the word. And?"

"He's probably paranoid. But he's no idiot."

"No, he isn't," Eekhaut said, whose thoughts lingered on a ticking timer of the bomb.

"He will assume we might find this access after we've found the closed doors."

"They might be waiting for us, you mean?" Prinsen said, behind Eekhaut.

She scanned the corridor with her flashlight and found what she was looking for. A small black box with a blinking LED. Hard to notice if you weren't looking. And to the left, no cables ran. Not part of the building's security's system.

"A sensor," she said.

"Doing what?"

"Don't know. Might set off an alarm or a bomb. Let's turn back and see if there's another entrance."

They climbed out of the niche again. She approached the technician. "There's also a ventilation duct," he said. "Runs over the ceiling. Ends in the main garage."

"Let's try that."

By the time they got to the ladder leading up to the ductwork, everyone was sweaty and dusty. "I hope this duct will hold us," Dewaal said.

"It's supposed to, ma'am. It's for cleaning and installing new filters," the technician said.

"All right then, up the ladder, everybody."

This time Prinsen led the way, and soon the six of them crawled through the ductwork. Al-Rahman went in last. The technician remained in the hall behind them.

Eekhaut, like the others, was trying to keep his flashlight focused ahead as they crawled through the ventilation ducts. There wasn't much room in any direction, so progress was difficult. Finally, Prinsen found a hatch in the bottom of the ductwork, carefully opened it after the others had killed their lights, and peered through it.

He went, feet first, through the hatch. The others followed, landing on a steel passageway high above the floor of the underground parking space. They squatted and scanned the large open area. A tanker truck, the size of a dinosaur and as conspicuous in the empty garage, hulked in the middle, under the harsh lights.

"I see no one," Prinsen whispered. Siegel and Binnendam slowly moved toward the end of the passageway. Prinsen got up and leaned over the railing.

A loud bang echoed through the hall. Metal and concrete fragments sprayed over Prinsen, who ducked down again.

"Gun!" Dewaal whispered, although there was no longer any need for silence. There was no cover. They had to get off the passageway as soon as possible. Two ladders, each in a different corner, led to the floor. Eekhaut had seen them as well. Siegel and Binnendam moved toward one, the others hurried toward the other.

Three more shots rang out, but they continued anyway, hurrying down the ladders and spreading out in the garage, looking for cover. The shooter remained well hidden.

A shot came from the other end of the garage. Al-Rahman aimed his pistol and fired three times in rapid succession. Eekhaut moved to the left, followed by Dewaal. Prinsen stayed with the colonel.

More shots came from the end of the garage. They saw muzzle flashes of at least one gun.

"Mind the tanker," Dewaal repeated.

She and Eekhaut avoided the vehicle.

They stopped behind a pillar. Eekhaut looked for possible hiding places.

"Keep your head down," Dewaal warned him.

"I will. I'm rather attached to it," he said.

Shots came from the other officers and, farther off, another gun. Then, at last, there was silence.

"Give it up, whoever you are," Dewaal shouted.

There was no response.

She stood up, behind the pillar. "We've got to move, Walter. We can't just stand here."

And she ran. He followed her and saw Al-Rahman and Prinsen at the other side of the garage, running, hiding, and running again.

They reached the hiding place of their opponent. A man in a black and yellow tracksuit lay on his back in a puddle of blood, with a pistol next to him. Dewaal kicked it away and quickly felt the man's pulse. "He's dead."

The other officers spread out, but the man had been alone.

"Colonel!" Dewaal called. "Defuse the bomb."

Al-Rahman moved toward the tanker, inspected the tractor, and, covered by the other officers, climbed inside the cabin. Eekhaut opened the other tractor door. Against the dashboard, on the passenger's side, a dozen cables in different colors led from a rectangular black box toward what looked like a large package wrapped in plastic foil.

"Timing device," Al-Rahman said, pointing at the box, and at the package, "Explosive charge." He slid a multifunctional tool from his jacket pocket. "Let's see how much time we still have."

He screwed open the box, peered inside, ran his fingers over some cables.

"How long?" Dewaal asked.

"One minute twenty," Al-Rahman said.

"Fix it," she said.

"It's in Allah's hands now."

"It's in your hands, Colonel," Dewaal insisted.

The colonel pushed the tool between the cables. A click, a snap. He sat up.

"Why do you doubt Allah's will, Chief?" he asked, looking at Dewaal.

"I wouldn't dare, but I prefer the dirty work here on Earth be done by soldiers and police officers."

"Well," he said, "in this case somebody made sure we're all safe."

She looked nonplussed. "Why is that?"

"The clock was ticking, and I wanted to make sure it wasn't connected to some other charge, so I disconnected it from the detonator. But the link between the timer and the rest of the contraption was already severed. There would not have been an explosion."

"We're no longer in danger then?"

"No, ma'am. We never were. Not after somebody sabotaged the whole thing."

They all got out of the cab. "I'm calling the bomb squad anyway, to make sure," Dewaal said. "Too many things around that can blow up by accident." She walked away from the truck to phone the others.

"The question is, who intervened?" Eekhaut said to Prinsen.

He shrugged. "Did us a favor."

"Maybe it's her informant, working on the inside. And all the while the chief claims not to know who *he* is. At any rate, it's a man she's talking about."

Colonel Al-Rahman approached Eekhaut while Prinsen and two other officers inspected the surroundings. "Do you know what the origin of the name Baphomet is, Chief Inspector?"

Eekhaut was surprised the colonel for once wanted to share information. "I have no idea, actually."

"It originates from the French, as it was in use many centuries ago. It was the name Christians used for the Prophet Muhammad. They struggled with the pronunciation of many names and words of Semitic and Oriental languages, which is why you are still talking about Avempace or Averoës. And Mohammed, or Mahommed, was corrupted to Baphomet." The colonel smiled. "Although the story might be apocryphal, like so many stories from older times."

"Is it not ironic that this name was chosen by an apocalyptic cult for the name of their leader? The name of the prophet?"

Al-Rahman agreed, glancing at the tool he was holding. "This is most ironic, indeed. But irony is not just a Western quality. The thing is, Chief Inspector, that both our cultures are plagued by the same problem, too little information about the other. "

"I'm sure that's true." Eekhaut wondered why the colonel was suddenly becoming talkative. A sign of improved relations between Christian and Islam cultures? Or a reaction to the tension?

"Many people in the Arab world see the West as greedy, shallow, devoid of spirituality, imperialist, obsessed with sex and violence. You might be aware of our clichés. But strangely enough, so many people in the Arab world admire your scientific and technological achievements and your popular culture."

"Except what is forbidden."

"Yes, but depending on the specific country, the Sharia is interpreted differently. Of course, the Wahhabites are stricter in their interpretation of the Quran than the Sunni brothers. But even in Saudi Arabia and in the Gulf States, private religious practice is allowed, although not the public practice of any religion other than Islam. But the West, these days, has become so . . . careless with its intellectual and historical values. This is not a matter of religion itself, but of morals and ethics. Both are lacking profoundly in Western culture. At least, that's how a lot of people in the Islamic world perceive it."

This, Eekhaut realized, was the colonel's longest speech. And though he knew these arguments, he felt a freshness in Al-Rahman's approach.

But then, he wondered, what sort of role was the colonel playing?

Why was he here?

Surely not for the sake of some all too evident cultural disparities between Islam and the West?

He noticed Dewaal walking back toward them, still on the phone. "Would you repeat that," she said, loud enough for the others to hear. She made a writing motion. Eekhaut found his pen and notebook and handed her both. She crouched down and began writing, keeping the notebook on her leg. "How long? Hello? Hello?"

She shoved the phone back into her pocket. "Disconnected," she said.

"Who was that?" Prinsen wanted to know.

"My informant. Could not talk long. Baphomet and some others seem to have gone into hiding." She handed Eekhaut his notebook back. "That's where they are at the moment. But probably not for long."

He saw an address.

The other officers had finished their tour. "Strange as it seems, Chief," Binnendam said, "there's no one else here. Maybe they found only one aspiring martyr."

"All the better," Dewaal said. "We have another appointment with these people. Eekhaut, show everyone the address. Let's move out at once, gentlemen. I want this scum behind bars as soon as possible."

"Bomb squad will be here in a moment," Binnendam said.

"We'll leave someone to guide them. Did you manage to contact Van Gils and Veneman?"

"Texted them again. They're outside, waiting for us."

While heavily armed police and a squad of special forces entered the area, the officers went out and found both missing colleagues. Dewaal ignored them. She asked Binnendam, showing him Eekhaut's notebook, "You know where this is?"

"*Het Kleine Water*? That's in the Veluwe. A place for families to go on vacation in the summer. Swimming, fishing, boating—that sort of thing. An inexpensive alternative to the Canary Islands, I guess. Never been there myself. There's a camping site and small family cabins. Remote, too. "

"How far?"

"Fifty miles, give or take."

"Five cars," Dewaal ordered. "Van Gils, Veneman, you're in as well. And armed assistance."

"Yes ma'am," Van Gils said.

"Where are we going?" Colonel Al-Rahman inquired.

"The Veluwe," Prinsen said. "Part of Gelderland Province and as far removed from Amsterdam as you could possibly want. Or not want. It's part of the Dutch Bible Belt, mainly agrarian, very thinly inhabited. People who still strongly adhere to traditional Protestant beliefs, often against the values of the secular society."

"Yes," Al-Rahman said. "I think I get the picture."

53

COURIER STOOD BESIDE THE body, gun in hand. Nobody had heard the shot. He had used the silencer. Not that many people were around anyway. This was a spot that attracted few, if any, visitors and none outside the vacation season. Not in the middle of winter. The ponds were partially frozen over, no waterfowl to be seen. The banks were damp and cold, the woods almost dark, even though it was early in the afternoon. Nature had ceased to make sounds. The cottages were like silent nocturnal animals sleeping through winter. Only the largest of them was now in use and heated. This looked like the least hospitable place in the whole of the Netherlands.

Courier glanced around. The kitchen was in the back of the cabin, facing away from the lake, next to the garden. Or what, during summer, would be a garden. He could drag out the corpse, and no one would notice. But then what? Drop it in the pond where it wasn't yet frozen over? He couldn't bury it, didn't have the time, and the ground would be hard. The pond wasn't deep, but if he weighted down the body, it would disappear for now. He didn't care if it was found later.

With his free hand, he felt the barrel of the gun. It was warm, not hot. He had only fired once. He unscrewed the silencer from the barrel and let it slide into his pocket. Then he pushed the gun under his belt, behind his back.

He knelt beside the dead man. The head was partially gone. A mess, but at least the man had been dead instantly. Courier found it comforting that he'd died without pain or regret. He had used a hollow point. The man had deserved a slow and painful death for his many sins, but Courier was merciful. Anyway, he had needed a quick and certain kill.

He picked up the phone lying next to the man. The display was dark, and nothing happened when Courier pushed a few buttons. Perhaps the phone was damaged. It didn't matter now. The man might have called the police earlier that day, but what could be done about it? Courier had heard him mentioning the name of this place. The police would be here soon.

It was a question of finding another hiding place. Did Baphomet have an alternative?

Courier rose when the door leading into the corridor opened. Baphomet stared at him, surprised. "I thought I heard something."

"You heard him falling down," Courier said thoughtfully. "You could not have heard the shot."

Baphomet peered at the body as if he feared the dead man might rise again. "Is that Metagogeus?"

"It is. Sorry about the mess I made. He was betraying us."

Baphomet didn't even ask about the evidence. *He trusts me. He knows I shot our fellow brother for a good reason.* "Only problem is what do I do with him? He was calling the cops, told them where we are. We might have expected a traitor among us, Baphomet. But Metagogeus? Maybe I am too gullible, but I hadn't suspected him. Nevertheless, he sold us out. The enemy will be here soon. We should leave at once."

Baphomet didn't seem perturbed. "Now why would he do that, betray us, why would he do that, do you think, Courier?"

Courier examined Baphomet carefully in the feeble light. The body didn't seem to upset him much. Neither did the betrayal. "What do you mean?"

"It is an obvious question, don't you think?" Baphomet said dryly. "Why would someone like Metagogeus talk to the police? Why would he betray us? He's as guilty as any of us, and he would have gone to prison for a very long time. There is no way he would be saved either if we cannot accomplish more sacrifices. He had a lot to lose, didn't he, in betraying us. And what would he gain?"

"He's an informer," Courier insisted. "Perhaps he was a police officer working undercover all these years. I don't know, Baphomet. I have no idea."

"You know this is nonsense, Courier. I have known most of you for a considerable time, and I know how faithful you all are. None of you could be working for the police. Certainly not Metagogeus. For years, he's been my trusted aide, my fellow traveler. His passion for the cause was without restraint. He did things—"

"You mean I killed the man without a good reason?"

Baphomet shook his head. "I imply nothing. I am only saying that you're the one holding the gun, and he's the one dead on the floor. The gun you used to kill an esteemed member of our society. This is what I see here. Nothing more, nothing less."

"But he was calling the police and telling them where we are. I wanted to stop him."

"The evil clearly had been done, Courier. He had already called them if that is what he did. So, there would have been no need to kill him. He would have been more valuable to us alive. Maybe as a hostage."

Courier was becoming distressed by Baphomet's stubbornness. Could the man not understand his reaction? Was he, Courier, now suspect in the eyes of Baphomet? "He was a traitor, Baphomet," he insisted. "We have treated traitors like this before. We have treated them worse than this."

"Yes, Courier," Baphomet said, "our tradition tells us clearly how to deal with traitors. But it also tells us not to carelessly decide about the lives of our own companions. We never take decisions too rashly. We think them over. We discuss. There resides our strength. And then, only after careful consideration, do we act. That's how it was done in the past."

"I may have judged too quickly, Baphomet, and for that I'm sorry. But we are persecuted, and we must act swiftly."

"*Persecuted*? Of course we are persecuted. What would you expect? We have just organized and performed the greatest purification in history. Thousands of humans sacrificed in one event. We would already have heard about it, had we not been isolated as we are. And does this matter, this persecution? No, it doesn't. Because very soon humanity will cease to exist, as was foretold, and even the universe might cease to exist. And then, we will be redeemed."

Courier didn't react.

"Now," Baphomet continued, "the question you need to ask yourself, Courier, is this: is there a reason to continue fleeing, or should we wait for the police and accept whatever fate they have in store for us?"

"We cannot expect anything good from captivity," Courier said.

"Of course not. We must remain free. Maybe the world will need more rituals still, and we are the only ones to provide them. Now tell me, dear Courier, was there any other witness to the conversation Metagogeus had with the police?"

"No. He was alone, and so was I."

"No one."

"He stood here, in the kitchen, and I caught his words, and my conclusion was—"

"You didn't give him the opportunity to explain himself?"

Courier said nothing.

"And of course," Baphomet concluded, "he no longer has an opinion to share with us. You made sure of that."

"Don't you believe me, Baphomet?"

Baphomet raised a revolver and held it to Courier's head. "I am not," he said, "inclined to believe you."

"There's no need for that gun!" Courier exclaimed.

"Are you afraid of guns, Courier? That is strange, since you just shot a man."

"This is going too far, Baphomet!"

The door behind Baphomet opened. He glanced over his shoulder. Serena stood in the doorway and stared at both men. "What are you doing?" the girl said. Then she saw the body on the floor. "God! What happened?"

"Our companion Courier claims Metagogeus was talking to the police," Baphomet said.

"And why would he do that?"

"That's exactly what happened," Courier said. "I'm telling the truth."

"Then why are you keeping your gun to his head?" she asked Baphomet.

"Because I do not believe his story. I don't believe Metagogeus was a traitor to our cause. Maybe Courier was mistaken in what he heard. Or maybe Courier can no longer be trusted."

"We have to go," Courier said. "Whatever your opinion of me, you know we have to leave."

"This place is isolated and more than an hour's drive from Amsterdam. I assume the police will have much more to worry about than us, with thousands of bodies and half the city in panic. Anyway, where would we go? The number of hiding places at our disposal is limited." Baphomet turned to Serena. "Go get the other companions."

Serena disappeared again. A few moments later, the other three members of the society stood in the main room, all of them young and willing to die for the greater cause, exactly why Baphomet had chosen them for this mission. He wasn't going to take any of the older members along except for Courier and Metagogeus—who might have been a spy.

"Jasper, Nemeth, there's a body in the kitchen. Carry it outside and try to clean the floor as much as you can. Courier will help you with that."

"They will find him . . ." Courier said.

"Let them find him, whoever *they* are. It will be too late anyway. We have come this far, and we have not been stopped. Do you care what happens to the body?"

"You want to be arrested," Courier said, his voice growing shrill. "You want to be arrested, don't you, so the world can see you and admire you or loathe you or whatever. You want to laugh at them from your cell."

"Perhaps I do," Baphomet said. "The time has come to confront the world with our passion. And with our message. Too few people are aware of our message. Now, for the first time, we might have their attention. We might even gain many converts when people realize their sole hope of redemption lies with us."

"You talk too much about passion, Baphomet," Courier said, exasperated. "You expect too much passion too. People are rational these days. They don't tend to—"

"No," Baphomet said. "Look at the news. Look at people. The time for Reason is over. Jasper, Nemeth? The body? And you, Courier."

The two young men entered the kitchen and carefully carried Metagogeus outside, into the cold and the dark. In the kitchen, Baphomet kept his gun aimed at Courier.

54

THE TEAM MADE GOOD time covering the fifty miles between Amsterdam and *Het Kleine Water*. The five big BMWs swerved through traffic, sirens blaring, lights flashing. Other cars moved out of the way. Dewaal was on the phone most of the time. She would concern herself with the paperwork later, but she needed at least verbal consent from the hierarchy for the operation and a couple of updates. The ministry finally gave its permission after the police chief had intervened on behalf of the Bureau. Only then did Dewaal stop cursing. "You'd like to believe we have some sort of federal police force unified under a single command, but far from it, goddamn it! I have to pass AIVD management, regional police chiefs, and even local police. Time for a change."

The last miles were the most difficult and the slowest. A provincial road meandering through sleepy villages and then something no better than a glorified track between trees. Like it had been in the Ardennes, Eekhaut thought, but without snow. He sat in the same car as Dewaal, with Al-Rahman riding shotgun, having reassured Dewaal and earned his place thanks to defusing an already defused bomb.

"Kill the lights," Dewaal instructed, and they drove the last stretch almost in the dark.

After a final slope, under the dramatically overcast sky, they spotted a dozen buildings on the edge of a darkening lake. The cars stopped at a safe distance, and the officers got out. They gathered around Dewaal, out of sight of the houses. Some of the officers had shotguns. Without the sound of engines, the surroundings seemed out of this world; not even wind moved through the naked branches. The cold began to creep into the officers' bones. Eekhaut knew it would be bad to get injured, with the cold and all. Hypothermia was a real danger under these circumstances.

Dewaal and some of the others observed the buildings, only one of which seemed inhabited.

"Three cars in the back," Prinsen reported.

"They might have heard our cars," Dewaal said. "And I can't depend on my informant. He might be dead anyway. This is where it all ends, as far as I'm concerned. Is that clear?"

"Yes ma'am," said Prinsen.

"Veneman?"

"Chief?"

"Take four officers to the right. Set them up just inside the woods over there, so they can't be seen from the cabins. Thijssen, take four others and do the same to our left flank. We'll assume they're still there, somewhere in those cabins. We'll assume they don't have a boat."

"Too much ice on the water for a boat," Van Gils said.

"Good. Move out, both teams."

Veneman and Thijssen left.

"Is this the Dutch idea of a vacation retreat or what?" Eekhaut asked. "No wonder everybody takes their vacations in Spain."

"All right, already," Dewaal whispered urgently. She kept her eyes on the cabins. "Keep your eyes peeled. Everyone in position? Who's got the megaphone? Ah, thanks."

Her voice echoed over the lake. "Maxwell! This is the police. We have you surrounded. Give yourself up."

They waited. Nothing happened. Some of the officers changed positions, but nothing else moved.

"Either they're not there—" Van Gils said.

"They are. Or they fled into the woods earlier, on foot," Dewaal said. "Either way, we'll catch them."

"We're sitting on our hands, that's what we're doing," Eekhaut grumbled. "Let's move in."

"What is the situation, Chief Inspector?" Colonel Al-Rahman asked, in English, unable to understand the Dutch spoken by the officers.

Eekhaut explained in a few words. "They'll be armed," he added.

"Perhaps we had better wait for reinforcements?" the colonel suggested.

"We catch them now, or we don't," Dewaal said.

"Baphomet, he is in there, in one of those cabins?"

"He is, Colonel. At least, that's what we assume." Dewaal considered her options. "Since we're not going to sit on our hands any longer, Walter, we'll have to move. Van Gils, Prinsen, three teams. Search every cabin, every shack."

"Right, ma'am."

The officers moved forward.

"You see what happens when we don't have control of things?" Courier said. They'd been waiting in the cabin for more than an hour, waiting for Baphomet to decide. But that decision had not come, and now they were surrounded by police. The indecision angered Courier. The three novices clearly were nervous and kept a watchful eye on their master.

"Keep a lid on it," Baphomet said. He didn't sound angry, seemingly not in the least disturbed by the unfolding events. Jasper had taken Courier's gun and sat on a chair by the window, with a partial view of the silhouettes of the AIVD officers all around the buildings. They knew the officers could not see them, since the lights were out. Just now a megaphoned female voice had told them they were surrounded. Nobody in the house had felt like responding, not even Baphomet.

"What's our next move?" Courier insisted. "Baphomet? Don't you see the madness in continuing? Why didn't we leave an hour ago when there was still time?"

Baphomet seemed distant. He took a moment to respond. "There is no need for excitement, my brother and companion. Our sins have now been forgiven. Eternal peace awaits us. What happens here is of no importance." He surveyed the room. "Aren't we at peace, Nemeth, Toth, Jasper?"

The three young men agreed silently.

"And what is your plan?" Courier insisted.

Baphomet smiled indulgently. "There will be time for the last sacrifice, Courier," he said. And he thought, *You are too weak to understand the importance of all this. You were always a trusted companion, a follower of the cult. But in the end, those are just meaningless words: companion, cult, follower. All is now devoid of meaning.*

He had a final plan. In the chaos and confusion that would soon erupt, he would disappear. His companions would have to find their own way out, however that might be. After this, both Maxwell and Baphomet would disappear.

At least for a while.

At least until the final reckoning would announce itself. Then he, the ultimate prophet, would claim his due, would claim his place in history.

Until then he would be a faceless man.

"It is the ultimate sacrifice," he said. "When the police enter these cabins, we will unite with our Creator. This will save us from the humiliation of a trial and prison. How can we be judged by mere mortals, anyway? We will go where mortals have no power over us."

He turned to Courier. "Or do you see yourself in a prison cell for years, Courier?"

Courier didn't reply. He could imagine a fate worse than prison, but he would probably not have a choice.

Serena sat in an armchair in the corner of the living room and watched the men. Especially the three young followers, who seemed unmoved by Baphomet's proposal. They were in his power, though, and would be until the end. They had been brainwashed and would follow him anywhere. They were afraid of him but more concerned about the purity of their souls.

Courier seemed to wake up. "What exactly do have you in mind, Baphomet? Another explosive device?"

"Unfortunately, a very ordinary bomb, yes," Baphomet said. He opened a cupboard and slid out a package the size of a laptop computer. It looked ominous, black with a few wires connecting different parts and a small display on top. He pushed a recessed button. "It's armed now. I couldn't come up with anything better on such short notice. I will be forgiven for such a lack of imagination. But it will be effective."

"They're coming," Jasper said.

Baphomet got up and joined him at the window. Dark figures, partially hidden by shrubs, shadows, and buildings closed in on them.

The two officers who first reached the building snuck around its corners toward the door and windows. They went slowly, keeping an eye on the other buildings.

"Too little experience," Dewaal whispered to Eekhaut as she eyed their progress. "These men haven't done much of this in a long time. And what about you?"

"I wouldn't be a good example for them, at my age," Eekhaut replied. "This wasn't the sort of thing I did in Brussels. No SWAT or anything. We occasionally kicked in a door, but you need little training for that."

They crouched behind a warped, rotten fence, observing the advancing officers. Eekhaut wondered about this place being a vacation camp. It was winter, but he couldn't imagine this would look much better in summer, desolate and downtrodden as it seemed in the dark.

Dewaal spoke into her radio. "Thijssen?"

"Yes?"

"Keep two officers outside, the rest go in. Every room, every cupboard."

"All right."

"They're armed, Thijssen."

"I'm aware of that, Chief. So are we."

"They won't surrender," Eekhaut whispered to Dewaal. "They'd rather commit suicide than be caught. They believe they'll be reunited with their creator or whatever."

"If that's what they want, we can arrange it," Dewaal said. "But try to concentrate, Walter. We move in, house by house." She spoke into the radio again. "Move, Thijssen." Then she got up and, followed by Eekhaut and other officers, headed for the nearest building.

Jasper whispered, "Here they come, Baphomet." His voice was raw with excitement.

Baphomet said, "And what is happening at the other buildings?"

"There's a number of cops moving toward the cabins on the east side. They're going in. I see lights."

"When they enter in here, we detonate the bomb," Baphomet said. "You, Courier, are allowed to press the final countdown button. Here, this one. It gives you ten seconds to consider your last sins."

Serena stepped up to him and grabbed his arm. "We can't go through with it, Baphomet," she said. "There's absolutely no sense in continuing this charade."

He looked at her in surprise. "And where is that passion you had before, my companion? The passion and the certainty I so much admired in you? Do you doubt our destiny? Are you doubting all we stand for? Now, at this ultimate moment?"

"We've done what we set out to do, in Amsterdam," Serena insisted. "That should be enough. We can be martyrs for our cause and explain our motives to the world at large, which is more important than dying here. Us dying here isn't even a statement, Baphomet. We should live and speak openly about the things we believe in. Even at a trial, even in jail. The world is waiting for us. There is no sense in being dead martyrs if you can be live ones."

"That does sound convincing," he said, smiling at her. "Very convincing. But you're on my turf now, girl. Living in shame, waiting for the end in the same way mere mortals do, that is not what we were meant to do." His face changed, his smile disappeared. "Courier here knows what to do. I will retreat to the back room, for my last thoughts. The bomb is powerful enough and will leave nothing but . . ."

"It's all a lie!" she exclaimed. And she pointed a small but efficient-looking gun at Baphomet's head. "You've lived so long with this lie, Maxwell, too long. It will end here."

Baphomet considered the weapon with a slight smile. "Prime the bomb, Courier," he said.

"No, Courier," Serena said. "Don't touch the thing. You don't want to die. Neither do I."

"You wouldn't want to live for a lie either," Baphomet reasoned. "We will be in the news for a short while, during the trial, and then we go to prison for the rest of our lives, and we will be forgotten."

"And rightfully so," Serena said. "Except in the memory of those who lost their loved ones. They will not forget." She looked at Courier. "He has brought us this far, Courier. Let us end this, but not as he intended. He is a madman. He condemns innocent people—"

"You were there as well, as I recall." Baphomet said.

"Like the others, I was used. By you, Baphomet."

Outside, police officers tried to get in, rattling the door and shutters. Voices demanded access. They heard pounding on the kitchen door.

"Courier!" Baphomet commanded.

"There was no sacrifice earlier today," Serena said. "The bomb in the ArenA didn't go off."

"Of course it did," Baphomet insisted.

But his face was pale now.

"I cut the wiring," Serena said. "I made sure it couldn't explode. There was no major sacrifice in Amsterdam today. I canceled your big event, Maxwell."

His eyes narrowed. "Who the hell are you?"

"I'm an officer of Interpol, Maxwell. And you're under arrest. And what a pleasure it is to say that!"

Baphomet didn't move. Neither did any of the others.

Except for Courier.

When Eekhaut and Dewaal stepped into the room, they were confronted with an unexpected situation. A young woman kept Maxwell at gunpoint and was, in turn, being targeted by one of the others present, a surly-looking man in his fifties whose contorted expression made it clear he was serious about the standoff.

Eekhaut and Dewaal were followed by Prinsen and Al-Rahman. Six guns were pointing at human beings.

"This is not going to end well, Commissioner," Courier said. "What we do is this: the girl and I step out with no interference on your part. We get into a car and drive away. She leaves her gun here, of course. Afterward, when I'm sure I'm not followed, I will leave her behind somewhere, and then I'll disappear. How about that for a plan?"

Maxwell, meanwhile, said nothing. He no longer seemed interested in the proceedings.

The young woman gazed at the officers. "You're late," she said. "I had hoped you'd found this place earlier."

"And who are you?" Dewaal inquired. She tried to focus on Maxwell and the thing on the table that might be a bomb.

Courier stepped toward the young woman and pushed his gun firmly under her chin. "Drop your weapon, bitch!" he hissed. "I'm fed up with all this."

"You'd better drop yours," Dewaal insisted. "You're going nowhere. What do you expect? Where will you go? Germany? Denmark? Police will be waiting for you everywhere you go. And who's the girl anyway?"

"I'm an Interpol officer, and I'm not a girl," the woman said.

It was Maxwell who spoke next. "We have been purified, Courier. You do not need to run. We will accept whatever punishment the world imposes on us. That world will not last long anyway."

But he sounded less certain, less inspired.

"Purified?" Eekhaut said. "You're a bunch of psychopaths and murderers, that's what you are. Your biggest plan failed. Everything you attempted, you and your Society of Fire, amounted to nothing."

"We are—" Baphomet sputtered. "We will all die now, and you will be part of this last sacrifice. You and your sacrilegious . . . Jasper, the bomb!"

Colonel Al-Rahman moved quickly toward the surprised young man and took the package from the table. Jasper didn't react.

"Master?" Courier inquired.

Baphomet turned his head toward him.

"Master, are we cleansed?"

"Yes, my dear, dear Courier, we are cleansed."

"Thank you, master," said Courier. He shoved his gun under his own chin and pulled the trigger.

55

SERENA MADE LITTLE EFFORT to wipe the blood off her face and neck. She didn't seem to be bothered by it. She sat across from Eekhaut at the kitchen table and drank water from a tall glass he had found in the cupboard. But Eekhaut noticed the slight tremor of her hands. He saw her as tough, but her body was telling her she had endured enough.

Al-Rahman was leaning against the counter, arms folded over his chest. Dewaal had ordered them both to remain in the cabin with the young woman while the other officers escorted the zealots of the society to the cars. Both corpses, including the one found outside the house earlier, had been taken to an empty shed, for later evacuation.

"Interpol," Eekhaut said approvingly. "Goddamn Interpol. And we weren't even advised. Left in the dark and all that."

Colonel Al-Rahman watched them both, impassively. Eekhaut wasn't sure how much he'd understood, but he was sure the colonel had gotten the main drift of the story.

"And how did Interpol get involved?"

Serena carefully set the glass on the table. "We have been after Maxwell for quite a while, Chief Inspector. Ever since he founded the society. We were familiar with the activities of the church as well, but they had renounced their former crimes and no longer posed a threat. Before that, well—there was hardly anything to prove, but that's old history. And then, well, you're familiar with the story, so I heard."

"You're Dewaal's informant."

"No, that wasn't me. He was in Maxwell's organization before I got in. Actually, I had no idea who he was. He's the man Courier shot earlier. You found his body outside. Nothing I could do for him, I'm afraid. We have been involved with the church for a long time. All this dates from before Interpol, when national security services tried to infiltrate the church. Tried but didn't succeed. We shifted our attention to the apostates when the church changed its policy twenty years ago. The psychopaths, like Maxwell. We needed to know what they were up to. Oh, he's smart, is he ever. We couldn't pin anything on him. And for years we couldn't get anyone in, until very recently." She grinned maliciously. "Want to run an organization well, hire a psychopath. We knew Maxwell would amp up the activities of his little organization."

"So, behind our backs—"

"Oh, no. The head of AIVD knew about us, of course. But since we weren't sure about who in the Bureau could be trusted, we decided to keep it at that. Not even Dewaal knew about me." She shrugged. "Basically, it's the big boys talking to each other in their big-boy network. As if it ever was any different."

"These things tend to get out of hand when we're all orbiting around the same object, unaware of each other," Eekhaut said. "What if we accidentally shot you?"

"Professional risks," Serena said. "Undercover agents know that can happen. We at Interpol try to avoid situations like these, but on the other hand I'm glad I followed Maxwell this close. Saved us all a lot of aggravation, didn't it?"

"How did you manage? To infiltrate, I mean?"

"Through one of his companies. He noticed me. Well, I made sure he would notice me. Me and my religious zeal. He was always on the lookout for new followers. His vanity, in the end, is what defeated him. That, and probably my looks too."

Even under the circumstances, Eekhaut was aware of her good looks. "It was the informant that gave us the coordinates of the Ardennes site."

"Yes. We got that one too late. The sacrifice, I mean. But we still had nothing on Maxwell."

"So, we went on a wild goose chase, while Interpol and the head of AIVD were after Maxwell all the time."

"Something like that, yes."

Al-Rahman, who couldn't follow what was being said, leaned in. "Can I assume," he said confidentially, "that the matter is now definitely settled?"

"It is, Colonel," Eekhaut replied, in English.

"We were wondering about your role," Serena said to the colonel. "Were you sent here solely because of the prince's murder?"

"Exactly, ma'am. I already explained to the chief inspector: the royal family was involved and much concerned, and therefore—"

"Yes, well," Serena interrupted him. "I've looked at your profile, Colonel, and sincerely, your presence astonished me. If that's the right expression. You're employed by the Saudi secret service, aren't you?"

"I never made a secret of that, ma'am," the colonel said.

"No, of course you haven't. But then, in your country, it is not easy to make the distinction between security services and the Mutaween, or even military intelligence."

"I'm Mutaween, as I adequately explained," Al-Rahman said. "It is, indeed as you state, a subtle distinction. But then, to us, religious matters and matters of state coincide to a high degree."

"Well," Serena said and got up. "I think I'd like to have a shower now, Chief Inspector. Not here, however. I need to return to Amsterdam at the earliest. Shower and report in that order. And then maybe something to eat."

Outside more AIVD officers and an armed response team had gathered. The five AIVD cars that Dewaal and the others arrived in stood nearby. The prisoners were dispersed among the vehicles, ready to be driven back to Amsterdam. A forensics team was examining the two bodies.

"I would like to ask Mr. Maxwell a few questions," Colonel Al-Rahman said, off-handedly. "Ahead of the formal interrogation, if I may?"

"I don't mind," Eekhaut said.

He noticed Dewaal talking to a gathering of officers and at the same time talking on her phone. Probably with the brass back home. Things would work out all right for her, he assumed.

The colonel walked toward the BMW, which had its passenger door open and Maxwell inside. Two uniformed police officers with submachine guns stood at attention.

Eekhaut gestured toward the officers. They stepped back. The colonel leaned inside. Eekhaut wondered what they would talk about. He wondered what exactly Al-Rahman had to ask Maxwell. It bothered him the colonel was still around. But then, such had been Dewaal's orders.

A muffled bang came from the car. Blood exploded against the back window.

Al-Rahman straightened up again, gun in hand.

The two officers stared at him, unable to move.

He showed them the gun, dangling from index and thumb. Then he dropped it in the dirt.

Dewaal was the first to react. She sprinted toward the BMW, opened the door on the other side, and peered in. Then straightened and faced the colonel, who looked back at her, unmoved.

"Holy fuck," Serena said.

A few hours later, back in Amsterdam, the detectives gathered at the second-floor working area of the Bureau. Nobody felt much urge to speak. Coffee was drunk, and occasionally someone went outside for a smoke. Sandwiches and donuts had been brought and eaten. Most members of the Bureau departed after a while, realizing there was nothing left to do. Only Eekhaut and Dewaal, Prinsen, Van Gils, and Veneman remained. And Serena. Dewaal had been in her own office most of the time. She had again been on the phone, and discussions hadn't been easy. She had kept the door closed.

Eventually, she joined the others.

"And what about the colonel?" Eekhaut inquired. He knew the subject had to be raised.

"He wasn't very talkative," Dewaal said. The colonel had been escorted from the scene by members of AIVD in another car, headed for another destination.

"He didn't offer an explanation for . . ." Veneman said, pausing, then: "For why he shot Maxwell?"

"Oh, about that, yes," Dewaal said. "He called it an execution."

"That's it?"

"Yep. And he's sure he will get away with it."

Van Gils snorted. "For murder? That's not going to happen. He'll get twenty years. Here, in Holland."

"I had his embassy on the phone just now," Dewaal said. "They're trying to make a deal with the ministry of foreign affairs. They might even claim the colonel has diplomatic status."

"And why did he shoot Maxwell? If the Saudis wanted him in front of one of their own judges, they should have asked for his extradition. They could have hanged him publicly in Rihad or wherever."

"They wouldn't have gotten an extradition. We don't extradite a Dutch national to a country where the death penalty is still applied," Dewaal said.

"Well, in the end, that's what he got, the death penalty," Eekhaut said. He surveyed the park outside, the benches already occupied by pensioners and their dogs. He looked at his watch. It was late.

And he said, "The serpent."

The others gazed at him.

"That's what he said, at some point, the colonel. The serpent needs to be beheaded when you want to make sure it's dead. I heard someone else say the same thing."

"Johanna Simson," Prinsen said.

"She did indeed. Prison would be out of the question for Maxwell at least. The church knew that. Ms. Simson knew that. Maxwell was much too dangerous to be simply incarcerated. They wanted to make sure the society would be cut off at the head. The head of the serpent. Well, Ms. Simson got her revenge in the end."

"You mean the colonel works for her?" Dewaal said.

"That's what it looks like. He works for the Church of the Supreme Purification, most probably. They're in on this together. Didn't Interpol know?"

"We have no information about any connection between the colonel and the church," Serena said evasively.

"I will, of course, consult your boss concerning this matter," Dewaal told her. "I'm not very happy about you Deus ex machinating the whole situation."

"Bad luck for Maxwell anyway," Prinsen said. "Onward to his creator, without a final sacrifice and all."

"I'm not sure he really believed all that crap himself," Dewaal said. "We'll never know, of course. Anyway, there we are. Seems like it's the end of the society."

"There are more than enough weird and insane people around," Eekhaut said, thinking of what Linda had told him she'd seen in Africa.

"Well, let's close up shop till Monday," Dewaal said. "This business will be in all the papers for the next few weeks, and I'm sure we'll notice the fallout. Anyone care for a drink at the pub? If we can find one open?"

Eekhaut excused himself to the surprise of the others. He insisted he had another appointment.

And he did.

He had given Linda a key to his apartment. The key hadn't been an invitation or a promise. It didn't work that way, at least not for him. He merely left open a few options. He left his door open. She could use his apartment whenever she wanted, wait there for him.

He wasn't in a hurry. Neither was she. They would let things run their course. He would arrive at his apartment and find her there, coffee already made the way he liked it. Or she might not be there, and perhaps she would arrive later. The decision would be hers.

But he knew what he wanted. He knew what he wanted from her. And he knew what he was prepared to offer her.